James Prior

Life of Edmond Malone

Editor of Shakspeare

James Prior

Life of Edmond Malone
Editor of Shakspeare

ISBN/EAN: 9783337415426

Printed in Europe, USA, Canada, Australia, Japan

Cover: Foto ©Raphael Reischuk / pixelio.de

More available books at **www.hansebooks.com**

LIFE

OF

EDMOND MALONE,

EDITOR OF SHAKSPEARE.

WITH SELECTIONS FROM HIS

MANUSCRIPT ANECDOTES.

BY

SIR JAMES PRIOR, M.R.I.A., F.S.A., &c.,

AUTHOR OF "THE LIFE OF EDMUND BURKE,"
"LIFE OF OLIVER GOLDSMITH," "THE COUNTRY HOUSE; A POEM."
ETC. ETC.

WITH A PORTRAIT.

LONDON:
SMITH, ELDER & CO., 65, CORNHILL.
—
M.DCCC.LX.

TO THE RIGHT HON. THE EARL OF DERBY, K.G.,

&c. &c. &c.

.

My Lord,

Amid the unavoidable contentions of political life, it is to be hoped that an hour may be occasionally spared to notice the pursuits of those who are less excitingly, though not unusefully, employed—I mean the scholar and literary inquirer, such as the subject of the following sketch.

These hours indeed cannot be many. Through life, the position of an English Statesman is peculiar. He must be, if he hopes to retain his standing in the country, pre-eminently a man of labour. Even removal from power ensures little remission from work. In office, he must originate the policy that distinguishes his country. Out of it, he is called upon to examine or to control the measures introduced by others. But in either case, by the conscientious exertion of large powers, he may establish a name that will die only with his country.

A 2

That your Lordship, whether in or out of office, may receive the honours fairly earned by fearless support of the integrity of the great institutions of the State, is the sincere wish of,

My Lord,

Your Lordship's most obedient

And most faithful servant,

JAMES PRIOR.

CONTENTS.

PREFACE.

He who has expended learning and industry in making
known the lives and labours of others, deserves the
record he bestows. It forms a debt of honour, if not
of gratitude, which literary men are bound to bestow
upon each other. The neglect of it is injustice to
their class. And in this instance, it would be to sin
against an eminent literary antiquary and critic, an
amiable man, and the intimate personal friend of
several of the very first characters of their time.

No name is more suggestive than that of Malone
whenever we take up a volume of Shakspeare, of
Dryden, of the history of the stage, of Boswell, or of
biographical sketches of a few eminent contemporary
friends who had just passed away. Upon Pope,
Aubrey, and others of a previous age, considerable
labour had been expended without having its results
ushered into light. While to works of more varied
general information, such as the *Biographia Dra-
matica*, he had contributed largely in personal
anecdote.

Of his own career I found little. The only connected sketch was an article in the *Gentleman's
Magazine* afterwards enlarged into a pamphlet, by

the younger Boswell, to whom in his illness he had assigned the duty of completing and issuing the enlarged edition of Shakspeare in twenty-one volumes. But this scant outline was only meant to allay the curiosity of the moment. Had that gentleman lived, no doubt we should have had a fuller account of a round of persevering studies in ancient poetic and dramatic literature by his friend, such as few other critical antiquaries have achieved.

Although I had been often impressed by the want of more satisfactory information respecting Malone, accident led to the present attempt to supply it. While at Brighton in 1856, in conversation with an eminent literary friend and likewise with a warm lover of letters, Mr. William Tooke, the latter mentioned having a resident friend there, the Reverend Thomas R. Rooper, a connection of the Malone family,* who possessed several of the books, letters, prints, and memoranda of Edmond, which he deemed worthy of close examination. I remembered that one of the letters of that gentleman to Bishop Percy had been quoted by me in the *Life of Goldsmith*, twenty years before, stating that he had once possessed some manuscript verses of that poet, which had been so carefully folded in one of his books that they could not then or afterward be found. It immediately occurred to me that the lost lines might be among these memorials. Mr. Rooper was applied to, who kindly assented to the search, which however proved vain. But the introduction led to some conversations on Malone's career and spirit of research,

* Nephew of Lady Sunderlin, wife to the elder brother of Edmond.

and eventually to the project of his life. Diligent inquiry and indifferent health have, however, postponed its appearance longer than I had anticipated.

In addition to the materials supplied by this gentleman, he was good enough to procure from the present Earl of Charlemont a packet of letters written to Malone by the late lord, and which Mr. Rooper had returned to the family. The letters of Malone *to* that nobleman during a correspondence of twenty years have disappeared—by some said to be lost, by others *destroyed.*

A contingency against which there is no provision, caused the dispersion of many other papers. After the publication of Shakspeare, an agreeable evening spent by the younger Boswell with the Malone family induced the ladies, at the suggestion of Mr. Rooper, to propose his acceptance of some memorial of their late brother. The most appropriate was deemed to be a box of papers, letters, and notes upon books, men, or miscellaneous subjects which his pursuits might turn to useful public account. A note to that effect was sent him next day. The box followed in a day or two more. No acknowledgment being made, the ladies, upon inquiry, ascertained to their surprise and regret, that his death had occurred the day after its reception. Unluckily, he proved to be in pecuniary difficulties; the creditors reckoned these papers among his property; and they became scattered at the sale of his effects in 1825.

For the manuscript anecdotes subjoined to the life, with free permission for their use, I am indebted to the Reverend J. H. Gabell, to whose father, the eminent master of Winchester School, they were given by the Misses Malone.

I am likewise obliged to the Reverend R. M. Jephson of Brentwood, for several letters of his relative, Robert Jephson, the dramatic poet, of whom and of his family, it will be seen that Malone was an attached friend. To the Honourable Mrs. Caulfield, Miss Jephson of Castle Martyr, Ireland, Mrs. Smith, Mrs. West, and a few others, including an attached intimate of the Malone family, I have to express my thanks for several useful communications. Nor should I omit to mention polite attentions received in the Bodleian Library from the Reverends Dr. Bandinel and H. A. Coxe.

Of collections made to illustrate literary history, some notice will be found at the conclusion of the *Life*. But Malone's fame as a collector will rest chiefly on the rare and valuable gift made to the Bodleian, which confers equal honour on his judgment, taste, and public spirit; while still closer examination of its contents will assuredly add to our estimate of its value.

LIFE OF EDMOND MALONE.

CHAPTER I.

1741—1765.

Family of Malone—Trinity College—Ode on the Nuptials of George III.
—Journey to England—Entered at the Middle Temple—Rev.
Mr. Chetwood—His Letters.

A THOROUGH Irish antiquary will find pleasure in searching out the history of the Malones. It is one of the most national of the country. No Saxon has anything to say to it. He may plunge into the un- known depths of Milesians and Celts; disport himself as wildly as Irishmen are said to do in the mysteries of races; and emerge with as little positive know- ledge of sober facts as any of his predecessors.

According to the famous Charles O'Connor, of Balanagar, the most recondite of moderns in such studies, it may be traced from a king of Connaught, Murray Mullathan (Murray the long-headed), who died in 701. His descendants assumed various names. Surnames were an innovation of the eleventh cen- tury, and adopted from peculiarity of person or cha- racter. Thus a descendant of the house being ton- sured in honour of St. John, received the name of

Maol Eoin, which soon became Malone—the former signifying bald, the latter John.   This branch had estates conquered for them out of the territories of the chief of Westmeath by their royal relative of the long head not far from the modern town of Athlone; and there their descendants continue.

From a junior branch of this race, which for some generations had practised the higher branch of law, sprang the subject of our notice.   His grandfather, Richard, while yet a student in London, had been sent on a mission to Holland by King William, on the recommendation of his friend, Ruvigny, Earl of Galway; and afterward gained wealth and celebrity at the Irish bar.   Four sons pursued the same profession in the same place during the career of the father; so that the family enjoyed a species of monopoly of the courts.*

* The family seat was purchased by this gentleman, of which the following account is given in Brewer's *Beauties of Ireland:*—" Baronstown, on the banks of Lough Iron, is the splendid seat of Richard Malone, Esq., inherited by this gentleman from his relative the late Right Honourable Richard Malone Lord Sunderlin, who died without issue.   The name of this place is derived from its ancient proprietors, the family of Nangle, Palatine Barons of Navan.   The estate was purchased of that family by Richard Malone, Esq., father of the celebrated forensic orator Anthony Malone, and of Edmond, the father of Lord Sunderlin.   Baronstown House is a capacious edifice of stone, chiefly built by the late Lord Sunderlin, under whose tasteful direction the demesne was enlarged and enriched with extensive plantations. . . . .

" At Kilbixy, on the Baronstown estate, and in view of Mr. Malone's mansion, is a small but beautiful church, erected under the auspices of the late Lord Sunderlin.   This structure is a very estimable example of the successful imitation in modern times of the florid style of pointed architecture, and will, we trust, remain to a very late posterity a proof of the exquisite taste and magnificence of its noble founder.   Kilbixy (locally pronounced Kilbisky) formerly contained a castle, and an Hospital for Lepers, of which last building some remains are still visible." —*Brewer's Beauties of Ireland.*

Of these, the most celebrated was Anthony, an orator, lawyer, and statesman of the first class. His name is even still mentioned with the reverence that belongs only to the great. To a commanding person, fine voice, an impressive yet conciliatory manner, temper rarely to be ruffled by an opponent, were added powers of argument and persuasion so effective, that it was once proposed to transfer him from the Irish to the English House of Commons, in order to oppose Sir Robert Walpole. The encomium of Grattan on this eminent person should not be forgotten.

"Mr. Malone was a man of the finest intellect that any country ever produced. The three ablest men I have ever heard were Mr. Pitt (the father), Mr. Murray, and Mr. Malone. For a popular assembly I would choose Mr. Pitt; for a Privy Council, Murray; for twelve wise men, Malone." This was the opinion Lord Sackville, the Secretary of [17]53, gave of Mr. Malone to a gentleman, from whom I heard it. "He is a great sea in a calm," said Mr. Gerard Hamilton, another good judge of men and talents. "Aye," it was replied, "but had you seen him when he was young, you would have said he was a great sea in a storm; and like the sea, whether in calm or storm, a great production of nature."

Edmond, second son of Richard, and father of the critic, was born in 1704. Intending to vary the scene of hereditary pursuit, he was called to the English bar in 1730; but removed from family ties and influences is said to have had indifferent success. In 1736 he married the daughter of Mr. Benjamin Collier, of

Ruckholts in Essex. One of the ceremonies on this occasion is recorded by his son on the authority of the officiating clergyman, and forms a curious peculiarity in past manners.

"He" (Dr. Taylor, of Isleworth, who gave the details in 1788) "married my father to Miss Collier in 1736. Old Mr. Collier was a very vain man who had made his fortune in the South Sea year; and having been originally a merchant, was fond, after he had retired to live upon his fortune, of a great deal of display and parade. On his daughter's wedding, therefore, he invited nearly fifty persons, and got two or three capital cooks from London to prepare a magnificent entertainment in honour of the day. When other ceremonies had concluded, the young couple were put to bed, and every one of this numerous assemblage came into the room to make their congratulations to my father and mother, *who sat up in bed to receive them:* ' Madam, I wish you a very good night! Sir, all happiness to you, and a very good night!'—and so on through the party. My father, who hated all parade, but was forced to submit to the old gentleman's humour, must have been in a fine fume; and my mother, who was then but seventeen or eighteen, sufficiently embarrassed."

In 1740, this gentleman removed to the Irish bar, and favoured by circumstances and application, soon obtained considerable business. A seat in the House of Commons followed. He became in time serjeant; and in 1766 found a seat on the Irish Bench as one of the judges of the Court of Common Pleas, which he filled till his death in 1774. His children were—

Richard, afterwards Lord Sunderlin; Edmond, of whom this memorial is written; Anthony and Benjamin, who died young; and two daughters, Henrietta and Catherine, who survived their brothers.

Edmond was born in Dublin, 4th of October, 1741. At an early age he was sent to a celebrated school in Molesworth Street, kept by Dr. Ford, where his brother Richard had preceded him. Among their school-fellows was Robert (Captain) Jephson, subsequently author of *Braganza* and other tragedies, with whom a very sincere and durable friendship was formed. Here likewise about the same period were found the future first Marquis of Lansdown, Lord Sheffield, General Blakeney, and others, afterwards of some note in the world. A favourite amusement of the boys was the performance of plays. Such was their reputation in this line, that much of the fashion of Dublin was found among the audience, and something of its gravity; more especially Lord Chancellor Jocelyn, who was observed to be no niggard of his praise. Macklin, the celebrated actor, sometimes conducted these exhibitions. In 1749, *Julius Cæsar* was brought out in very good style, two of the Jephsons taking the parts of *Brutus* and *Cassius; Marcellus,* by the late Lord Lansdown; *Casca,* by General Blakeney; *Anthony,* by the late Rev. Thomas Robinson; *Portia,* by Richard Malone. Edmond was then too young to exhibit in public, but succeeded in due time to similar honours; and it is believed that in his instance, as was the case with Jephson, Shakspeare and the drama were never afterwards forgotten.

A promising career here carried him to Trinity College, Dublin, in 1756, where in due time he became bachelor of arts. Richard, his elder brother, had been entered in 1754, and in 1758 removed to Christchurch, Oxford. The talents of Edmond were more than respectable; he ran the race of competition among fellow-students with considerable applause, particularly in an *Ode on the Marriage of his Majesty George III.* This offspring of juvenile loyalty occupies more than one hundred and fifty lines; was published in Dublin in a thin quarto in 1761, with ten others from the University on the same theme; six of which (two in Latin) were by his chosen friends, then, as in after life, Kearney, Hussey, Southwell, and Chetwood. I have in my possession a prize volume of poetry, Somerville's *Chase*, given him in 1760. Likewise some of his exercise books, gleaned from among the old book-shops in London. The ode will be found at the end of this volume.

Steady, rather than shining powers, formed his characteristic feature. He had determined to accomplish anything he took in hand—to take a comprehensive view of subjects of study, and not to quit what he had once begun till the details or principles were mastered. This quality, the basis of all solid knowledge, is rarely popular with youth. Light minds are content with light or superficial acquisitions; and the sedate student occasionally found himself open to the jest or the neglect of more volatile companions. He might be considered then as shadowing forth symptoms of the future critic.

He was a remorseless inquirer. Nothing would be taken upon trust where minute examination was practicable. Thus, while at college might be found that keenly inquisitive spirit which nearly fifty years afterward induced him to write to Bishop Percy in terms I have mentioned elsewhere—" Give me but time, place, and names, and the genuineness or falsehood of any story may be easily ascertained."*

A mind judicially constituted in essentials, seemed to be cut out by nature for the bench. He was therefore destined for the family profession, to which some time in Dublin was given in initiatory studies. Added to the esteem earned by steady talents, he had won warm affection from several fellow-students, who through life expressed for him the strongest regard. Among these were the very distinguished Fellows of the University, Doctors Michael Kearney and John Kearney (afterwards Bishop of Ossory), Dr. Wilson, Rev. John Chetwood, Henry Flood, John Fitzgibbon (afterwards Earl of Clare), and others, some of whose letters will be found in his correspondence.

The climate of Ireland appearing not to agree with Mrs. Malone, her husband—now Mr. Serjeant Malone, M.P.—and Edmond, accompanied her to England in the summer of 1759. Highgate was selected for a time as her residence. Hence she writes to her husband, taking an occasional glance at the society of London by visits to the family of her relative, Lord Catherlough, an Englishman with an Irish title. Ultimately she removed to Bath,

---

* *Life of Goldsmith*, vol. i. p. 126. 8vo. 1837. In allusion to some of the poet's stories to his relatives.

where, gaining partial relief, she continued for some years. In the meantime, when comfortably settled with her relatives, the serjeant considered the moment favourable for giving his son a view of the interior of England. A tour was therefore undertaken through the Midland Counties, much to the gratification of both.

They did not reach Dublin till towards the end of the year—the serjeant to his usual labours in the four courts, with occasional trips to a country residence and farm named Shinglass; and Edmond to college studies preparatory to further examinations. His father had formed a favourable opinion of his talents and diligence. His disposition was affectionate, his temper genial, his attachment to his mother and sisters devoted, to which the former more than once alluded; and there reigned between the brothers a degree of regard which appears never to have been interrupted. Their letters, as well as surviving testimony, render it apparent that there could not be a more united family. From the country retreat of his father, when taking a turn at farming, we have the following sensible admonitions to Edmond, January, 1760 :—

MY DEAR NEDDY—I am very much obliged for your letter of last Sunday, which was a great treat to me, in this lonely place. I often wish for your company, but at the same time am glad that you made the choice you did, of sitting down to read for next examinations, as you will by that means soon recover the time lost by our English expedition last summer.

The seeing you and your brother both so diligent in the pursuit of the necessary means for your own happiness and success in the world, is the greatest joy and pleasure of my life, and makes amends for a thousand troubles I have from other causes ; and if it shall ever be in my power to reward you for it as I wish to do, I'll show you all the affection and kindness the most deserving child can expect. But as human events are so precarious, there is no trusting to that chance. Continue, therefore, my dear child, the same course of industry you are in, in order to qualify you to get your own bread, and to make your own way in the world. God Almighty always blesses the diligent and industrious ; He has been pleased to endow you with a good understanding, and many other advantages, which can't fail to succeed when properly applied. I came here on Friday from Mr. Magan's, and have been quite alone ever since. I live much as you do, upon a bit of mutton every day, and occupy only one room in the house, except the chamber I lie in. I found both tea and sugar here,* and Mrs. Magan gave me a pound of sugar. . . . The weather, last Saturday, was so very bad I could not stand out ; but Monday was a fine frosty day, and I was abroad all day long, and am very busy in my farming, which mightily wanted my presence here. There fell a great deal of snow on Tuesday, which kept me a prisoner that day, but I think the air is a great deal warmer for it.

I send the enclosed cover to your mamma open to you, that you may send anything you please under the same cover, and then seal it and send it away next Saturday. I hope to see you on Sunday night ; but, as I must dine on the road, I would have you dine at your uncle's, as usual ; and, if I come at any reasonable time to town, I'll call upon him that night. Tell him that nothing but the severity of the weather shall prevent my being in town to my time.

In 1763, he was entered of the Inner Temple. London possessed charms to a young and ingenuous

---

* Irish villagers were then sadly deficient in the usual supplies now required for civilized life, so that a pound of sugar became a provision against accidents.

mind, which found amusement not in its dissipations, but varieties. To him, fresh from a narrower sphere, it was indeed seeing the world—a preparative to enlarged intelligence and liberal studies. Unlike Dublin there was no provincialism, none of those views or misapprehensions which smaller or partially isolated communities take of their own or others' affairs. He saw none of that secondhand influence —few of those second-rate men who, busy or ambitious, always needy, often corrupt or instruments of corruption, influenced or governed his country less for its interests than their own. In London these things were better veiled or less practised. There he found the centre of that society always to him a main source of delight—literary and dramatic persons —or what formed a substitute as constituting a large admixture of both to a young man without ties of home—namely, coffee-house society. The "Grecian" in the Strand was then and long afterwards the favourite resort ; and, to strangers in the metropolis, an irresistible evening attraction.

Glad was he likewise in opportunities of paying to an affectionate mother the duty of a good son, to which allusion is made in her letters. She had continued at Bath, unable to walk without assistance, and died there in the beginning of 1765. Lord Luxborough, now become Earl of Catherlough, thus writes to her husband from Golden Square, January, 1765 :—

You would have received my most sincere condolence on the melancholy event that has happened, but that, till last night, by a letter from your dear son, I imagined you would have come to Bath; but now I hope your journey hither has been prevented, and that all your children will mix their tears with yours at Dublin, for the irreparable loss we have all sustained. I say *we,* because I most affectionately loved and esteemed my late dear kinswoman for the many good and valuable qualities she had. . . . I wish to my heart you may have fortitude of mind to support you under this calamity. You have the comfort of your most deserving children, and that they may all live to be a blessing to you is the sincere wish of, &c. &c.

Edmond, who continued for some months in London, thus adverts in a letter to his father to a delicate topic of the day—the first mental illness of George III.—which had been studiously kept out of sight. Nor are the attractions of the Grecian Coffee-house, even for an Irish chief justice, forgotten.

London, March 2, 1765.

HONOURED SIR*—As I imagined you would be entirely taken up with business during circuit, I have not troubled you with a letter for some time past, and, indeed, should not now, but suppose you will by the time you receive this be returned to town, and this is the last opportunity of paying my respects before I see you in London. My brother, I think, in his last letter informed you of the death of Mrs. Weaver. We have heard nothing further from Lord Catherlough on that subject, so that we may bid adieu to the prospect of any share of her personal fortune. I have not heard to what it amounts, but suppose it can't be less than 6,000l. . . .

I have little public news to send. The K—— has had a slight fever, which has alarmed people so much that it is said a Regency will be formed in case any accident should

---

* This deferential phrase which also concludes the letter, was likewise used by Burke in addressing his father. What examples for a modern Templar!

happen to him. Everything goes on very smoothly in the House of Commons, the Opposition being inconsiderable in numbers, and without a head, for Mr. Pitt has not been in the House the whole winter. Hence it is imagined that the motion for an address, to know by whose advice General Conway was dismissed, in which he has certainly promised to assist them when health would permit his attendance, as it has been so long deferred, will not be brought on this session.

Lord Chief Justice Aston arrived here yesterday, and found his way very soon to his old friends at the Grecian, among whom I fancy he will be much happier than with all his dignities in the Council Chamber of Dublin. . . .

An affectionate reply, in a wise and fatherly tone, adverts to the neglect of the deceased relative in her will.

"By not suffering the events of life to affect us, we shall by degrees become superior to all calamities. I well know that one thousand pounds a-piece to my children would have been a great benefit; but after all, their happiness depends more on the wisdom and virtue of their own minds than on that or any other sum. So let us, my dear child, think no more of it."—He had just returned from Kilkenny assizes on his way to preside (by order) over those of Wicklow. Whiteboyism then disturbed the country; no less than eleven were capitally convicted. Five more were acquitted for what was called "high treason," and he agreed in opinion with the jury. Yet, in proof of the exasperation of public feeling against such offences thus absurdly said to be trea-sonable, he dared not, he said, make the avowal of their innocence to any but his own children. He postponed a journey to London to wait the arrival of Lord Hertford from Paris, who was nominated to succeed Lord Northumberland in the viceroyalty.

Among the intimate and lasting friendships formed at college has been mentioned that of Chetwood, who soon afterwards took orders. His family, settled near Chester, were connected with Ireland, and had destined him for the church of that country. Imbued with taste and imagination, fond of poetry and music, with a lively sense of the advantages of polished and intellectual society, he felt and regretted the rudeness of the country in which his lot was cast, and occasionally could ill repress gentle repinings at his position. This was but natural to a sensitive mind. But to live among people mostly of an alien and exclusive creed—to labour with the certainty of few fruits to be reaped, no honours to be won— to have the motives of kindnesses towards poorer neighbours suspected, and charities almost repelled, or to find indifference forced upon him, and yet charged as negligence or barbarity—these are the conditions upon which a Protestant clergyman must often take his position in Ireland.

Letters to his friend under such circumstances formed one mode of relief. But he possessed the Irish faculty of *hoping*, or in other words, that the chances of life would eventually turn out in his favour; and thence with a light heart threw forth his thoughts in an agreeable strain. For Malone he had contracted a strong attachment. He loved his temper, thought highly of his capacity, applauded his tastes and pursuits, sought fre-

quently at his hands for literary information and
opinions, and their correspondence continued, though
often with long intervals, till nearly the close of life.
Just at this period he had quitted his charge on a
visit to the paternal abode near Chester, whence he
thus writes:—

Plasissa, July 30, 1765.

It is time, my good friend, to thank you for your last
letter, which I received some weeks before I left Ireland.
You will be surprised to hear that I am still in the same
kingdom with you.   I am sorry to think, however, that I am
not likely to receive much pleasure from diminution of the
distance between us.   We are still too remote to render a
meeting very practicable, unless my stay here were longer
than I believe it can be.   Three months, I fear, will be the
utmost that prudence will allow me to enjoy the beauties of
the scene before me.

I committed my flock at Rockfort to the care of a temporary curate, and sailed from Cork to Bristol about three
weeks ago.   I devoted a few days to the Hotwell; a few
more to Bath and its purlieus; took a most delightful tour
through Gloucestershire, Worcestershire, and Shropshire;
and am now arrived at my father's, where I want nothing to
brighten my happiness except the addition of *my* friends
Edmond and Southwell to my party.

Were it not inconsistent with your present pursuits, how
glad should I be to have your company whilst I remain here.
I would venture to pronounce that the situation of this place
would inspire you with that exalted enthusiasm that a fine
rural scene so naturally suggests.   But you have been so
long an Englishman, that the hanging grove, the open lawn,
the winding river, the distant sea, are objects that, perhaps,
from their frequency, have lost their force upon you.

To me, who have come from an uncultivated world, where
rude nature reigns without a rival, each minutest beauty is
so far from being lost, that I often fancy I view everything

around me through a magnifying glass,* and that every tree
spreads at least a quadruple proportion of foliage before my
eyes beyond its real produce. At present, I can truly say I
pass nothing unadmired. I am in the situation of one caught
in love ; my heart—my poor heart—my Edmond, is caught,
and the Sylvan Deities have engaged all my attention. The
great Berkeley, upon his return from Killarney, told the
friend to whom he was describing its beauties that the utmost
exertion of all the powers of art might repair a ruined Ver-
sailles, but that God alone could make a Killarney. I never
felt' the spirit that I am sure then warmed his lordship so
strongly as I have done since my last arrival in England. I
would prescribe previous banishment to any one who had a
mind to enjoy real solid pleasure from the prospect of natural
or artificial beauties. But I shall fill my paper before I
say a word upon any other topic than that of rural beauty.
You think me mad already, in all probability. I heard from
Southwell† just when I left home ; he was then well, and
going upon a ramble into the country with his father.

I met Fitzgibbon‡ at Bath, on his road to the Hotwells.
His unparalleled effeminacy, I am now convinced, is uncon-
querable. Change of kingdom has, I think, rather increased
his unnatural delicacy of manners. His dishabille was not
by any means remarkable after a long journey from Oxford,
but it gave him great concern that I should meet him in such
an undress. *Risum teneatis.*

I hope, my dear Ned, to hear from you immediately.
Direct to me at Crewe Chetwood's, Esq., at Plasissa, near
Chester. If I return by way of Bristol, which as yet is not
determined, I shall perhaps be in London for a few days ;
and for that purpose, shall leave home a fortnight' sooner

---

* This graphic sketch of Ireland at that time came from a strong
imagination. So backward was she in *moral*, or, in other words, civilized
influences, that it seemed to affect things *physical*—not even the trees
appeared to produce their due proportions of foliage !

† A relative of Lord Southwell, to whom there are future allusions.

‡ Afterwards Earl of Clare, so well known in the disturbed periods of
Irish politics. His character, whatever his dress may have been in future
life, exhibited anything but effeminacy.

than if I go through Dublin. This depends upon accidents which I cannot yet be informed of, so that our meeting is not absolutely impossible. Adieu. God bless you, my dear Ned, and believe me ever, &c.

The first days of the return of this cheerful friend to his post—Rockfort, near Bandon—were employed in persuasions to Malone to release his muse from supposed durance, and exhibit her to the world. Literature, and the persons and topics connected with it, formed at all times his favourite theme. And among youthful writing associates, whenever prose is not forthcoming, the presumption seems to be that the candidate is addressing the Goddess of Song. Most of them would have it that nature had cut him out for a poet; but circumstances afterwards hardened him into a critic.

Rockfort, Nov. 15, 1765.

Our friend, Southwell, transmitted your letter to me by the last post, which I had expected with impatience before my departure from Dublin. It arrived here, however, before I did, as if it was meant to welcome me to my rural abode. I received my friend with that ardour that its hospitable intentions merited; and you see, I take the earliest opportunity of returning the visit.

I feel a little like a schoolboy upon his reviewing the scenes of scholastic discipline after the dissipation of Christmas holidays. I enjoy the sensations that a poor bird does when clipped in his wings; and I fancy, that no lover ever sat down to pen a sonnet on the charms of his mistress with stronger inspirations from the power of song than I now could to tack together a few wretched couplets of wretched topics on rusticity and retirement. But, however, as you are my friend, and have not offended me, I will not punish you at present by inflicting torments brought from the inquisition of the Muses. I long much to see you, if it were for no other

reason than to examine the recesses of your escritoire.   I am
sure, my friend, that that warm brain of yours can never find
enjoyment in inaction.   The forms of beauty, either moral or
personal, solicit it too strongly to suffer it to be at rest.   No
law jargon, no collection of statutes, not all the Pandects in
the world, can even avail to extinguish the passion for the
muse when she has taken legal possession.   " *Naturam ex-
pellas Colo, tamen usque recurret,*" said one of the best philosophers that ever united that character and the poet's together.
If you resolve to keep them close concealed—I mean those
compositions that you most penuriously have hoarded up and
concealed from public inspection—Shakspeare's curse attend
you.   Never pray more; abandon all remorse; on poems' heads
poems accumulate; and never reap those unfading laurels that
their publication would ensure you the possession of.

You inquire about Tom's* mistress.   She is not tall, nor
yet very low of stature.   She is not a beauty, though she has
a red and white complexion that I much approve of, and her
features are rather delicately formed.   She is well made, and
brimfull of virgin modesty.   When she casts an eye towards
her little hero, she blooms like the rosy bosomed morning.
But yet I know not whether her happy fortune has destined
her to the participation of our friend's bed.   There may be
obstacles that tend at least to retard, if not prevent, the union;
and Tom, though not in love, is not perfectly at ease on this
account.   Adieu! God bless you, my dear Malone, is the
constant wish of your faithful and affectionate friend.

* Mr. Thomas Southwell.

CHAPTER II.

Introduction to Dr. Johnson—Letters from Avignon—Promotion of his
Father—Called to the Bar—A Love Story—Spa.

LED by attachment to Shakspeare and the natural
desire of an intelligent mind, he had at this time in
London formed the acquaintance of Dr. Johnson.
The introduction took place through one of his
friends of the Southwell family, younger brother of
the peer of that name, whose manners Johnson so
highly commended for " freedom from insolence."
" Edmund Southwell," said Malone, " lived in intimacy with Johnson for many years. See an
account of him in *Hawkins' Life*. He died in
London, November, 1772. In opposition to the
knight's unfavourable representation of this gentleman, to him I was indebted for my first introduction
to Johnson. I take this opportunity to add that he
appeared to me a pious man, and was very fond of
leading the conversation to religious subjects."

Doubtless, he was proud of an honour valued by
men of the highest attainments; and the event was
duly communicated to Irish friends. His letters to
Chetwood, descriptive of such incidents, are unluckily

not to be found; for to those of others he often gave
that preservative care not always bestowed upon
his own. But the replies of this friend let us into
the main events of this period of his life, so that
we are not left wholly uninformed. Chetwood writes
thus in November, 1765:—

You see, my dear Malone, that I am not of the number of
those correspondents who never write but to answer their
friends' letters, and who think it a work of supererogation to
address two successive letters to the same person without the
regular intervention of a reply. However ceremonious I
may wish to be with others in this respect, I want no encouragement to make me think every circumstance a favourable
one that gives me a pretence for employing my pen to you.
An opportunity that I have just met with by accident, of
sending this free to Bath, is the reason for writing to you at
present; and I am not without hopes that a passport thence
to the Grecian (coffee-house) will be procured by the gentleman to whom this is enclosed. Were I to write a long letter
you might say that I had more compassion for your pocket
than yourself. . . . .
How happy are you who can sweeten even confinement with
the company of men and works of genius! I envy you your
intimacy with the editor of Shakspeare, and the opportunities you have by your situation in London of collecting
books. I wish you may have sufficient influence over Mr.
Johnson to urge him to continue his writings. His *Prince of
Abyssinia* has been of use in the world enough to encourage
him to prosecute the theme of morals. You amaze me by
accusing him of indolence. I imagined from the perusal of
his dictionary, that his application was at least equal to his
abilities. I have received a few hours' entertainment from a
dialogue of Hurd's, upon the uses of foreign travel, which I
take for granted you have seen long ago. I should be highly
obliged to you if you would give me an account of anything
that appears in the literary world, worth notice. Books of
the highest reputation may be read over half the globe

c 2

before the fame of them is published in this unilluminated
region. This is no small loss to me, who have a great deal
of time to devote to study. It obliges me to employ my
attention very frequently upon productions from which it is
difficult to glean any useful knowledge amidst rude heaps of
barbarous language and uninteresting events.

I suppose by this time Hussey and Burgh are resettled in
the Temple. I saw them both in Dublin, and have in my
possession a stronger proof than I ever saw before, of the
poetical genius of the former. With all his irregularities,
and with his many hasty and undigested sallies, there is an
original softness and elegance of sentiment in him that I
never found in Hammond or even in his master, Tibullus.
He has sometimes, too, a strength and beauty of expression,
particularly striking in him who is in general inattentive to
the dress of his thoughts. I fear he is too volatile to apply
very assiduously to any study, unless it be of poetry; and a
man of imagination, possessed of a passion for the Nine,
should never be licentious in the indulgence of either, if he
means to be deeply learned in the intricacies of law. Such
is the severe tax upon the ingenious of your profession.

I received this morning a long letter from our friend
Southwell, which you may imagine was no small comfort to
me in my retreat. This may possibly induce one of your
humanity to lose no time in following his example, though I
am in hopes when your next arrives I shall enjoy it in perfect sanity of body as well as mind, which the remains of a
sore throat prevent me from enjoying at present. I fear Tom
is not yet so near the verge of matrimony as I imagined him
to be some time ago. There are circumstances that may
perhaps totally prevent, or at least procrastinate, his hoped-for
union. I think you had better say nothing to him on the
subject in your letters, as I know he is uneasy when he thinks
or is put in mind of it. It has given me much more material
concern that his constitution is not what I could wish it
were. . . . .

The difference that subsisted for some time between his
family and Lord Southwell, contributed at intervals to make
him unhappy; and after the reconciliation took place, the

hurry of perpetually visiting that right dishonourable and ignoble Peer deprived both me and him of a much more friendly intercourse. For several days I scarce ever saw him after breakfast till the hour of dressing for dinner. I must add a second caution—not to give him the least hint that I mentioned anything to you about his health. I don't know whether I told you in my last letter that I had frequently seen Beresford and my friend Eliza. She is really improved and not in the least affected by her change of state. Were she unmarried, I could almost relapse into my quondam friendship for her. All appearance of vulgarness seems banished from her manners and speech. Adieu! It is well for you my paper is filled, for otherwise, I should have no mercy on you to-night.—Yours ever, J. C.

The " Grecian," the Temple, and law studies were occasionally diversified by excursions into the country, or a short visit to Ireland. There he found his lively friend, Chetwood, diligently fulfilling parochial duties, while enjoying, with all the elasticity and vivacity of the national temperament, such amusements as a confined sphere permitted. Of these, added to literary tastes and desires—the latter always a favourite topic —some notice occurs in one of his letters, written from Bandon in August the following year. Nor is the allusion to the lady of the " thick legs " and his friend's susceptibility of heart altogether without interest, as we shall find in a future page.

My dear Ned,—At last your long-expected epistle is arrived. It contains an excuse for delay so very reasonable, that I most heartily signed your acquittance from any imputation of neglect as soon as I had read it. I began to suspect that your plea would have been of another nature, and that something more interesting than even filial or fraternal affection had engaged your attention; for, from

my intimate knowledge of your genius, I was convinced
that your soul is as impregnated with fire as the flint, and
that both, when struck, are equally prone to produce pain.
I began to consider that even a glance was sufficient to
unman a breast so susceptible of the least impulse, and
concluded, in consequence, that some happy fair one —
possessed of all the accomplishments, and as thick legs as
the once favoured Elliott—had enslaved my friend's affections. "Ever prompt to blaze at Beauty's sacred call." So
that, from motives of pity, I had pardoned your omission to
me before the receival of your excuse.

I am sorry you had not an opportunity of communicating
all the handsome things I had penned for Mrs. Jeffries ; but
as she is fully convinced of my profound adoration and respect
for her and her sister without the proof of Panegyride, the
loss of so superfluous a compliment is not very material.

I despair of ever bringing our friend Southwell to a proper
sense of his duty as a correspondent. I wrote him a long
letter, and have not yet received a line in answer, but suppose
his Donegal expedition, and his intention of assuming the garb
of sobriety which you say he is resolved upon, has obliterated all epistolary thought. Where is he gone to, in so
remote a part of Ireland as Donegal ?

I still remain very comfortable and snug, and pleased with
my situation. I begin to like the people of the country rather
more than I did. I ride about as much as I can, and have
lately been two or three days at Mallow, which is a most
lovely situation as I ever saw. I met many people there
whom I knew ; among the rest, Mrs. Coote, the dowager,
and Mrs. Anketell, her daughter. Dissipation, as Martin
would say, reigns perpetually there. Nothing but dancing
and public breakfasting, and such riotous customs, are practised. I propose going there again soon, and mixing a little
with the *beau monde*, by way of recreation.

I received a letter lately from poet Hussey, who is study-
ing the law hard with Foster in a little retirement in Surrey.
It was half poetry, half prose. There are some good lines,
the best of which I will just transcribe for you, as you are
one of the wooers of the tuneful ladies. In praising my " idle

life," as he terms it, in comparison of his laborious one, he
says :—

> " No wrangling Bar or busy strife
> Shall chase the peaceful muse from thee;
> She loves to live from toil and trouble free,
> Basks in the sunshine of an idle life,
> But flies averse from business and from me."

Now I am speaking of poets, you have often heard me
mention a very particular friend of mine in Oxford, by name
Bagot, many of whose productions I have shown you. He
has been obliged to have recourse to Lisbon for the recovery
of his health, from whence I received a long letter from him
a few days ago.   He informs me he is better in that climate
than when he left England; but I much fear he will fall a
martyr to severity of study.   Adieu! dear Ned.

In April, 1766, Edmond writes from London to
his father, who he regrets had a " new commission"
to return to some duties at Clonmel—" Mr. Pitt is
very ill with the gout at Hayes." The conclusion
notices two personages once well known at the
" Grecian " and in theatrical circles—" I am at
present writing in a coffee-house, in the midst of
so much noise and bustle—the celebrated anti-
Sejanus (Mr. Scott*) on one side and Mr. Macklin
on the other—that I can't add anything more at
present."

It will be seen by previous letters that an intimacy existed with the family of Lord Southwell.   In
the autumn of this year he accompanied, as a friend,
the son and grandson of that nobleman to the south
of France.   Marseilles formed their original destination.   A halt arising from illness, occurred at
Avignon which continued to be their abode; and
where his friend by the death of his father soon

---

* Author of well-known letters under that signature in the newspapers.

afterward succeeded to the peerage. The first
impressions of the spot are addressed by Malone
to his father, December 3, 1766:—

It gave me great pleasure to hear by a letter which I
received yesterday from my brother, that your affairs in
England were at length settled to your mind, and that you
were soon likely to be freed from the disagreeable task of
court solicitation. I take it for granted that before this time
your patent is passed, and that this letter will find you safe
arrived in Dublin.

I have been here near a month. Mr. Southwell, when we
arrived, had no thoughts of staying longer than one day, but
his son unhappily was seized with illness, which has continued
upon him ever since. He was so miserably weak previously,
that this new attack was very near destroying him; but as he
has borne it so long, he may perhaps get through, and it may
possibly be of service by carrying off the cause of the disorder
that has afflicted him so many months. We were for a good
while in a very disagreeable way in an inn; but for the last
week have been in private lodgings, where probably they
will remain for the winter; for they seem to have no hope
of being able to reach Marseilles. It is unlucky that we
were not able to reach that town, as by all accounts it is
a lively and agreeable place, which is of no little consequence
to an invalid.

Avignon is very far from being a place one would wish to
settle in. It has no sort of trade or business, no public enter-
tainments, and is besides an old, straggling, ugly town. It
was rendered famous for some time by the residence of the
old Pretender, and in the year 1746 his son retired hither after
the rebellion. He lived very magnificently, but so void of
gratitude, or even common decency, as to give a grand ball,
at which he danced, at the very time he well knew his party,
Lords Balmarino and Kilmallock, were losing their heads in
London.

The Duke of Ormond spent the last twenty years of his life
in this town; and at this time it is the residence of two or three

families who were attached to the same cause. They have probably chosen it for the sake of more easy correspondence with their friends at Rome, this town and the adjacent country being under the dominion of the Pope. I don't know whether you ever heard of a brother of Lord Mansfield's. He was governor to the present Pretender, and was created, if it may be called a creation, Lord Dunbar. He is an agreeable old man, and we are glad sometimes to see him, for want of other English company. By this account you may see if a man's principles were any ways doubtful it would not be very safe to pitch his tent in this place.

We received the account of Lord Southwell's death last night. Mr. Southwell was infinitely obliged by your letter, and takes it extremely kind of you to have concerned yourself so much in his affairs. His father was so worthless a man, that I believe he has not left many wet eyes after him. It appears pretty plain how friendless he must have been, from having appointed none of his own family his executors, and being obliged to have recourse to two persons with whom they are entirely unacquainted.

I beg you will tell my sister Kitty that I received her letter yesterday, and will answer it by the next post. I long much to hear that you and my brother have got safe over the Irish Sea, which is sometimes very rough at this season. I wish most heartily all health and happiness, &c.

The business which carried his father from Ireland to London was expected removal from the Bar to the Bench. One of the channels used for that purpose was the Earl of Bristol, first husband of the famous Miss Chudleigh, who afterwards giving her hand to the Duke of Kingston, figured in the celebrated trial for bigamy. At this time he was expected to become Viceroy of Ireland. The Malones had become known to him; and the serjeant judged it becoming to pay his personal respects to so in-

fluential a friend in England. His suit proved
successful, though the Earl did not become Lord
Lieutenant.

His son, in the first of the following letters, duti-
fully laments some delay which had occurred in the
transit to the seat of justice. In the second, we
hear of what was no doubt the first feat of his
own in the business of law—making a will; and,
the late difficulty in promotion being conquered by
his father, he is not a little pleased to change the
address from " Mr. Serjeant " to " The Honourable
Mr. Justice Malone, Stephen's Green, Dublin."

Avignon, Dec. 29, 1766.

I little imagined some time ago that my letter would find
you in London in the beginning of January; but by one
that I received from my brother yesterday, I find this may
possibly overtake you, before your departure for Ireland.
I need not tell you how concerned I am at the occasion of
your stay. It was, indeed, a great mortification to me, for
I had flattered myself that after you once had got my Lord
Bristol's absolute promise, and only waited for Judge Mar-
shall's letters, nothing could have prevented you from succeeding. It shall be a lesson to me never to believe in any
great man's word, unless coupled with performance, and to
aspire by every honest means at the greatest blessing of
life, independence.

Possibly, however, your powerful friend may still be able
to effect something for you; if that has been the case, I hope
you will be so good as to write me a few words before you
leave London. I have written to you two or three times
since I came to this town; but imagining you would be in
Ireland about the middle of last month, addressed all my
letters to Stephen's Green. My Lord Southwell, on the
same supposition when he answered your letter, directed to
the same place. He sent you two advertisements; one of
thanks to the county Limerick, and the other for his son,

to be inserted in the public papers; but luckily at the same time forwarded duplicates to his agent in the country. So that, notwithstanding your absence, they have probably appeared. He desired me to give you a thousand thanks for your kind letter.

I am extremely obliged for the 25*l.* you have permitted me to draw, which I shall do very unwillingly, because I fear it may distress you; but I shall be in absolute need of it to carry me home. I must draw upon you instead of Norton, for my credit at Foley's, which I got from Nesbit when I was leaving England, is on you, and not on him. I shall draw a bill on you for 40*l.*, the 25*l.* you have been so good as to give me, and 15*l.* which will remain due to me on the 1st of February, the rest of that quarter being gone in chamber rent, &c.; and at the same time write to Nesbit to send the bill to Mr. Norton, who will I suppose, accept instead of sending it to you in Ireland.

I mean to go next week for a few days to Marseilles with a gentleman of this town, who has offered me a place in his chaise. There I must receive my money, my credit from Foley being on the banker of that place, and where Lord Southwell thought to spend the winter, but which he will probably not now visit, as he has got a house in the town, and is now settled here. His son is surprisingly better within this fortnight; and I have now great hopes of him. I am so hurried in order to overtake the post, that I can only add that I am, dear sir, &c.

I intend to leave this about the 10th of February. Be pleased to direct to me here.

Avignon, Jan. 28, 1767.

I have been so unsettled for some time, that this is almost the first opportunity I have had of thanking you for yours of 16th of last month, which I received about a fortnight ago, and of congratulating you on your having at length succeeded to the bench. I received your letter at Marseilles, whither I went about three weeks ago with a French gentleman, who, happening to be going thither, offered me a place in his chaise. I found there a great number of English, and much more

entertainment than this town affords.   It surprised me, however, a good deal, to meet many young men of fortune who
have it in their power to go either towards Italy or to Paris,
in either of which I should think they might spend their time
more profitably, as well as more agreeably, than in a remote
provincial town like Marseilles.

Nat Clements' second son, and a General Sandford, who
are settled there, were very civil, and made me dine whenever
I was disengaged.   Mr. Clements has found much benefit by
bathing in the sea, which he does whenever the weather per-
mits, to the astonishment of the French who have no notion
of such hardiness.   The climate at Marseilles is I think
much better than at this place, the town being tolerably well
sheltered from the north wind, which here cuts through and
through.

Though I did not carry any of my law-books with me, yet
I can't say I was wholly idle at Marseilles; for Lady Macclesfield, who is now there, did me the honour of entrusting
me with her will, and requested me to draw up a codicil to it,
by which she made many alterations.   She has left four
nieces who travel with her very good fortunes.

I drew upon the banker there for 25l. which you were
so good as to give me, for which I am extremely obliged.   I
should be very sorry to put you to the least distress, but so
much of my money has gone in clothes to make a decent
appearance in this dressing country, where everybody down
to the peruke-maker puts everything he is worth on his back,
that I am afraid I shall be obliged to make use of the indulgence you were so kind as to give in the latter part of your
letter, and draw for 20l. when I get to Paris.

I intend to set out hence about the 15th of next month, and
will travel in the cheapest manner that I can.   There is a
coach hence to Lyons, but it goes so exceedingly slow, being
four or five days doing about 140 miles, that I think of proceeding with the courier, to which method there is no exception but his going rather too quick.   But that is I think a
better extreme than the other.   From Lyons to Paris there is
a tolerably good stage-coach, which performs the journey in
six or seven days.

My Lord Southwell received your letter very safe, and, imagining you would be in Ireland, directed his answer thither. He desires his best compliments, and will trouble you soon with some law queries, which however he says he would equally have done had you remained in your former situation. His son is daily mending, almost beyond our warmest hopes. If I should be under the necessity of troubling you, I'll draw upon Norton. I take it for granted this letter will find you in Dublin, where I suppose you were this week invested with your dignity. I have only to wish health and many years to enjoy it, and to assure you that I am, dear sir, &c.

I hope you got the letter that I addressed to Tom's coffee-house the latter end of last month.

In March, 1767, he reached London. A letter to his father in the following month returns thanks for a present (of money) paid him by Lord Catherlough; adverts to the parliamentary exertions of his friend Lord Northington; to the debates, &c., on American disturbance; and requests that he will not insist upon his residing in town in summer; "for studies in a farmhouse, far from obstructing, would advance their progress;" concluding with the promise—"It is my firm resolution to apply as closely as possible, till I go to Ireland, to the study of law and the practice of the Court of Chancery; and hope soon to make up for the time I have lost."

Soon afterward he was called to the Irish Bar. Such a profession, in either country, seems one of the hazardous casts in the lottery of life. Patience is one of its requisites, and family funds to fall back upon in case of failure, another. Time, diligence, and aptitude, can alone untie the tongues and store the bags of the youthful, the silent, and the briefless.

To the few it affords all that men can wish—rank, wealth, and honours ; to the many, but a dreary attendance, unenlivened by calls to employment. The stream of success sweeps by unfelt by the large majority of candidates, who, like wrecks upon the shore, remain objects of pity or spectacles to gaze at, till disgust drives them from a scene of failure and mortification to some other occupation. Ingenuity indeed has found out other spheres for exertion for the helpless of the profession. A " barrister of seven years' standing," although unknown to fame, unheard of in the courts, is often deemed fit for anything ; and he who never held half-a-dozen briefs, or showed himself in the courts, may at last, by the favour of friends, stumble into a lucrative office. " Life at the Bar " may make a title and promising theme for the ingenious novelist.

His hopes we may believe, were as vivid as youth and good connections could make them. But law did not close his heart against letters. London. associates and conversations were not forgotten ; politics certainly were not. They became a necessary condition of Bar life, as forming the main road to its higher offices ; and at the tables of his father and uncle were found those who could aid in bestowing such things, as well as others who were fated, if not fitted, to receive them.

But some restraint was thrown upon the reception of certain political guests at particular tables shortly after this period. The wits of Dublin on the popular side had combined against the government of Lord Townshend. Missiles, in the form of jest, story, ridicule, and banter, were shot forth against it in the newspapers, in which he took part, and these were afterwards collected into a volume (*Baratariana*) with some effect. We have an indistinct glance at Edmond after he had been some time in Dublin through his friend Chetwood, who seems to have been transferred to a new scene in the south of Ireland, little in unison with his tastes.

Skull, near Shibbereen, Feb. 10, 1768.

At last I address you from my own abode, heartily sorry to write to you from any greater distance than from the college to George Street, for I am sick of solitude and a sequestered rural life already. I was concerned at the necessity I was under of leaving town without seeing you; and the more so, as I had something which I wished to converse with you upon before my departure from Dublin. But that must be the subject of a future interview, or of a future letter. I heard from our friend Southwell last week; his account of himself is a very favourable one, and he seems to write in good spirits. I hear Lord Southwell is to be created Earl Belingsly.

I know you repine at your change of situation from London to our metroplis—not without reason. This ought to raise your compassion for me who am removed in effect out of the world, and as it is in your power in a great measure to introduce me into company, I can't help being so unreasonable as to beg you will do it by informing me what is transacting in life, of parliamentary anecdotes particularly, of which I don't know a man better informed.

I am at present quite out of spirits; I am ashamed to own it, but cannot help it. Philosophy does not always avail to correct constitution. I exert the little portion I can. I believe at last I must have recourse to one of my garrets and the Muse, to induce an *oblivium vitæ præteritæ*. Adieu! Write to me soon, and in the meantime believe me, my dear Ned, your unalterable J. C.

From this presumed familiarity with political matters, his feelings became about this time diverted into a widely different channel. He became in love. Sensitive as the national temperament is said to be to the attractions of the softer sex, he allowed it to influence and colour the whole tenor of his future life. Scarcely anything could expunge the fair object of it from recollection.

Chetwood, as we have seen in a former letter, jests upon his susceptibility of heart toward the lady of the " thick legs." Who this damsel may have been is now unknown. But that either she or some new love exercised the very strongest sway over his heart and conduct we have his own testimony. By reference to dates, this attachment appears to have commenced in 1769. Why it was not gratified in the usual way— whether from humble birth, deficient fortune, family dislikes, or some unhappy flaw in character—does not appear. But matrimony was deemed inexpedient. He however shall tell his own story.

Lord Charlemont, in a letter to him in London in December 1781, thus writes : — " I will not trouble you with our politics, as I know you are not much addicted to that science, and as you probably have constant accounts of all that passes here." The reply in the following month quite undeceives his noble friend. It is ample confession of weakness, yet loses him none of our respect, and forms almost a literal fulfilment of his master Shakspeare's description.

" *He* let concealment,
    Like a worm in the bud, prey on *his* damask cheek."

You say, my Lord, you will not trouble me with politics, as I am not much addicted to that science. I was once deeply engaged by it; but a most unfortunate attachment, which never could have contributed much to my honour, and has ended most unhappily, has estranged me from that and almost everything else, except a few friends, the recollection of whom is one of the last sentiments I shall part with.

I endeavour to employ my thoughts with books and writing, and when weary of them fly into company; and when disgusted with that return back to the other. But all will not do—there is little chance of getting over an attachment that has continued with unabated force for thirteen years; nor at my time of life, is the heart very easily captured by a new object.

You see how frankly I confess my weakness. But if I am not much mistaken you will make some allowance for the extravagance of this sort of sensation, which is allied, however remotely, to some of the best feelings of the heart. I am a very domestic kind of animal, and not at all adapted for solitude.

From the moment it became inexpedient, from whatever cause, to gratify this passion, his feelings became painfully depressed. Whether any objection arose from his family does not appear. They were strongly attached to him; and his father, who was at this period in ill-health, had always evinced the most affectionate regard. To divert the current of thought, he was recommended to travel. His brother had gone to Spa the preceding year, and he joined him there in the summer of 1769.

To a companion of his former excursions, Mr. Thomas Southwell, who continued at Avignon and ultimately became a convert to Romanism, he wrote in April in a desponding tone without specifying the cause. His friend suspected it, and in a strain of pious earnestness thus hints his suspicions in the following month :—

I have turned and re-turned all the words and expressions
of your letter, in order to get some insight into the cause of
your distress, but am still as much in the dark as ever.   The
effects of it appear but too visibly in your manner of writing,
and in your so long silence, as I had written twice.   .   .   .
I mentioned this to Chetwood lately.   He assuredly knows
nothing of your grief, or at least mentions nothing of it to
me.   Would to God I were near you !   Perhaps I might
comfort you, or give some counsel, or hit upon some expe-
dient to extricate you from this distress.   At this distance I
have only prayers to offer that God will in his great mercy
give you that help and consolation you desire.   But you
must address yourself zealously to that great Fountain of
mercy.   .   .   .   I wish you could be more particular (in
statement), except it be something absolutely improper for
me to know.   At present I have formed but one reasonable
conjecture, which is that it is something of a love affair
which you have not been able to bring about.   I wish again
I were near you.   .   .   .   I hope there is no disagreement
with your father.   .   .   .

His elder sister thus writes in August following :—

I beseech you, dear Ned, to recover your spirits.   I own it
is a very hard task, but the greater the difficulty, the more
merit you will have in conquering it.   I wish you would
partake of all sorts of diversions ; for though I do not expect
they can afford you in your present situation any amusement
at the time, yet I believe dissipation is the best remedy
against low spirits ; though I must confess I do not think
it the pleasantest.   .   .   .   Adieu ! my dear Ned, and let
me once more entreat you to strive to get the better of your
melancholy as well for your friends' sake as your own ; for
it is impossible we ever can be happy when we see you
otherwise.

Catherine, the younger, who through life evinced
extreme affection for her brother, writing in Sep-

tember, is less explicit: "I am very glad to find that you are in better spirits than when you left us. Remember, I charge you that they be very good when we meet, which I hope will be soon."

At a later date, another warm friend (the Rev. W. Jephson) is unable to sympathise with the sufferer: "We talk of you (with his sisters) like true lovers: begin generally by abusing, and assuredly end by praising you. Why will you not enjoy the affection that is lavished upon you, and manfully slight that which you cannot obtain or ought to scorn? No man, I verily believe, ever deserved the love of sisters more than you do, and I am certain no man ever possessed it more perfectly. And such sisters, my dearest Ned! But I have done with this. I never throw away the hope of seeing you one day or other think and act like yourself."

His admiring friend Chetwood, who now understood his real position, writes in September 1771: "As to a part of your last letter I shall be silent, because I have some doubts whether this letter will arrive in Limerick by the time you propose leaving it. I cannot however resist my inclination to entreat that you will give me the solid satisfaction of informing me of the departure of —— to America as soon as you know it. I never wish that person to be in the same quarter of the globe with you; for as long as that is the case, I see plainly that you are not master of one atom of resolution."

An eminent political friend, Mr. Denis Daly, of whom some account will hereafter appear, adverts to the same theme from Dublin, April 1779 : " As to Mecklenburgh Street, you are quite wide of the mark. In spite of all your devotees, I am still of opinion that it is in the power of a *man of resolution* to be in or out of love, just as he thinks proper. The difficulty does not lie in succeeding in the attempt, but in making it. I am glad, however, that your resolution is not put to the test, and that the lady remains upon this side (Ireland) of the water."

Poor Malone ! what sympathy can the devoted but unlucky lover expect from his own, the coarser part of creation ? Smiles, perhaps, or sneers, or other provoking proofs of indifference. They are too busy in matters of profit or worldly advancement for those deeper and unseen emotions which once shook their own firmness, but have been forgotten or thrown off as the folly of youth. But how different is it with woman ! From her the sufferer may expect gentleness, kindness, and sympathy to soothe those feelings which, perhaps, cannot be healed. She can understand the distractions which encumber such a state. The life of man is business—to earn the bread he eats, or keep the station in society which he holds. The life of a woman is love—love for her parents, her husband, her children ; the indulgence in short of those softer and devoted feelings which make her the comforter and civilizer of human life. And upon her, in the persons of two most attached sisters, devolved by unwearied assiduity the duty of cheering the sorrows of an amiable brother.

CHAPTER III.

1769—1777.

Law Studies—Irish Duels—Death of his Father—Candidate for the
  Representation of Trinity College—Edition of Goldsmith—Death of
  his Uncle—Literature of the Stage—Removes to London—The
  Shakspeare Mania—Lord Charlemont—George Steevens—Letter
  from his Brother.

His return from Spa, improved by the excursion, took
place ere winter set in. To Dublin he proceeded
without delay—thence sought the courts for as much
employment as attorneys and clients would bestow;
and joined the Munster circuit. Here he remained
four or five years with the usual fortune of a young
barrister—sometimes occupied by a case, sometimes
by the state of the nation, always an important business to men who have little else to do. Allusions to
Dublin business occur in his correspondence. One
friend wishes to "hear of him in long pleadings in
Chancery." Another inquires after "briefs" in
which he was interested. It is likewise remembered
by the lady who now occupies Baronston, that in a
suit between her father and the then Marquis of
Drogheda, Edmond, who was engaged in the cause,
exhibited abilities which promised future eminence.

No diligence to this end was neglected on his own
part. A manuscript volume of his law studies now

lies before me, indexed for reference like a merchant's
ledger. It consists of about one hundred and sixty
pages, for the most part closely written, strongly indicative of the pains taken upon other subjects with a
specific purpose in view.*

His chief correspondent at this period was Chetwood, who invites him from Cork to "Skull" to the
"enjoyment of such music as he may not often hear."
He likewise sends verses to relieve the "soporific
influences of law." And of one of their chosen mutual
friends, a young barrister on the same circuit, and
also a "verse-man," thus writes:—"I should lament
your fate on every circuit much more than I do had
you not such a companion as Hussey. You may talk
of wretchedness, but you can neither of you be unhappy together. His petit extempore is delightful,
as is all that he either writes or thinks." On another
occasion he mentions warmly "Hussey's admirable
Epithalamium."

In 1771 a short visit was paid to England, led by
some instinct to map out the ground on which he
was ultimately destined to abide. Hence he sent
Chetwood Dr. Johnson's pamphlet on the *Falkland
Islands;* when, as an example of the erroneous views
formed by even educated persons in remote districts
of eminent men living in the world, he asks whether
the great moralist "is not venal?" He writes likewise
for the best edition of the celebrated anonymous hero

---

* The title is, *A Table of the several Statutes in Ireland respecting
Treasons, Felonies, and the power of Grand Juries since Poyning's Law.*
At the end of the alphabet are added abstracts from the State Tryals
concerning the Criminal Law.—Edmond Malone.

of the day, adding :—" However insecure Junius may be from criticism, Johnson is still more so."

Ill health overtook him while at his father's country residence, Shinglas, Westmeath, in 1772, and occasioned some months' confinement. The devoted attention shown by his sister Catherine on this occasion was never forgotten. It would appear also that this incident added strength to the regrets that ill-fortune still condemned him to the hapless condition of a bachelor.

In Dublin, the absence of briefs produced divided allegiance between the newspapers and the Forum. He who could not officially talk law, might talk or write politics; and those paper squibs and crackers to which allusion has been made, found vent in abundance. To these, Malone makes allusion in some of his letters, but without such distinctness as serve to mark his own, excepting one. It is ironical; and produced probably from some new ideas started on political economy. He laments in a well-handled paper the notorious improvidence of so poor a people as the Irish, who devour eggs by millions, which if permitted to become fowls would be of more than twenty times the value! For papers of more serious import, he calls upon the great orator and patriot of the day, Henry Flood, to testify to his industry when addressing a Dublin constituency on his own account, soon afterwards. He was of course patriotic in opinions. Who at such an age is not? And what theme more prolific to Irishmen than Ireland?

Toward the beginning of 1773, his brother, then in London, communicated details of a war among the

Peers,—no less than five of that order, and an honourable, being concerned—Lords Townshend, Bellamont,
Ligonier, Ancram, his friend Charlemont, and Mr.
Dillon.   The former two had quarrelled in Ireland.
No fighting however could take place with a Viceroy
in office.   But after the usual complications on such
occasions, it was settled in Marylebone Fields by
Lord Bellamont being shot in the side, very narrowly
escaping death.   Lord Charlemont had a commission
as mediator, but prudently avoided the thankless re-
sponsibility of second.   No allusion to this occurs in
his biography ; although he and Lord Ancram disclosed their part of it in the newspapers.

The reply of Edmond, February, 1773, written in
some anxiety, was no less warlike.   He describes in
a long letter a duel in Dublin between Colonel
Blaquiere, who had just arrived in Ireland as Public
Secretary, and Mr. Bagnell, a fiery member of a
Tipperary family.   Nothing could have been more
unprovoked by the former or more unwarrantable on
the part of the latter.   But the account shows the
stuff of which duels were commonly made—a san-
guinary spirit, ferocity, misconception, ill-temper,
pride, irritability, and—nonsense.

The interest of Malone in his brother's account of
the affair in England, arose from the implication of his
friend—for near acquaintance had now ripened into
friendship with Lord Charlemont.   All Ireland took
a similar interest in him.   In return, he entertained
the strongest attachment for her ; and certainly no
country could point to a more honest, amiable, pure-
minded man.   Edmond and he first met at the tables

of his father and uncle, where much of the genius and wit of Dublin were to be found. Their politics and tastes were then similar; and substantial private qualities ripened into sincere regard. The topics of the moment, as being too exciting, were often forgotten in their correspondence. Literature, criticism, and rare books, frequently superseded politics, poetry, and law. In fact, the former three in quiet times formed the natural tastes of both; sought by one as relief from private disquiet, by the other in order to forget for a time those ferments in which commercial injustice and parliamentary control from the sister island had embroiled his country.

Possessed of sound common sense, his lordship had likewise that moderation of tone in which Irishmen are sometimes deficient. He would go as far as prudent men may fairly go, but no farther. He was the drag-chain that kept that mighty engine, the volunteers of 1782, from running over their leaders. Altogether he was, perhaps, the most popular man ever seen in Ireland—but he wanted one faculty to become the greatest—that was the gift of public speaking. The want of it threw him back upon his books and pen. He wrote, it is said, pretty largely; but from timidity and reserve shrunk from the honours of the press. His letters, however, make us fully acquainted with the man. An epistolary intercourse with Malone commenced soon after the removal of the latter to London, which continued nearly to the close of life. These furnish evidence of scholar-like propensities, pursued in those useful and innocent hours which thought and intelligence can win in its library when the outside world is contentious or adverse. Notices of these will hereafter appear.

In the spring of 1774 Malone lost his father, who evinced undiminished affection in the gift of an income which insured moderate independence. Politics were still kept in view; but in exchange for squibs and pamphlets he sought the usual family destination, a seat in Parliament. He even aimed at the University of Dublin. Among his papers is the draft of a speech in his own handwriting, spoken on that occasion, which rattles away in choice candidate-style to the constituent body.

In this he speaks of his nomination and address in the previous summer; and of his relationship to Anthony Malone, admitted to be one of the most wise, able and disinterested men living, who, unlike most others in Parliament, had done everything for his country and nothing for his connections. Yet even of him he was independent. "For, a few months ago, I obtained, at too high a price indeed, an honourable independence; nor shall any motive on earth induce me to forfeit it." He would regard no private tie, no relative in public affairs, but deem himself a trustee merely for the people; that he had testified this spirit in a private capacity in opposing the corrupt government of Lord Townshend—to which the worthy friend, nominated at the same time as himself, and another gentleman, the greatest orator in this or, perhaps, any other kingdom, would bear testimony.* He thus

* Meaning, no doubt, Henry Flood, of whom some notice will hereafter appear. He had warred much against Lord Townshend's government, joined by many witty or popular men, whose ephemeral sallies

characterizes the mass of public men of the day: " Who are most unqualified for their offices—who accumulate place upon place, sinecure upon sinecure —who are so eager to obtain the wages of the day ere the day has passed over them, as to be emphatically, and not improperly, termed ready-money voters ? "

If this be even a tolerably correct picture of Irish peers and commoners—and most Irish writers unfortunately agree in the sketch—who, however they may abuse it, can wonder at the Union ? What honest man can regret the extinction of a mass of corruption that formed a standing national disgrace ?

From newspaper paragraphs and essays, the next usual step of candidates in letters is to editorship ; and this office he now assumed. It was an edition of Goldsmith's works, commenced in 1776, printed in Dublin the following year, and republished by Evans, a London bookseller, in 1780. Here we find his characteristic love of accuracy. He first drew forth from Dr. Wilson, Fellow of the College, memoranda of the poet and his tutor (February 24th, 1776), which came into my hands in the search for materials for his biography, and are noticed elsewhere.*

In 1776, the death of his celebrated uncle, Anthony, without issue, gave Baronston his seat, and a fortune to his elder brother.† For a time this produced no

---

were collected in the volume already mentioned. Malone, by this confession, appears to have been one of the number.

  * *Life of Goldsmith*, vol. i. p. 63. Murray, 1837.

  † The will of Anthony Malone, made in July, 1774, gave all his estates in the counties of Westmeath, Roscommon, Longford, Cavan, and Dublin, to his nephew, Richard Malone, eldest son and heir of his late brother Edmond, in the utmost confidence that they will be settled and continue in the male line of the family and branches of it, " according to

change in the arrangements of Edmond. But having now none whose wishes it was necessary to consult, or whose opinions carried control, he seems to have contemplated withdrawal from the Bar, and the adoption of a more quiet and studious career.

The turmoil of contentious life, the power to bait or to endure daily baiting in the courts, was probably not to his taste. It was provoking to take the side he was paid for, not that which he preferred—to enter for hours on a warfare of words which should endeavour to make that *right* which he could not but suspect or know to be wrong. He had not yet, perhaps, arrived at the conviction, that those were mere tricks of trade, of being to the ear what conjuring is to the eye, efforts to make things appear as they are *not;* and therefore adverse to the taste of a straightforward man. The state of his heart—that impressible and unsophisticated organ as it proved to be—no doubt had its weight; and when these were balanced against London society, authors, letters, libraries, and repositories of every learned pursuit for learned or studious men, we cannot wonder at the preference at length given to the English metropolis.

Of his early attachment to the literature of the stage we are left in no doubt. During his visits to

priority of birth and seniority of age." These estates, all acquired by the practice of law, have become largely the prey of law. Richard (Lord Sunderlin afterward) did not strictly fulfil his uncle's injunction. Upon his death in 1816, his sisters claimed the estates. Their right became contested; and when 10,000*l.* had been spent in legal proceedings, a compromise gave them 3,000*l.* a year for life, upon surrendering the estates. Further litigation ensued, as successive deaths occurred, between claimants legitimate and illegitimate; and the estates have been at intervals, and are still (1859), before Parliament and the courts of law.

London, persons who were familiar with it formed his
favourite friends. Among others was George Steevens,
the editor of Shakspeare; who found in his young
Irish acquaintance, in the same pursuit, no probable
cause for that rivalry which might be apprehended
from others of more name and experience. He even
lent him to copy, while still resident in Ireland, his
own transcript of Langbaine's *Dramatic Poets*. These
volumes, largely annotated, had belonged to Oldys;
were bought by Dr. Birch at the sale of his books
and papers; lent to the Reverend Mr. (afterwards
Bishop) Percy to copy; by him lent to Steevens for a
similar purpose; and by the latter to Malone, whose
interleaved copy with large additions, now in the
Bodleian Library, forms another monument of un-
flagging industry.

He writes his name at the commencement of the
work, 1777, with a short notice of Langbaine. At the
conclusion of the fourth volume it is added—" Mem.
—Finished this transcript, March 30, 1777," with his
name. At a later period, the handwriting still his, but
more unsteady, it is further noticed—" I left Ireland,
May 1st, 1777, and settled in London." In another
place we find—" Since it (the transcript) was made in
1777 I have made numerous additions to it—1787."

The date of his advent to London, about which
there had been some doubt, is therefore settled by
himself. His first abode was No. 7, Marylebone
Street, where he continued till 1779. Thence a
change took place to 55 (often written 58), Queen
Ann Street, East, re-named subsequently Foley
Place, where he continued for the remainder of

life the pursuit of studies insuring content and reputation, and the society of friends, many of them the most distinguished men of the age.

His correspondence with Lord Charlemont commenced about this busy political period. Yet amid great national excitement (in Ireland) their subjects were almost exclusively literary. Politics gave way to books, war to criticism, heroes to writers. While volunteer armies, American reverses, and threatened French invasions, had nearly withdrawn the native country of these philosophers from her allegiance to England, they—one of them soon afterward a conspicuous actor in the scene—scarcely permitted the heats of the time to be distinguished in their letters. At length the Commoner found courage to disclose to the Peer that his criticisms, disquisitions, and letters were likely to become books;—their subject, Shakspeare.

Little connected as the subjects may seem, frequent explorations of black-letter law—fond as he was of going to the basis of all things—led him onward to the taste for its poetry and dramatic literature. "The love of things ancient," says Bacon, "doth argue stayedness;" and between a staid lawyer and staid critic, both being devoted to the balance of evidence, there is perhaps less difference than at first view may appear. On previous visits to London, Johnson and Steevens' *Shakspeare* was full in the current of popular favour. No subject was more likely to attract a young man of literary predilections; while occasional personal glances obtained at the master-critic himself tended to confirm his reverence. The topic was open to moderate as well as to the highest talents; and distinguished men of at least two previous ages had attempted explanations of the obscurities of the great poet, or often mystified what they could not successfully explain. Ample room yet remained for trials of skill by others. Every discussion added to the fame of the subject. But simple admiration was deemed insufficient without comment. Several therefore wrote upon him who were little entitled to write upon anything—and as the worm thrives upon the carcase of the author, critics sought their peculiar nutriment or distinction by fastening and fattening upon his fame.

Time has so little diminished this passion, or rather mania, that it has grown nearly to a literary nuisance. Editors and commentators upon Shakspeare appear at every turn in all societies. In the club-house we meet three or four of a morning; in the park, see them meditating by the Serpentine, or under a tree in Kensington Gardens; no dinner table is without one or two; in the theatre you view them by dozens. Volume after volume is poured out in note, comment, conjecture, new reading, statement or mis-statement, contradiction, or variation of all kinds.

Reviews, magazines, and newspapers, repeat these with so little mercy on the reader, as to give occasional emendations of their own. Some descant upon his sentiments, some upon his extravagances, some upon his wonderful creations or flights of imagination, some upon his language or phraseology. Several suppose that he wrote more plays than he acknowledged; others, that he fathered more than he had written. While the last opinions are still more original and extraordinary—that his name is akin to a myth, and that he wrote no plays at all! Every new aspirant in this struggle for distinction aims to push his predecessor from his stool. Hero-worship sinks to nothing compared with this interminable author-worship. We are not permitted for a week together to think for ourselves, but so crammed by successive volumes as to have no power of literary digestion left. And, however worthy of all honour the object may be, we become weary of such busy, yet useless or trifling adorers, and are tempted to exclaim in an agony of impatience—when is this clatter of criticism to end?

Men of talents can often throw interest into even a hackneyed subject; and thus Dr. Johnson did not disdain to participate in the work of inferior writers. But he looked at the poet as a great whole. He felt his vastness and saw his weaknesses, but would not place him upon the literary dissecting table to be sliced into a thing of words, syllables, or phrases, for the gratification of the carrion critics around him. Taking the range of a capacious and original mind, he has said in that preface, which will endure as long as the volumes it introduced, all that one great man can say in honour of another still greater. Inferior artists were left to hunt up smaller matters. Research, such as the occasion required—long, laborious, minute, often irksome—defied his eyes, his patience, and his time of life.

Upon his colleague in the edition, Mr. George Steevens, devolved this portion of the duty. As a critic, he had several qualifications—a scholar, a wit, of ready perceptions, an appetite for work, and not indisposed to those antiquarian pursuits required by the undertaking. He did not, however, intend so wide a range in research as the subject of this Memoir had in view ; nor was he of course so successful. Neither did he in a private capacity win the favourable opinion of contemporaries. He had the unhappy art of making enemies. He is represented as sarcastic, ill-natured, jealous, envious, self-sufficient, and while occasionally prone to a kind or generous action, quite as ready to evince bitter malignity for small or fancied offences.

Malone, from the first, seems to have felt that exclusive of what had been done for Shakspeare, there were several topics yet untouched, or scarcely touched, open to a devoted inquirer. The chronology of his plays, the stories on which they were grounded, the history of the stage during his occupation of it, the poetry and dramas of other writers of the time, the incidents of their lives, successes, and discouragements—all tended to throw light upon the principal figure.

Upon this extended canvas he set to work with characteristic zeal. No publication of the age of Elizabeth, her predecessors or successors, in the form of poem, drama, pamphlet, or miscellaneous tract, was neglected. Manuscripts, wherever found, were carefully consulted ; no expense or application was spared to exhume something like truth and substance out of the graveyards of time. Collectors, antiquaries, and college men, whose lives had been spent in storing their shelves or their memories with knowledge of the past, were solicited to disburse such acquisitions as could be turned to account.

Who, fond of literature, shall not sympathize with such an inquirer—his hopes, discoveries, disappointments? How often is he befriended by chance! A date, a name, a fact, an allusion, a reference, however slight, even to an unpromising object, suddenly starts from some obscure corner to gladden his eye and heart, and give assurance that he who works diligently shall not work in vain. Even when positive facts fail, there may be ground for plausible conjecture. A slender clue may track a labyrinth. History is made up of such discoveries, accidents, or combinations; biography is often so. *Haud inexpertus loquor.* Yet how often is it that some destroying agent, or rather barbarian, careless of the interest, or ignorant of the value of written memorials of the facts of life or history, have consigned them to destruction! * And how many of those slighter details, occurrences, projects, or intrigues, that link small matters with great—how many points of manner, conduct, temper, or peculiarity that make up the sum of human character, are thus lost, of which we would gladly be informed! But, under every disadvantage, the hard student, like the daring soldier, must occasionally adventure

---

* Almost at the moment of penning this, I had heard from my late friend, Commissioner Charles Phillips, that the whole, or nearly the whole, of the papers of an eminent Irish peer, statesman, and lawyer, had been committed to the flames soon after his death. Many names, in many ways, would, it seems, have been compromised by their preservation. Surely, in this indiscriminate paper-massacre, the curious and unoffending could have been separated from the obnoxious? I had not long before heard of a similar immolation of a series of letters of a deceased literary man, descriptive of London life, letters, and society, because a few were objectionable in portions of the details!

upon a forlorn hope, and like him not unfrequently be rewarded by success.

Few difficulties were encountered by Malone in his new sphere of residence but what London connections readily overcame. He was proud to meet her celebrities—happy to receive their civilities—happier still in not being destined to mount to eminence through the rugged paths of penury, tracked as hunters do wounded animals by the pain and suffering commonly attendant upon friendless adventurers in letters.

In commencing the subject of study, he judiciously resolved to begin at the beginning; to trace out in the first instance the chronology of the poet's plays. A temporary diffidence, however, overcame him. He imagined that something of ridicule or prejudice might attach to one whose recent profession had been so dissimilar. Happily it occurred to him to consult Lord Charlemont, whose taste in letters he found reason to respect; and his lordship's approval was immediately given. It is the first letter which I have met with in their correspondence, and forms a fair example of what it continued for twenty years.

Marino, August 18th, 1777.

My dear Malone.—I cannot give you a stronger proof of my approbation of the subject which procured me the pleasure of your letter than by thus sitting down to answer it, though scarcely able to write from the effects of a disagreeable nervous complaint in my head and eyes. That some wise ones may smile at your lucubrations, I doubt not; but let them smile. There is nothing more despicable than their censure. For surely that wisdom may be accounted folly which would cut off one principal source of innocent amusement from a state which seems to stand in need of every such assistance to render it tolerable. One of the Roman emperors is said to have offered a reward to any one who should invent a new pleasure; and if to pleasure he had added the epithet *innocent,* I should highly approve of his design, certain as I am that such invention would do more real service and much less injury to mankind than all the wise speculations of philosophers from Epicurus to Voltaire.

For my own part, I will never be laughed out of my amusements till they shall have proved hurtful to society, but will boldly proceed in those pursuits which, though they cannot be deemed the fruits of literature, may at least be styled its flowers. Such is my opinion of the more trifling literary amusements. But your undertaking, my dear Ned, needs not any such apology. The history of man is on all hands allowed to be the most important study of the human mind; and what is your chronological account of the writings of Shakspeare other than the history of the progress of the greatest genius that ever honoured and delighted human nature?

And now to proceed in answer to your queries. Allured by the title-page, I long since read Green's play,* with the view you mention, but could not find in it the most distant resemblance to the fairy part of the *Midsummer Night's Dream.* The plan of it, in brief, is this: Bohan, a Scot, disgusted with the world, has retired to a tomb where he has fixed his dwelling; and here he is met by *Aster Oberon,* king of the fairies who entertains him with an *antick,* or dance by his subjects. These two personages, after some moral conversation, determine to listen to a tragedy which is acted before them, and to which they make a kind of chorus by moralizing at the end of each act—a circumstance which so early in the English drama may perhaps be curious.

The edition which I possess of Sir David Lindsay's works, though printed so early as 1581, is not the original, but is said in the title-page to be *turned and made perfect English from Poems compiled in the Scottish tongue.* In this collection

* *James the Fourth, a Scottish Story.*

there is but one poem with the title you mention, viz., *The Tragedy of David Beton*, late Cardinal and Archbishop of Santandrons, so written for St. Andrews.

I received by Dick Marlay* the *King John* in two parts, and return you many thanks for your goodness to me. In order to render my old edition of Spenser complete, I wish you could procure the first quartos of the following pieces:— *Two Cantos of Mutability; Amoretti, or Sonnets; Prothalamion and Epithalamion; Four Hymns; Daphnaida, an Elegy on Douglas Howard; Britain's Ida* (this not by Spenser, yet bound with his works); *A View of the State of Ireland; Some Letters between the Author and Mr. Harvey.*

Did Upton ever publish his third volume of Spenser's works in quarto? I wish also that you could procure for me the collection of Lord Essex's letters.

You see what it is to encourage a troublesome correspondent. But relying on your goodness, and on the resemblance of our pursuits, I doubt not but that you will pardon

Your very affectionate and obedient humble servant,

CHARLEMONT.

Don't forget to send me a copy of *your* " Shakspeare " (for such I love to call it) as soon as it shall be published. Remember me to all friends; and if your friend Mr. Steevens should recollect a person who had once the pleasure of dining in his company at poor Goldsmith's entertainment,† please to present my compliments to him. Has Percy published his new edition of Surrey's poems? Don't let Sunning Hill seclude you too much from the world. Retirement is a good thing, but certainly too large a dose of it is not suited to your constitution. It is very possible that I may be able to see you in spring. I should like it much, but it depends on many circumstances. Adieu.

The allusion of his lordship to Steevens arose from the intimacy now prevailing between that gentleman

* Well known in literary circles in London and Dublin. Afterwards Bishop of Waterford.

† This dinner I have noticed in the Life of that poet early in 1774.

and his correspondent. Between the critics existed also a free interchange of letters. Not less than twenty with dates, and nearly as many without, passed from the senior to the junior within a short time, which became scattered at the younger Boswell's sale,—their subjects, as may be supposed, Shakspeare and Shakspeare-men from Capell to Warton, criticism, notes to plays, and passing circumstances bearing on such themes.

Steevens likewise adverts at this time (1778) to an intended trip of Malone to Dublin. In jest, as was often his habit, or with marvellous good-nature, he requests in such case, that " his notes may remain behind —*ne quid detrimenti capiat respublica.* St. George's Channel has had its share of literary spoil.* Seal up your criticisms, however, for I shall not venture to examine them till your return."

This journey, whether actual or only contemplated, arose from the persuasions of his family. A hard student in a strange land seems, and often must be, in a state of uncomfortable isolation ; and so his sisters thought. Whether he felt so may be doubted. Men of resolution aiming at distinction in a specific pursuit, will seldom be turned from it by minor considerations ; but sisterly affection sees such privations in a different light. They therefore pressed his return.

The following to the same effect from his brother,†

---

* In allusion probably to the loss of scarce works of Mr. Dennis Daly on the same voyage, collected by Malone.

† This gentleman was himself fond of the society of London, and paid it an annual visit. He became member of the Irish Parliament for Granard in 1768 ; for county of Westmeath in 1782 ; returned also for a borough in King's County ; in 1778, married Philippa, elder daughter of

evinces the truest regard. He sketches for him a scheme of life, which, as usual with kind relatives, had worldly, not literary, advancement in view.

Dublin, Nov. 10*th,* 1777.

I received your letter of the 24th October this day sevennight, a few hours after my arrival in town; and should have been sorry your expectations of seeing me suddenly in London, as indeed you had reason to do, should have prevented your writing. It is in vain I think to stop any more letters to me, for as surely as I do, some new matters occur to retard my journey. I had better therefore, I believe, say that it will be a *long* time before I shall see you, and then probably I shall appear at a moment when you least expect it.

But jest apart, I now really hope to embark in a few days, not that I can yet name the particular time. A Mr. Cahill, whom you remember we went with one day last spring, to Mr. Wolfe's, is preparing to file a bill against me. Glasscock thinks, as indeed I do, that it will be best, if possible, to prevent the addition of another law-suit, and is now reading the case, which has been laid before him. When I find in what manner it is proper for me to proceed with regard to that affair, I shall quit this; and at all events shall not suffer that business to detain me here for any considerable time. I have attended the courts pretty constantly since I have been in town, but though I despair to get rid of, I hope at least to get *out* of them.

Some of your friends, whom I have seen there, and indeed at other places, lament your having quitted the kingdom at this time, as they think, and I believe with reason, there never was so favourable an opportunity for a young man of any abilities rising at the bar, as at present. The defalcation of the great lawyers that has happened here of late, is indeed astonishing. Tisdall's death has in its consequences occasioned the retirement of two men of the most eminent that remained, Hutcheson and Radcliffe. The former, become

Godolphin Rooper, Esq., of Berkhampstead; in 1785, raised to the Irish Peerage as Lord Sunderlin. His seat, Baronston, Westmeath, is forty-seven miles from Dublin.

Secretary of State, has bid adieu to the bar, and the latter, just appointed Judge of the Prerogative Court, has also (by agreement) quitted the practice of the Hall; so that in the space of less than three months, all the capital lawyers almost to a man are gone off. Tisdall, Dennis, Hutcheson, and Radcliffe, not to say a word of my uncle, who led the way so recently before. I am convinced that were you to return here you could not fail of the most rapid success in the profession; and really wish—could you in any sort reconcile it with your other schemes of happiness—that you would once more adventure in a pursuit, which there is no doubt would now be attended with the greatest advantages to your fortune, if that is a matter you consider as any object.

The only thing I can see wanting absolutely to insure success, would be a seat in Parliament, which might easily be obtained, and should be immediately done by me, if you choose it, with the greatest pleasure. One obstacle, I know, would occur to you in such a proposal, which is the difficulties you might imagine it would lay me under; but to entirely remove any objections or scruples you might have on that head, you shall hereafter, if you please, repay me the expenses attending it if you meet with the success that I hope. If not, whatever the disappointment may be (of which I think there is little probability), the loss I am sure will be to me *temporary* and *inconsiderable;* but the reflection of having endeavoured to contribute my mite to a scheme that bids fair for promoting your prosperity, will certainly afford me a pleasure that I well know will *always* continue.

Perhaps, among other objections you might have, would be the awkwardness in returning to a place, which you seemingly had relinquished—that, I think, is no obstacle, if there were no other in the way. Upon a little reflection I think it would appear to you as undeserving of attention, because your coming into Parliament of itself would be considered by every one a sufficient motive for the change of your intentions, if indeed in their eyes there wanted any; for you are too well acquainted with the people of this country, not to know that your returning to a place which they consider as containing everything desirable, would not be to them a matter of the smallest surprise. Upon the whole, I most ardently wish that you would have it in your contemplation, and for my own part think you might adopt this scheme, without by any means bidding adieu to the other kingdom, or sacrificing your happiness to your interests, which I should be one of the last persons to recommend.

You do not seem very fond of the *pleasures* of London, and probably will not hereafter pass much of your time there. Why should you not then keep the place in the country you now have, and spend the principal part of the summer vacations there; besides occasionally visiting it, as well as London at such other times as may be agreeable. At all events you would have it as a place ultimately to retire to, should you find a return to this kingdom either not answer, or any residence here so irksome upon trial, that you should think the sacrifices made by the exchange more than a balance for the greatest advantages that might arise from it. But I hope very soon to see you, when we can talk more at large upon the subject. I only wish now to recommend it to your consideration: for, notwithstanding what I have said, you will believe, whatever may be my own sentiments, I only wish you to pursue that path of life which, upon due deliberation, you may think most likely to lead to your happiness.

I have so little time to go to the House of Commons, that I can give you no account of what is going forward there; and if I could, you probably receive intelligence of it through other channels, from those who know more of the matter than I do. Everything is certainly going on very quiet there, and I believe likely to continue so.

Since I wrote the above, Glasscock has been with me. He would fain keep me till McEvoy's affair comes on, which he is in hopes will be in a few days. He seems to have fears that we shall want sufficient proofs to disclose the iniquity of this transaction, and wishes me if possible to be present; yet I think if it does not come on by the middle of next week, nothing shall induce me to stay here a moment longer: but I have expressed the same so often before, that you may truly say, " I hear, but can believe no more."

CHAPTER IV.

1778—1781.

An Attempt to ascertain the Order in which the Plays of Shakspeare were written—Irish Politics—Mr. Denis Daly—Sir Joshua Reynolds — Supplement to the Edition of *Shakspeare's Plays* by Samuel Johnson and George Steevens—Hogarth's Widow—Lord Charlemont—Rowley's Poems—Jephson's Count of Narbonne—Epilogue.

AGAINST three such lures—a seat in Parliament, no rivals of note in the courts, and residence in his native country—all irresistible to an ambitious man —his philosophic spirit was proof. Fame might be otherwise secured. Wealth and honours were not worth the slavery endured in the pursuit. Certain feminine temptations might be avoided. And the cultivation of sober, sedentary letters became therefore his deliberate choice.

In January 1778, came out *An Attempt to ascertain the Order in which the Plays of Shakspeare were written*. A few of his opinions upon this subject were subsequently modified; but the main were republished in the prologomena to his edition of the poet in 1790. He had the satisfaction likewise of securing the assent of such a fastidious judge as Steevens, who thus writes in his second edition:— "By the aid of the registers at Stationers' Hall, and such internal evidences as the pieces themselves supply, he (Malone) hath so happily accomplished his undertaking, that he only leaves me the power to thank him for an arrangement which I profess my inability either to dispute or to improve."

Uninfluenced by this successful opening into literary life, intimate friends in Ireland could see little advantage in his selection. They thought well of his talents, and wished for their exertion in a more stirring sphere. Politics formed the great game of all the Irish gentry; and he who declined to play it was thought to have spent his life to little purpose, or wanted spirit for the pursuit. As his brother had failed to move his resolution, others now tried their powers of persuasion. Among these were John Fitzgibbon, afterwards distinguished as Earl of Clare; one or two of the Fitzgeralds; and Mr. Denis Daly. All wished for his influence, or expected much from the soundness of his advice in a crisis they saw at hand.

The state of Ireland at this time had assumed a new and threatening aspect. As national misfortune will ever engender discontent, the disasters of the American war led Irish politicians to look narrowly into the condition of their country, in order as well to withstand a foreign enemy, as to place the ties that bound them to England in an improved condition. Her great and undoubted grievances were—restraint upon her originating laws for her own guidance, dependence of her Parliament upon the Ministry and Parliament of the sister state, and the imposition of very selfish and ungenerous restrictions upon her commerce by that state. England, above all countries in the world, would never for a moment have submitted to anything

of the kind herself; but as the stronger party, she
thought fit to inflict them upon a weaker for three-
fourths of a century. The law of the strongest, however, is one not fated to last. Neither has a single
opinion been advanced since in support of the justice
or policy of a system long retained and unwillingly
surrendered.   Ireland, therefore, seized upon the
moment to extricate herself from a thraldom at once
tyrannical and insulting.

To do this, however, cost no ordinary effort. There
was England to alarm or to convince of her error;
Ireland to arouse to the point of resistance without
risking absolute separation ; a force to organize in
order to give weight to her remonstrances ; a spirit
of true patriotism to instil into her crooked-minded
or wavering statesmen ; and the whole influence of
government in Ireland and England to overcome.

One of the leading men in accomplishing these
patriotic objects was the writer of the following letter,
Mr. Denis Daly. Educated at Christchurch, Oxford,
returned member for the county of Galway at twenty-
one, he is represented by Sir Jonah Barrington as
" a man of great abilities, large fortune, exquisite
eloquence, and high character." Hardy, in his *Life
of Lord Charlemont*, gives the highest praise to his
oratory ; and of one of his great efforts on the embargo
question says : " It was the most perfect model of
parliamentary speaking that, in my opinion, could
be exhibited." Lord Charlemont himself writes to
Malone, January 11th, 1779, shortly after its delivery : " Your friend Daly has lately outdone himself ;
I never heard in any house of Parliament a better

speech than his upon the embargo." In 1779, he retired with Grattan to the village of Bray, about ten miles from Dublin, to concert those measures which, however opposed at the moment, and carried ultimately with difficulty, experience proved to be wise and effectual. They gave content, free trade, and independence of her Parliament to one country, without inflicting the slightest loss of any description upon the other.

To Malone he bore a strong attachment. They were good scholars, fond of books, read them attentively, and collected the best authors and first editions zealously, of which it appears he did not always gain possession after making the purchase. Lord Charlemont tells Malone, about 1779: "You have, I suppose, been informed of the evil destiny of Daly's books. The ship in which they were embarked foundered off Beachy Head, and all his first editions are gone to the bottom."

In addition to personal friendship, their families were intimate. Daly's sister, a very clever person, had selected Henrietta and Catherine Malone as her chosen friends; and through this channel, no doubt, the persuasions of her brother to his friend to return to the land of his property and family became stronger. The mention of unhappiness alludes to his love affair. We have a glance, likewise, at some Irish statesmen; but the scene described at the conclusion we may consider rather as a sally of Irish vivacity than grave matter of fact.

Dublin, February 22nd, 1778.

MY DEAR NED.—I wrote to you about a month ago to beg pardon for my want of punctuality, and to plead guilty to us much idleness as you please to lay to my charge. I do not attempt to make any excuse of the business of Parliament, for very little has been done there; and I have been every whit as indolent with respect to that as to my correspondence. I put off writing to you, as I do about everything else, from day to day, intending to send you a very long letter, partly respecting you, and partly myself. But what I have heard from Fitzgerald lately has hurried me a little, and interested me enough about you to make me very impertinent.

I do most solemnly assure you that you have not a friend in the world more nearly concerned in everything that can happen to you than myself, and you may be sure that I cannot hear of your being unhappy, without being sincerely afflicted. When a man of good sense is completely master of a matter that concerns him—when nothing prevents him from seeing it with all its circumstances in its true light, it is the height of absurdity for any other person to pretend to advise him on the subject. And yet when I consider how warmly all your friends here wish to have you among them, and how very little pleasure or advantage you receive by being absent, I can hardly help entreating you to return, and not to sacrifice us all to so very little purpose. Depend upon it, however, you may pass over a year or two at your present time of life; you will find it more comfortable, as well as more respectable, to pass the principal part of it where your property and *all your connections* are, than at a distance from both. '

If you are angry at the liberty I take, I shall soon be with you to make my excuses in person; and I do assure you a very principal inducement will be to see you, especially at present. Though you have deserted all your friends, you shall not be able to accuse them of deserting you. Our business here will be pretty well over at Easter, and I have no other, at least of a pleasanter kind, to detain me.

Our friend Burgh has played the most comical part in the world for a minister. He has laboured hard to keep up his character with both parties, but he has been very unsuccessful. He has acted against Government on one or two occasions, but has taken special care that the questions should be of no sort of consequence. In everything of importance

he has stuck close to Administration, sometimes at the
expense of his consistency. I do not find that he has convinced many persons of his disinterestedness, and has only
persuaded his present patrons that he is a very inconvenient
minister. The Attorney-General seems to grow into confidence. You can have no idea what a speaker he is at present,
and how infinitely he falls short even of his former miserable
rhapsodies. Burgh himself has been pretty bad upon the
whole; and Flood hardly ever opens his lips except to convey
an oblique censure upon the present Administration by
praising the last. You may guess how matters stand in our
House when I do assure you Opposition fairly out-talks the
Ministry. As for myself, I got drunk last night with the
Primate, the Speaker, and Mr. Secretary Heron.

I hope in a very few weeks to trouble you to take lodgings
for me; and am, my dear Ned,

Ever yours sincerely and affectionately,

DENIS DALY.

I am now nominee for Bushe in his Petition for Kilkenny.
When it is over, I will let you know.

Neither personal nor epistolary persuasions displaced the critic from his stool. London he had
decided should be his home, and by that resolution
meant to abide. Daly therefore paid his visit, but
the voice of the charmer sounded in vain.

In the following year he gives Malone the Irish
view of the state of affairs, and of the English
Opposition.

Dublin, April 26th, 1779.

I suppose you have heard that all my *Editiones Principes*
are gone to edify the fishes off Beachy Head.* Pray let me
know what I am in Mr. ——'s debt, that I may remit to him,
and direct to me at Dunsandle,† as I mean to retire thither

---

* Alluding to the foundering of the ship that contained them on her
passage to Ireland.

† His seat in the west of Ireland.

the moment Henry Grattan returns, whom we expect every day. In his letters to me, he does not seem to have acquired a high opinion either of the principles or eloquence of the British Parliament, especially of the Opposition.

It gives me great satisfaction to find that our independent companies (volunteers) raise some serious apprehensions both in the English and Irish Administrations, for I am convinced that this country will be indebted to their fears alone for any favours received. If I am not very much mistaken, our next session will be as turbulent as ever Charlemont himself could wish. Lord Buckingham is, of all men upon earth, the most unfit for the present crisis. He and all his coadjutors are timid to a ridiculous degree; and his public economy, necessary as it is, has made so many men his enemies that I have a strong suspicion that something in the way of a very strong address will be procured at the meeting of Parliament. I wish sincerely we may have hopes of seeing you at the opening of it. Surely London will have as great charms in October.

Your brother, sister, and all your friends here, are perfectly well except poor Charlemont, who is still terribly troubled by the rheumatism. You have heard, I suppose, that Fitz (Gibbon) is third Sergeant, Carleton, Solicitor (General), and Heller, a Judge in Tenison's place.

When you write, let me know something of your literary pursuits. Consider that I am just going to be shut up for six months without any employment but composing panegyrics for the House of Commons; that I still feast upon every article of intelligence you send me; but, whether idle or occupied, always, my dear Ned,

Yours most faithfully and affectionately,

DENIS DALY.

Absence from Irish friends naturally induced the wish to replace them by others within easy reach of association. His connections, pleasing manners, and social qualities, found free access to such as could estimate classical knowledge, added to considerable attainments in Italian, French, and general literature.

To Johnson, Steevens, and many others of note, he soon added Tyrwhitt, Dr. Lort, the two Wartons, Isaac Reed, Dr. Farmer, Dr. Francklin (of Cambridge), Burney, and several more.

At what period he first knew Burke does not appear, though doubtless before settling in London, through the introduction of mutual Irish acquaintance. The date assigned in his private memoranda to intercourse with Sir Joshua Reynolds is 1778 ; in a printed statement, 1777. But there is little doubt that he knew him, though not intimately, at a still earlier period. In the President's memoranda, as Mr. Cotton obligingly informs me, *Mr.* Malone paid the first instalment for his portrait (36*l.* 13*s.*) in May 1774 ; the second, a similar sum, in July 1778. The same memorial states that an equal sum remained then due for the portrait of *Chancellor* Malone (Anthony) ; so that the former appears to have been Edmond or his elder brother.

The intimacy with Sir Joshua became, after some time, cordial attachment. Each exercised that gentleman-like hospitality which gives to London life one of its powerful attractions. They often met at the houses of mutual friends, and sometimes took short country excursions together. Both were men of sterling worth, of social habits, good-natured, well-informed, attached to literature and literary men as sources of rational enjoyment, and esteemed by all who had admission to their society. Both were, as Malone has minutely recorded, of similar stature and weight, and although of considerable difference in age, each fond of testing his physical vigour as a pedestrian.

At a later period, the painter occasionally sought Malone's opinion on minor points connected with the composition of his discourses ; and he did the same probably with Johnson and Burke. Hence a most ungenerous rumour found circulation, that he was indebted for much of their matter as well as manner to the Irish orator—an opinion which I have combated at some length in another place.*

Nothing indeed can be more unjust, under any circumstances falling short of positive proof, than to surmise away the honest reputation of any man of undoubted talents, such as Reynolds, because he associates with another of still higher genius and attainments. That men improve in mind by communication with greater minds, is the common attribute of our nature. We should be wanting in capacity, in observation, in common intelligence if it were not so. But it does not thence follow that the lesser intellect owes all its acquisitions to the greater. I find the following short note in Malone's correspondence, in proof that the President did not always ask even Burke for those smaller critical offices which friends are free to exact from and render to each other :—

December 15th, 1786.

My dear Sir,—I wish you could just run your eye over my discourse, if you are not too much busied in what you have made your own employment. I could wish that you would do more than merely look at it; that you would examine it with a critical eye, in regard to grammatical correctness, the propriety of expression, and the truth of the observations. Yours, &c., J. Reynolds.

* *Life of Burke*, p. 360, 5th edition.

Resuming the line of inquiry commenced in his first work, the labours of Johnson and Steevens at this time came under review. Those gentlemen had not in their edition of Shakspeare introduced either his poetry or doubtful plays. This omission Malone proposed to supply. Of the former he says, though " near a century and half have elapsed since the death of Shakspeare, it is somewhat extraordinary that none of his various editors should have attempted to separate his genuine poetical compositions from the spurious performances with which they have been so long intermixed, or taken the trouble to compare them with the earlier editions."

Two years were occupied in the laborious researches necessary for this work. Lord Charlemont, deep in the love of old poetry and plays, encouraged the design, clapped him on the back as he proceeded, and in regard to one of his own corrections in a disputed play, pays a handsome compliment to his friend. —" Exclusive of the quartos of Shakspeare, I am extremely glad you are getting on with your supplementary volumes. It was you know, always my opinion that the imputed plays ought to make a part of every complete edition ; and the poems are absolutely necessary. With regard to my correction in *Pericles*, you may make what use you please of it, though if you do not choose absolutely to father it, I would rather go down to posterity by the appellation of a friend of yours, than by the far less honourable one of my own name."

In 1780, appeared in two volumes, each of more than seven hundred pages, " *Supplement to the Edition of Shakspeare's Plays by Samuel Johnson and George Steevens."*

Half the first volume is occupied by what he terms " Supplemental Observations" on the plays, actors, and theatres of the time, with a variety of notes which became afterwards in part embodied in a history of the stage; and a reprint of the scarce old poem *Romeus and Juliet,* taken from the Italian by Arthur Brooke. The other half contains *Venus and Adonis, Rape of Lucrece, Sonnets, The Passionate Pilgrim, A Lover's Complaint,* with notes throwing such lights upon each as he possessed.

The second volume gives us seven doubtful plays— *Pericles, Locrine, Sir John Oldcastle, Lord Cromwell, London Prodigal, Puritans, Yorkshire Tragedy.* Of these, several he pronounced to be undoubtedly spurious. *Pericles* at first was judged to be of the same class. Further consideration induced the belief that, if not wholly, it was in part, a genuine though early production, for which his reasons are assigned; and subsequent editors have agreed that he had at least a share in its composition.

This change of opinion, before being printed, he communicated, like most other of his impressions on such subjects, to Steevens. The latter, in return, detailed his reasons for a contrary belief. Malone prints both in the most amicable spirit, using an apologetical tone for differing from his friend; but to differ with him was not the way to his favour. Their intercourse hitherto had been friendly and frequent. The younger editor poured out freely his thoughts, discoveries, and accumulations to the elder, who in return confessed himself pleased and instructed. As expressive of his obligation, he even went so far as to quote from the subject of their mutual admiration :—

> " Only I have left to say,
> More is thy due than more than all can pay."

But this spirit did not continue. A few more differences of opinion, and eventually the design by Malone of printing an edition of his own, threw him into disfavour with one whose rivalries and resentments were easily roused and difficult to allay.

Among others occasionally consulted on points where critics may fairly differ, or who may possess more ancient treasures for the elucidation of truth than their neighbours, was of course Lord Charlemont. He writes in reply, May 1779, and appears to arrive at Malone's ultimate decision :—

I am not possessed of any ancient copy of the *Venus and Adonis*. If I were, you certainly should have the use of it.

In consequence of your last letter but one I read over *Pericles*, and am strongly of opinion that by far the greater part of it is the genuine work of Shakspeare. I cannot, however, join with you in thinking that it is all of his composition, as there are some parts so very absurd, that I think it hardly possible he should have been capable of writing them. As it was the fashion of the time for poets to club their wits, I should rather suppose that some foolish poetaster had been concerned in it, and that the whole had passed for the production of Shakspeare, as the principal author and the most popular name. The quarto copy is so very incorrect that you will, I fear, find the publication attended with some difficulty. There are many passages which appear to me scarcely intelligible. I have made some guesses at the sense of one or two, but they are so little satisfactory as not to be worth communicating to you. One, however, I will mention, though probably the same guess may have occurred to you. Diana's speech toward the end of the play I would read thus. . . . .

Has Johnson received an Irish-English curiosity which I sent him by Lord Carysfort? It is a pity you could not procure the two plays of Massinger to make the volume complete.

During the following year, their literary intercourse continued pretty active. In the genuine spirit of a collector, what his lordship sought were rare things and of repute, and therefore to such inquirers valuable. Old poetry, plays, histories, pamphlets, first editions, quartos and octavos, as it might be, odd volumes to make up sets, deficient leaves to be made up by manuscript copies, Italian and French standard works of the same description of the older writers, formed his usual commissions. Numberless apologies are made for the trouble thus imposed. "If your friendly feelings were not sufficiently strong to get the better of every latent principle of indolence, you would, I am sure, shudder at the sight of my name signed to a letter—as from long experience you may safely conclude that some fresh trouble is at hand." On another occasion: "You see how impudent I am. In the beginning of my letter I ask your pardon, and peremptorily demand your trouble in the conclusion. But I know you well enough to be sure that you will forgive this and a good deal more to your ever affectionate CHARLEMONT."

It may be doubted whether his lordship derived most pleasure from receiving these acquisitions, or Malone in making them.

Sometimes kinder offices were sought by either, an instance of which affected the interests of the widow of one to whom the Peer had been a considerate patron. This was Hogarth—a name scarcely less popular— shall we say national?—in its way than that of the great poet, the object of their mutual adoration. One was indeed rather an ancient, the other a contemporary; and therefore perhaps not yet arrived at his full measure of fame. Both were eminently men of the people; both exercised their respective talents upon society at large—not upon classes or sections, but upon the masses, in the hope of shaming and correcting vices and improprieties. Both possessed the clearest views of human nature in its various aspects. They could unveil without reserve the peculiarities of life—its characters, follies, offences, motives—and depict its actions each in his own way, with a power acknowledged by their countrymen to be almost exclusively their own. The pencil of the one was nearly as expressive and intelligible as the pen of the other—sometimes indeed more sarcastic—and each remains in his way unapproached and perhaps unapproachable.

A wish had been expressed in London for an extension of the better class of prints of the artist, with such additions as the possessors of original pictures might choose to supply. Lord Charlemont was known to possess a few of these. Malone was in consequence requested to sound him. The reply forms another specimen of the various topics on which they loved to dilate :—

Dublin, June 29th, 1781.

Thank you for your letter, thank you for your purchases, and thank you over and over again for your kind and constant remembrance. But the King of Prussia, when he beat the French and travelled post a thousand miles in order to beat the Russians, was not more hurried than I am.* My letter must, therefore, be very short, and I proceed at once to business.

Surrey's *Sonnets* was the book of all others that I most desired. I am also extremely glad that you have got the *Gascoyne,* and return you many thanks for the means you are pursuing to perfect it, which I beg you would do, if possible, in print. But if any imperfection should still remain, I request that you will take the trouble to get it supplied in handwriting. And this I would entreat you to do with any imperfect book you may hereafter purchase for me. Do you not mistake when you say that the two plays which you had omitted to bind with my two volumes of B(eaumont) and Fletcher's, would make my quartos complete? I have in' all but sixteen plays, exclusive of the two you mention. Were there then no more than eighteen published in quarto? However, should you happen to have made a mistake, the two unbound plays will make a beginning for a third volume.

Elmsley † is, I am sure, mistaken with regard to the *Natural History* of Buffon. His birds were certainly printed on a very large paper and coloured. It was the price of these I was desirous of knowing, as well as the relative cost of the uncoloured and small paper.

That men of taste should wish for good impressions of Hogarth's prints is not at all surprising, as I look upon him to have been, in his way, and that too an original way, one of the first of geniuses. Neither am I much surprised at the rage you mention, as I am, by experience, well acquainted with the collector's madness. Excepting only the scarce portrait, my collection goes no farther than those which Mrs. Hogarth has advertised, and even of them a few are wanting, which I wish you would procure for me, viz., *The Cock-match, The Five Orders of Periwigs, The Medley, The Times, Wilkes,* and *The Bruiser.* As my impressions are remarkably good, having been selected for me by Hogarth himself, I should wish to

---

* At this period the Volunteers of Ireland were in full activity; and his duties, as their general, not a little arduous.

† A well-known bookseller.

have these the best that can be had; and if Mr. Steevens, who promised me his assistance, should happen to meet with any of those prints of which I am not possessed—I mean such compositions as do honour to the author, as, for instance, *The Satire on the Methodists, The Masquerade,* &c.—I should be much obliged to him to purchase them for me. To that gentleman I beg my best compliments. Should he purchase anything, you will be so good as to account with him.

I have no objection to suffering *The Lady's Last Stake* to be engraved, but on the contrary, should be happy to do anything which might contribute to add to the reputation of my deceased friend. But then it must be performed in such a manner as to do him honour; for otherwise I should by no means consent. One great difficulty would be to procure a person equal to the making a drawing from it, as the subject is a very difficult one. Hogarth had it for a year, with an intention to engrave it, and even went so far as almost to finish the plate which, as he told me himself, he broke into pieces, upon finding that, after many trials, he could not bring the woman's head to answer his idea, or to resemble the picture.

Here this subject dropped for a time, but was resumed in July, 1787, when his lordship writes to Malone for the information of the widow :—

I have this moment received a letter from Mrs. Hogarth, requesting that if *I should permit any one to make an engraving of " The Lady's Last Stake," I would give the preference to a young gentleman who lodged in her house, as by such preference she should be greatly benefited.* Of this application I consider it necessary to immediately inform you, as the affection I bore towards her deceased husband, my high regard for his memory, and, indeed, common justice, will most certainly prevent me from preferring any one else whatsoever to her in a matter of this nature. At the same time I must add, that whoever shall make a drawing from my picture must do it in Dublin, as I cannot think of sending it to London.

Will you, my dear Malone, be so kind in your morning walk as to call upon this lady, and read to her the above paragraph, as such communication will be the most satisfactory answer I can give to her letter. The same time, you will be so kind as to mention the circumstance and my resolution to the person in whose behalf the postscript in your letter was written. Perhaps matters may be settled amicably between him and Mrs. Hogarth, in which case I have no objection, provided the execution be such as not to disgrace the picture or its author, that the drawing be made in Dublin, and that Mrs. Hogarth be perfectly contented, and shall declare her satisfaction by a certificate in her own handwriting. I know your goodness will pardon all this trouble from, &c. &c.

Don't forget to worry Elmsley about the *Life of Petrarch.*

In December (1781), his lordship forwards to his friend for publication in the newspapers a protest originating with him in the Irish House of Lords. It is accompanied by a political letter not necessary to find place here, but contains the passage already quoted, which drew forth Malone's avowal of the state of his heart for so long a period. In the middle of it we find an outbreak of one of the prevailing passions :—"If you should happen to meet with Fleming's *Bucolics and Georgics* of Virgil, London, 4to, 1585, and Phaer's *Æneid,* first edition of seven books only (I have the second), I should be glad to purchase them, as I would bind them with Hervey's fourth book. I should wish also to procure an edition of Surrey's translation, which as I am told, contains the first and fourth books. Mine has only the fourth, and is, I believe, the first edition."

Familiarity with Shakspeare led our critic onward to a still more remote age, in a tilt against the poems of Rowley. The fate of their alleged discoverer,

Chatterton; the doubts and denials thrown upon
their authenticity; their actual merits compared with
others of their own or a subsequent age; and the
improbability of their forgery by a mere youth, drew
a large share of attention. Cool inquirers deemed
them not genuine. Easy or less suspicious minds
arrived at an opposite conclusion. Poetical imposture was not new. Ossian had already set the
watch-dogs of criticism on the alert, ready to fly at
any intruder in such questionable shape as Rowley.

Tyrwhitt had published an edition of the poems in
1777, in which and in an appendix, he had arrived
at an adverse conclusion. But on the other hand,
Dean Milles (of Exeter) and Jacob Bryant, whose
learning was unquestionable, had taken the field as
champions of their authenticity—the former in a
quarto edition of the works; the latter in two octavo
volumes of observations.

Against the latter gentleman, Malone, as a tenacious stickler for truth, was not slow in giving battle.
His remarks, couched in good-humour and occasional
ridicule, appeared first in the *Gentleman's Magazine*,
shaped afterwards into a pamphlet, *Cursory Observations on the Poems attributed to Thomas Rowley, a
Priest of the Fifteenth Century.*

He contends for their spurious origin on four
grounds: their versification, imitations of more
modern authors, numerous anachronisms, besides the
handwriting of the manuscript and state of the parch-
ments. He considers it—and therefore implies some
personal qualification for the task he had undertaken
—"a fixed principle that the authenticity or spurious-

ness of the poems attributed to Rowley cannot be decided by any person, without a moderate at least, if not critical knowledge of the compositions of most of our poets, from the time of Chaucer to that of Pope."

Thomas Warton, who followed him in a pamphlet in support of his original views, calls this "a sensible and conclusive performance." Tyrwhitt, also, in a "Vindication" of above two hundred pages, reiterates his disbelief, and refers with commendation to Malone's quotations of the opening lines of several old poems of that and subsequent dates, as certain evidence that the supposed Rowley had not caught either the language, versification, or manners of the time.

Volunteers rushed to the fight on either side. Burnaby Green, Dampier, Hickford, Rev. J. Fell, and others, in support of Milles and Bryant. On the other, we have Warton, Tyrwhitt, Steevens, Malone, Pinkerton, Chalmers, Scott, Southey, Croft, Jameson, and many more. Conviction could be scarcely doubtful where facts stood upon one side, and ingenious conjectures, added to a large store of belief, on the other. Even within a few months past the question has been revived; but life has not been breathed into it sufficient for critical resuscitation.

He wished the subject, however, as an interesting literary question, not to be forgotten. Everything written on it—tracts, reviews, magazines, and newspapers—was therefore collected, as his habit was on several other occasions, and bound together in volumes for reference. These, said to be complete on the subject, passed into the hands of a collector at the sale of his books in 1818.

From this contest of criticism he was summoned to render aid to a tragedy by an old friend. This was the *Count of Narbonne*, brought out at Covent Garden in November 1781.

Robert Jephson, author of this and two previous tragedies, was son of a beneficed clergyman in Ireland, a friend of the Malone family and schoolfellow of the sons. Quitting Trinity College without a degree, he obtained a commission in the army; served at Belleisle; retired from his regiment unable to face the climate of the West Indies; found some friends in Dublin; whence he soon sought London as the general mart for disposable talents. An attachment to the drama introduced him to Garrick; and this led to acquaintance with Mrs. Cibber. Thence probably arose some hankerings after dramatic fame in the form of authorship; at least he had the address to persuade the former at one time with the promise of a play, to lend him 500*l.*; supposed to be then no ordinary feat of generalship with the economical manager.

One of his London friends was the well-known single-speech Hamilton, at whose villa at Hampton he spent much time, and who in fact made over to him a pension on the Irish establishment which had been given to Edmund Burke, and was soon extorted from that gentleman under the plea that he had withdrawn his services from Hamilton.* His employment here was that of an amusing literary friend. He had several qualifications for social enjoyment: one particularly in being an admirable mimic; so

---

* *Life of Burke*, 5th edition, p. 71. *See* also a subsequent page of this work.

that in future life, any person who had once heard a debate in the Irish House of Commons had no occasion to ask the names of the parties imitated.

Well received in the upper circles of London, he found an introduction to Charles Townshend, then a member of the Ministry. One of the occasions proved to be a convivial entertainment protracted till the dawn of morning. The chief provocative to this excess was an amusing display of the talents of Jephson. He exhibited with remarkable fidelity and humour representations of persons with whom the parties present were familiar—the Duke of New-castle, Lord North, Lord Northington, Alderman Beckford, Glover (author of *Leonidas*), and others of note. So well was this done that Charles Towns-hend, in a fit of admiration, started from his chair, embraced him with rapture, and vowed to make him his secretary. This enthusiasm passed away with the moment; but he was not forgotten. When his brother, Lord Townshend, went to Ireland as viceroy, Jephson was put upon the list for an office in the household, and soon became Master of the Horse. A seat in Parliament followed. In the society of the "Castle" and its chief, amid the wit, talents, and hospitality which then shone pre-eminent in Dublin, he found the position fitted above all others for that species of enjoyment where the "flow of soul" was aided by liberal streams of claret and whisky punch.

But he possessed some higher merits. That taste for poetry and the drama already alluded to which had been early imbibed, became fostered by intimacy with the leading actors of London. In the Irish

House of Commons his humour shone so often to the general amusement as to procure him the name of the " Mortal Momus." In the press he was equally diligent with Courtenay and others, in a series of satirical papers directed against the writers of " *Baratariana*," the opponents of Lord Townshend's government.

But he aimed at fame through a more general audience. In 1775 he brought out the tragedy of *Braganza;* in 1779, *The Law of Lombardy;* but, not content with writing tragedy, displayed also his powers in acting it in the private theatre of the Phœnix Park. Lord Charlemont thus writes to Malone, in January, 1779:—" The nineteenth of this instant is to be presented, at the new theatre in the Park, the tragedy of *Macbeth.* The part of *Macbeth* by Jephson ; *Lady,* by Mrs. Gardiner ; *Macduff,* by Mr. Gardiner,* &c. &c. With the *Citizen* for a farce ; *Maria,* by Miss Flora Gardiner. Here your assistance will be much wanting."

He had now ready for the stage *The Count of Narbonne,* taken from Horace Walpole's *Castle of Otranto.* The diplomacy then necessary to introduce a new play to the theatre was not small. Every species of friends were pressed into the service—statesmen and states*women,* poets and players, peers and commoners ; so that the unhappy author, after spending two or three years in the composition of a piece, passed perhaps as many more in procuring its representation. On this occasion Malone was solicited to render his obstetric aid. Theatrical studies and acquirements

* Afterwards Lord Mountjoy.

pointed him out as fitted rather to command than
entreat the good-will of a manager. Aided by Horace
Walpole, whose good offices were likewise sought,
and who felt interested in a scion from his own
stock, he succeeded. It was performed on November
17, 1781; ran nine nights in succession, and for
twenty-one during the season.* Malone to his other
services added the following epilogue, of which his
friend the Rev. W. Jephson writes in March, 1782:—
" I believe I never told you how much we admired
your epilogue. We all agree that it is complete. I
really did not think you could write such good verses,
at least upon a very short warning. I do not suppose there are more than three in the language that
come near it. We hear that you spend much time
with Mr. Walpole. I hope it is the case. Such
company is exactly to your taste."

EPILOGUE TO THE "COUNT OF NARBONNE.'

Spoken by Miss Younge.

Of all the laws by tyrant custom made,
The hardest sure on dramatists is laid :
No easy task in this enlighten'd time
It is, with art "to build the lofty rhyme,"
To choose a fable nor too old nor new,
To keep each character distinctly true ;
The subtle plot with happy skill combine,
And chain attention to the nervous line ;
With weighty clashing interest to perplex,
Through five long acts—each person—of each sex;

---

* Geneste, in his *History of the Stage*, says nineteen. Walpole himself
was not a little elated by its success. Next day (Nov. 18th) he writes to
General Conway of " tending and nursing and waiting on Mr. Jephson'
play. I brought it into the world, was well delivered of it; it can stand
on its own legs, and I am going back to my own quiet hill, never likely to
have anything more to do with the theatre."

And then at last by dagger or by bowl,
To freeze the blood and harrow up the soul;
All this achieved, the bard at ease carouses,
And dreams of laurels and o'erflowing houses;
Alas, poor man! his work is done but half,
He has made you cry—but now must make you laugh:
And the same engine, like the fabled steel,*
Must serve at once to wound you and to heal.

   Our bard of this had ta'en too little care,
And by a friend he sought me to appear.
" Madam," he said, " so oft you've graced the scene,
An injured princess or a weeping queen,
So oft been used to die in anguish bitter,
And then start up to make the audience titter,
That doubtless you know best what is in vogue,
And can yourself invent an Epilogue.
You can supply an author's tardy quill,
And gild the surface of his tragic pill;
Your ready wit a recipe can bring
For this capricious serio-comic thing."
A recipe for Epilogues! " Why not?
Have you each vaunting chronicle forgot?
Have we not recipes each day, each hour,
To give to mortal man immortal power?
To give the ungraceful timid speaker breath,†
And save his quivering eloquence from death.
Have we not now a geometric school
To teach the cross-legged youth to snip by rule? ‡
When arts like these each moment meet our eyes,
Why should receipts for Epilogues surprise?"
" Well, sir, I'll try." I first advance with simper,
Forgotten quite my tragic state, and whimper.
Ladies, to-night my fate was surely hard,
What could possess our inconsiderate bard
A wife to banish that his miss might wed,
When modern priests allow them both one bed.

---

* The spear of Achilles.
† In allusion to a quack medicine recommended for its efficacy in calming
the nervous agitation of some public speakers.
‡ A tailor has lately informed the public that he fits his customers by
geometric rules.

Thus I'll begin : but it will never do,
Unless some recent anecdotes ensue :
Has no frail dame been caught behind a screen ?
No panting virgin flown to Gretna Green ?
Have we no news of Digby or the Dutch ?
At some rich Nabob can't I have a touch ?
Or the famed quack,* who, but for duns terrestrial,
Had gain'd the Indies by his *bed celestial.*
" Bravo, Miss Younge !—the thought my friend will bless,
" This modish medley must insure success."
Won by his smooth-tongued flattery I've dared
To do what ev'n our fluent author fear'd.
If I succeed to-night the trade I'll follow,
And dedicate my leisure to Apollo.
Before my house a board shall straight be hung,
With—" Epilogues made here by Dr. Younge ! "
Nor will I, like my brethren, take a fee,
Your hands and smiles are wealth enough for me. †

---

* Dr. Graham, from his " Temple of Hymen," had announced that " if it were not for unprecedented cruelty, he would in a few years have been one of his Majesty's richest and most respectable subjects."

† In addition to these and other tragic pieces hereafter to be mentioned, the sister muse was not forgotten. He is recorded to have written the *Hotel*, farce, 1783 ; the *Campaign*, opera, 1785 ; *Love and War*, 1787 ; *Two Strings to your Bow*, 1791, only the last of which met with popular favour. But I have met with no communication on these pieces to his critical confidant in London, the letters to Malone being probably returned, as in other instances, to the family.

CHAPTER V.

1781—1783.

Horace Walpole—Literary Club—Dr. Johnson—Lord Charlemont—
Shakspeare—Steevens—Rev. Mr. Whalley—Henry Flood.

PLAYS, however, even when successful, seldom run
altogether smoothly. There are too many tastes to
to consult—and opinions in which to agree. Happy
the man never condemned to pass through such an
ordeal of patience and temper as the theatre ! To
write *up* to the ideas of one man and *down* to those
of another; to find a manager of one opinion, and
the performers directly opposed to it; to be denied
credit on points to which he himself has given much
consideration, and they who differ from him, probably little or none; to omit this and alter that—is
the every-day fate of a dramatist by a decree as irre-
versible as a law of nature. Some alarm of this
description influenced the author, at which Walpole
hints in the following letter to Malone, written a few
days after the representation :—

Strawberry Hill, Nov. 23rd, 1781.

SIR,—I have just received the honour of your letter, and
do not lose a minute to answer it, though my hand is so nervous and shaking so much, that I have difficulty to write.

If you remember, sir, Mr. Harris sent for me out of
the box on the first night. I found Dr. Francklin in the
green room, and some of the players. The former was just
come out of the pit, and said the audience there disliked the
death of Hortensia, and thought it most unnatural that she
should die so suddenly of grief. The actors, too, agreed

with him, and it was proposed that she should be carried off, to leave it at least doubtful whether she was dead or not.

I am sure I have never taken the liberty of making any alterations in Mr. Jephson's excellent tragedy. It is as true that I have not set up my own judgment against those who have, and must have, more knowledge of stage effect; and, whenever I have acquiesced with them, it has been with the sole view of serving and contributing to the success of the play, or with the view of contenting Mr. Harris in little points, who had so readily consented to bring out the play. I flatter myself, too, that it has not suffered by those little compliances of mine.

It is likewise true, sir, and I have no objection to Mr. Jephson's knowing, that I approve the alterations you have made, and which you do me the honour of proposing to me, to be inserted in the printed copy; but I fear I am not at liberty to agree to that idea, as, since I saw you, I have received another letter from Mr. Jephson, in which he desires me to deliver the last copy to you, sir, which I had done, and adds these words, "that he (Mr. Malone) may be requested not to suffer any alteration of the text, excepting as to printing, which he understands better than I do." I confess I think Mr. Jephson too tenacious. He has produced such a treasure of beauties, that he could spare one or two. My frankness and sincerity, sir, speak this from the heart, and not in secret. I would not for the world say one thing to you and another to Mr. Jephson; and, therefore, have no objection to your communicating my letter to him. You have shown yourself so zealous a friend to him, and I hope have found me so too, that I am sure you will understand what I say as it is meant, and not as flattering to either, or as double dealing, of which I trust I am incapable.

I read with pleasure in the papers, sir, that your epilogue succeeded as it deserved; but I am much surprised at what you tell me, that the audiences have been less numerous than there was every reason to expect. If any burlesque of what is ridiculous can erase taste for genuine poetry, the age should go a little further, and admire only what is ridiculous.

I am much obliged to you, sir, for the notices you are pleased to send me, which I shall certainly insert in my own trifling works.

Voltaire's letter to me was printed in one of the later miscellaneous volumes; I do not recollect in which. I do not doubt but that it will be reproduced in the general edition preparing. Hereafter, perhaps, another letter of his may appear, in which that envious depreciator of Shakspeare and Corneille may be proved to have been as mean and dirty as he was envious. I have the honour to be, sir, with great respect, your most obedient humble servant,

HOR. WALPOLE.

The next note refers to some complimentary lines applied to him by Mr. Gardiner, already noticed as one of the theatrical amateurs of Dublin:—

December 22nd, 1781.

I am very sure, sir, that the four lines with which Mr. Gardiner has honoured me, are much too great a compliment, and will be thought so by all who have not some friendly partiality for me. I am not a poet; and though I have written verses at times, more of them have been bad than good. However, as next to vanity I should dislike to be thought guilty of affected modesty, and as I have no right that, in compliment to either, Mr. Gardiner's beautiful lines should be suppressed, though he was so obliging as to sacrifice them at the representation, which I confess I could not have stood, I will take no more liberties, nor object to the publication. Yet should I be taxed with consenting, I must comfort myself that I did not acquiesce till I had no right to refuse.

I very seldom go out in a morning, sir, but will certainly have the honour of waiting on you soon: and am, sir, with great respect,

Your most obedient humble servant,

HOR. WALPOLE.

At what period and through whom this acquaintance commenced does not appear; probably after the publication of the supplement to Shakspeare. Walpole was then well on in life; had retired a good deal from general society; was of delicate health, and sought amusement in his "Castle" of Strawberry in reading, writing, and *printing* of books. He had the reputation of being somewhat exclusive in the selection of intimates. Malone soon became on the most friendly terms; paid him and often received morning visits; found in his visitor those stores of details of men and manners of his earlier days, or of those recently removed from the world, which have equally informed and amused readers of every class. Few persons or events, as we find in his letters, appear to have escaped observation at some period of life. Those with whom he associated he seems to have known well; so that if not always accurate or absolutely impartial in his sketches, he is rarely ignorant; and none can be more amusing.

What Malone first thought of him we find in his memoranda :—

"When Mr. Horace Walpole came from abroad about the year 1746, he was much of a *Fribble* in dress and manner. Mr. Colman, at that time a schoolboy, had some occasion to pay him a visit. He told me he has a strong recollection of the singularity of his manner; and that it was then said that Garrick had him in thought when he wrote the part of *Fribble*, in *Miss in her Teens*. But I doubt this much; for there is a character in a play called *Tunbridge Wells*, in which that of *Fribble* seems to be evidently formed. However, Garrick might have had Mr. Walpole in his thoughts.

" This gentleman (Mr. Walpole) is still somewhat singular in manner and appearance; but it seems only a singularity arising from a very delicate and weak constitution, and from living quite retired among his books, and much with ladies.   He is always lively and ingenious; never very solid or energetic.   He appears to be very fond of French manners, authors, &c. &c., and I believe keeps up to this day a correspondence with many of the people of fashion in Paris.   His love of French manners, and his reading so much of their language, have I think infected his style a little, which is not always so entirely English as it ought to be.   He is, I think, a very humane and amiable man.

" He regrets much that he wrote the tragedy of the *Mysterious Mother;* he printed only a hundred copies of it at Strawberry Hill, and cannot be pre-vailed upon to suffer it to be published.   But it is in vain now to think of suppressing it, for these one hundred copies being dispersed immediately after his death it will certainly be reprinted.*   No work of his does him more credit.

" He has printed, I believe, at his own press a complete edition of all his writings in quarto.   On examining the late Mr. Cole's papers, a sheet of this new edition was found among them, which he took (it is imagined) without the knowledge of Mr. Wal-pole from Strawberry Hill."

In 1782 Malone was elected into the Literary Club —an object of ambition to the most eminent men of the day.   Temper and taste had well fitted him for supe-

* It was reprinted in Dublin in 1791.

rior associations of this description. The suavity of
Burke, Reynolds, Nugent and Percy, curbed the
sourness or coarseness of inferior men, such as Hawkins; while the reproofs of Johnson kept in check
the wildness of wit in Beauclerc and Colman. Conversation and argument ran freely—not always perhaps unruffled—but like pebbles in the brook, just
sufficient to impart animation to the scene.

Before publication of the supplementary plays, he
had hinted the wish for admission to Lord Charlemont,
who in reply wrote: "For my own sake I wish you
every success in your endeavours to get into the
Turk's Head Club. Why am I not in London to
vote for you?" It is rather remarkable that this
celebrated social assemblage of talent might almost
date its origin from the Irish Peer. Some words had
dropped from him on the subject to Reynolds.
The latter mentioned it to Johnson, proposing his
lordship as one of the first members. "No," was
the reply; "we shall be called Charlemont's Club;
let him come in afterwards."

Just about this time a letter came from that nobleman to Queen Anne Street, complaining of incessant
duties, civil and military—the latter as general of Irish
Volunteers. Such were the claims upon his time that
he had scarcely a moment even to open one of the last
packets of books received from his critical friend—for
it appears that whatever else was in hand, the acquisition and examination of old authors was not intermitted.

"Gascoigne," he says, "notwithstanding his ominous
setting out, arrived safe and sound, in excellent plight,

and perfectly uninjured by their long journey—a piece
of good fortune which, considering their great age
and consequent debility, was rather to be hoped than
expected.

"I know but of one thing you have omitted—that
is, to send me some sheets of Spenser, containing his
letters to Sir W. R. (Raleigh) and the commendatory
verses. These were meant to complete my first edition
of the *Fairy Queen*. You, I remember, set it apart
for me, but have I suppose forgotten it, as well you
might in the multiplicity of matters undertaken for
me. You have sent the second volume of Warton's
Pope. I once had the first, but have lost it, and must
beg that you will procure it for me. The size of the
old plays exactly matches—the colour rather paler,
and the gilding something different. One may be
easily altered; time no doubt will change the other."

The Club formed a new tie to intimacy between
Malone and Dr. Johnson. In the spring of the year
he invited the latter to meet Dr. Farmer and others
at dinner, and sent him his pamphlet on Chatterton.
The invitation Johnson could not accept, on account
of illness. For the pamphlet he is thankful; comments
on the wild adherence to Chatterton as even more
strange than that to Ossian; and hopes to be able
soon to meet his friends in society. Boswell dilates
upon the esteem felt by his great friend for Malone,
"whose elegant hospitality" he compliments, and
truly adds, "who the more he is known is the
more highly valued."

Previous to this, both critics appear to have had
several communications on certain anecdotes and no-

tices on *Shakspeare* and in the *Lives of the Poets*, of
which only a few remain. Malone considered Johnson
right in some disputed notes, as in " Asses of great
charge," and wrong in " To be, or not to be."   Like
Johnson and Pope, he deemed rhyme necessary for
the full effect of English poetry.   Like the former,
he entertained dislike to the politics, temper, and
conduct of Milton; and on another occasion is violent against Milton's master, Cromwell.   He told
Johnson that he had censured Lord Marchmont
wrongly for not taking care of Pope's papers; for
Lord Bolingbroke alone had been entrusted with
that charge.   But Johnson forgot on this as on
some other occasions to make the necessary corrections in a new edition. He corroborated the fact
tated by Johnson though doubted by others, of
Addison having put an execution into Steele's house
for debt.   Burke was his authority; he having heard
the story from one of Steele's personal acquaintance,
Lady Dorothea Primrose.

All communication with the great moralist added
to his veneration for one so worthy of it; and to
familiar friends often became the subject of conversation in future life.   A lady now resident in
Ireland, who more than twenty years afterwards
accompanied her father on a visit to Malone in
London, thus adverts to the subject in a communication to the writer :—

" Next to Shakspeare, Dr. Johnson appeared to be
the great object of his admiration. He had often
visited him in Bolt Court, and in a morning's stroll
took me to view the exterior of the house. On one

occasion, the doctor, during the decline of his health, proving unusually silent, Malone rose to retire, believing him to be in pain or his presence inconvenient. 'Pray, sir,' said Johnson, 'be seated. I cannot talk, but I like to see you there.' On two or three occasions, also, he had managed the breakfast tea-kettle when Levett was absent or otherwise engaged. Mr. Malone had several engravings of Dr. Johnson in his study."

It is probable that admiration of Johnson's conversational powers first led Malone about this period, to new employment for leisure hours. This was to record his occasional remarks—those impressive droppings of wisdom and genius which left something on the mind for future remembrance, and use at fitting moments. Often pithy, always powerful, they were conveyed in language which most of his auditors felt to be elegant and aimed to preserve. At this time, Malone knew not Boswell, neither probably had heard of his biographical projects. But they became intimate soon afterward; and the collector freely furnished the biographer with such notes as were new and useful for the purpose he had in view.

Further consideration on this subject induced desire on the part of the critic to give notes of anything remarkable heard from other eminent men.— Not personal matters merely, but on books, manners, general and literary anecdotes, historical facts, matters amusing or instructive, yet too unimportant for more methodical record. Several of these in the form of diary, written down at the moment, naturally make part of the present narrative. Others, of more

miscellaneous character, will be found at the conclusion of the volume.

Almost the first passage in these " Maloniana," as
he designates them, is given to Johnson :—

" *March*, 1783.

" Dr. Johnson is as correct and elegant in his
common conversation as in his writings.   He never
seems to study either for thoughts or words; and is
on all occasions so fluent, so well-informed, so accurate, and even eloquent, that I never left his company
without regret.   Sir Josh. Reynolds told me that
from his first outset in life, he had always had this
character; and by what means he had attained it.
He told him he had early laid it down, as a fixed rule,
always to do his best, *on every occasion* and in *every*
company, to impart whatever he knew in the best
language he could put it in; and that by constant
practice, and never suffering any careless expression
to escape him, or attempting to deliver his thoughts
without arranging them in the clearest manner he
could, it was now become habitual to him.

" I have observed, in my various visits to him, that
he never relaxes in this respect.   When first introduced I was very young; yet he was as accurate in
his conversation as if he had been talking to the first
scholar in England.   I have always found him very
communicative; ready to give his opinion on any
subject that was mentioned.   He seldom however
starts a subject himself; but it is very easy to lead
him into one.

" When I called about two months ago, I found him

in his arm-chair by the fireside, before which a few
apples were laid. He was reading. I asked him
what book he had got. He said the *History of
Birmingham*. Local histories, I observed, were generally dull. 'It is true, sir; but this has a peculiar
merit with me; for I passed some of my early years
and married my wife there.' I supposed the apples
were preparing as medicine. 'Why, no, sir; I
believe they are only there because I want something
to do. These are some of the solitary expedients to
which we are driven by sickness. I have been confined this week past; and here you find me roasting
apples, and reading the *History of Birmingham*.'

"I asked him if he had seen Mr. Mason's translation
of *Du Fresnoy* (which was just then published), and
what he thought of it. He said he had read some
pages, and that he thought it was executed with as
much fidelity as was consistent with taste, and with
as much elegance as could be employed without
departing from fidelity; but that the epistle to
Sir J. Reynolds was a very poor thing.

"Mr. Cole, of Milton near Cambridge, had died
a few days before. He was a great antiquary and
collector of books. On examining his library, his
books* were found to contain a great many sarcastic
remarks against persons now living, and with whom
he had lived in intimacy, particularly Mr. Horace
Walpole, who had been at school with him (as
Mr. Walpole himself told me), and who used to send
him a copy of every piece printed at Strawberry Hill.

---

* They were sold to Benjamin White, the bookseller, and resold by him
in one of his annual catalogues. Mr. Steevens picked out the most curious.

" On mentioning this circumstance to Dr. Johnson, he said that 'if Mr. Cole had scribbled in the margin of his books merely to give vent to his thoughts, it was a very harmless amusement; but then he ought to have ordered them to be burnt at his death : that if it arose from malignity, it argued a very base disposition, especially in the case of Mr. Walpole, with whom he kept up a friendly correspondence to the last. If however a man found he could not restrain his ill-humour within bounds, it would be much the shortest and fairest way' (he added, with a smile) ' to keep one fair paper-book, for the purpose of abusing all his acquaintance.'

" This Mr. Cole had another practice that seems hardly justifiable* in the extent to which he carried it. He kept all the letters he received, especially from literary persons, and pasted them into a large book. This, with all his other manuscript collections, he has *devised* to the British Museum, but ordered them not to be opened for thirty years. By that time, the anecdotes they contain will have little value; and most of those who take an interest in them will be dead. I should like much to see Mr. Walpole's letters, he being a very lively and entertaining writer. My friend, Mr. Jephson, the author of several excellent tragedies, has had many letters from him, some of which I have seen, containing much good criticism on plays and play-writers."

---

* Why not? Literary history without them would be of little interest. How much should we lose in authentic contemporary history and anecdote, were those of one of the parties mentioned here (Walpole) suppressed?

On a subsequent occasion we are informed :—

" In a conversation a few days ago with Dr. Johnson (April 24th, 1784), I asked him whether he was personally acquainted with Mr. Colley Cibber. He said he had not lived in any intimacy with him, but had sometimes been in his company ; and that he was much more ignorant even of matters relating to his own profession, than he could well have conceived any man to be who had lived nearly sixty years with players, authors, and the most celebrated characters of the age.

" I asked also whether he could recollect all the pieces written by him since he first came to London ? He said he believed he could ; but this I doubt very much. I mentioned his proposals for a translation of Father Paul's *History of the Council of Trent.* He said such a thing had been agitated, but he very soon relinquished the design. However, Mr. Henry, partner with the late Mr. Cave, Johnson's first employer and patron, positively says that he saw six sheets of it actually printed, as Mr. Nichols, Henry's present partner, informed me."

Amid patriotic fervours nearly at the boiling point, yet with all the good nature that made them amusing, Lord Charlemont found time for a letter on those graceful and peaceful pursuits calculated to smooth even the rugged front of political contention. Thus he writes from his beautiful villa on Dublin Bay :—

Marino, October 4th, 1782.

MY DEAR MALONE,—You will probably be surprised and perhaps a little displeased, at being so long without an

answer to your last kind letter. Indeed, I would not wish
you to be entirely satisfied, and I cannot desire you should
bear any apparent neglect on my part without some degree
of displeasure ; yet when you reflect on the busy scene in
which I have been a principal actor, or the various occupations, civil and military, which have occupied my mind
and body, you will, I doubt not, pardon and perhaps pity
me, whose whole time has been taken up in occupations
different from those you know to be my favourite amusements; more especially when you consider that I have been
thus obliged to interrupt a constant correspondence which has
ever been one of my most pleasing occupations. But my
comfort is, that I have been doing my duty. From that I
trust no fatigue either of mind or of body shall ever be able
to deter me. I have now, however, a moment of leisure,
indeed but a moment; and that I give to you and to our
own pleasing subjects of literary intercourse.

Since I last wrote, I have had time only to peruse two
books, idle ones indeed, and that by snatches : Warton's
Pope, and Bryant's *Rowley*. The former is, I think, the
most extraordinary work I ever read, and is indeed everything but what it promises. The writer seems to have
copied, and impudently enough printed, his commonplace
book of anecdotes and remarks upon various writers. Some
parts are indeed critical, but his criticisms are not in my
opinion always just, and there is but little anywhere to be
found that can be called new.

As to Bryant, he ought, I think, to be answered by some
of your Chattertonians, or Rowley may still have some
chance with posterity, though the laugh be now against him.
The arguments of his defenders are sometimes weak, but in
many instances, if not answered critically, and not merrily,
are strong enough to support a claim at least to some part of
what is attributed to him. Indeed the whole controversy
appears to me in some respects like that of Boyle and Bentley
respecting the *Epistles* of Phalaris. All the wit and genius
are on one side, together with some good argument, but the
weight of proof seems to be on the other. In the case of
Phalaris, wit supported the supposed imposture, which in the

present controversy it endeavours to lay open ; but the laugh
is now forgotten, and the arguments remembered.   Phalaris,
after the reign of a few years, has lost his station, and perhaps
in the same manner Rowley may resign his rank among
English bards.

Now for the topic which has already given so much trouble.
It is impossible for me at present to send you the catalogue
you mention.   Indeed I have not time to make it out, so that
you may still purchase upon the hazard of your memory.   I
have a copy of Lydgate's *Troy*, printed by Must.   If that,
however, which was offered to you be an earlier edition, I
should be glad to have it ; I cannot insert your fragment of
Spenser without unbinding a very well-bound book, so I
should be glad if you could procure any other piece of that
author which I have not already, either in prose or verse, to
which I might affix it, so as to form a supplemental volume.

Will you be so kind to ask Mr. Walpole how many
numbers were published of the *Strawberry Hill Collection*, of
old [Greet's ?]   He gave me two, and I should wish to make
up the lot ; and if there be any more, beg you would procure
them for me.   I forget how much I owe you; please to let me
have it in your next.   Send me also in the next parcel
Potter's translations, and Chatterton's avowed works, the
former well-bound, and the latter in boards, as I wish to bind
uniform.

The ladies desire their best compliments.   My most affectionate and sincere good wishes to my dear Mr. Walpole;
and the best compliments to all friends, particularly my
brethren of the Club, and most particularly to Sir Joshua.

His brother, in the annual spring visit to London,
came furnished with more than the usual number of
recommendations from affectionate relatives to the
wanderer to return.   But this was more hopeless
than ever.   He had tasted of new life in a new
region; and as certain animals cannot contentedly
forego food to which they have been once accustomed,

so neither could he resign those mental feasts enjoyed in London libraries and societies.

Poor Dublin! what could she yield in return? Whiteboys (in her vicinity)—faction-fights—hostile religions—homely, if not coarse manners and customs—little literature—angry party spirit—narrow views—and now with an army of volunteers, influenced by genuine patriotism indeed, but without great care on the part of their leaders, likely to run wild and try to disconnect themselves from the only country that could advance their wealth and civilization. Amid her wit and her ease she was merely provincial; and provincialism is but another name for inferiority of every description, from a halfpenny ballad to an epic poem! Bishop Percy, in one of his letters, had injured the island materially in his opinion:— " In this remote part of the kingdom (Dromore) nothing could afford me a higher gratification than to be honoured with a few lines from you or any other of my good friends, to inform me what is doing in the literary world, of which I can seldom get intelligence sooner than it would reach to the East Indies."

Toward the latter part of the year was commenced the main business of our Critic's life—the edition of Shakspeare. A pretty long course of preliminary training, as we have seen, pointed to this as the natural result of the days and nights, the thought and research, devoted to the study of the poet and his age. Whatever new light had been thrown upon either, much obscurity remained. A steady, persevering advance into the mists of antiquity could alone render objects distinct. Connecting circumstances likewise demanded all the sagacity of the most deliberate inquirer. Each topic touched upon inevitably led to another. From the few known incidents of the poet's life, it was necessary to glean and analyze such as were doubtful; to investigate the chronology of his plays; to furnish notices of the stage; of actors, authors, managers, facts, names, dates; and of family as well as of theatrical history. The subject necessarily grew by what it fed on. To keep each within moderate compass—to throw the clearest light upon the times, language, and allusions of the great writer without overpowering the patience or memory of the reader—became the test of the artist's skill.

Antiquarian reading became a daily duty; but zeal made it a labour of love. His range proved unusually extensive. No sportsman followed the chase with more spirit than he did black-letter authorities; and if the game thus bagged did not always prove of the value he hoped, no question existed of the energy shown in the pursuit. Histories, poems, plays, pamphlets, letters, every species of paper, printed or manuscript, before, during, or after the age of Elizabeth, were sought out and consulted for such incidents or anecdotes as they could supply. He particularly dreaded being misled by careless predecessors. In the true spirit of such as write for futurity, no second-hand statements satisfied him where original authorities were known to exist.

The labour thus incurred became extreme. He travelled from library to repository; from private papers to public records; from universities to the

British Museum and Stationers' Hall in order to be exact. His heart yearned to his theme. Unlike the task set before the necessitous or unwilling workman, whose position incites a hasty glance and a running pen, he sat down deliberately to the enjoyment of his tastes amid the pleasures of social life, good company, and pecuniary ease. He was cut out for the work, and the work for him. To such men, when we can conveniently find them, seems of right to belong the business of research in matters critical, antiquarian, or of doubtful authority. They best can afford the leisure where leisure is essential to the elucidation of truth ; and where, as in the instance before us, labour is seconded by judgment and discretion. If not always the highest effort of mind, inquiry is indispensable to the acquisition of accurate as of useful knowledge.

No obstacle appeared to stand in the way of the undertaking,—no rival was now in the field to confront. Steevens, by his own account, had been disgusted—"I never mean," he wrote to Malone, "to appear again as editor of Shakspeare ; nor will such assistance as I am able to furnish go towards any future gratuitous publication. Ingratitude and impertinence from several of the booksellers have been my reward for conducting two laborious editions, both of which are sold."

In April, 1783, he goes further, and recommends Malone in a long letter to edit Shakspeare, as he has quite done with the pursuit. He is offended with Isaac Reed ; requests his correspondent to draw up the account for the *Gentleman's Magazine*, which he

will transcribe " so that not even Nichols shall know
the author."

Towards the end of the year Malone was applied
to by the Reverend Mr. Whalley, then preparing an
edition of *Ben Jonson*, for such assistance as he could
afford. But he had formed no love for that writer or
his productions. Other commentators have expressed
similar feelings. Some believe him to have been a
personal enemy of his great contemporary—jealous,
envious, and spiteful toward a genius superior to his
own. This is perhaps unfair to "rare" Ben after the
excellent poem written to his great contemporary's
memory. While living, indeed, many unhappy contentions arise among brethren; but after death,
comes, or should come, truth. Yet little as either
of their lives are known, it is scarcely fair to affix
the passion of envy upon one who in the rivalries of
a theatre may believe he has just cause for complaint. A passage from the reply of Malone fairly
states his views: " I shall with great pleasure add
my mite of contribution to your new edition of *Ben
Jonson*, though I have very little hopes of being able
to throw any light on what has eluded your researches. At the same time I must honestly own
to you that I have never read old Ben's plays with
any degree of attention, and that he is an author so
little to my taste that I have no pleasure in perusing
him." It appears by the same letter that he was then
busy upon the " *Second Appendix to my Supplement
to Shakspeare.*"

Accession to office of the Coalition Ministry gave
him new occupation in trying to allure one of his

friends into its ranks in Ireland.   This was the celebrated Henry Flood—one of the men of whom she
boasts; but who appears to have been deficient in the
temper or tact necessary to attain the very highest
success in political life.

Born in 1732 previous to the marriage ceremony,
he was the son of Warden Flood, afterwards Lord
Chief Justice of the Irish King's Bench, and the
first native who obtained that honour.   The accident
of birth did not mar his fortunes.   From Trinity
College, he removed to Christ Church, Oxford, under
Dr. Markham, afterwards Archbishop of York; became from an idler a man of study; delighted in translating Greek orators and poets; and at length was
said to read Greek as fluently as English.   He also
wrote good verses; a few fellow-students deemed his
genius marred by entry at the Middle Temple; but a
summons to Ireland meant him to represent his native
county in Parliament, or if that failed, the borough
of Callan.   Fond of the drama, he commenced at
Farmley, his father's seat, near Kilkenny, a course
of private theatricals which have since become
more celebrated ; married Lady Frances Beresford,
with a fortune of ten thousand pounds; and by the
deaths of a brother, sister, and of his father who died
in 1764, inherited a fortune of five thousand pounds
per annum.

Such an outset in life left no opening for the lures
of the Irish Secretary.   He chose his seat upon the
Opposition benches, assumed a lead upon all Irish
topics; and acting with moderation, his patriotic reputation rose with his fame as an orator.   Inconsistencies

were laid to his charge, but the then complexities of
Irish politics render it difficult to form an opinion.
He opposed strenuously the government of Lord
Townshend; and Malone, as we have seen, became
an occasional assistant. But an unhappy event, then
too common in Irish life, awaited him. He killed
in a duel an opponent in the borough of Callan,
Mr. Agar, who, having escaped in one encounter
with him in the field, unluckily insisted upon a
second.

In 1775 he accepted the office of Vice-Treasurer,
and became Privy Councillor in both kingdoms.
Under Lord Buckingham and Mr. Secretary Heron
(1781) he resigned; no attention having been paid, as
he urged, to certain previous stipulations. While in
office he was nearly silent. Out of it he became an
active opponent; till at length, in consequence of stre-
nuous efforts against Lord Carlisle's government, he
was recommended to be dismissed from the honours of
the Privy Council both in England and Ireland. On
this occasion, the friendship of Lord Charlemont,
which had cooled during his retention of office, broke
forth with fresh enthusiasm on its close. In writing to
Malone he says : " With Flood on our side, it is impossible to despair. Our sun has broke out from the
cloud with redoubled lustre. His unparalleled conduct would scarcely be believed but by us who know
the man; and his abilities are, if possible, greater
than ever. Yet Grattan still shines with unabated
brightness ; and if numbers be against us, we have at
least the satisfaction of having the weight of abilities
entirely on our side. You may judge, as you know

my heart, of the pleasure I feel from my friend's conduct, from my friend's return!"

It is creditable to the enlarged views of Flood,
that he early contemplated removal from the Irish to
the English House of Commons.   First-class men
are often lost in secondary positions ; and local legislatures, such as was that of Ireland, must ever be
so considered.   They lie under the disadvantage
of contracted views ; are hampered by family interests, local influences, mistaken opinions, and are
rarely in communion with the great interests of
nations.   How much would not the genius of Burke
have been stunted had the chances of life thrown him
into the Irish House of Commons?   That wisdom
which throughout his career made the politics of
Europe but the echo of his opinions, would have
fallen unheeded among an oligarchy of his country
obedient to power, and a democracy pursuing place—
where it has been said by native writers there were
but sixty of the representative body independent of
the influences of Administration.   Isolation among
such would be fatal to the utility of superior men.
Great assemblages often bring forth, while they support, great intellects.   A useful or an ambitious man
should seek his station as near as possible to the
fountain of power.   Thence he may best distinguish
the mistakes and dangers which obstruct his career.
Who does not climb the hill for the largest extent of
view?   Who is content to disport in a pool with the
open sea before him ?

So early as 1767 he hinted the wish for removal to
Lord Chatham through Mr. John Pitt, but it came

to nothing. Other attempts also failed. They were renewed when the star of Grattan became in the ascendant and his own proportionably declined, till in 1783, the Duke of Chandos procured his return for Winchester. The dissolution consequent on the dismissal of the Coalition again sent him adrift on the popular waters; and his Grace was said to have shuffled out of a positive engagement so unfairly that a challenge from his Irish acquaintance was the result. Seaford was then tried; and on the third election he succeeded.

Fortune failed him in rendering the change conducive to increase of fame. Why, it is not easy to say; excepting that the reputation earned in one place does not necessarily accompany its possessor to another. He reached St. Stephen's for the first time during the discussion of Fox's India Bill. Insufficiently prepared, he was imprudent enough to take part against it;* and on avowing such insufficiency, paid the penalty of frankness to the ridicule and sarcasm of one of his countrymen (Courtenay†),

---

* Horace Walpole's sagacity in immediately foreseeing the result of this imprudence upon Flood's future reputation, is not a little remarkable. He writes to the Earl of Strafford, December 11, 1783:—"Mr. * * * (Flood), the pillar of invective, does not promise to re-erect it (the character of Parliament)—not, I conclude, from want of having imported a stock of ingredients, but his presumptuous *début* on the very night of his entry was so wretched, and delivered in so barbarous a brogue, that I question whether he will ever recover the blow Mr. Courtnay gave him. A young man may correct and improve, and rise from a first fall; but an elderly formed speaker has not an equal chance."—*Private Correspondence*, vol. iv. p. 357. 1820.

† Well known in the political and literary societies of London. He had been in the army; afterwards held office in Ireland under the Marquis of Townshend; also under Whig administrations in England; mostly in Parliament. He wrote *A Poetical Review of the Literary and Moral*

who concluded the debate by telling the House, among other severe things, that here was an honourable member who by his own confession had just arrived from violent party contentions in his own country, and now, without the loss of an hour, exerted all his powers to embroil the senate of another!

From whatever cause, his advent became a failure. This—and perhaps the conviction that he stood alone in the House unconnected with either party—may have repressed future exertion save on important occasions. These were chiefly the Irish propositions, French commercial treaty, and reform in Parliament. Upon the latter he had previously laboured in Ireland, and Fox now pronounced his present measure the best yet proposed on that subject. On all these, his speeches were as good, his vigour and ingenuity as great, and his political views such as he had usually professed. But the claim of perfect independence of all party ties left him, as may be supposed, without supporters from either.

Without doubt, he was one of the ablest men which Ireland had produced—learned, acute, logical, earnest, and bold; his manner in debate perhaps more slow and sententious than is usual in England. As a statesman of general powers, he was often mentioned by Curran as far superior to Grattan.* He was probably self-willed, difficult to manage, desirous to

---

Character of Dr. Johnson, and other works. Became a great friend of Malone, though their politics after the French Revolution differed essentially.

* So I have been told by my late eminent friend, Charles Phillips, to whom Curran often spoke of him with high praise.

think on all things for himself. Something of this escapes in defence of his tenure of the vice-treasurership against the invective of Grattan: "I felt myself a man of too much situation to be a mere placeman. If not a minister to serve my country, I would not be a mere tool of salary. What was the consequence? I voted with government in matters where they were clearly *right*, and against them in matters of importance where they were clearly wrong. In questions of little moment I did not vote at all."

He was transplanted, too, at fifty, when new roots are difficult to strike. He saw the scene occupied by men of vast abilities whom he could not expect to surpass or displace. He had been a leader, and could not gracefully descend to the condition of subordinate. Or he may have refused to modify those opinions which, having long enunciated as truths in Ireland, he could not now unsay, however at variance with the larger and clearer views of another—and it must be admitted superior—assemblage of statesmen.

CHAPTER ,VI.

1783—1786.

Correspondence with Flood—Second Appendix to Shakspeare—Prepares to become Editor—Horace Walpole—Bishop Percy—Goldsmith—Steevens—Elevation of his Brother to the Peerage—Boswell—John Kemble—Walpole and Rousseau—Lord Charlemont.

SUCH was the friend upon whom Malone had some time previously ventured to try his skill in political negotiation. Who the original prompter was on this occasion does not appear. Perhaps Burke, also an old friend of Flood ; perhaps indirectly Windham, just nominated Irish Secretary, likewise a friend of Burke and Malone, although the latter had not seen him since his accession to office. But the letter implies some—although indirect—authority for the proposal.

London, April 24th, 1783.
Queen Anne Street East.

DEAR FLOOD—You will probably, before you receive this letter, have heard that Lord Northington is appointed Lord Lieutenant of Ireland, and Mr. Windham, of Norfolk (not Lord Egremont's brother), a gentleman of good fortune, his secretary.

This new appointment is the occasion of taking up my pen at present for the purpose of asking you whether you mean to come to England shortly, or have any wish or intention to form any part of the new administration in the next session in Ireland. I trouble you with these inquiries, not from idle curiosity, but because I am well, though not *officially*, informed that the new Government is thoroughly impressed with a sense of your importance; and, of course, I should think, would wish to make an arrangement that should be the means of obtaining your friendship and assistance.

I shall not enlarge further on this business till I hear from you what your intentions or wishes are. Among other things that I have reason to believe are attainable, I have great grounds for believing that the office of Chancellor of the Exchequer may be vacated; and if any office is an object to you, I take it for granted that must be one.

It is so long since I have seen you that I am entirely ignorant whether such an office or any other is at present an object of your wishes; and I am also aware that you may have particular reasons for not choosing to disclose your intentions to any one. I request, therefore, you will be so good as to communicate or withhold your thoughts from me on this subject, as you please. If you think fit to employ me, I think it may be in my power to put things in such a train as will be agreeable to you; and you know there are occasions in which a middle-man is a useful one.

You will, I am sure, readily believe that I have no other object or interest in this business but doing you, and the public at the same time, a service. I must, however, once more repeat that what I write is neither at the desire nor even with the knowledge of any person concerned in Government; but is merely in consequence of my putting together a number of things that have lately fallen within my private observation, and in which I think I cannot be mistaken. Mr. Windham, the new secretary, is an acquaintance of mine, but I have not seen him since his new appointment. He is a man of strict honour, and does not go to Ireland with any view to emolument, it being with great difficulty he was prevailed upon to accept of his present employment.

I am doubtful where you are at present, but will direct to Dublin. I wish either business or inclination led you a little more to this part of the world; being, my dear Flood, with perfect truth,

Your sincerely affectionate
EDMOND MALONE.

The voice of the charmer to office—how rare is such a result!—sounded in vain. Quite as powerless was that of his former tutor, Archbishop Markham, the following week ; yet *he* wrote avowedly from personal communication with Lord Northington, that any position selected by Mr. Flood should not be withheld. Why he declined can only be conjectured. Perhaps an impression of the instability of Ministry—that a weight evidently forced upon the Royal shoulders would be thrown off at the first fitting moment, and he necessarily as part of the burden. By the reply, it appears he could not have accepted his former office:—

Farmley, near Kilkenny, May 5th, 1783.

DEAR MALONE—I have just received your favour of the 24th of April, and am equally concerned that we are not oftener together. I attempted your door last summer when I was in London.

I have been a friend to Irish rights to the best of my poor power, it is true, and upon the fairest grounds. Some people said it was to recover my office, which I could have kept had that been an object. The late suspense with respect to one of those appointments revived this tale, and I never thought it worth my while to tell them what I said long since to Mr. Eden, viz., that if I were dismissed from the vice-treasurership, I never should resume it. I will keep my word ; I am apt to do it. At the same time I am sincerely disposed to English Government. This you will readily believe who know my principles and my situation, neither of which I will abandon. They are above vulgar faction and vulgar ambition. I was suggested into office on higher motives. I embraced administration with an unsuspecting credulity. I felt it was their interest to act as they spoke ; but I found myself deceived. I do not know the author or motive to this. You know the consequence.

I take your communication to be precisely such as you

state. I have no immediate inducement to go to England; and, if you have none to come to Ireland, let us at least correspond. I am perfectly assured of your good wishes, and I flatter myself you are equally so of mine.

I am, dear Malone,

Yours faithfully and affectionately,

HENRY FLOOD.

You write to me as if I was a Privy Councillor.*

Two notes succeed this, one in June, in which the classics take their turn; another in November, in which hints are dropped of the little familiarity in Ireland with the less prominent shades of English politics. Nor was England better informed of the tendencies of her weaker sister. So marked was their little familiarity with each other, or so imprudent the policy pursued in the face of passing events, that a stranger might have doubted whether both were members of the same kingdom. Such mistakes and misapprehensions are unavoidable with two Parliaments sitting in two divisions of one empire :—
" A thousand thanks for your literary selections. I am still better pleased that we are to meet this summer in Ireland. That implies of necessity a visit to Farmley, which will open all its doors to you. For fear, however, of being seduced to Dublin or Westmeath, I counsel the road of South Wales, Milford, and Waterford to you. I mentioned in my letter another translation of Euripides, lately advertised, of which, however, I have never heard any character, and I suppose by your silence it deserves none. England exhibits at present a strange scene to one at

* It will be remembered he had been struck off the list of both countries.

a distance from it. I do not, however, pretend to judge very decisively on it for that reason."

Soon after the publication of the supplement to Shakspeare in 1780, he saw cause for various emendations, and followed it up by an appendix. In the spring of this year (1783) came out *A Second Appendix to Mr. Malone's Supplement to the last Edition of the Plays of Shakspeare.* This extends to nearly seventy pages: reference is always made to " Mr. Steevens' last excellent edition of 1778 ;" and it is introduced by a passage from Roscommon, whose critical advice seems to have been ever present to his mind—

> " Take pains the genuine meaning to explore;
> There sweat, there strain; tug the laborious oar;
> Search every comment that your care can find :
> Some here, some there, may hit the poet's mind.
> When things appear unnatural and hard,
> Consult your author with himself compared."

The fact communicated to him by Steevens himself of having ceased to be a commentator, led to the wish of supplying the vacant place. Such necessity he probably conceived to exist some time before, but about this period the design was finally formed. In August he had occasion to write to Mr. Nichols, the zealous and intelligent editor of the *Gentleman's Magazine,* on other literary points, and requests that he may be announced as " preparing a new edition of Shakspeare, with select notes from all the commentators." He adds—" I am just preparing to set out for Ireland for a few months. My address there is Baronston, Mullingar."

No details of this journey, which we have seen was

likewise announced to Flood, appear among such of
his papers as I have personally examined, or are
noticed in remains found elsewhere. This may be
explained by their extensive dispersion in book and
autograph sales. But probably it may have been
postponed; unless some rumour reached him that
in the literary office in which he had engaged, certain stores of antiquity were likely to be forthcoming
in some of its historical recesses.

In 1784 the journal of anecdotes commences by
noting a conversation with Horace Walpole, who
repeats in some of his letters what he also freely
communicated in personal intercourse. To Strawberry Hill were taken such of Malone's friends as were
desirous of viewing its rarities; but the fastidious
owner, with the whim inherent in the man, would
admit only four persons in a party, although gratified
by the general curiosity to examine its contents.

For this regulation he apologizes in a note to
Malone written in the spring. Her Royal Highness
the Princess Amelia, he says, was graciously pleased to
assent to it as reasonable, although some proposed
visitors were to come from her house. But " he will
willingly send Mr. Malone three tickets for four each
for any day after next Monday."

One of his visits to the owner of this classical
abode drew forth a few anecdotes of his father, which
appeared to be as well remembered as pleasantly told
by the son.

" Having called on Mr. Walpole this morning
(March 30th, 1784), I took occasion to mention
Lord Hardwicke's new work, entitled *Walpoliana*, a

I

small quarto, containing some anecdotes relative to
Sir Robert Walpole, of which I believe only a few
copies were printed for his friends. They have not
been published. Mr. Walpole said it was a very
extraordinary performance, and he wondered much
that a nobleman who lived so near the time would
send forth anything so imperfect and inaccurate,
when he might so easily have obtained better information.

"This account (he said) of Sir Robert's becoming
Minister to George II. was entirely erroneous. The
truth of the matter, Mr. Walpole said, was as follows :—On the death of George I., Sir Robert, who
was then First Lord of the Treasury, went to the
Prince, at Richmond, to announce the event. He
knew he was no favourite there (Sir Robert having
attached himself to George I., between whom and
his son there was a quarrel), though he believed
the Princess (afterwards Queen Caroline) very well
inclined to him. As soon as admitted,* and he told
the new King what had occurred, he further informed
his Majesty that the first thing necessary to do was
to assemble the Privy Council, and to make a speech
to them. Sir Robert then asked him who should
draw it up, or, in other words, who was to be his
prime minister? The King desired him to apply
to Sir Spencer Compton (afterwards Lord Wilmington), the speaker of the House of Commons. Sir
Robert accordingly did so. Sir Spencer, a few hours
afterwards calling upon Sir Robert, honestly owned

---

* Sir Robert went to Richmond with such speed that he killed two of
his coach-horses by fatigue.

that he could not draw up a proper speech, and requested Walpole's assistance, which the latter good-naturedly gave him. When this matter came to be known, Queen Caroline urged to the King how very improper it was to make any one his prime minister, who so far from being equal to the office was forced to seek assistance from the very person whom he was about to displace. The King, struck by the observation, continued Sir Robert in his old station.

" Having got upon this subject, I expressed my suprise to Mr. Walpole that he had not himself given the world some memoirs of his father's life and times. He said that, at the time his father was principally concerned in the administration of affairs, he was at college or abroad; that he came home about the year 1740 or 1741; that Sir Robert died about three years afterwards; and at that time of life he troubled himself very little in inquiring after such historical anecdotes, &c. If, therefore, he undertook the task at all, he must rely on the information of others. Independent however of this, he thought the world would be little inclined to pay attention to what a son should say of his father. All his statements would be deemed coloured and partial; even where he should be most simple and nearest to the truth.

" He proceeded to mention a singular anecdote of Dr. Kippis, editor of the new edition of the *Biographia Britannica*. Mr. Walpole in his *Royal and Noble Authors* had said of that work, that ' it ought rather to be called *Vindicatio Britannica*, for that it was a general panegyric upon everybody.'

In an additional note to the new edition, Dr. Kippis, quoting this passage, added, ' that whenever the editors should come in the course of the new publication to the article of his father, Sir Robert, he might probably find that the work was *not* a panegyric upon everybody.' Notwithstanding, however, this threat, Dr. Kippis a few days ago waited on Mr. W., with whom he had no acquaintance, to request *he* would furnish the new work with his father's life. He replied, that he certainly should not, giving the reasons he assigned to me that he should trust his father's memory to the justice of posterity. If, however, when Dr. Kippis had drawn up his account he would lay it before him, should anything be grossly misstated, he should point out such mistakes, but not go a step further.'

" Among the anecdotes of Sir Robert Walpole, I wonder the following should not have come to the knowledge of Lord Hardwicke. In the height of Pultney's opposition, an old gentleman had constantly voted with the minister, and often attended his levee ; but never asked him for any favour. Sir Robert, who was plagued with daily solicitations, felt some surprise at this, and at length observed to him that he was much obliged by his support, and should be happy to know how he could serve him. The other replied, that he wanted nothing. Sir Robert, who believed every man acted from interested motives, exclaimed, ' How then, my dear sir, comes it to pass that I am honoured with your support ? ' " Why, I'll tell you," said the old gentleman, ' I have lived a great deal in foreign countries where

an arbitrary government prevails. I hold such a
government to be the best that ever was devised;
and all your measures appear to me admirably well
calculated to render this Government arbitrary, and
the king at the head of it despotic. On this principle, as long as ever you continue minister, you may
rely upon my voice.'

"I heard this story many years ago, and mentioning it long since to Mr. Andrew Stewart (author of
the admirable letters to Lord Mansfield), he said it
was certainly true; and that the gentleman was a
Scotchman, a Mr. Falkiner, of Selkirk, as well as
I recollect."

The literary club cemented sincere friendship with
Dr. Percy, Bishop of Dromore, familiar to students of
old verse by *Reliques of Ancient English Poetry*. Frequent correspondence ensued and continued through
life, even when the Bishop becoming blind was obliged
to employ the pen of another. Literature formed the
usual topic—dear to both in old books, editions, plays,
ballads, fragments of criticism on the older writers,
inquiries as to the new, loans of what the other did
not possess, and of course emendations of Shakspeare.
"As I shall soon have an opportunity," writes the
prelate in February, 1785, "of having a parcel of
books sent me from London, if you have no particular
wish to retain the second edition folio of Shakspeare
longer (otherwise I withdraw my request), I should
be much obliged if you would be pleased to send it
well packed up, directed for me."

The same letter gives a sorry picture of difficulties

in the culture of literature in Ireland. He always
writes with a species of enthusiasm of the " Club"—
the enjoyment he derived from it, asks what new
members have joined, desires remembrance to the old
—and rarely forgets to conclude with, " *Esto perpetua!* "   " In this remote part of the kingdom,
nothing would afford me a higher gratification than
to be honoured with a few lines from you or any
other of my good friends, to inform me what is doing
in the literary world; of which I can seldom obtain
intelligence sooner than it might reach to the East
Indies.   How is the Club attended?   What names
have been added to it?   These questions I am tempted
to trouble you with, though sensible that your time
may be better employed.   But my obligations will be
the greater."

Accident occasionally enabled the Bishop to return
something in the way of anecdote.   One of these
relates to Swift.   It is characteristic of that eccentric
and scarcely intelligible man, whose conduct even
when kind always differed from that of others in
the mode of displaying it.   I have not seen the story
elsewhere, and therefore transfer it to a note for the
amusement of the reader.*

* " I was exceedingly astonished at what you told me concerning the
charge brought by Dr. Calder at this late day against Dean Swift, and
thought with you it was most incredible and absurd. And yet, yesterday,
chance procured me an unexpected opportunity of inquiring into it.
  " At Dromore church appeared a genteel clergyman, a stranger. I invited him to dine with me. After dinner he said he possessed the prebend
in the adjoining diocese of Connor, which was the first ecclesiastical pre-
ferment of Swift—the prebend and parish of *Kilroot*—which he was believed to have held with another small vicarage called *Maghera Moran*
in the same diocese and near Kilroot. He told me that when Swift came
to take possession of these two benefices given or procured him by Lord

Another object now occupied the Bishop, which furnished several letters to Malone. This was to collect—or to make others do so—materials for a *Memoir of Goldsmith* to prefix to an edition of his works. Of this tedious operation, occupying no less than sixteen years, I have given the history elsewhere.* The aim was to benefit the poorer relatives of his old friend. He had already given them occasional supplies drawn from various quarters; but being indisposed to biographical labour himself, or deeming it inconsistent with high ecclesiastical functions, he turned over the duty at different periods to four or five other persons. Their united inquiries passing from hand to hand from 1785 till 1801, furnished at length but the loose elements of a life, mainly from the personal recollections of his lordship, and such anecdotes as his birthplace and relatives could very inadequately supply.†

Capel, about 1694 or 1695, he, with that odd humour that always distinguished him, entered the house of a neighbouring vicar, a Mr. Winder, and without ceremony took up his quarters there, living with him a whole year without offering payment for his board, &c. He at last took French leave, nor did his host know whither he had gone, till he received a letter from him from Dublin, saying he had resigned the vicarage and procured the presentation of it for him. This anecdote the relator told me he had from a near relation of Mr. Winder's, who outlived Swift thirty years, and died at Lisburn at an advanced age in 1774 or 1775." Here follows the story of the alleged attempt of Swift to commit a rape in his parish, brought forward by Dr. Calder; but which, upon minute investigation, turned out an idle rumour. The refutation is in the *Gentleman's Magazine* for 1790, p. 189.

* Preface to *Life of Goldsmith*, 2 vols. 8vo, 1837.

† This imperfect tribute to the genius of the poet could not be deemed satisfactory to any of his admirers. One of his townsmen (Reverend John Graham, late rector of Tamlaghtard in the diocese of Derry), also a poet and friend of the writer of the present work, suggested to him to furnish, if possible, a full and satisfactory biography, with such circum-

The year 1785 seems to be a blank in his record of anecdotes. He was, however, diligent in pursuit of notations on the text of Shakspeare; and among others heard that Horace Walpole, then ill of the gout in Berkeley Square, indulged his taste that way. To an application for the favour of their perusal, he replies in February: "They are at Strawberry Hill, and till he removes thither they cannot be got at, but as soon as that can be done he will look them out and send them to Mr. Malone."

Some misunderstanding of the rules enforced in visiting his country retreat drew forth another letter of explanation to Malone, on the annoyances given and experienced by sight-seers. A show-house is not always a comfortable possession. Visitors sometimes expect their curiosity to be gratified even against rules; the owner, that his regulations shall be observed. If good nature prompt him to oblige a few, offence will probaby be taken by the many; and censure rather than praise be the result of an accommodating disposition. Of the discontented spirit of

stances as time had revealed, and inquiry should trace during a career much of which remained little known. The proposal was adopted. I made excursions to his native spot; to Athlone, Ballymahon, Longford, and their vicinities, where relations were found who contributed a variety of original matter. In Dublin and London equal diligence discovered much more. Several letters, occasional verses, essays, prefaces, tracts, introductions, agreements with booksellers were found; added to bills of board and lodgings, tailors' bills, with the prices received for copyrights and various small performances. Several things not known to be his, amounting to more than fills an octavo volume, and printed in my edition of his works, 1837, I first discovered. Others of doubtful origin were ascertained. In short, I found a loose sketch of a life, of something more than a hundred pages; and by zealous research added nearly a thousand more of original matter. I shall not here allude to the unwarrantable piracies to which *all* its contents, without exception, have been subjected.

neighbours he gives a sketch in the letter alluded to, which is in a somewhat formal style :—

Strawberry Hill, July 10, 1785.

I am much obliged to you, sir, for the favour of your letter, to which I was extremely sorry to have given any occasion, and of which I beg you will give me leave to send you this account.

I live here in so numerous and gossiping a neighbourhood, that I am not only tormented daily by applications for tickets, but several persons have quarrelled with me for not complying with their demands. Nay, I have received letters reproaching me with indulging some of my particular friends with a greater latitude than four; for they are so idle as to watch and count the carriages at my gate. The very day you was here last, sir, a gentleman and his wife, who came from a neighbour's, were in the house, and I knew would report that I had admitted six, if the carriages were seen; and yet, out of regard to you, sir, I could not think of disappointing your friends. You was extremely good to favour me; and I hope, by this relation, will see how much I am distressed, though very desirous of obliging. As numbers come to see my house whose names I do not even know, I must limit the number, and I offend if I break my rule. Therefore, last year, I printed those rules, and now should give still greater offence if I did not adhere to them; while the only advantage that accrues to myself is that my evenings are free, and that I keep the month of October for myself.

I beg your pardon, sir, for troubling you with this detail, but it was due to your politeness, and will, I hope, convince you that I am, sir, &c. &c.

Hitherto Steevens and Malone had gone on well together; but in the edition of *Shakspeare* superintended by Isaac Reed which appeared about this time, Malone had inserted some notes which controverted a few by Steevens, and gave offence. The latter wrote to him, desiring they should be retained in their then state whenever his own edition should appear, and he would reply to them. This Malone declined to promise, reserving to himself the right in his future book to alter or expunge anything of his own that further consideration should deem erroneous. But he should transmit to him such alterations before they went to press—that Mr. Steevens should have the privilege of answering them, which he (Malone) would print without reply. This very fair arrangement, with characteristic irritability, was declined. Thenceforward, the offended commentator said, all intercourse on the subject of Shakspeare should cease. It has been stated that among all the friendships of Steevens, not one but those of Dr. Farmer and Isaac Reed continued uninterrupted.

In June 1785, he had the satisfaction of seeing his brother raised to the Irish Peerage by the title of Baron Sunderlin of Lake Sunderlin in Westmeath. Richard had been many years in Parliament. So were several of the family during the preceding half century. Their general character stood high; they had filled some important positions; and the honour now conferred evinced desire to repair the injustice shown to one of the number, the eminent Anthony, by dismission from high office for voting patriotically, and as it afterwards appeared strictly constitutionally, against hasty measures of the Irish Ministry. The nephew already inherited the estate, and Baronston, the mansion of his uncle; and at length now gained what should have been the title of the latter. He had married in 1778, Philippa, elder daughter of Godolphin Rooper, Esq., of Berkhamstead.

With Joseph and Thomas Warton he kept up a

brisk correspondence during the year. Their topics, as usual, literary and antiquarian—old poets, plays, interludes, epitaphs, sonnets, *Venus and Adonis*, Marlowe, Milton, Lord Southampton, and Shakspeare. How warmly to such things yearns the heart of an intelligent antiquary!

In this year likewise (1785) he had the pleasure of making a new acquaintance,—very soon transformed into a friend. This was Boswell; and the place of meeting no less appropriate—Baldwin's printing-office while examining a proof-sheet of the *Tour to the Hebrides*. An intimacy ensued, which like most of the critic's friendships continued undisturbed through life, though faults and follies scarcely attempted to be concealed impaired respect for his new companion. To many the now renowned biographer appeared then a jumble of contradictions—sense and nonsense, shrewdness and good humour, cunning and simplicity, vanity, yet with kindness and generosity; a tone of flattery to the great in order to make way in the world, combined with feelings of rectitude and firm regard to truth in biographical statements. Few gave him credit during life for the talents he really possessed. He puzzled even Dr. Johnson, who while in Scotland wrote of his companion "that he possessed better faculties than I had imagined."

The devotion shown to the great moralist has perhaps tended to diminish the respect due to the writer of his life. He made him almost too sincerely the hero of worship; never for a moment swerved from his allegiance; sought him at all hours; evinced reverence in every way; and submitted patiently to reproofs which were ungracious even if deserved. The follower kissed the rod, and has not hesitated to confess the punishment; he had a fixed purpose in view, and therefore, much to our advantage and to his own fame, "stooped to conquer." For this deference toward great knowledge, pre-eminent abilities, and moral worth, he has been denounced with extravagant violence as if guilty of a moral offence. Hard names have been freely applied to what has unquestionably proved to be disinterested attachment. Yet who has contributed so much to our amusement? Where shall we find in our own or any other language one who has shown equal talent and industry in recording so much wit, wisdom, and acquaintance with life for the instruction and amusement of mankind? Such a book is not the product of chance. He had no model to follow; but with that happiness of thought, which if it does not imply genius certainly falls little short of it, struck out one for himself. As there has been but one Johnson, so there certainly is but one Boswell. He stands alone in the plan and execution of a work which has won the admiration of every description of reader.

Malone, who appears to have mentioned Boswell's design to a Dublin correspondent so early as 1787, became more impressed in his favour by the reply. Unluckily the name is detached from the letter; but this Irish friend appears to have had keen insight into character, and evidently figured among the higher class of literary men of that city.

"You will think me very passive that I should never have read the illustrious Hawkins,* but I have

* *Life of Dr. Johnson.*

seen so many extracts and criticisms that I am no stranger to his merits. . . . . Boswell's work I am anxious for. I will answer for it we may depend upon his fidelity. I knew him intimately many years ago when he was in Dublin. He had not then appeared as an author; he was an amiable, warm-hearted fellow, and there was a simplicity in him very engaging."

A writer upon the life and works of Shakspeare must take interest in the performers as well as in productions of the modern stage. Among the former, John Kemble took the lead. About 1783, Malone selected him as a man of education and gentlemanly manners, with whom a few agreeable hours could be spent on their favourite topics. The actor understood the value of such an acquaintance, and soon learned to esteem his amiable private qualities. Pleasant dinners, amid amusing and intelligent companions, gave zest to their discussions; and among Malone's letters is an apology from Mrs. Siddons, who cannot fulfil a previous dinner engagement to him by the unexpected arrival of two dear friends from abroad. A note from her brother to the critic at this time (March, 1786) postpones a friend's dinner invitation while jesting upon the fate of an unlucky play—forgetting that what proved sport to him was dramatic death to the luckless author. He was a clergyman, Dr. Delap, once curate to Mason, the poet, and whose name occurs in his letters to Gray. He wrote no less than seven tragedies. Three were represented and failed. The others only escaped from a country printing-office to pass into immediate and total oblivion. Who may not admire the perseverance of such an author? Yet who venture to exhibit such devotion to ill-success?

> DEAR SIR,—I will send Mr. Byng word, very early in the morning, that I hope he will excuse me to-morrow, and command me to wait on him either Wednesday or Friday next week, as you find it most convenient.
>
> The *Captives* were set at liberty last night, amidst roars of laughter.* I see the doctor publishes it this week. If his reverence should be severe, the best thing that we can hope is, that all who read the preface may read the play.
>
> Cadell bought this sublime piece before it appeared, for fifty pounds, agreeing to make it a hundred on its third representation. It has been played three times, and I dare say old Sanctimony will have no remorse in taking the other fifty.
>
> Your very obedient and obliged servant,
J. P. KEMBLE.

Two or three notes from Walpole occur early in this year. He had forgotten to execute some commissions for Malone, and pleads seventy years in excuse. One of these was a deed connected with the theatre or with Shakspeare, in the possession of Mrs. Garrick at Hampton, which he wished to inspect through the intervention of that gentleman. Another is of more interest by its reference to Vertue's remains, and the interest taken by Malone in Lord Roscommon the poet, part of whose estate, it will be remembered, fell into his possession :—

> Mr. Walpole sends his compliments to Mr. Malone, and assures him he has looked for the source whence he mentioned a picture of Lord Roscommon by Carlo Maratti, but

---

* *The Captives :* a Tragedy, by John Delap. Brought out at Drury Lane, March 9th, 1786.

cannot find it. He concludes it was some note of Vertue; but at the distance of so many years cannot be sure. All Vertue's memorandums were indigested, and written down successively as he made them in forty volumes, often on loose scraps of paper, so it is next to impossible to find the note; nor, were it found, does it probably contain more than Mr. Walpole has copied into the Anecdotes.

The same correspondent in a morning's conversation, gave him the following account of a celebrated quarrel :—

" Mr. Horace Walpole, who sat with me some time this morning (Jan. 28, 1786), gave a particular account of the origin of his letter to Rousseau in 1765, which in fact was the occasion of the quarrel between that madman and David Hume. He happened to be at the house of a French lady in Paris with Helvetius, who observed that Rousseau seemed to court persecution. Mr. Walpole said that if he would go to Berlin, the King of Prussia would persecute him as much as he pleased. On this thought, he afterwards sat down and wrote a French letter in the name of the King of Prussia to Rousseau. The lady was delighted with it ; and copies, as is often the case in Paris, flew through the town rapidly. Mr. Walpole was invited everywhere, and the *devotees* particularly paid court to him as espousing the cause of religion against philosophy. He had even invitations from several Abbesses ; but at last they made so much noise about a small matter, that he grew tired and thought it ridiculous. There were two faults in the French of his original letter, which the Duke de Nivernois and Helvetius pointed out to him, and they were corrected.

" Mr. Hume happened to lodge in the same hotel with Mr. Walpole, and often proposed to introduce Rousseau to him; but as author of a paper written to ridicule him, he thought it would be unhandsome to suffer Hume to make their acquaintance. A few days afterward Hume and Rousseau left Paris for London, when the letter in question having got into some of the French *Mercures*, was printed in an English newspaper.* Rousseau aware of Hume and Walpole being friends; that Hume was secretary to Lord Hertford, cousin to Walpole; and that he had often been with Walpole at the time this letter first appeared, suspected that Hume had some hand in the publication. But Mr. Walpole assured me he never showed it to Hume; and publication arose solely in consequence of many copies being handed about. Rousseau could not divest himself of this suspicion. Hence the origin of his subsequent quarrel with Hume. The latter became so distressed on the occasion, that he requested Walpole to write him a letter, avowing sole authorship in the offensive piece, which he did.

" This acknowledgment was published by D'Alembert in his account of the dispute between Rousseau and Hume. Mr. Walpole complained to me that Hume had garbled his letter, for it began: 'Your friends, the literati, have acted like fools as literati generally do;' but this paragraph was suppressed.

" Such was Mr. Walpole's acount; but the true solution of the quarrel is that Rousseau was mad.— M."

---

* See it in *Saint James's Chronicle*.

In the spring, Lord Sunderlin, his lady, and sisters, reached London on their way to the Continent. Edmond and his family delighted in each other; but as he could seldom visit Ireland without impeding the progress of the "book," so he could not be tempted to participate in their excursion. Catherine however gave him an occasional journal of proceedings, and in one of her letters from Nice where several Irish friends had made a halt, gives an alluring sketch of the spot, still with the hope of drawing the critic from his task and his home.

" Both she" (Henrietta, usually called Harriet, her elder sister) " and Lady Sunderlin like the place extremely. Indeed it is an absolute paradise. A thousand paths we have to walk, and for miles without an inclosure, in the midst of orange-trees and all kinds of sweet shrubs. If the lower rank of people properly enjoyed their situations, they would be much above us, for most of their cottages are placed in the most beautiful and delightful spots that can be conceived. But their inhabitants see not as we do, and wonder at us for admiring them."

With the ruling passion strong within him, Lord Charlemont, as usual, solicits his good offices in the acquisition of books, negotiations with booksellers, and occasional criticism :—

" Your acquisition for me is magnificent, and what is still better than magnificence though seldom allied to it, extremely cheap. You are certainly the best book-jockey that ever existed. I long to see my new old treasure, and expect it daily. Payne,* however,

* The Bookseller.

K

has not been quite as active as you have been, for I do not find that he sends some of the principal on my list.   The best quarto of Dante is surely to be had in London.

"Have you endeavoured to make Elmsley send me a complete third volume of *Petrarch*, instead of the imperfect one I had from him?   You see how I tease you, but you may thank your own goodness for my unreasonable importunity.   .   .   .   .   I have the nineteen volumes in large paper of Provost's *Hist. de Voyages;* but imagined that a supplement had been published.   .   .   .   .   My old and dear friend Burke, after having made us happy by his unexpected arrival, has now made us as miserable by too speedy departure."

A succeeding letter from his lordship is filled with Shakspearian details.   Among the doubtful plays he would have *Pericles* stand first, as showing un-doubted evidence of the hand of Shakspeare; and *Titus Andronicus* last, as having little of the master. A hint had been previously dropped to his noble friend, of doubts as to Shakspeare's share in the three parts of *Henry VI.*, and his design of writing a dis-sertation on the authorship.   The reply then was that the creed of his lordship on the subject was not finally settled.   He now says: " The more I consider it, the more confident I am in opinion that they were not originally written by Shakspeare.   The second part has most of him, though even here much of the tragick wants that peculiar colour which even in his worst writing is always discernible.   *Jack Cade* is certainly his.   Much of the third part is strongly

marked for his own, and I really think that with due
attention to all these plays, one might with tolerable
certainty select his gold from the dross of the original
writer."

The examination of the three plays in question
appeared duly in the edition. Theobald and Warburton had deemed them spurious. Johnson and
Steevens thought otherwise. Farmer did not believe
them *originally* written by Shakspeare; and Malone,
after entering thoroughly into the question, arrived at
the same conclusion. To do this, however, cost him
much study and no slight critical sagacity. Whoever
reads his dissertation appended to those plays will see,
that not content with ordinary assurance, he enters
heart and soul into the work of solving difficulties
which had perplexed or mastered men of no small
reputation, yet still remained matters of doubt.

He appears to prove that all three plays came
originally from other hands. The first our great
poet touched but lightly; the second and third he
new-modelled, added to, altered, and in part re-
wrote, rendering such traces of the master as left
no doubt of the infusion of his spirit into both.
The inquiry extends to nearly fifty closely printed
pages; for he had made up his mind not to be
repelled or foiled; and that others should be as fully
convinced as himself. He thus, among others, satisfied Professor Porson—the least practicable man of
his day perhaps—that, in his own words, "he considered the essay on the three parts of *Henry the
Sixth* as one of the most convincing pieces of criticism that he had ever read."

CHAPTER VII.

1786—1789.

Jephson's *Julia, or the Italian Lover*—Prologue by Malone—Lord Charlemont—Horace Walpole—Correspondence with Rev. Mr. Davenport
of Stratford—John Kemble—Pope and Warburton—Lady M. Wortley
Montague—Visit to Burke.

So obliging a correspondent as he proved was not
left long unemployed by his Irish friends. Lord
Charlemont assails him with the usual solicitations,
apologizes for the trouble given, and increases it by
further requests.

Not less importunate is Bishop Percy for books,
transcripts from the British Museum, inquiries as to
Ritson's censures and criticisms upon portions of the
Reliques, with such varieties, new or old, in literature as excited notice or promised interest. He
likewise asks for "Baretti's *Tolondron*, and whatever
answer my friend Bowle published in reply; and
favour me with a little insight into that curious
controversy."

Again the Bishop returns to the charge: "I thank
you for the particulars of the last hours of my much
honoured friend Tyrwhitt. A few more such losses
would thoroughly wean me from all desire to visit my
native country, especially if you and a few other friends
would enliven this solitude by sending me now and
then such a letter as your last, informing me what
you are doing yourself, and what attracts the atten-

tion of the literary world. I shall be truly anxious to see your edition of *Shakspeare*. When it comes, I will set to read his works with attention, which may suggest something for a future edition."

He desires to thank Boswell for an obliging letter. He had promised a few anecdotes of Johnson's earlier life, but now thinks them too trivial, or anticipated by Mrs. Piozzi. One however he tells, which Boswell has not failed to chronicle : " I have heard him observe that, at Lichfield, he learnt nothing from the master, but a great deal in his school ; and at Stourbridge, that he learnt a great deal from the master, and nothing in his school."

The muse of his friend Jephson had again become pregnant—and again was the critic seduced into consultation on the best mode of ushering the " interesting stranger " into light. In short, he had written a new tragedy. The birth of a play or poem, like that of heir to an estate, usually brings the .family together in council in order to relieve the affectionate anxieties of paternity.

While in progress, it had been submitted to Malone who suggested various alterations. Jephson replied in a well-filled sheet of foolscap, so early as January, 1785. He adopts most of the suggestions, allows lines to be dropped, words to be altered; dwells on the stage business, incidents, order of the scenes, more or less prominence of characters—always keeping Mrs. Siddons pre-eminent—weighing the proper allowance of stabbings and poisonings so that too many dead shall not encumber the stage at the same moment ! In short, we are let into all the agonies of

a tragic playwright. Even the title must be sacrificed in order not to let the public too soon into the
mystery of the story. First it was *The Cruel Lover.*
Then *Julia, or the Fatal Constancy.* The author
also objects to one of the actors, although of good
repute in theatrical history—" Gentleman Smyth,"
as he was usually called; and begs his correspondent
to keep out of the play " that most detestable of all
actors and coxcombs.".

Many who knew the writer amid the pleasures,
politics, and wit of Dublin, wondered how he could
be studious enough for a tragic subject. The talent,
however, was within him, and the way to the London
stage smooth. None of the perplexities of an unknown author could be felt where the manager, the
first tragic actor of the day, and an eminent dramatic
critic figured as his personal friends. To Malone
was confided preliminary matters and the prologue;
to Courtenay, the epilogue; to the manager, all his
moral influence over performers; and to Kemble and
his great sister, the embodiment of sentiment and
situation in the principal characters. To prepare
the way more favourably, the *Count of Narbonne*
was played shortly before; and a new edition printed,
edited by Malone.

On the 17th April, 1787, appeared at Drury Lane,
Julia, or the Italian Lover. A brilliant audience
received it well. Kemble acted the principal character admirably, and also spoke the prologue; he is
said on that night to have even outshone the talents
of his sister, and by his exertions to have brought on
serious illness. Delay became, therefore, unavoid-

able; it was withdrawn for the season; and possessing perhaps no inherent vitality, lost place upon the stage.

The following is Malone's chief contribution; but Courtenay, being idle or otherwise occupied, left half the epilogue also to him :—

PROLOGUE TO "JULIA, OR THE ITALIAN LOVER."

From Thespis' day to this enlightened hour
The Stage has shown the dire abuse of power;
What mighty mischief from ambition springs,
The fate of heroes and the fall of kings.
But these high themes, howe'er adorned by art,
Have seldom gained the passes of the heart.
Calm we behold the pompous mimic woe,
Unmoved by sorrows we can never know.
For other feelings in the soul arise,
When private griefs arrest our ears and eyes;
When the false friend, and blameless suffering wife,
Reflect the image of domestic life.
And still more wide the sympathy, more keen,
When to each breast responsive is the scene;
And the fine chords that every heart entwine
Dilated vibrate with the flowing line.
Such is the theme that now demands your ear,
And claims the silent plaudit of a tear;
One tyrant passion all mankind must prove,
The balm or poison of our lives—is love.
Love's sovereign sway extends o'er every clime,
Nor owns a limit or of space or time;
For love the generous fair one hath sustained
More poignant ills than ever poet feigned;
For love the maid partakes her lover's tomb,
Or pines long life out in sad soothless gloom;
Ne'er shall oblivion shroud the Grecian wife
Who gave her own to save a husband's life.
With her contending see our Edward's bride,
Imbibing passion from his mangled side;
Nor less, though proud of intellectual sway,
Doth haughty man this tyrant power obey—
From youth to age by love's wild tempest tossed;
For love e'en mighty kingdoms have been lost!
Vain—wealth and fame, and fortune's fostering care,

If no fond breast the splendid blessings share,
And each day's bustling pageantry once past,
There—only there—his bliss is found at last.
   For woes fictitious oft your tears have flowed,
Your cheek for wrongs imaginary glowed.
To-night our Poet means not to assail
Your throbbing bosom with a fancied tale.
Scarce sixty years their annual course have rolled,
Since all was real that our scenes unfold;
To touch your hearts with no unpleasing pain,
The Muse's magic makes it live again.
Bids mingled characters, as once in life,
Resume their functions, and renew their strife;
While pride, revenge, and jealousy's wild rage,
Rouse all the Genius of the impassioned stage.

Literary and antiquarian correspondence diversified his own peculiar pursuits. Thomas Warton amused him with references to the poems of H. Constable of Elizabeth's time; and on the changes of proprietors of Tichfield monastery, which came afterwards into the hands of Lord Southampton. Lord Charlemont writes no less than four letters. He taxes him with silence, yet sympathizes with an allusion from his heart-stricken friend, who had not yet escaped from the tyranny of Cupid, as we may presume by his own axiom in the preceding prologue,—

    "One tyrant passion all mankind must prove,
    The balm or poison of our lives—is love."

"But the best hearts are the weakest," adds his lordship, "and their weakness is but too apt to prevail over the strength of the most vigorous understanding. *Experto crede Roberto.* Yet one remedy there is which has not yet, as I believe, been tried. Vacuity is probably the source of the disorder. Why is not the void filled up? When a picture has gotten a dint, the best method of cure is by *new lining*."

From love his lordship flies off to dramatic business. Shakspeare, he says, is an unanswerable excuse for everything.

"Many thanks for your kind and persevering attention in supplying my literary wants. The number of my last volume in small quarto is thirty-three; in the larger size, twenty-nine. The Morocco volume contains:—*Hamlet* (no date), *Henry V.* (1608), *Henry VI.* (no date), *Midsummer Night's Dream* (1600), *Merchant of Venice* (1600), *Merry Wives of Windsor* (1619), *King Lear* (1608). What others of my Shakspeares have you got, and what have you been able to procure?" Another letter relates to Italian writers. One also to Mrs. Hogarth, which has been previously noticed. A fourth coincides in almost every point with Malone's dissertation, which he had now perused, on the parts of *Henry VI.*

To the inquiry of his friend as to the first theatrical performances in Dublin, his lordship says no satisfactory information could be given. Mr. Cooper Walker, well known in the literary circles of Dublin, had done all he could. The records were few and scanty; but the result, such as it was, is, for the information of the curious reader, transferred to a note.*

---

* He can find nothing in the Auditor-general's office relative to plays acted at the Castle. The most ancient theatre of Dublin appears to have been a booth erected in *Hoggin Green*, now College Green, where mysteries principally were acted, to which the Lords Lieutenant were frequently invited. A theatre in Werburgh Street succeeded to this, which was open till 1641, and the last play there exhibited was *Landegartha*, a tragi-comedy, by Henry Burnell, an Irish gentleman. Respecting the

Another Dublin correspondent, whose name does not appear to his communication, sketches his lordship and a scene at the Royal Irish Academy, then recently instituted by his means, showing his harmless nationality, though not at the expense of amiability or good temper.

Our Academy will venture abroad this winter. The different essays were all determined upon before I had the honour of being admitted a member, and I have not yet learned either their numbers or the subjects. But I am not without some panic about them. This being the first publication (of the *Transactions*), a preface became necessary, the writing of which was consigned to the youngest man in the society. That was a good leading step! Such a rant on the heroism, genius, learning, and arts of Ireland as would have given the *coup de grace* to our reputation. We had a warm battle—a division at last, in which Bishop Percy, Mr. Kirwan, and I were left to ourselves by a vast majority. However, they cooled a little, and, at the next meeting, Mr. Kirwan prevailed to have two-thirds of the preface expunged. . . . . There has arisen in Ireland, within a few years, such a spirit of extravagant, fulsome self-adulation, that it exceeds everything human vanity has heretofore made pretensions to. There cannot be a stronger bar to improvement, and every sincere rational friend to the public should discourage it.

Our amiable friend, the president (Lord Charlemont), is more wild and boisterous on the subject of Ireland than you can conceive. Many a warm dispute we have. I told him,

---

rejoicings mentioned by Ware:—In a MS. in the library of Trinity College is the following passage—"In the Parliament of 1541, wherein Henry VIII. was declared King of Ireland, there were present the Earls of Ormond and Desmond, the Lord Barry, MacGilla Phadrig, chieftain of Ossory, the sons of O'Bryan, MacCarthy More, with many Irish lords. And on Corpus Christi day they rode about the streets with the procession in their Parliament robes, and the *Nine Worthies* was played, and the mayor bore the mace before the deputy on horseback."

not long ago, that my motto was " *Nil admirari*," and that I was determined to combat all their cloud-capped notions about their country, shake every idea that tends to set one race above another, 'or promote national distinctions. His lordship said I should have enough to do, but we have agreed much better ever since.

A morning visit from the fastidious genius of Strawberry Hill elicited some of his usual free and forcible remarks upon the public characters of a previous day.

" *December* 29*th*, 1787.—Mr. Horace Walpole, while he sat with me this morning, mentioned a singular anecdote relative to the late Mr. West, whose rage for *collecting* varieties was such, that what he could not otherwise procure he *stole*. He was one of the executors to Lord Oxford (Harley), and is thought, on very good grounds, to have secreted a great many curious letters and papers belonging to that statesman.

" It is well known that all the proceedings against Lord Oxford by the House of Commons were very suddenly stopped. This was effected by Harley's writing a letter to the Duke of Marlborough, reminding him that he (Harley) had in his hands authentic proofs of the Duke having been in *treaty with the Pretender* in order to seat him on the throne. The letter was carried by Lord Duplin to the Duke, whom Duplin found walking on the Pantiles at Tunbridge Wells almost in a state of dotage. When he received it, he burst into tears, and very soon afterwards the prosecution was stopped.* This

* See a further notice of this subject in he subsequent anecdotes.

letter, of which a rumour had got abroad, the
Duchess of Portland made a long search for among
her father's papers, but it was not to be found. Soon
after his death, Mr. West was brought into Parliament for the borough of St. Albans by the Duchess
of Marlborough, and it was generally supposed that
his giving up the original letter, in Lord Oxford's
handwriting, to her grace was the price of his seat.
And not being found among the Harley papers
appears to justify such an opinion.

" When Mr. West died, the Duchess of Portland,
desirous to recover such other papers of her father
as this gentleman had secreted, sent to the widow,
offering any reasonable price for them, if that were
an object : but she did not like to furnish proof of
her husband's criminal conduct, and refused. However, some years afterwards they were sold by Mr.
West's daughter to Lord Shelburne (now Marquis of
Lansdown) for a *thousand pounds*."

In pursuit of materials for Shakspeare, it will not
be supposed his native town was overlooked. The
date of the critic's first trip thither does not appear,
nor were visits thither at any time frequent. His
inquiries were chiefly epistolary, addressed to the
vicar, the Rev. Mr. (afterwards Dr.) Davenport,
whose patience and politeness in reply appear to
have been exemplary. Nineteen long letters were
written to him on this fertile and favourite theme,
from the commencement of the correspondence
in April 1788, to the publication of the edition
in 1790; twelve in 1793; and several others
at intervals, making together, thirty-six. To the

vicar as to the critic, it must have been a labour of love.   He replied to innumerable questions requiring laborious and tedious investigations in a spirit of zeal and good humour, which to the end won the gratitude and friendship of his correspondent.*

The latter, at the end of a long letter, and in re-membrance of the scene where the mulberry-tree stood, warms to the theme, drops the cold pen of criticism, and seizes upon the lyre to propitiate the owner :—

In giving an account of Mr. Hunt's garden, I could not help breaking out into a poetical rhapsody, which may per-haps render him more propitious to my inquiries. I fear these lines are entitled to the reverse of Ovid's description, *Materiam superabat opus*. However, such as they are, let them make some small amends for this very tedious letter. I wish them not to *wander out* before my "books" which will not be ready for some months.†

> "In this retreat our Shakspeare's godlike mind
> With matchless skill surveyed all human kind.
> Here let each sweet that blest Arabia knows,
> ' *Flowers of all hues, and without thorn the rose,*'
> To latest times their balmy odours fling,
> And Nature here display eternal spring."

These lines, with an account of New Place, then the residence of Mr. Charles Hunt, appeared in print. But the destroyer of the Mulberry Tree, and indeed of Shakspeare's house, is well-known to have been the Reverend Mr. Gastrell.   It is difficult to account for such an act of human perversity; but the re-searches of Malone appear to make it an act of divided delinquency.   To Mr. Davenport he writes

* For the communication of these I am indebted to their owner, Mr. Hunt, of Stratford.

† This was written in April, 1788, and the edition did not appear till November, 1790. But what chance have literary resolutions against the innumerable obstructions which continually occur to mar them?

in May 1788, what it would have been inconvenient to put forth in print.

"A friend of mine read me yesterday part of a letter of a lady from Lichfield who is in great wrath at Mrs. Gastrell, whom she describes as little better than a fiend. Having had some disagreement with a lady to whom she had let a place, called I think Stow Hill in the neighbourhood of Lichfield, she has turned her out, and resolved that the poor, to whom this lady was very charitable, shall not derive any benefit from *any* inhabitant of that house; for that it never shall be let again, but remain empty. The rent was, it seems, one hundred guineas a year. The writer of this letter speaks of it as a known thing—that it was this lady and not her husband who cut down the celebrated Mulberry Tree. Perhaps she was only an accomplice. If this Lichfield story is not exaggerated, this lady and her husband seem to have been well-matched."

Correspondence with Mr. Davenport drew attention from one of his humbler neighbours, Mr. John Jordan, a carpenter and wheelwright, commonly known there as the "Poet." What his productions were I have not seen.* But his tastes rose above his occupations. He amused himself with the study of ancient memorials, inscriptions, ballads, family anecdotes, and such similar lore as may flash across the path, or enliven the hours of a rural genius. But more especially was he devoted to such points as were

---

* Mr. Halliwell obligingly informs me that he published a poem, *Welcombe Hills*, in 4to, about 1770, anonymously. He is not aware of anything else of his in print.

available regarding his illustrious townsman. Malone's inquiries further stimulated his exertions; and having wants to supply as well as information to communicate, he early in 1790 forwarded a packet of papers on that subject to the Critic in London.

One of the letters of Jordan—April 1790, in Mr. Rooper's collection, with its truth vouched by the Vicar of Stratford—offers his services in any mode of research likely to be useful, but prefaces it by a history of his life. Like so many unlucky followers of the Muse, it had been but a series of evils. He had experienced neglect, disappointment, misfortune, poverty, sickness, starving and scarcely-clothed children; reduced from master-tradesman to journeyman at nine shillings a week by an "ungrateful brother, who basely usurped the business during a long illness arising from quotidian ague." He is refused by a rich sister-in-law even a shilling a week for the schooling of his children; "is overwhelmed by misfortune, misery, and wretchedness." Even the Rev. Mark Noble, a near relative of his wife, and author of *Memoirs of the Cromwell Family*, had promised aid and some small place under government, but both expectations remained unfulfilled. "Alas!" he cries, "I am unnoticed by the world, oppressed with affliction, and wrecked with despair; the anchor of hope has totally forsook me; I am dashed by the waves of a boundless sea of trouble, sorrow, and misery, which brings to my mind an expression of Shakspeare, that

> " Misery trodden on by many,
> Being low is not relieved by any."

This melancholy detail had due effect upon the heart and purse of the Critic.

The latter appeared rather surprised at the variety of small facts noted by his correspondent; and in return, always alive to the chance of imposition upon an inquisitive antiquary, questions him minutely on the origin of each. More than fifty queries as to date, name, and source whence obtained, occupy three or four of the first letters. Several hundreds succeeded during the first year. "Good Mr. Jordan," as he was styled, had ample employment in fulfilling the requests of his precise and inquisitive friend, which did not cease till the edition of *Shakspeare* had appeared. In return, the hints of pecuniary distress and a "family," already quoted, were not forgotten. Malone gave him good Christian advice, and added a more substantial soother of uneasiness in a note for forty pounds raised among his friends in London. Nor did his kindness cease there. Occasional correspondence continued; and a small post in the Excise was procured him, but being over age he proved to be ineligible for the place.*

---

* Our critic, and other prosaic people, had been zealously at work in attempting to discover *earthly* facts of the Poet's life. But inquirers of another order aimed to ascertain how the *heavens* were affected at the moment of his birth. Such a genius could scarcely arise, thought astrological pundits, without the stars having some hand in it, as the reader may be amused to hear:—

"By the amazing intellectual faculties," says Mr. John Bolton to the Shakspeare Club at Stratford in 1829, " and surprising, as well as unexampled depth of genius of the immortal Bard, as well as his poetic powers, retentive memory and other mental gifts, which have, like the refulgent Sun, shone far and near, and victoriously surmounted the mightiest efforts of all other dramatic writers. These most astonishing powers are well denoted by the Moon, Mercury, and Mars being in cardinal signs; by the opposition of the Moon and Mercury; the trine of the Moon and Venus; the

Of some of his favourite associates at this time, and of the promised *Shakspeare*, we have glimpses in the letters of his friends. Boswell writes to Bishop Percy, February 1788:—"I dined at Mr. Malone's on Wednesday, with Mr. W. G. Hamilton, Mr. Flood, Mr. Wyndham, Mr. Courtenay, &c. . . . . Malone flatters himself that his *Shakspeare* will be published in June. I should rather think we shall not have it till winter. Come when it may, it will be a very admirable book."

An amusing letter from John Kemble, then in Dublin, incites the Critic to play off a trick not wholly new upon his friend Jephson, then said to be on his way to London with a poetical production in hand. This was to commit to memory the passage sent in the letter, repeat it when Jephson presented the poem, and then gravely accuse him of having stolen it from a previous writer! Theatricals appear at that moment not to have been in the ascendant in the Irish metropolis.

Dublin, No. 7, Essex Bridge, July 19th, 1788.

DEAR SIR,—I am mad till I give you an occasion of surprising Jephson, when he sends you his poem, which will be, no doubt, very soon after he has shown you himself. Here is the character which he gives of Virgil, and which you may pretend to have seen before:—

---

position of Venus and Luna in scientific signs; but more especially the approaching great conjunction of Saturn and Jupiter, the two superiors in the regal sign Leo in trine also to Mercury. The square of Mercury and Mars was undoubtedly the cause of his early misfortunes, his being obliged to leave his native home, and subsequently was the cause of his pecuniary troubles; and yet, but for this restlessness, I expect the dramatic world would have probably been without the matchless writings of this illustrious Poet."

L

> " Hush'd be each ruder breath and clam'rous tongue,
> Apollo listens to the Mantuan's song.
> Yon chief who feels bright Inspiration's flame,
> With mighty Homer's palm divide his claim;
> Fav'rite with me of all the tuneful choir,
> A boy, I felt him, and a man, admire.
> When grief or pain my anxious mind engage,
> Secure of case, I search great Maro's page;
> For deep and rankling sure must be the pain
> That finds no balm in his mellifluous strain:
> As Jesse's son Saul's phrenzy could compose,
> The madness sinking as the musick rose;
> The oil, diffused by philosophic skill,
> At once the agitated waves can still;
> This gentle magick o'er my senses glides,
> The charm prevails and all my rage subsides.
> From Tityrus, stretch'd the beechen shade beneath,
> To Turnus, shrinking from the uplifted death—
> Some careful Muse presides o'er every line,
> And all is sense and harmony divine."

I have committed no robbery, I assure you, for the Poet gave me free leave to take as much of his work as I could carry off with me. Never was town so empty as Dublin is now, since Mark Anthony was left alone in the market-place with the air which was uncivilly tempted also to forsake him.

The Count of Narbonne, however, brought all the country round into the play-house, and will be acted to another crowded theatre, I dare say, again on Saturday. The ragamuffishness of the players, and the filthy meanness of everything behind the scenes (I don't know how I can say scenes, when there are none) of the *New Theatre Royal* surprises even me, who lived two years at Smock Alley, in what I thought very reasonably good idleness, drunkenness, and dirt.

The city itself is, in every particular which my observation can reach, incredibly improved. The lights are as regularly sustained by night as they are in London. They affect to be oppressed in various shapes by the institution of the police, but I know they keep the streets ten thousand times more orderly and quiet than the old watchmen ever did. They do permit some frail beauties to walk their charms along the wood pavement of Dame Street, but then they are very still in their solicitations, *leves sub nocte susurri* are the loudest violences they offer to the solemnity of silence and dignity of municipal institutions.

Peg Plunket is, dying. Do you know that H—— has a pension on this establishment? Poor Mr. O'Neill is very ill. Mr. Greville hardly hoped for. Mr. Sheridan* has one foot in his grave. By Mrs. Lefanu's account, he is no more than sixty-six. He sailed yesterday with Miss Sheridan and Mrs. Crewe for England, to consult in London upon his case (dropsy and jaundice they say) with Dr. Turton. Between you and me, Mrs. Lefanu told me she firmly believed that, finding himself too old and weak to undertake the direction of the county schools, which do not exist anywhere but in his own brain, this disappointment of his whole life's hopes had contributed more than disease to destroy his nerves and debilitate his faculties.

Have you seen Mr. Hitchcock's *History of the Irish Stage?* It is the first volume of a work commencing at the earliest and proceeding to the latest date of theatres in this kingdom. It is full of wretched blunders in facts, and stuffed with whole pages of follies in opinions.

I fancy Jephson is the only one of my acquaintance you have in London now. Pray give him my best compliments, and believe me, dear sir, most sincerely your servant and friend, J. P. KEMBLE.

Two letters from Lord Charlemont form his contributions for the year; one mentions the transmission of a translation from the Italian. His name is not to be affixed, and it is to be "corrected without mercy." His idea of rendering one language into another is perfectly just, were it always practicable.

" Not content with giving the sense of an author, I would always wish, if possible, to communicate his manner. This is, in my opinion, best done by, as far

---

* Mr. Thomas Sheridan, father of Richard Brinsley.

as the difference of idiom will permit, copying his phrase; a mode of translating hostile to elegance but friendly to fidelity. I would at all times rather choose to be faithful than elegant. Above all things, the characteristics of the original should be preserved, which in the case before us has a certain simplicity or *naïveté*, and this I have endeavoured to copy, though in so doing I may very probably have rendered my language so faulty as to require much correction."

The second adverts to the paucity of corrections in the piece so transmitted, which he attributes to Malone's delicacy. He asks, as usual, for further supplies of books:—Dante, in large paper; some of the *Delphine Classics; Gatt's Travels; Ford's Plays*, "to which I am very partial;" and some others. He glances also at the trial of the then great Indian delinquent—"As a man, and for the sake of human nature, I am happy that Hastings has been so ably attacked. As a friend, I am delighted at Burke's success. When next you see him, tell him so from me. It is, I think, impossible that even partiality can screen the tyrant of the East from punishment; and the disgrace will be greater in proportion to that partiality."

All writers who have spoken of Dr. Warburton's career have usually dwelt upon his good fortune in meeting with Pope. But by the following account, the latter would appear to have been the greater gainer of the two by the intimacy. The Poet made the Divine a Bishop, and the Divine made the Poet a Christian.

"*January* 18*th*, 1789.—Dr. Joseph Warton, talking last night at Sir Joshua Reynolds's of Pope's *Essay on Man*, said that much of his system was borrowed from King's book on the *Origin of Evil*. This was first published in Dublin, in Latin, in 1704, and translated into English by Bishop Law, in 1731, not very long before the *Essay on Man* was written. Dr. Warton mentioned that Lord Lyttleton told him that he lived much with Pope at that time, and that Pope was then undoubtedly a Free-thinker; though he afterwards either changed his opinion, or thought it prudent to adopt Warburton's explanation and comment, who saw his meaning as he chose to express it, ' better than he did himself.' Dr. Warton forbore to state this in his *Essay on Pope*."

The subject of the following conversation has been so much the theme of animadversion in talk, in writing, in verse, and in prose, that notwithstanding her talents, there is too much reason to believe she opened the way for a large share of that scandal which fastened upon her fame in life and has clung to her in the grave. Unlucky, indeed, must that person be against whom Pope and Walpole united in the bitterest censure! Some further particulars will be found in the note subjoined to this statement, made to the hero of our story.

"*March* 8, 1789.—Mr. Horace Walpole remembers Lady M. W. Montague perfectly well, having passed a year with her at Florence. He told me this morning that she was not handsome, had a wild, staring eye, was much marked with the small-pox, which she endeavoured to conceal, by filling up the depressions with white paint. She was a great mischief-maker, and had not the smallest regard for truth. Her first gallant after her marriage was Lord Stair, our ambassador at Paris.

"Worsdale, the painter, told Mr. Walpole that the first cause of quarrel between her and Pope was her borrowing a pair of sheets from the poet, which, after keeping them a fortnight, were returned to him unwashed. She had a house at Twickenham, near Pope's.

"The line of that poet—

'Who starves a sister or forswears a debt?'

alludes to two of her most disreputable actions. Her sister was Lady Mar, who resided some time at Paris. After her coming to England she went mad, and Lady M. W. Montague had the custody of her person. She put her under the care of one who was used to that employment, but allowed so scantily for her maintenance (though the Court of Chancery had furnished her with means for the support of the lunatic), and paid so little attention to her, that her keeper, to save trouble, used to put the three meals intended for her into *one*, and then lock her up, that she might be free herself for the rest of the day. When Lady Mar's daughter, Lady Mary Erskine, came of age, she applied to the Court of Chancery, got her mother out of Lady M. W. Montague's custody, took her into her own house, and carefully attended to her till her death.

"The latter part of the line—'who forswears a

debt'—alludes to another unprincipled transaction. Soon after Lady Mary W. Montague's return from Constantinople, she fell in love with a French gentleman who was very fond of her, and to whom she gave her person while she remained in Paris. He followed her into England with about two thousand pounds in his pocket, which soon after his arrival, she persuaded him to put into her hands to dispose of in the English funds to the best advantage, lest from ignorance of our customs he might be imposed upon. Soon afterwards she assured him her husband had discovered their intrigue, and that he could not stay longer in England without danger to his life. The poor Frenchman in vain begged to have his money; but she said that withdrawing it from the funds would take up too much time; and that he must fly instantly. He fled accordingly, and solicited in vain afterwards to have the money remitted. Lady M. W. Montague had the impudence to disown the whole transaction; and even to write to her sister, Lady Mar, to incite her husband, or Lord Stair (Lady Mary's old lover) to punish the Frenchman for defamation.

" On her death-bed she gave seventeen large volumes in MS. of her letters, memoirs, and poems, to the clergyman who attended her, with an injunction to publish them; but Lady Bute, her daughter, being very desirous to prevent this, prevailed on her husband, who was then Prime Minister, to give the clergyman a good Crown living. For this bribe he broke his trust, and surrendered the letters, which will probably never see the light.

" Of twelve of her letters, however, addressed to Lady Mar at Paris, there are copies in the hands of Colonel Erskine, Lady Mar's grandson, which will probably some time or other get into print. He has also a copy of a very curious letter of Lady M. W. Montague's, giving an account of a private society that used to meet about the year 1730 at Lord Hillsborough's in Hanover Square, where each gentleman came masked, and brought with him one lady—either his mistress, or any other man's wife, or perhaps a woman of the town—who was also masked. They were on oath not to divulge names, and continued masked the whole time. There were tables set out for supper, artificial arbours, couches, &c., to which parties retired when they pleased and called for what refreshment they chose. This letter is not one of the twelve above-mentioned. This institution probably lasted but a short time. The late Captain O'Brien told me that his father, Sir Edward, was one of the members.

" *Aviennus and his wife*, in Pope's verses, were Wortley Montague and Lady Mary. *Wordly* was also Mr. Wortley.

" Lady W. Montague had two children by the Frenchman alluded to, and this amour was the cause of being separated from her husband.

" (From the information of Colonel Erskine.)" *

---

* Whether these statements, even from a relative, be true, will now be difficult to decide. Walpole, however familiar with her history, was certainly very hostile to her in feeling; yet he could scarcely descend to invent and string together such a tissue of offences, however he may have given a ready ear to rumour or exaggeration. Much in her history is no doubt difficult to explain. She often lived in equivocal society, and

Occasional excursions to the country varied the
enjoyments of town and of the club.   One of these

her reputation must pay the penalty; for her friends, by destroying her
papers, have left complete vindication impossible.

For the story of the children, mentioned on the authority of the colonel,
no sufficient foundation appears.   No record marks separation from her
husband, so as to admit the birth of two children from the time of their
return from Constantinople till her departure from England on a twenty
years' exile.   She was then forty-nine years old.   Time, therefore, would
seem to acquit her at least of child-bearing.

It is certain from admissions in her own letters that a Frenchman,
who professed the strongest attachment, and who we must suppose was
a previous acquaintance, wrote from France, requesting permission to
join her in England.   This after some time was conceded.   He was not,
however, to come empty-handed.   With his money, or a joint sum, purchases were made in the funds; but disagreement arising, she wished
him to quit England leaving his investment behind.   He would not go.
She sought the return of her letters from him, which were refused; he
even made communications to her husband, which she had ingenuity
enough to intercept; and then, it is said, threatened him with personal
violence, if not assassination.   In return he threatened the publication of
her letters.   This produced agonies of terror, as evinced in communications to her sister, such as are not known in any of her writings.   Exposure, no doubt, would have been ruin, but her good genius prevailed in
staying its execution.

Lady Mary, it appears, kept a journal from her earliest years to their
close.   Her sister, afterward Countess of Mar, destroyed it on her elope-
ment with her husband, Mr. Wortley.   After marriage, the practice was
resumed and continued.   At her death—whether procured, as stated,
from the clergyman in attendance does not appear—it fell into the hands
of Lady Bute, who ever after kept it under lock and key.   Occasionally
she would read passages to her family and friends, but would not trust
any portion of it out of her own hands, except a few of the early copy-
books, which she allowed one of the family, Lady Louisa Stuart, to read
alone, on condition that nothing should be transcribed.   Shortly before
her death, Lady Bute burned the entire journal, to the great grief of the
junior portion of the family.

What disclosures or explanations were made in those papers, none can
now tell.   Unquestionably they must have been curious in a high degree
in literature, morals, wit, anecdote, and sketches of personal character,
from one who saw so much and described so freely in her journey
through life.

Lord Wharncliffe, in his edition of her works, puts the best construction on unexplained points.   This is natural and charitable.   We
readily go with him where we can, though not at the expense of truth.
We would all desire to see genius as pure in conduct as noble in attri-

was to his distinguished countryman in Buckingham-
shire, of which we have a few details.

"*July* 28, 1789.—Went to Gregoriess, near Beaconsfield, the seat of Mr. Burke, with Sir Joshua
Reynolds, Mr. Wyndham, and Mr. Courtenay, and
passed three days there very agreeably.

"As I walked out before breakfast with Mr. B.,
I proposed to him to revise and enlarge his admirable
book on the *Sublime and Beautiful*, which the
experience, reading, and observation of thirty years
could not but enable him to improve considerably.
But he said the train of his thoughts had gone
another way, and the whole bent of his mind turned
from such subjects; that he was much fitter for such
speculations at the time he published that book (about
1758*) than now. Besides, he added, the subject was
then new, but several writers have since gone over the
same ground, Lord Kames and others. The subject
he said had been long rolling in his thoughts before
he wrote his book, he having been used from the time
he was in college to speculate on the topics which
form the subjects of it. He was six or seven years
employed on it, and produced it when he was about
28 or 29 years old—a prodigious work for such a
period of life.

"On Thursday, 30th, we went in the morning to

butes—willing to exalt our common nature, untainted by those vices that
drag them down to the level of the unprincipled and vulgar. Should the
reader wish further details, he may turn to the *Quarterly Review*,
No. 115, in the notice of Lord Wharncliffe's volumes—written no doubt
by the late Right Hon. J. W. Croker.

* It should be 1757. The anecdote had been communicated to me
in substance many years ago.

Amersham, to see Mr. Drake's very noble seat. He has some of the tallest trees in England; two particularly fine, a beech and an ash, that are as straight as the mast of a ship, and the former several years ago was 112 feet high to the top of the branches. It is now much higher of course.

"Mr. Drake has a few good pictures, particularly four very fine by Vernet, as Sir Joshua Reynolds said. They were done in the early part of his life, as he observed, with great care, and in his opinion were worth 500l. apiece. Vernet is still alive and very old. All his later works, in consequence of the great business he has had and his great age, were done very carelessly; yet for these latter he has received a great price; for the former a very moderate one.

"There was a portrait here of Lord Chancellor Hatton, said in the Catalogue to be done by Jameson, the Scotch Vandyke; but this must be a mistake, for Jameson was born in 1586, and Hatton died in 1591. Possibly however it might be a copy by Jameson.

"There was also a portrait of Queen Elizabeth, said to be done by Hilliard, which by no means qualified the high praises given him by his contemporaries. Like most of the other portraits of the queen, this has not the least shade to the face, and her hair is quite red.

"We dined this day at Hall-barn, as it is now called, though Dr. Johnson, in his life of Waller, calls it Hill-barn, and I took another look at Waller's portraits. I did not before observe, that on that by

Cornelius Jansen is written ' Ann. ætat. 23 *vitæ vix primo.*' Sir J. Reynolds said it was done with great care, and probably was an exact resemblance; but that it had the fault which all Jansen's pictures have—the flesh has too much the appearance of ivory. He thought the portrait of Waller, in his old age, was done by Kneller in his first and best manner. When Kneller came first from Italy (he said) he painted much more carefully than afterwards, and was less of a mannerist. In his latter works he gave every woman pouting cherry lips, as Lely gave all his ladies a sleepy eye.

"Sir J. Reynolds found out another portrait of Waller here, which he supposed to be done by Lely in his first manner, when he imitated Vandyke so closely that some of his pictures have been mistaken for those of that master. Afterwards, he too became a mannerist. Lely was born in 1617, and came into England in 1641. He at first painted landskips (*sic*) as well as portraits, and he gave some designs for ornamental engravings prefixed to books. One of his designs of this kind may be found in Lovelace's Poems. He died in 1680, at sixty-three. Kneller was born about the year 1648, went to Italy in 1672, remained there for some time, and came to England in 1674. He died October 27, 1723, aged 75."

CHAPTER VIII.

1789—1791.

Revision of Boswell's *Johnson*—Baretti—Visit to Waller's former mansion—John Kemble—Publication of Shakspeare—Burke—Reynolds—Mrs. Piozzi—Relique of Elizabethan Poetry—Visit to Burke—Abbé Raynal—Burke, in allusion to Hastings' trial.

AMID much good society, to which there are several contemporary allusions, added to a long visit to his brother and sisters in Hertfordshire, he was pushing on *Shakspeare.* He had destined the work for an earlier birth; but time will leave the most diligent labourer behind.

Even friendship conspired to increase the delay. Boswell was equally busy upon the life of Johnson; and having the strongest faith in the judgment of Malone, claimed his assistance not only in contributions to notes and text, but in revision of the whole work. This rather serious tax upon attention was met in his usual spirit of active good-will. His notes to that work form ample evidence of the interest in it which he felt; and there were introduced numberless suggestions which do not publicly appear. But the private acknowledgments of the biographer display pretty strongly the extent of his obligations.

On the 10th of January 1789, he writes to his chosen friend the Rev. Mr. Temple: *

* See the letters recently published.

Whenever I have completed the rough draft, by which I mean the work without nice correction, Malone and I are to prepare one-half perfectly, and then it goes to press, where I hope to have it early in February so as to be out by the end of May.* I do not believe that Malone's *Shakspeare* will be much before me. His brother, Lord Sunderlin, with his lady and two sisters, came home from a long tour on the Continent in summer last, and took a country-house about twenty miles from town for six months. Malone lived with them; so his labour was much intermitted.

July 3, 1789.

I may perhaps come to you in autumn if Malone goes to Ireland, so that the revising of *Johnson's Life* cannot proceed till winter.

October 13-14, 1789.

Malone, who obligingly revises my *Life of Johnson*, is to go to Ireland when his *Shakspeare* is published, which will be about Christmas. I am therefore to get as much of his time as may be while he remains, as he may not return from Ireland till the summer. Yesterday afternoon, Malone and I revised and made ready for the press thirty pages of *Johnson's Life*. He is much pleased with it; but I feel a sad indifference, and he says I have not the use of my faculties.

How often is it that gloomy anticipations of failure come over authors during the progress of the most successful works! Often, on the other hand, what lively expectations of success where utter disappointment awaits the writer!

November 28, 1789.

My apology for not coming to you as I fully intended and wished, is really a sufficient one; for the revision of my *Life of Johnson*, by so acute and knowing a critic as Mr. Malone, is of most essential consequence, especially as he is *Johnsonianissimus;* and as he is to hasten to Ireland as soon as his *Shakspeare* is fairly published, I must avail myself of him *now.* His hospitality and my other invitations, and particu-

---

* It did not appear for two years afterwards.

larly my attendance at Lord Lonsdale, have lost us many evenings. . . . . The week before last I indulged myself by giving one dinner. I had Wilkes, Sir Joshua Reynolds, Flood, the Irish orator, Malone, Courtenay, Governor Penn, grandson of old William, who brought over the petition from Congress which was so obstinately and unwisely rejected; and my brother David. We had a very good day. Would I were able to give many such dinners! Malone gives them without number. Last Sunday I dined with him, with Sir Joshua Reynolds, Sir Joseph Banks, Mr. Metcalf, Mr. Windham, Mr. Courtenay, and some of Johnson's friends, to settle as to effectual measures for having a monument erected to him in Westminster Abbey.

A few other acknowledgments appear early in the following year.

February 8, 1790.

It is better that I am still here; for I am within a short walk of Mr. Malone, who revises my *Life of Johnson*. . . . . 13*th.*—I drink with Lord Lonsdale one day, the next I am quiet in Malone's elegant study, revising my *Life of Johnson,* of which I have high expectations, both as to fame and profit. . . . .

July 21, 1790.

Though my mind felt very sick, I soon felt relief in London. I dined that day quietly with Malone. On Sunday I was at St. George's Church, Hanover Square, and dined again with Malone.

An evening's walk home after dinner with an intelligent companion furnished the subject of this work with the following anecdotes of Dr. Johnson :—

" Baretti, with whom I dined at Mr. Courtenay's (Sunday, April 5, 1789,) mentioned two extraordinary instances of Dr. Johnson's wonderful memory. Baretti had once proposed to teach him Italian. They went over a few stanzas of Ariosto's *Orlando*

Inamorato, and Johnson then grew weary. Some years afterwards, Baretti reminded him of his promise to study Italian, and said he would give him another lesson; but added, I suppose you have forgot what we read before. 'Who forgets, sir?' said Johnson, and immediately repeated three or four stanzas of the poem. Baretti was astonished, and took an opportunity before he went away of privately taking down the book to see if it had been recently opened; but the leaves were entirely covered with dust.

"The other instance was as remarkable. Dr. James had picked up on a stall a book of Greek hymns. The author's name I forget. He brought it to Johnson as a curiosity, who ran his eyes over the pages and returned it. A year or two afterwards, he dined at Sir Joshua Reynolds's, where also Dr. Musgrave, the editor of *Euripides*, happened to be. Musgrave made a great parade of his Greek learning, and among other less known writers, mentioned the hymns of ——, which he thought none of the company were acquainted with, and extolled them highly. Johnson said the first of them was indeed very fine, and immediately repeated it. It consisted of ten or twelve lines.

"When Johnson had finished his *Rasselas*, Baretti happened to call on him. He said he had just finished a romance—that he had no money, and pressingly required some to take to his mother who was ill at Lichfield. He therefore requested Baretti to go to Dodsley the bookseller, and say he wished to see him. When he came, Johnson asked what he would give for his romance. The only question was what number of sheets it would make. On examining it, he said he would give him 100*l.* Johnson was perfectly contented, but insisted on part of the money being paid immediately, and accordingly received 70*l.* Any other person with the degree of reputation he then possessed would have got 400*l.* for that work, but he never understood the art of making the most of his productions.

" Baretti made a translation of *Rasselas* into French, which is I believe in print. He never, however, could satisfy himself with the translation of the first sentence, which is uncommonly lofty. Mentioning this to Johnson, the latter said after thinking two or three minutes, ' Well, take up the pen, and if you can understand my pronunciation, I will see what I can do.' He then dictated the sentence to the translator, which proved admirable, and was immediately adopted.

" Baretti used sometimes to walk with him through the streets at night, and occasionally entered into conversation with the unfortunate women who frequent them, for the sake of hearing their stories. It was from a history of one of these, which a girl told under a tree in the King's Bench Walk in the Temple to Baretti and Johnson, that he formed the story of Misella in the *Rambler*."

The introduction by Burke to the occupier of Hillbarn, procured an invitation for Malone to revisit it, and run over again more at leisure those objects, chiefly portraits and books, which had been the property of the poet.

" *Saturday, July 3rd*, 1789.—I went to Hill-barn near Beaconsfield, the seat of Waller the poet, and

M

spent two days with Mr. Blair, its temporary possessor.   The house was built by Waller himself, but
there have been considerable additions.   Mr. Waller,
the present owner, is a young man, the sixth I believe
from the poet; and being straitened in circumstances,
the estate being now not more than about 1,500*l.* per
annum and much encumbered, has let this house
and domain for three years to enable him to pay
debts of his father's to some amount, which, however,
he is not under any *legal* obligation to pay, but means
to discharge from a sense of honour.

   " There are here two original pictures of the poet,
one when he was twenty-three, painted I think by
Cornelius Jansen.   That in Lord Chesterfield's collection appears to have been a copy from this.   I
have never seen it, but the print made of it by Bell
(engraved by Cooke) has no resemblance to the picture at Hill-barn, though the dress shows that it was
done from some copy of that picture.   The other
was painted in his old age ; and I should have
supposed it the portrait from which Vertue engraved
his half sheet print, and also that for the quarto
edition of Waller's works, but that Vertue's band is
plain, and that in the picture just mentioned is laced.
In all other respects the print and picture correspond,
except that I think the character of the face is not so
nicely preserved in Vertue's print as it might be.

   " I may say the same of the print which has
been just now engraved by Sharpe from a portrait
of Henry, Lord Southampton, for my edition of
Shakspeare: in which though it is tolerably faithful,
the character of the face is not so nicely preserved

as I could have wished. If Sacharissa was not handsomer than the portrait which is shown for her at Hill-barn, she was not worth half the verses bestowed upon her.

"There is a very good library here, partly consisting of the poet's collection, which has been greatly increased by his successors. I found his name written in many of the books. As he is said to have formed his versification on Fairfax's *Tasso*, I was curious to examine it. But it contained not a single remark in the margin, nor even his name. It was the second edition of 1624, it was remarkably clean, and had no appearance of being much read.

"In the first leaf of the Duchess of Newcastle's *Philosophical and Physical Opinions*, folio 1663, he has written these lines which describe her book very truly :—

> "'New castles in the air this lady builds,
> While nonsense with philosophy she guilds.'

"In his *Chaucer*, folio, 1560 :—

> "'jam monte potitus
> Ridet anhelantem dura ad vestigia turbam.'*

"Sidney's *Arcadia* one should suppose would have been read by him at an early period of life; but he does not appear to have read it till he was near seventy; for in the title-page of his copy, which is in folio, printed by Ponsonby in 1613, he has written 'Ed. Waller, 10s. 1674.' In the title-page of his copy of Sir William Davenant's works, I found 'Edw. Waller, 01l. 00s., 1673,' which I mention only as it ascertains the price of the book.

* The lines were written by Camden, and are found in the old edition of Chaucer, printed in 1598.

" The first folio edition of *Shakspeare* was probably sold for the same price. This was not in the library, nor any ancient edition but that of 1685, which was bound in three volumes. His name was not in it. Waller died in 1687. Is it possible that he did not possess a copy of Shakspeare's Plays till two years before his death? His *Ovid* by Sandys contained nothing; but in Sandys' version of the Psalms he has written *Ex dono Authoris.*

" I was surprised to find that a very thick volume of quarto tracts, which contained a great number of detached speeches made in Parliament in 1642 and 1643 and printed on single sheets, did not contain Waller's own speech in his defence when his plot was discovered."

An application made to Kemble for some theatrical information, and the acknowledgment of the actor for some literary attentions from the critic, produced a characteristic letter from the former while absent from London on one of his summer campaigns :—

Liverpool, July 7th, 1789.

MY DEAR SIR,—Your letter found me confined to bed by a pleurisy, and utterly incapable of moving. This is the eleventh day of my illness; but, thank God, I am on the mending hand, and hope to be on horseback to-morrow.

I wrote to Mr. Westley, the treasurer of Drury Lane Theatre, by this post, and shall mention your desire very particularly. I have inclosed a line to him here; he lives in Charlotte Street, Bedford Square just behind me; I don't know the number of it, but his name is on the door; and nine in the morning or four in the afternoon is the likeliest time to find him within.

I am very much obliged to you for having thought

of the manuscripts for me; and am sorry to think I should leave town without a valedictory gripe of your hand; but Mr. Sheridan had me in waiting from one at noon till almost one the next morning, and as I was obliged to be in my chaise by four, prevented my making my last compliments to all my other friends. We did a good deal of business at last, however, and I passed a very agreeable day. We should have had a very triumphant season but for my unfortunate illness which has prevented our acting our most attractive plays—*Macbeth, Othello, Hamlet,* &c. Huzza! Shakspeare for ever!

Pray give my compliments to Jephson; and believe me your obliged and faithful servant,

J. P. KEMBLE.

Lord Charlemont, as usual, pursues his friend for acquisitions in poetry, the drama, and criticism, with that zeal which is so pleasant to witness in one who, though but an amateur, gives his hours to the pursuit.

He writes for a title-page for Turberville's poems * in Malone's hand-writing from the want of one in print; for one of Shirley's plays, in which his set is deficient; for a volume of Green's works; and a second copy of the plays attributed to Shakspeare. "I wish to have them, as I do everything that bore that sacred name. . . . My MS. plays are all of them written in different hands, and from many interlineations and corrections, are likely to be the original copies. I believe Lady *Mob* has been mistaken for Lady *Moth.* The mistake however is not

---

* A note of Malone in Warton's *History of Poetry,* vol. iii. p. 383, alludes to some comic tales of this writer, from whom, it is supposed, Shakspeare took the fable of *Much Ado about Nothing.* He is also supposed to be (instead of Fairfax) the first translator of *Tasso:* p. 392, v. iii. of the same work. Ed. 1824.

mine, but that of some former proprietor, who has given in the first page an imperfect list of the plays."

In 1790 little appears of his correspondence, and nothing in the *Anecdote Journal.* *Shakspeare* occupied close attention; and eight years' gestation had brought it to the verge of birth. " When I first undertook to give an edition of his works," he says in a pamphlet written soon afterwards, " it did not appear to me so arduous a work as I found it." Very few but the experienced, calculate the time or the labour necessary to a book, of which research and conflicting opinions form the distinguishing features. It had been long expected by the host of Shakspearians who flutter in the press either as admirers of the poet, or rivals of every new editor. His friends occasionally gave hints of their expectations ; and we may readily believe that he was willing enough to take rest for a time from a labour, the ramifications of which on relative points had extended far beyond his original conceptions.

Toward the end of the year (November) appeared *The plays and Poems of William Shakspeare* in Ten Volumes. In fact there were eleven ; the first being divided into two parts for the introduction of preliminary matter necessary to the comprehensive view taken of all the bearings of the subject.

The preface occupied above seventy pages; followed by that of Dr. Johnson ; Steevens' Advertisement ; ancient translations from classic authors, chiefly by Steevens ; Pope's preface ; dedication and preface of Heminge and Condell ; Rowe's life of Shakspeare augmented by the Editor ; anecdotes of

Shakspeare from Oldys' MS.; Shakspeare's will; mortgage made by him in 1612-13; commendatory verses on Shakspeare by writers of more or less eminence; ancient editions of his plays and poems; detached criticisms upon him; entries upon the books of the Stationers' Company, chiefly by Steevens; essay by the editor on the chronology of the plays, with additions; a paper on Shakspeare, Ford, and Ben Jonson. In the second part of the first volume is a historical account of the English stage, occupying above three hundred pages, to which Burke and critics of every class have rendered high praise. It exhibits the most active and persevering research.

Little need be said here of a work so long before the public. Beyond doubt it formed the best and fullest edition which had appeared; and as the desire for improvement did not cease with publication, the additions made and the reproduction of the work in twenty-one volumes by the younger Boswell in 1822, ensured it a place on the book-shelves of all reading men.

The amount of research was at once apparent. Most known sources of information had been diligently explored. We cannot open a page without being impressed by the sifting and winnowing of authorities,—the variety, extent, minuteness of his reading,—which left little doubt on the mind of the reader, that if accuracy were attainable, he had exerted every means within reach to attain it. Not but that an ample field of doubt still remained, and will remain, open upon various points, in which a dramatic antiquary might disport himself at pleasure. Any argument may be maintained when nearly all the lighthouses and landmarks of facts have been swept away by time.

Released from the duties of the press, he sought relaxation in a long-promised visit to Ireland. Relatives and old acquaintance equally vied in dispensing the national hospitality to one who, viewed by some as an idle wanderer, had returned the possessor of no inconsiderable fame.

From England likewise followed warm approval of his labours by devoted Shakspearians. Among these were Warton, Farmer, Bishop Percy, and many others. While men of more general celebrity, like Burke, Windham, Reynolds, Sir William Scott, Courtenay, and a few more, gave testimony which might almost have made a reputation. With the public he was no less successful. In fifteen months a large edition was nearly sold. So unequivocal was the encouragement, that for those who objected to the rather unsatisfactory nature of the paper and type, he was induced to offer proposals for another edition in fifteen royal quarto volumes, of which we have an intimation in a pamphlet published soon afterward. But it was never executed.*

---

* He says: "A splendid edition of the plays and poems of our great dramatic poet, with the illustrations which the various editors and commentators have furnished, is yet a desideratum in English literature. I had, ten years ago, sketched out the plan of such an edition, and intend immediately to carry a similar volume into execution. It is almost unnecessary to add, that the same gratuitous zeal which induced me to undertake the former edition, will accompany this revisal of it, and that no diligence or care of mine shall be wanting to render this new edition of my work, which is to be ornamented with engravings, and to be printed in fifteen volumes royal quarto, worthy of our greatest English poet. The first two volumes are intended to be published next year."

The adoption of the particular paper and type were the results of ill advice ; for his great labours were gratuitous.   They taxed not only the eyes of others but his own, the object being to accommodate the masses, who sought the greatest quantity of matter within the most moderate compass. Taste was thus sacrificed to partial convenience. " His sight," said Boaden, " had never been very good ; and unfortunately to keep the works of Shakspeare within any reasonable limits, he had in the year 1790 done the greatest possible injury to his eyes by selecting types both for text and notes for his edition painful and distressing to the great majority of readers."

The letter of approval by Burke is too characteristic of the master not to find place here :

(No date.)

My dear Sir,—Upon coming to my new habitation in town, I found your valuable work upon my table. I take it as a very good earnest of the instruction and pleasure which may be yet reserved for my declining years. Though I have had many little arrangements to make both of a public and private nature, my occupations were not able to overrule my curiosity, nor to prevent me from going through almost the whole of your able, exact, and interesting history of the stage.

A history of the stage is no trivial thing to those who wish to study human nature in all shapes and positions. It is of all things the most instructive to see not only the reflection of manners and characters at several periods, but the modes of making their reflection, and the manner of adapting it at those periods to the taste and disposition of mankind. The stage indeed may be considered as the republic of active literature, and its history as the history of that state. The great events of political history when not combined with the same helps towards the study of the manners and characters of men, must be a study of an inferior nature.

You have taken infinite pains, and pursued your inquiries with great sagacity, not only in this respect, but in such of your notes as hitherto I have been able to peruse. You have earned your repose by public spirited labour. But I cannot help hoping that when you have given yourself the relaxation which you will find necessary to your health, if you are not called to exert your great talents, and employ your great acquisitions in the transitory service to your country which is done in active life, you will continue to do that permanent service which it receives from the labours of those who know how to make the silence of their closets more beneficial to the world than all the noise and bustle of courts, senates, and camps.

I beg leave to send you a pamphlet which I have lately published.* It is of an edition more correct I think, than any of the first; and rendered more clear in points where I thought, in looking over again what I had written, there was some obscurity. Pray do not think my not having done this more early was owing to neglect or oblivion, or from any want of the highest and most sincere respect to you; but the truth is (and I have no doubt you will believe me) that it was a point of delicacy which prevented me from doing myself that honour. I well knew that the publication of your *Shakspeare* was hourly expected; and I thought if I had sent that small donum, the fruit of a few weeks, I might have subjected myself to the suspicion of a little Diomedean policy, in drawing from you a return of the value of a hundred cows for my nine. But you have led the way, and have sent me gold, which I can only repay you in my brass. But pray admit it on your shelves; and you will show yourself generous in your acceptance as well as your gift. Pray present my best respects to Lord and Lady Sunderlin, and to Miss Malone. I am, with the most sincere affection and gratitude,

My dear Sir,

Your most faithful and obliged humble servant,

EDMUND BURKE.

* *Reflections on the Revolution in France.*

During the latter part of 1790 and beginning of the following year, Boswell wrote several letters to Malone on their respective topics—Shakspeare and Johnson.* He was full of his forthcoming book, of anxiety, hypochondriacism, and pecuniary difficulties. The critic formed a most friendly depository for his thoughts; and these letters give us curious revelations of his hopes, doubts, social meetings, and involvements at the time, though it is only necessary to notice here such as relate to our immediate subject. After a round of dinners and *sobriety*, as he describes—

And now for my friend. The appearance of Malone's *Shakspeare,* on the 29th November, was not attended with any external noise; but I suppose no publication seized more speedily and surely on the attention of those for whose critical taste it was chiefly intended. At the Club, on Tuesday, where I met Sir Joshua, Dr. Warren, Lord Ossory, Lord Palmerston, Windham, and Burke in the chair, Burke was so full of his anti-French Revolution rage, and poured it out so copiously, that we had almost nothing else. He, however, found time to praise the clearness and accuracy of your dramatic history; and Windham found fault with you for not taking the profits of so laborious a work. Sir Joshua is pleased, though he would gladly have seen more *disquisition* —you understand me! Mr. Daines Barrington is exceedingly gratified. He regrets that there should be a dryness between you and Steevens, as you have treated him with great respect. I understand that, in a short time, there will not be one of your books to be had for love or money.

Three days afterwards, he writes—

I dined last Saturday at Sir Joshua's, with Mr. Burke, his lady, son, and niece, Lord Palmerston, Windham, Dr. Law-

---

* These, or rather extracts, were communicated to Mr. Croker for his edition of *Boswell,* from Upcott's collection.

rence, Dr. Blagden, Dr. Burney, Sir Abraham Hume, Sir
William Scott.   I sat next to young Burke at dinner, who
said you had paid his father a fine compliment.   I mentioned
Johnson, to *sound* if there was any objection.*   He made
none.   In the evening, Burke told me he had read your
Henry VI. with all its accompaniments, and it was "exceedingly well done."   He left us for some time; I suppose on some
of his cursed politics; but he returned.   I at him again, and
heard from his lips what, believe me, I delighted to hear, and
took care to write down soon after:—"I have read his *History
of the Stage,* which is a very capital piece of criticism and
anti-agrarianism.   I shall now read all *Shakspeare* through, in
a very different manner from what I have yet done, when I
have got such a commentator."   Will not this do for you, my
friend?   Burke was admirable company all that day.   He
never once, I think, mentioned the French Revolution, and
was easy with me, as *in days of old.*

In January he is in great straits for money, but
tells Malone it is *no hint,* as he is aware he cannot
assist him.   Of another obligation, he says, "Your
absence is a woeful want in all respects.   You will, I
dare say, perceive a difference in the part which is
revised only by myself, and in which many *insertions*
will appear."

Toward the end of the month, he writes again in a
melancholy tone, and apologizes for it.   "But your
vigour of mind and warmth of heart make your
friendship of such consequence, that it is drawn upon
like a bank."   He adds the history of a purchase of
old family property, and is quite destitute of money to
pay for it—is at his wit's end—asks whether he would

* The meaning of this is not very clear.   What objection could Burke
have, excepting, perhaps, some coolness towards Boswell, who had talked
and exhibited some attachment to Hastings on his trial?

recommend him to accept of one thousand pounds which had been offered for *Johnson's Life?*—adding, " Your absence has been a severe stroke to me. I am at present quite at a loss what to do. . . . . As I pass your door I cast many a longing look. . . . . I shall be very anxious till I hear from you."

In February, two more letters dwell upon his embarrassments, his book, and the Club. Has purchased part of a lottery-ticket for Malone and his sisters—also one for himself, which fancy at one moment conjured into a prize. Asks his friend whether he will join with him in a bond for one thousand pounds, which he must pay in May; but it is added that a refusal will not in the least interfere with their friendship.

March furnishes two letters on similar subjects: the disposal of the book forms a sad puzzle. Did Robinson positively propose one thousand pounds for it, or only supposed that sum was its worth? Tells how his "inexplicable disorder" (depression of mind) had for a time taken a turn. Solicits his friend as to various particulars in the title-page of the forthcoming work—what should be said and what omitted?

Such are the labours, the doubts, the anxieties of an unhappy author! But Boswell lived to receive the honours which were his due, even if he did not share so fully as he had a right to expect in the reward which should belong to the author.

While in Ireland, the following reached Malone from Sir Joshua Reynolds. It appears to have been written under the influence of a very unnecessary fit of humility, as if an erroneous construction were liable to be put upon the civilities of a man of his character and eminence:—

London, *March 8th*, 1791.

MY DEAR SIR,—It requires some apology to expect you to distribute the enclosed books.* I believe the persons to whom they are directed are all your friends. I am sorry to hear Lord Charlemont has been unwell, which gives real concern to all that know him. I am afraid to express my particular esteem and affection, as it would have an air of impertinent familiarity and equality; and, for another reason, shall say nothing regarding yourself for fear of the suspicion of being a toad-eater—a character for which we gentlemen about town have great abhorrence, and are apt to run too much on the other side in order to avoid it. However, I will venture to say thus much, that you are every day found wanting, and wished for back. And by nobody more than your very sincere friend and humble servant,

J. REYNOLDS.

To-day is Shrove-Tuesday, and no Johnson. I beg my most respectful compliments to Lord Sunderlin.

The allusion to the great moralist may imply that they had been accustomed to meet on that day, or, perhaps, to the slow advancement of his monument. Differences of opinion on that subject had arisen among the committee—namely, Burke, Sir Joshua Banks, Windham, Metcalfe, Boswell, and Malone— duly communicated to the latter while in Dublin. The site, Westminster Abbey, was to be relinquished for St. Paul's, which, as he expressed it, was too modern—too cold and raw to lie in comfortably, but in a century or two hence, would look more habitable!

* Supposed to be copies of his *Lectures*.

Doubts also occurred as to the nature of the memorial among the general body of the Literary Club.
Some, our critic writes to a friend, were for a picture
in mosaic, some for a bust, some for a statue, some
for neither, but for emblematical figures. The objection to a full-length arose from the supposed uncouth
formation of Johnson's limbs. But Sir Joshua maintained that to be a mistake. He had paid attention
to the members in question ; and far from being
unsightly, he deemed them well formed.

Dublin, Baronston, his brother's seat in Meath,
Shinglass, his own property, and visits to the south of
Ireland to recall old friendships or lay the foundation
of new, formed his chief resorts. In the capital,
meetings of the Royal Irish Academy were duly
attended with Lord Charlemont. There, some new
acquaintances were also found—men learned but
unobtrusive, who as retiring as their studies, often
require to be dug out of their recesses in a capital, on
certain public occasions, rather than found in ordinary scenes of resort. One of these was Mr. Andrew
Caldwell, and a few others whose names are defaced
or torn away from their letters.

Malone, it appears, had caught the general distaste
of the Johnsonian circle towards Mrs. Piozzi for
throwing off her celebrated inmate after the death of
Mr. Thrale. The marriage with her music-master,
and something like literary rivalry afterwards with
Boswell, added to the main offence. Occasionally we,
even still hear of the circumstances in a tone of reproach. Yet it is difficult to conceive how she could
have done otherwise to one who, with no other tie

than that of friend, had become not only in familiar phrase, but almost in fact, while resident in her house, her " master."

Excellent in every solid quality of man, Johnson was not a guest for every house. He had not, and probably could not be, schooled into system. Conformity to usual domestic arrangements is a condition exacted by most ladies from those who aim to be agreeable inmates. With this he could rarely comply. He had no method at home, and found it difficult to accede to one abroad. His hours were late ; his temper often irritable, sometimes rude, to host and hostess as well as to visitors ; his remarks sharp or sarcastic upon trifles, so as frequently to give offence ; yet borne with exemplary forbearance. His reproofs, as stated in her *Anecdotes,* evince their genuine origin. There is no mistaking the master. Like a spoiled child, he was permitted to have his way, and impunity occasionally made him offensive. Yet she is not censorious. Liberal allowance is made for all his infirmities ; every virtue to which humanity can pretend is allowed him ; and she congratulates herself, " with Mr. Thrale's assistance, to have saved from distress at least, if not from worse, a mind great beyond the comprehension of common mortals, and good beyond all hope of imitation from perishable beings."

No praise can exceed this. Yet there may have been substantial reasons for not selecting him—if the idea ever existed—as partner for life. If a woman is at any time permitted to have a will of her own, surely it may be conceded when she is of mature age and a widow. But such seems not to have been the idea among Johnson's friends, even in a matter so purely personal. Our Critic becomes positively peevish, if not ill-natured in his notes upon the *Anecdotes*. Her economy, rather ill-judged perhaps upon one occasion, increased this irritation. Mr. Cator of the Adelphi, who as guardian of the daughters was interested in the affairs of the family, wrote to Mrs. Piozzi in Italy in 1785, that for Dr. Johnson's monument two guineas only would be accepted from subscribers; and that sum he had paid for her and for each of her daughters. Proving however insufficient for the object, further aid became necessary, and Malone writes: " The committee for the monument of Dr. Johnson applied, among others, to Mrs. Piozzi. She had gained 500*l.* by this book (*Anecdotes*) and 600*l.* by publishing his letters. The answer sent me by this worthless woman with three guineas 4th February 1791 or 92 was—' Mrs. Piozzi sends her compliments to Mr. Malone, assuring him that she has already subscribed two guineas for this purpose, and has now sent three guineas more to make up five.' "*

Toward the end of the year, a present from a friend put him in possession of a small volume of ancient English verse, of which by an alluring table of contents, an admirer of that age might reasonably be proud.

"*Diana* or the *Sonnets of H. C.* (Henry Constable) 1592 or 1594; Daniel's *Sonnets*, with the

---

* From the copy of *Anecdotes*, obligingly lent me by J. H. Markland, Esq., who purchased it at the younger Boswell's sale in 1825.

Complaint of Rosamond, and the *Tragedie of Cleo-patra,* 1594 ; Barnefield's *Sonnets,* with the *Legend of Cassandra,* 1595 ; *Fidessa,* Sonnets by B. Griffin, 1596 ; *Diella,* Sonnets by R. L., with the *Poem of Dom. Diego and Genevra,* 1596 ; *The Poem of Poems,* or *Sion's Mase,* by J. M. (Jarvais Markham) 1596 ; The *Tragedie of Sir Richard Grinville, Kt.* by the same, 1595."

Here were treasures for a poetical antiquary! Poetry of vigour, elegance and originality thrown off in the age of Elizabeth, with a power which may cause the uninitiated an occasional stop in perusal to consider how in those days they could write so well! The volume is very small, just fit for the waistcoat pocket —four and a half inches long by three broad, pretty thick, well printed, in good condition, the date 1592. The story told of it is no less interesting than the little work itself, and deserves here the record he desires to preserve, as verifying its origin and career—

" The history of this book is curious. It was sold at the sale of Dr. Bernard's books in 1698 for one shilling and threepence. Afterwards probably passing through many hands, it came into the possession of a broker at Salisbury, where about thirty years ago, Mr. Warton found it among a parcel of old iron and other lumber, and I think purchased it for *sixpence.* Since his death, his brother, Dr. Joseph Warton, very kindly presented it to me ; and I have honoured it with a new cover, and have preserved above the name of my poor friend Mr. Thomas Warton which was written at the inside of the old cover, as a memorial of that very elegant and ingenious writer.

" This is the book I have mentioned in the preface to my edition of Shakspeare, and such is the variation in prices of pieces of this kind, that if it were now to be produced at an auction, it would undoubtedly be sold for three or four guineas.

"The very rare copy of Shakspeare's *Venus and Adonis*, 1596, originally made part of this volume, but on re-binding it I took out that piece in order to place it with my other early editions of Shakspeare's pieces.   I have also changed the place of Constable's *Sonnets*, which originally did not stand in the front of this little volume.

"EDMOND MALONE, Dec. 1, 1791."

This curious miniature rarity is numbered 436 in Malone's contribution to the Bodleian. A pencil note attached to the *Tragedie of Sir Richard Grinville*, says — " This poem alone was purchased by Mr. Grenville at Mr. Bindley's sale for 40*l.* 19*s.*" Though termed in the title *Tragedie*, it is a poem in one hundred and seventy-four Spenserian stanzas. The subject, the engagement near the Western Islands of Sir Richard with the Spanish Armada ; his heroic conduct, wounds, and death. Of two or three introductory *Sonnets*, one is to "Henrie Wriothesly, Earl of Southampton and Baron of Tichfield," whom he addresses as—

" Thou glorious laurel of the Muses' hill,
    Whose eyes doth crowne the most victorious pen,
  Bright lampe of Vertue, in whose sacred skill,
    Lives all the blisse of cares—inchaunting men."

A visit to Beaconsfield gives us a sketch from authority of Abbé Raynal, reputed author of a once

famous work, *History of the East and West Indies.*
The account of him while in England sufficiently explains why his work has lost credit as an authority
with us, and even in France. The other anecdotes I
had long since noted in another place.

"*At Mr. Burke's, near Beaconsfield, Sept.* 6, 1791,
General Conway, an officer in the French service,
said that the Abbé Raynal's book on the *European
Settlements in India,* like many other modern French
productions, was a work of contribution ; that he had
seen many of the different numbers of that work,
which were written by various persons. Raynal himself was by no means equal to it, as his contemptible
account of the Parliament of England evinced. He
added, that after the work was originally compiled,
the Abbé introduced a due portion of infidelity into it
to please the *esprits forts* of Paris.

" Mr. Burke entirely agreed with him in his opinion of this writer. He said, when the Abbé was in
England about eight or ten years ago, he had often
seen him ; he had visited at Beaconsfield ; and did
not show the least curiosity about either the literature,
the politicks, or the commerce of England. Mr. Burke
had offered to accompany him through various publick
offices, and to explain the details of each, but the
Abbé declined his offer. When he went to Bristol,
Mr. Burke recommended him to some friends who
would have displayed the whole arrangements and
operations of that great commercial city ; but when
there, he simply inquired of one of the gentlemen to
whom he was recommended, whether there was a
playhouse in the city ? An answer in the affirmative

took him to see the performance; and no further information was sought of the gentleman to whom Mr. Burke's letters were addressed.

"During his stay in England Mr. Gibbon the historian, mentioned to him that many inquiries had been made in our Parliament relative to India; and that he would send him various reports of the committee of inquiry from which much information might be obtained. The Abbé asked their size, and being told they amounted to seven folio volumes, he said that Mr. Gibbon need not give himself the trouble of transmission, as a friend who had been in India had given him a full account of the English possessions in that country, by which he should abide. This *full* account consisted of a single sheet of paper.* All the details concerning the French East Indies which are found in his book are authentick, and may be depended upon, the author by order of the government having had admission to the public offices in Paris where information on this subject could be obtained. This piece of information I had from Mr. Gibbon, who considered that the most valuable part of the work.

"On a subsequent day (September, 1791) when no one but Sir J. Reynolds and myself were present, Mr. Burke, after dinner in the freedom of conversation said, that if there was one day of his life more brilliant than another and which he should wish to

* The Abbé Raynal seems to have been of the same opinion with Father Daniel, who, being shown in the Royal Library at Paris a large collection of MSS. relating to the history of France from the time of Louis XI., spent only an hour in looking over them, and declared he did not want those *paperasses*.

live over again, it was the day when he appeared at
the bar of the House of Lords with the censure of the
House of Commons in his hand, relative to the conduct of the managers on the impeachment of Mr.
Hastings.

" He had from a sense of decorum and propriety
absented himself from the debate in the Commons,
and went down to the house at an early hour the next
day to learn what had been done. He first desired
the Resolution to be read to him, then demanded a
copy of it ; and immediately afterwards determined on
the part he should take. This was *not* to relinquish
the prosecution, as Mr. Fox strongly urged him to do
on account of the indignity they had suffered from
the house, and as Mr. Pitt certainly *hoped* he would
have done. He had but an hour to prepare himself before he appeared at the bar of the House of
Lords.

" The second most brilliant day of his life he
esteemed the day when he was attacked by his own
party in the House of Commons in May, 1791, relative
to the French revolution ; and was very feebly supported by Mr. Pitt though he pretended to agree
with him in sentiment.

" It is remarkable, that many of the persons who
have written answers to his book on the *French
Revolution,* were of his particular acquaintance.
Mr. Paine had been strongly recommended to him
from America, and pretty frequently became a guest
at Beaconsfield. He had also shown many civilities
to Mr. Thomas Christie, another of his answerers ;
and to a Mr. Bousefield of the County of Cork, in

Ireland, who is peculiarly virulent as I am told against him.

"Of Mr. Burke's first book on this subject, just *eighteen thousand* have been now sold, as he told me this day. Twelve thousand of the French translation have been sold in Paris. It is done by Mons. Dupont, an *avocat* of the parliament of Paris."*

* All these circumstances I had learned from his family, in many conversations which Mrs. Haviland, his niece, had communicated to her son, Mr. Haviland Burke. But it is satisfactory to have such a matter-of-fact witness as Malone to their accuracy.

" *January 6th*, 1792. — A call from Dr. Joseph
Warton produced a conversation respecting Spence,
author of the *Anecdotes*, who he maintained Dr.
Johnson had under-rated.

" He told me that Spence once intended to publish
his *Anecdotes*, and had actually sold them to Robert
Dodsley for a hundred pounds. Before the matter
was finally settled both Spence and Dodsley died.
Spence's executors, Dr. G. Ridley and Dr. South,
late Bishop of London (who mentioned this circumstance to Dr. Warton), on looking over the *Anecdotes*
found there were so many personal strokes affecting
persons then living, that suppression at least for a
time was deemed the more prudent course.

" James Dodsley, brother to Robert, relinquished
his bargain, though he probably would have gained
400*l*. or 500*l*. by it, being unwilling that anything
should appear prejudicial to the memory of Spence.
The executors sealed up the papers and delivered
them to Spence's patron, the present Duke of New-

castle, in whose hands they remain. They were lent to the late Duchess Dowager of Portland, and to Dr. Johnson while he was writing the *Lives of the Poets;* and have also passed through other hands. They are, Dr. Warton says very entertaining, and full of curious information."

In issuing an edition of *Shakspeare,* Malone could not expect to escape the usual lot of the author and editorial race—contradiction and censure. Accordingly, there came out a pamphlet of a hundred pages early in 1792—*Cursory Criticisms on the Edition of Shakspeare, by Edmond Malone.* The writer was judged and proved to be, the unhappy Ritson, whose many eccentricities, literary and otherwise, added to morbid tendencies to find fault with all his brethren, terminated in insanity.

"*A Letter to the Rev. Richard Farmer, D.D., &c.,*" in April 1792 with his name affixed, gives Malone's reply. He is sufficiently triumphant; sometimes a little prone in return for ridicule and sarcasm, to charge his critic with the usual tricks of such a trade.—"Fraught with the usual materials of hypercriticism, that is, with unblushing cavil, false argument, and false quotation." . . . .

" When my admiration of his (Shakspeare's) innumerable beauties led me to undertake an edition of his works, I then thought it my duty to exert every faculty to make it as perfect as I could, and in order to ensure a genuine text, to collate word by word every line of his plays and poems with the original and authentick copies—a task equally new and arduous. By this laborious process I obtained

*one thousand six hundred and fifty-four emendations
of the text.*"

The number of lines collated in the plays, he tells
us, amounted to nearly *one hundred thousand.* The
errors alleged by his critic are *thirteen;* but as five
are his own mistakes, the actual numbers are *eight.*
So enormous a tax on industry has been rarely so
successful in its results.

However unanimous our national love of Shakspeare,
no love whatever exists among those who make him
a theme for the exercise of their ingenuity. All his
editors, critics, and commentators *agree to differ*—
nay, not differ only, but wage war upon each other
with all the fury of the celebrated genus of *Kilkenny
cats,* who fight till not a fragment is left of either
combatant! Utter extinction of an adversary—in
pen and ink I mean—is the aim of most Shakspeare-
men—and why? Each has a new view, a new inference, a new conjecture, a new explanation, which,
whether with or without a basis, he expects shall fill
the post of honour and be alone accepted as truth.

Apparitions of such volumes haunt the reader's
path in every shop or stall of books. The eye
scarcely rests upon one when another aims to thrust
it into oblivion. To displace it is scarcely enough.
The book and the writer must be gibbeted if it be
only for inadvertence, as if he had committed one of
the deadly sins. "Another and another still suc-
ceeds," and meets with a similar fate. "Come like
shadows, so depart," is the rule for these pugnacious
candidates for distinction. Few happily are destined
to survive the contest. Were Shakspeare still more

delightful than he is, the fact of having, however unintentionally, overshadowed the land with an army of commentators ever at war with each other and often with staid, good sense, is of itself a serious drawback to the gratification derived from perusal of his works. *

Previous to this critical attack, he had lost by the death of Sir Joshua Reynolds one of those endeared friends whom the chances of life even in a great metropolis, seldom allow us to meet, or when lost to replace. The pursuits of the editor enjoyed the favour of the President; while the public merits of the latter commanded that distinction which is due to eminent genius when it carries its owner far beyond his fellows.

Still more cordial if possible was the painter's association with Burke. It had commenced thirty-four years before, when neither could anticipate that career of celebrity which both were destined to run. The pursuit of one was already fixed. Not so that of the other. Fate was hovering over him, doubtful as yet whether to make him a literary man, a lawyer, a consul,

---

* Among the more recent editions of *Shakspeare* of the highest character, many esteem, as preferable, that of the Rev. Alexander Dyce. The notes are not oppressively numerous; they are placed at the end of each play; and tact and experience have enabled him to profit by the mistakes of others so as to acquire credit for the best text of the poet.

Not less industrious in research is Mr. Halliwall, in his truly splendid volumes. The *fac-similes* of Shaksperian documents, and the uncommon elegance of typography, must give his edition—if copies are to be had—a place in every select library in the kingdom.

Mr. J. P. Collier would appear, by some letters from the British Museum, to have been subjected to imposition in his celebrated volume of emendations. The fact is sufficiently mortifying to an industrious labourer in the cause, without admitting the charge of inattention or any participation in the deceit.

or cast him as she eventually did, into a life-long line
of political contention and enlightened statesmanship,
embracing not only the interests of our own nation,
but of the world. Yet this trying process had no
effect in deadening his affections. More than once
his tears and his pen, while executing the trust reposed in him as executor by the departed, proved that
the same warmth and worth that had stamped the
little-known man of letters in 1758, imbued the great
statesman at the summit of fame, in 1792. His *Hail
and Farewell* to the artist forms a literary portrait of
the highest order.

Goldsmith, nearly twenty years previously, had
judged Reynolds not less kindly than justly in the
jocular epitaph in *Retaliation*—

> " He has not left a wiser or better behind,
>   By flattery unspoiled ——" *

Nor should it be here omitted that a fourth worthy
son of Ireland, Lord Charlemont, participated not
less warmly in these feelings. In his visits to England, hours were given to conversation with Reynolds
upon art and Italy in which he was well informed.
He occasionally dined with the President to meet
Burke, Malone, and other men of note and literature;
had his portrait painted; received for private perusal
the MS. of Reynolds's *Flemish Travels*, until frequent communication instructed both that nature had
tinctured their minds with kindred elements of good

---

* It is not unlikely that this unfinished line may have been the last
from his pen. It had been carelessly omitted in his printed works,
although noting another fine quality in the deceased, till I recovered
and introduced it in the edition in four 8vo. volumes (including above
a volume of new matter) in 1837.

taste and mutual respect and esteem. In writing to
Malone, his lordship had often desired to be remembered to his Club-mates, "more especially and affectionately to Mr. Walpole and Sir Joshua;" and when
his death was announced, replied immediately to Malone (March 1st, 1792) in the following strain :—

How erroneously do we judge of our own happiness!
Here have I been for many years past regretting and
lamenting the situation into which Fate and my duty have
plunged me, principally because I have been thereby almost
totally deprived of all possible society with the greater part of
my early connections. Yet experience has now demonstra-
tively shown me that this very privation, by me so long
regretted, has in its effects been fortunate. Since, however,
I may be sincerely grieved at the loss of those early friends,
my grief would certainly have been much more pungent, if
the circumstances of my life had allowed me continually to
increase and to fortify those friendships by constant and
endearing intercourse.

Poor Sir Joshua! How good—how kind—how truly
amiable and respectable! The best of men—whose talents,
though an honour to his country, were the least of his qualifications! Indeed, I most sincerely lament him, and ought,
perhaps, still more to grieve for you, my dearest Edmond,
who have lost the society of a friend so justly dear, of a companion so truly valuable. Yet let us not repine. All is
surely for the best; and perhaps our own dissolution would
be scarcely tolerable to us, if our life were not from time to
time, as it were, habituated to death in the persons of our
friends. . . . .

Send me in your next cargo the octavo edition of our
friend's lectures. Compleat also, if you can, my collection of
the quartos, which he sometimes forgot to send me.

What were Malone's immediate thoughts upon this
regretted event we find in his memoranda, which are
here in part transcribed :—

"The dear friend so often mentioned in these papers, Sir Joshua Reynolds, died at his house in Leicester Fields, last Thursday evening (Feb. 23, 1792), at half past eight o'clock. So much have I been employed for some days past, he having done me the honour to make me one of his executors, that I have not been able till this moment to set down any of the particulars of that sad event.

"I became first acquainted with him in 1778, and for these twelve years past we have lived in the greatest intimacy. The morning after his death, Mr. Burke drew up a short character of him which was inserted not quite correctly, in *The Gazetteer*, and in *The Herald* the following day.* It is so perfectly just, appropriate, and discriminative, that it is not easy to add to it. He was blessed with such complacency and equality of temper, was so easy, so uniformly cheerful, so willing to please and be pleased, so fond of the company of literary men, so well read in mankind, so curious an observer of character, and so replete with various knowledge and entertaining anecdotes, that not to have loved as well as admired him would have shown great want of taste and sensibility. He had long enjoyed such constant health, looked so young, and was so active, that I thought, though he was sixty-nine years old, he was as likely to live eight or ten years longer as any of his younger friends.

"On our return from an excursion to Mr. Burke's at Beaconsfield last September, we alighted from his

* It was afterwards interwoven with other matter by John Nichols, and published in the *Gentleman's Magazine*, March, 1792.—*Malone.*

coach, and while the horses baited at the half-way house, we walked five miles very smartly in a warm day without his being fatigued. About three years ago he found some defect in his sight whilst painting the picture of Lady Beauchamp, if I remember right, and then determined to paint no more. Soon afterwards he entirely lost the sight of his left eye. From that period he became very apprehensive of losing the other also, yet his uniform cheerfulness never forsook him till very lately.

"I cannot help thinking that we should not have lost this most amiable man for some years, had there not been want of exertion, combined with some want of skill in his physicians. In September, he was much distressed by swelling and inflammation over the lost eye, owing as has been since thought, to some extravasated blood. For this Mr. Cruikshank, who was called in as surgeon, bled him with leeches, purged and blistered him repeatedly, all in vain; for the swelling and pain in that part remained till the period of death. This pain led him to fear that the other eye would be soon affected; and from this or other causes, his spirits became depressed and his appetite daily decreased. In this state he continued in the month of November. The physicians who then attended, Sir George Baker and Dr. Warren, assured him that his remaining eye was in no danger, and that with respect to any other complaint, if he would but exert himself, take exercise, and think himself well, he would be well.

"Unfortunately, they paid little attention to his loss of appetite and depression of spirits. Even

while he was gradually wasting, their constant language was—' What can we do for a man who will
do nothing for himself?' At the same time they
owned they could not discern his disorder, though he
was ready and willing to follow such prescriptions as
they should direct.　All this while, that is during the
months of November, December, and January, they
made not the least *attempt* to investigate the seat or
origin of his disease; nor did they call for the aid of
a surgeon to examine his body minutely, and thus
discover the latent mischief.

"Dr. Blagdon (Secretary of the Royal Society,
who had studied physic, and practised for some time
in America) *alone* uniformly declared he was confident the complaints of Sir Joshua Reynolds were not
imaginary, but well founded, and that some of the
principal *viscera* were affected.　His conjecture
proved but too correct; for on his body being
opened, his liver which ought to have weighed about
five pounds, had attained the great weight of eleven
pounds.　It was also somewhat scirrhus.　The optic
nerve of the left eye was quite shrunk, and more
flimsy than it ought to have been.　The other, which
he was so apprehensive of losing, was not affected.
In his brain was found more water than is usual in
men of his age."

One of the legatees of Sir Joshua was the poet
Mason—his gift, *The Miniature of Milton by Cooper.*
The announcement made to him produced the following letter to Malone, which from one filling a prominent place in English literature, deserves record here—

Aston, May 26th, 1792.

SIR,—I have for some time expected to receive from my friend Mr. Stonehewer the valuable miniature which Sir Joshua Reynolds bequeathed me, and which he received from Miss Palmer; but as he has lately written to tell me that he waits for a safer conveyance than he has yet met with, I will not defer answering your most obliging letter any longer, and returning my thanks for your having settled matters with Mr. Cadell respecting *Du Fresnoy* in a manner more than satisfactory to me.

I have to thank you also for the trouble you have taken in sending me so much information relative to the controversy concerning Milton's portrait, and for giving me your own opinion also concerning the writing affixed to it, which with you, I think to have been written much later than Sir Joshua imagined.

My supposition is, that Deborah Milton might have been, before her father's death, in possession of the picture in question. Cooper might himself have painted it at her request, after her father was blind, and it might have been her property before she was on bad terms with him. There is great probability also for thinking that either her indigent circumstances or of those she left behind her, might have induced them to sell it to some unknown person at a low price, and that it might have got into a third hand, who wrote on hearsay the memorandum which certainly contains blunders, if not falsehoods. I have, however, no doubt but that Cooper painted it and that Milton sat for it.

Sir Joshua says, in his letter to Urban, that the " *drop serene* is not visible in the miniature," but for myself, I have long been of a different opinion, and when I was last in residence in York, I sent a young, blind musician to my friend Dr. Burney, with a recommendatory letter, and requested (at a time when I was ignorant of poor Sir Joshua's danger) that he would contrive he might be a living *argument* on my side of the question. And I am persuaded that were you to see the unfortunate youth, you would perceive a similar cast of eye in his countenance. It is this very cast and indirect glance which gave the portrait that shrewd cunning look

O

which you justly remarked in it, and which I fairly believe
neither Milton nor the young man had before the *gutta serena*
was confirmed. Perhaps what I have said may induce you to
speak to Dr. Burney on the subject, who if you wish it, would
easily give you an opportunity of seeing the person I have
mentioned.

I have for many years neglected to examine the various
editions of Shakspeare which have been published since Warburton's. I must therefore take shame to myself when I
own that I have not seen more of your edition than a great
turning over some of its volumes has given me, which, however, has convinced me that you have taken such minute,
accurate, and laudable pains in restoring the text, that I
think you might well have spared the trouble of taking notice
of so poor an antagonist as you have in the pamphlet you
have done me the honour to send, and to whom I think you
have given more than ample confutation.

I guess him to be the same person who a few years ago
treated the late Mr. T. Warton with the same sort of scur-
rility, but I neither knew nor wish to know his name. I
should (were I you) have contented myself with calling him
in Shakspearian phrase—

A captious and unteemable sieve (illegible).

But here, you see, I adopt a reading which you have dis-
carded for this reason. To teem or team (I know not which
is the right spelling) is a northern verb used for pouring one
thing through another, or into another. That species of sieve
or (illegible) which separates flour from bran is with us called
a *temze.* Hence, therefore, the word might be altered to
untemzible, a sieve which will let nothing pass through it;
and though I cannot, in *All's Well that Ends Well,* find the
passage, and therefore am ignorant of the context; yet the
epithet captious leads me to think that Shakspeare meant to
say that the person spoken to was so captious that he would
let nothing pass, like a sieve of too close a fabric or texture.
I by no means, however, wish you to adopt either of these
readings in your next editions, lest they should be laid to the
charge of that Mr. Mason, some of whose notes you have

already admitted, and which I have heard were supposed to be mine, and whom I take to be the gentleman who published an edition of Massinger.

The engraving * which you favoured me with is extremely elegant, and I have only to wish that I had better right to it by having attended the funeral of our excellent friend. The great distance I am from town, and some other reasons which disincline me from going there, were I assure you, the only reasons which prevented me. I beg you to present my best respects to Miss Palmer; and that you would believe me to be, with all sincerity, your highly obliged and very faithful servant, W. MASON.

If I can persuade myself to revise my translation again, I shall send you that revision in due time.

In the summer he made a journey to Oxford, in order as he would term pretty diligent work, to be idle. Business and pleasure were however conjoined; for while the mornings were passed in examining old books and manuscripts, the evenings called forth those hospitalities which several acquaintance familiar with his table in London were desirous to repay.

Several letters from Lord Charlemont during this year, indicate a pretty active correspondence His lordship smiles at Malone's idea of idleness— turns to Burke from whose politics he differs widely, being a strong Whig, yet a still stronger admirer of the great powers of his old friend—and concludes an interesting letter (August 20th, 1792) upon the stock subject of literature and prints.

* To each of the gentlemen attending the funeral of Sir Joshua a print was presented, engraved by Bartolozzi. It was a female figure clasping an urn, accompanied by the genius of painting, holding in one hand an extinguished torch, the other pointing to a sarcophagus, on the tablet of which is written—

"Succedet fama, vivusque per ora feretur."

If I could grudge you any pleasure, I should think with some degree of envy on your fortnight spent at Oxford, as exclusive of your particular business there, I know of no place where much time can be spent with more satisfaction. Ten times at least have I visited that venerable seat of the Muses, and could with delight revisit it ten times more; perfectly agreeing with a travelled friend of mine whom I have heard declare that, after having seen the whole world, Oxford was most worthy of a traveller's attention.

You have, it must be confessed, much work upon your hands, and are undoubtedly right in allowing yourself to be idle for a few weeks; but surely your idleness is of a whimsical kind; and if poring over old manuscripts with eyes already well nigh worn out in the service be a relaxation, I can scarcely guess what you would call labour.

Burke is, indeed, a young man of his years. But the reason I take to be, that if age should deprive him of one half of his ideas he would still have more left him than any man of five-and-twenty. If he has really given up politics— a cession which I wish heartily he had made twelve months ago—literature will be his only resource, and he will yet be able to delight and to inform mankind. I cannot, with you, however, recommend a revisal of the *Sublime and Beautiful*, since, notwithstanding the miraculous texture of his brain, thirty years I fear may have taken from him more in fire and fancy than they have given in experience.*

When I mentioned Fabricius to you, I was, as you may recollect, desirous of possessing a copy of all his works. They are all of them curious, and in my present course of study necessary for consultation. A Dublin bookseller, now on the Continent has promised if possible to procure them for me.

Boydell's second number I have, thanks to your brother, safely received. I do not see why people should be disappointed, as the large prints appear to me excellent, and the small ones

* Here we see the party politician at war in opinion with the great majority of persons at home and abroad. The power of his friend over the politics of Europe became nearly universal; while "fire and fancy" threw all other writers into the shade.

are, I am told, to be engraved anew. The difference, indeed, between the proofs and the ordinary prints is inconceivable— a not unusual trick with London engravers; and this may, I doubt not, have depreciated the work.

Respecting the Milton to be chosen, you leave me undecided, and your brother is not in town. Milton does not seem to me a bad subject for prints, though, indeed, a very difficult one. The Paradisaic scenes most certainly give the fullest scope to the genius of the landscape painter, and the figures, though but two, might be beautifully varied. Heaven and hell might also produce incomparable pictures, but the genius of the artist must be in some degree analogous to that of the poet, a coincidence, I confess, not easily to be found. Dramatick poetry is, however, far better fitted for picturesque representation than the epodée, since the peculiar business of the former is to speak to the eye as well as to the ear, and every scene ought in effect to be a picture. . . . . I have procured here the *Loves of the Plants;* but your having procured it for me in London will be of no consequence, as I can easily get rid of that I had. The East India books will be highly acceptable, and I wish to have them as soon as may be.

Three other letters from him to the same friend touch upon Royal Irish Academy matters, book auctions, prices, *Bibliotheca* of Fabricius, *Asiatic Researches, Institutions of Timour, Boydell's Shakspeare,* and the question " What are these Miltons? Which is the best?" The amiable writer, as usual, makes numberless apologies for occupying his correspondent's time; but invariably concludes by adding to the tax. It was the happy spirit of two good-natured men anxious to please and be pleased with each other.

Occasional correspondents also from Dublin amused him with lighter topics of the day. Among these was Mr. R. M. Jephson, nephew of the drama-

tist, who thus sketches (February, 1793) two persons
of no ordinary note in that country, one of whom
figures unhappily in the page of history.   This was
Lord Edward Fitzgerald.   He had it appears previous to this time, termed the Lord Lieutenant
(Westmoreland), and the majority of the House of
Commons, " the worst subjects the king had ;" and
would make no other apology than that he was sorry
he had used words contrary to parliamentary usage.
" He is turned," says Jephson, " a complete Frenchman—crops his hair,* despises his title, walks the
streets instead of riding, and thence says he feels
more pride in being on a level with his fellow
citizens."

I was fortunate enough to get a sight of the celebrated
Pamela, as I happened to be sitting with Lord Charlemont
when they both came to see his library.   She is elegant and
engaging I think in the highest degree, and showed the most
judicious taste in her remarks upon the library and curiosities.
The Dublin ladies, I understand, wish to put her down. . . .
She promised Lord Charlemont with great good humour, to
assist him in keeping her husband in order.   She seems something about the size and figure of Mrs. (Scot?) but rather
plumper.   She was dressed in a plain riding-habit, and came
to the door in a curricle.

Robert Jephson, to whose tragedies he had stood
in the position of second parent, now aimed to put
his skill and patience to a new test.   He was about
to launch a poem.   To revise the plan, scan the
characters, revolve the sentiments, correct the language—in fact, to put that mental machinery into

* This fashion became ultimately, in Ireland, the distinction of a
rebel, or at least a person of such opinions.   Hence a celebrated air, in
1798, among Loyalists there—"*Croppies lye Down !*"

motion which can alone produce a finished piece, and then to carry the whole through the press, were the duties expected from the critic. Alas! how rarely is this done faithfully. The delicacy of the operation precludes even a friend from doing what even the poet himself in all sincerity may wish, in order to secure his path to immortality. But he has not the heart to pull his offspring to pieces. A man may write non-sense in prose, yet in time become aware of the fact and amend it. Not so at all times with verse; it is a more cherished kind of offspring. The one is the son, the other the daughter of his fancy; and with all natural partiality for the more delicate and beau-tiful party, sees not her faults or tries to excuse them. He views her with admiration and tenderness, soothes her with a father's care; and if direct praise from him be not admissible, takes care to show de-voted though silent attachment to the child of his imagination. Who may venture to disturb this com-placency by hinting to the parent unpalatable truths?

The poem was *Roman Portraits*. Malone, although busily occupied in researches connected with stage history, and in meeting the cavils or indirect censures of Steevens, gave his time freely to the task. Fre-quent correspondence as to the necessary alterations ensued. Many of these letters lie before me, of which the following is the first. But the piece did not issue into life until the following year, and has not retained hold of public opinion.

Dublin Castle, May 16th, 1793.

MY DEAR EDMUND,—I was very glad yesterday to receive your letter of the 11th, accompanied by a proof sheet. I think *nor* in the eleventh line of Lucius Brutus should be *not*, and in the short quotation from Valerius Maximus the last word *valuit* should be *maluit*. I see no other mistakes you have not corrected. If those two I have mentioned are too late for the copy, they may be put in errata.

I have no doubt of the malignity of Steevens. I have always heard him described as the most malevolent of human beings. I hope you will not spare him, and I think your forte in writing is personality. You could not possibly have a more worthy subject for its exercise.

It gives me great concern to hear such a bad account of your sight: there is one certain way of preserving it, by abstaining from what has injured it; don't go on poking into small crabbed manuscripts, or you will be as blind as Tiresias. Can't you get some young lusty Epidaurian-eyed drudge to make out the text for you, and so save your own peepers? I agree with you entirely, that a man who has a relish for literature need never look to old age with despondency. It is that prospect which comforts me; and so long as there are books, and I keep my relish for them, time may be too short for me, but I shall never last too long for time. I know some worthy friends who depended upon field-sports for their amusement, and being now grown infirm, their existence is a load, because they have no substitute to fill up the space which was once devoted to bodily exercise.

It gives me the greatest satisfaction to hear that you have resolved upon getting engravings. Twenty, as you mention, will be sufficient. I shall be very impatient to see some specimens, and flatter myself you will not fail to send them to me with the earliest opportunity. They will make it look handsome, and with such paper, type, and engravings, the book will have at least the outside of a gentleman. I forgot in my distribution of copies in presents, two persons very material; one the Marquis of Townshend, the other the Prince of Wales. To the latter I wish you could contrive in my name to present it yourself, or consult Mr. Hamilton* what will be the most respectful and proper manner of doing

---

*   * Right Honourable William Gerard Hamilton.

it. His Royal Highness was very gracious about me when I was in England last.

My Scipio whom you ask about is the conqueror of Hannibal, at the battle of Zama, and I believe the same as in Melmoth's translation of the *Dialogue*, but it is not in the least material, and I am glad you have got a good head to copy from. You know that there were many Scipios—the two most illustrious are those Virgil refers to:—

Duo fulmina belli

Scipiades.

I think 750 a very small number of copies, but I must submit. I flatter myself it will bear more than one edition. The price of the book, with such paper and engravings, should be at least one guinea; what is it to be fixed at? I don't see the number of lines marked on the margin, as you said you would order.

I send with this some new lines for *Augustus,* and for the Augustan age; also an extract from the *Confessions de Jaques Batiste Couteau, Citoyen Français,** from which you may form some notion of the performance. I have, as you recommended, translated into English as much as I had originally written in French, and the mere manual operation of writing in a print hand has been very tedious. About ten chapters in both languages are finished—about a hundred pages of paper, something less than this (foolscap). Two persons who paid me my income as agents are broke, and the profits of a book at present are very material to me. I shall be for a long time in a deplorable way about money. I hope you have not suffered by the times.

I am glad to hear that Courtenay is become less outrageous. He had a great deal of republican frenzy to spare, and yet enough left to qualify very well for an apartment among Moorfields collegians. Adieu! my dear Malone. I am ever most sincerely yours,

ROBERT JEPHSON.

I can't be aware even what small matter I have left for your objection in the preface.

* Also written by Jephson against the French Revolutionists.

Among the anecdotes with which I have diversified the conclusion of the present work, are several gleaned by Malone at the Club. Few there but had mingled largely in society, knew the most noted public characters, or were intimate with those who did. One of these was Bishop Douglas, detector of Lauder's forgery concerning Milton, and a successor in the see of Salisbury to a more celebrated name, of whom he found a few remaining anecdotes. His memory in historical, biographical, and literary incidents of the previous half century, appeared unusually well-stored, and were freely drawn forth by a little judicious prompting.

"*Tuesday, February* 12*th*, 1793.—We had a very good club, only eight—Bishop Douglas, Nuncliff?* Percy, Marlay, Mr. Langton, Mr. Boswell, Mr. Steevens, and myself. On the preceding meeting we had fifteen members—much too numerous to be pleasant.

" Dr. Douglas, talking of Burnet, mentioned that several of his characters were softened down by his son the judge, chiefly by omissions. The person who had been employed as amanuensis, a clergyman I believe of Salisbury, was not faithful to his trust, and some of these omissions appeared afterwards in a pamphlet which the Bishop possesses. He has some more in manuscript which are not in that pamphlet.

" Burnet, he said, was extremely passionate and violent in his resentments. He piqued himself on preaching without book. Some of his sermons, however, are in print. At one of his visitations, when

* *Sic* in MS., but who meant is unknown.

the name of a very old clergyman was called over (of whom a private complaint had been made that the parish could not endure him, he gave such bad sermons), he gravely chided the poor parson—'I am told, Mr. ——, that your parish is very well satisfied with you in many respects, but they are much discontented with your sermons. Now there is no excuse for this; for instead of preaching extempore, as I am told you sometimes do, or giving them your own compositions, you have only to preach good printed sermons, and they will have no cause for complaint.'—'May it please your lordship,' replied the clergyman, 'you have been wholly misinformed. I have been long in the habit of preaching printed sermons, and those I have preferred are your lordship's!'

" When Burnet once rated his son, afterwards the judge, for something indecorous that he had done, ' Lord, sir, I can't help it; I was forced to do it for bread.'—' Get you gone,' replied the Bishop, ' it was for drink.'

" Bishop Douglas, it appears, was principally concerned in issuing out the *Life and Continuation of Lord Clarendon*, at Oxford in 1759. He says that Lord Clarendon's character of Monk was much stronger coloured (*i.e.*, he was more censured by his Lordship) than appears at present. But such alterations as were made in the manuscript—which were chiefly to soften the characters—were made by Lord Clarendon's heirs before it came to Oxford.

" Lord Onslow has from his father, all the castrated sheets of Burnet's *History*. The judge promised to put his father's MS. into a public library, but never did. Bishop Douglas said he was assured, from good authority, that he had been accustomed to read parts of his work to some old people of a former age, and to make alterations which they suggested, when in fact they were wrong and he right. He yielded in this way often to Lord Portmore.

" Bishop Douglas told us, the same day, that old Dr. King, of St. Mary Hall, prophesied, before he died, that when the Hanover family were securely established on the throne, and the pretensions of the Stuarts comparatively at an end, the Whigs of England would become Republicans. This prophecy is in some measure verifying in our own days; particularly since the new and accursed doctrines of equality, &c., have been broached by Paine in England and the French savages on the Continent."

At one of these club meetings, though probably of more recent date than this year, an instance of ill-nature was alleged against Malone by Rogers the poet, as I am informed by a distinguished literary friend.* In the height of revolutionary proceedings in France, Rogers, not at all reserved in giving full swing to Whig opinions of the day, came forward as candidate for the Club, and was blackballed. This he attributed to Malone—whether truly or not is doubtful, as the ballot leaves no clue to trace the party. But strong opinions from any one were likely to give offence to many members; and there was something perhaps of reprisal in the result; for Dr. French Laurence, the intimate friend of Burke, had

---

* Rev. Alexander Dyce, editor of *The Table-Talk of Samuel Rogers.*

been previously rejected by other dissentients. Boswell however on one or two occasions privately to our Critic, pointed at Steevens and Sir Joseph Bankes as sometimes showing their distaste in this manner.

The diligence of Malone had not ceased with the publication of Shakspeare. Time added daily to his stores relative to the Poet, the stage, the language, and allusions of former days, as illustrative of the text. He had become also fully alive to the mechanical defects of the previous work—small print and a close page. All these imperfections he sought to correct; and ambition even aimed at "royal quartos with engravings," to which Jephson alludes in the previous letter.

In pursuit of all possible knowledge for this project, his friends at Stratford were not forgotten. To Dr. Davenport he writes in April 1793 :—

"For my own part, after having for two years reposed from Shakspearian labours, I am now once more going to resume them, and to put a splendid quarto edition to the press, of which I enclose you the prospectus. This is the occasion of my giving you the present trouble, as the first work I mean to set about is the *Life of Shakspeare*. For this I have a good many materials already in print, to be woven together into a connected narrative with the addition of some information obtained too late for my octavo edition. Will you allow me once again to resume our Shakspearian disquisition,— 'Age cannot wither it, nor custom stale its infinite variety.' "

To his humble friend Jordan he is equally commu-

nicative later in the same year,—says it is long since
they have had any Shakspearian talk, "for that càn
never tire;" sends him also a prospectus of the proposed "new edition of the Poet, in fifteen volumes,
royal quarto, embellished by Heath from paintings
by Stothard;" afterwards announces that "he will
be at Stratford to-morrow (Nov. 19), on his way to
Ireland, and means to call upon him," and finishes,
as usual, with a good supply of queries.

The reference to Steevens in the following letter
from Lord Charlemont, as in that from Jephson,
arose from the unhappy disposition of that gentleman
to pursue in bitterness of spirit any supposed adversary or rival.   Although he had at one time, as we
have seen, recommended his then friend to edit
Shakspeare, compliance with this wish extinguished
his favour, if not friendship.   The younger Critic became in his eyes offensive, because he could not acquiesce in all opinions of the elder.   The results were
actual hostility to Malone, whom in order to annoy,
he re-published his own edition in 1793, to prevent
any re-issue by one now considered by him an intruder.

I have lately seen (October, 1793),—for Heaven forbid
that I should have bought!—Steevens's last edition of Shakspeare.   You know I always disliked the man, and certainly
the manner in which he mentions you has by no means
diminished my dislike.   In all he says there is but too visibly
a feeble, though, thanks to his slender abilities, a fruitless
attempt to damn with faint praise, which is certainly the
species of satire least creditable to its author.   Besides, that
a publication at this period has at least the appearance of
being meant to check the progress of your intended quarto,

and indeed he has taken care to preserve for himself the only
advantage he can ever have over you, by making his edition
far more legible than that which you last published.   The
quarto however will not I trust, be affected by it: indeed,
I now wish for its success more ardently than ever.   Yet it is
whispered here among the booksellers that the present state
of the times may possibly retard its coming forth.   I hope
otherwise.

A month later his lordship writes again :

—— " Labor vincit omnia."

Improbus—with your ardour, talents, and indefatigable
diligence, my dearest Malone, it is utterly impossible you
should fail of success.   We may now flatter ourselves that
we shall shortly know all that ever can be known of that
first of bards, whose writings alone would have rendered the
poetick fame of his country immortal.

All I dread is that your sight—with which mine has a sad
fellow-feeling—will never hold out to the end of your pursuit; and the bare idea of your having examined *three thousand antique papers*, the greater part of which were legible
with difficulty, makes, I confess, my poor eyes ache. . . . .

He adverts again to the quarto edition, and learns
from Mercier, " an intelligent bookseller in Dublin,
that some of the plates are already finished and well
executed."   But this information proved erroneous.
The times also would not admit of expensive editions
such as the quarto with plates; nor even the quarto
form without plates, as he next proposed.   Two
years, 1794-95, were spent in various projects between him and the booksellers, without satisfactory
results.   His first edition had been some time exhausted.   All that was done to replace it was a
cheap reprint, in seven small volumes, without the
dissertations or poems ;—so insignificant in his view,

as to take the trouble to disclaim connection with it in the journals.

At length in 1795, another plan of publication found favour, which may be considered in effect after long delay, great labour, and some changes of design, the one ultimately adopted, though he did not live to bring forth what was nevertheless all his own. His views, such as they then were, will be found in the prospectus.*

* "Reverting, however, to his original idea (from which he was very reluctantly induced to depart), that of giving a new and splendid edition of the plays and poems of the author without engravings, he intended to present the public with a second edition of his former work, in twenty volumes, royal octavo, on a larger paper and type, both for the text and commentaries, than have ever been employed in any edition of *Shakspeare* with notes. The first six volumes will be ready for publication in 1796; and the remainder of the work, in two deliveries of seven volumes each, will be published with all convenient speed.

"The first volume will be appropriated to an entirely new *Life of Shakspeare* (compiled from original and authentic documents), which is now nearly ready for the press; the second and third to Mr. Malone's *History of the Stage*, considerably enlarged, and his other dissertations illustrative of the poet's works; together with the prefaces of former editors, to which some new elucidations will be added. The twentieth volume will comprise Shakspeare's poems, and the remaining sixteen his plays which will be arranged in the order in which they are supposed by Mr. Malone to have been written; with the editor's commentaries as well as those of his predecessors, and several new annotations.

"To the plays it is not proposed to annex any engravings; but the *Life of Shakspeare* will be ornamented with a delineation of his bust at Stratford, of the head of which Mr. Malone is possessed of a *fac-simile*, the engraved portraits of Sir Thomas Lucy and Mr. John Coombe, from drawings made on purpose for his work, in 1793, by Mr. Sylvester Harding; also, with an engraving of Shakspeare, not from factitious or fictitious representation of that poet, but from a drawing of the same size as the original, made in 1786 by Mr. Humphry, from the only authentic portrait now known, that which was formerly in the possession of Sir William D'Avenant, and now belonging to the heir of the late Duke of Chandos."

CHAPTER X.

1794—1797.

Jephson's Poem and Letters—Another Tender Attachment—Death of Boswell—Aubrey's Papers—The Irelands Shakspeare Forgeries—Letter of Burke—Lord Charlemont—New Tragedy by Jephson—Lord Orford—Reynolds' Memoir and Works—Death of Burke.

IN the office of literary accoucheur to *Roman Portraits*, a reminder occasionally dropped from the parent to keep him up to his work. Here we are permitted to witness the throes of the poet in the act of delivery; for alas! who fated to cudgel his wits for the entertainment of the public can forget the self-imposed toil of the process! He writes from Castletown (Ireland) early in January 1794 :—

You are by this time, I suppose, returned from Cheshire,—I heartily hope with your health improved, your eyes strengthened, and again assailable by letter. In my last, I gave my opinion that it was not necessary to make any alteration in the first couplet of Cicero's character; but if you don't think so, the following line (pretty nearly your own words) may do, viz. :—

> " But all these desperate parricides concealed
> A woman's tongue," &c.

I am glad you are pleased with the note upon the poor Queen of France. Pray alter it as little as possible, for it runs so well in its present form that it drew streams of tears down the cheeks of two or three very sensible ladies who read my copy of it here. It gives me pleasure to think that in a work of mine there will be at least one striking passage

P

which belongs to you properly.   I have a long and, I think, very good concluding note for Julius Cæsar ready to send when you give me advice it may be time for it. · I have also made great additions to Augustus and the Augustan age, which I believe I have not yet sent you; and a very long note, or rather short essay, upon the Roman Constitution, for the conclusion of all.

I have added an entire new character of Octavia, sister of Augustus and wife of Anthony, to be inserted immediately after Anthony and Cleopatra.   She was by all accounts a most amiable creature, and forms a good contrast to her husband's harlot, Cleopatra.   I hope you will like it. I see the speedy publication of Conteau* again advertised in the *Whitehall Evening Post,* but I have not heard from Reeves this long time. . . . . I send you Octavia, and hope you will treat her better than Anthony did.

Several letters follow upon the same theme. Additional notes were necessary; new lines to be introduced; re-arrangement of passages made; words altered for others of superior elegance or force; in short, all the processes common to inventive labourers in the workshop of literature.

In the summer of 1794, though at the end of the book season, the poem, closely revised, came out in an expensive form.   The author wanted money much, but buyers were then few, and he must be content to wait for a more propitious moment.   To Malone, who had taken a trip to Brighton for recreation, his obligations were freely acknowledged.   They were now increased; for this good-natured friend had to send presents of copies to several influential noblemen; to propitiate or answer reviewers; circulate favourable notices; and

---

* *Confessions of James Baptiste Conteau,* also by Jephson, written in exposure of enormities of the French revolutionary leaders.

gain for the work fair play at least, if not favour.* Lord Orford in July received his copy through Malone, for which he returns due thanks, and afterwards sends a criticism to the author. At the same time, he writes— "Lord Orford will be much obliged to Mr. Malone for a print of himself, and another of Mr. Jephson."

Whether our Critic at this moment expected Government patronage, is not clear; but the occasional necessities of an Irish landlord over unpunctual tenants render such boons very agreeable. That a place would have been accepted many years afterwards, his letters disclosed. At either period, his intimate friend Mr. Windham was to have formed the channel to office. Yet it never took effect. Jephson touches upon the subject in one of his letters in October 1794.†

* Two of the noblemen whose good opinions were sought were Lords Orford (lately come to the title) and Mornington. The account of the latter may not be uninteresting, as he was known for keen literary tastes, though not, like Walpole, a professed writer.

"I expected rather more praise from Lord Orford, and much less from Lord Mornington (Marquis Wellesley). The latter is the most fastidious of human critics, and though he has great literature, keen sagacity, and a well-formed taste, praise comes from him like drops out of a still. Besides, we have never (though once I think he loved me like a brother) been cordially reconciled, I mean on his part, since he has known my aversion to that most proper object of it, the M. of B. (Marquis of Buckingham). He and his family were the first patrons and friends of the young Mornington. However, he has said a great deal and well. With Lord Orford's letter you ought to be particularly pleased, as you see how much he is struck with the note on the Queen of France, all the materials for which, and not a little in the wording, I had in letters from you. The merit of the note is its strength and conciseness. Strong facts in strong words."

† "With most fervent earnestness I pray that some considerable improvement in your situation may result from the new Government coalition. The Secretary of State has a multitude of lucrative sinecures at his disposal; and if Windham with such advantages as he at present possesses does not contrive speedily to put you quite at your ease, you must allow me to say he is the most frigid, nominal friend that ever

But another tender attachment affected him more nearly than any disappointment of place. Toward the end of 1794, a tour in Lancashire and Cheshire, to which Jephson refers in one of his letters, had unexpected results. Again he became a victim to the tender passion. Criticism and time had not steeled the heart to love. And shall we be cold enough to blame him? Although once unsuccessful in a suit that lasted nearly a life, why not be permitted to try again? Are the young and the gay alone privileged to seek again and again the tenderest ties of human life? Is a smile all the sympathies we can bestow upon the suitor of sedate age when disappointed in his endeavours to participate in those affectionate endearments which it is the province of woman to bestow? He tried however and again failed. He had once loved " not wisely but too well," and did so a second time. Cupid and his stars had no compassion on a

pretended to the virtue of friendship. How could the D. of Portland refuse him a request, urged as it should be in favour of the most learned man in England (as I really think you are), and universally beloved and respected ? I am very happy to find you have engaged Mr. Gerard Hamilton in the same office ; for he has great zeal for a friend, and delights in negotiating."

Again, in the following month—

" Have we any more intelligence to expect about Lord Fitzwilliam ? If he does not come, perhaps Lord Spencer may ; and with either I think you might be Usher of the Black Rod, a very gentleman-like place, which is attended with no trouble, leaves you at liberty to return to England the moment the session of Parliament ceases, is worth at least 600*l.* per annum, and gives an excellent claim to a sinecure of at least half the value when the administration of a friendly Lord Lieutenant is over."

. . . . The following passage is not very complimentary to two well-known men in Irish politics:—" Disturbing such a character as Lord Fitzgibbon might gratify such men as Mr. Philpot Curran or greasy Jack Egan, but it would be felt by every honest suitor and liberal gentleman at the bar as a national insult and national injury." Curran is mentioned very contemptuously by two or three other Dublin correspondents of Malone—party politics often became there personal antipathies.

kind and affectionate heart eminently fitted for domestic companionship, yet condemned to drift down the stream of life a solitary however unwilling traveller, notwithstanding his own lines evinced the high estimate formed of domestic affection—

> Vain—wealth and fame and fortune's fostering care,
> If no fond breast the splendid blessings share;
> And each day's bustling pageantry once past,
> There—only there our bliss is found at last.

The lady, it appeared—and it is nearly all we can hear of her—was a Miss B——, well known to Mr. Windham, possessed of all the necessary qualities of a good wife; but difficulties now unknown stood in the way. A younger Jephson, nephew of the poet, hopes (November 21, 1794) the case is not so desperate as Malone thinks. "I have heard as high an account of her as can be given of woman. The portraiture you sent me was very pleasing and satisfactory. . . . . Nothing but your evil genius, who seems to have discovered with cruel sagacity where you are most vulnerable, could have dashed so fair a prospect." In the same strain, Lord Charlemont, Chetwood who knew her personally, the two Jephsons, uncle and nephew, allude to the subject in their letters of this date, and regret the result, for the sake of both parties. Fate had decreed him irreversibly a bachelor!

A characteristic homily upon love from the noble peer, a happy papa of sixty-seven, to the despairing bachelor of fifty-four, reached the latter in July 1795.

Tant pis pour elle! My dearest Malone,—She has been able strongly to attach you, and must therefore be a woman of excellent sense; neither do I in the least doubt that she is possessed of every amiable quality, and of every elegant

accomplishment. Yet one thing I am sure she wants —
namely, prudence. Since of all the men I ever knew, you
are the best adapted to make happy the woman of your
choice in the state of wedlock. *Tant pis donc pour elle.*

As for you, amusement and consequent forgetfulness are
your best remedies. The specifics, however, are, I am well
aware, not easy to be procured, but your literary turn, in a
town like London, can scarcely, I should hope, fail in pro-
viding you with the first; and Shakspeare may, perhaps,
now be more profitable to you than ever he has yet been.
That I most sincerely feel for you, and with you, is most
certain. For never having but once in my life suffered love
in your way, I never could have been precisely in your pre-
dicament. I have still known enough of the passion to be
thoroughly acquainted with all its effects.

Why will she not give you reason to be angry? *Dépit* is
sometimes, though indeed not often, a tolerable resource.
But this, I find, is denied you. Still, however, you are not
without hopes. Neither am I. For I think it scarcely
possible that a woman, such as you describe, should not
finally return the passion of a man such as I know you to be.
Should this happen, which I by no means think improbable,
hang me if I would not, for some short time at least, endeavour to repay her in her own coin. But this, with you,
I suppose is heresy.

Bewildered by what would appear the vacillating
conduct of the lady, alarmed by the results of the war,
doubtful of Irish loyalty, and the consequent stability
of his property in that country, he proceeded in a
moment of fright, and unknown to his family, to ad-
vertise it for sale. From this he was soon dissuaded.
Good-nature had caused some temporary difficulty;
rents were irregular; small loans had been advanced
to friends on pressing emergencies, and not repaid; so
that he was less at ease than usual; and this may have
given the first idea of accepting, if offered, some suit-

able place.   In the meantime, always careful of his
friends, he had secured a small office at Gibraltar,
through the interest of Mr. Windham, for one of the
younger Jephsons, who in action with an enemy's ship
on the passage thither, had an opportunity, as a volunteer in working a gun, of distinguishing himself, and
was complimented on the occasion by Lord St. Vincent.

Early in 1795 death unexpectedly carried off his
friend Boswell, whose volumes have ensured fame,
while among the waspish professors of criticism they
have scarcely given him character.   Between the biographer and his labours some have drawn a very wide
distinction.   One has taken rank among the undying
productions of our country.   The other is absurdly
alleged to have been a simpleton, a toady, a flatterer,
almost a fool.   Nay, undoubted independence and truth-
telling even made him enemies at the moment.   " I will
not pare my tiger's claws down to those of a cat for any
one," was the manly declaration regarding Dr. Johnson's sarcasms.   An opportunity was, therefore, taken
in one of the newspapers after his death, and recently
in works of more pretension, to sketch him unfairly ;
to take measure of the workman, not of the work ; to
lower the greater to the standard of the less.   But
Malone flew to the rescue ; and as we might expect
from a kindly spirit, rendered due credit to an erring
nature of many foibles, but with talents beyond dispute.*   Nay, the departed seemed almost to have
expected something of posthumous aid from his good-
humoured friend ; for Bennet Langton thus writes to
Malone in August, 1795—

* *Gentleman's Magazine*, June, 1795.

I have not had any information of the Boswell family since an affecting letter from Sir William Forbes of Edinburgh, giving an account of his attendance at the last solemn office of our poor friend's interment at Auchinleck. I find, sir, the poor man had referred to you, jointly with Sir William and Mr. Temple, the friendly task of judging which and what parts of his writings left behind him may be thought of for publication.

Absence from town was frequent during the year, caused, perhaps, by attachment to the lady in Lancashire, of whom his old friend Chetwood thus writes in January, 1795—

My wishes for your success in your matrimonial pursuit were strong when I saw you, and much stronger afterwards when, in the neighbourhood of Warrington, I heard a character of the lady that attracted me most warmly to her. Among other traits, I was charmed with one—namely, that she is almost adored by the poor of that country.

In March of the same year, the monument to Dr. Johnson being nearly ready for erection, Malone, as an active member of the managing committee, wrote for the epitaph which had been promised by Dr. Parr. An assenting answer was given, to which early in April Malone replies—

" I am sure it is unnecessary to tell you that it was not from any want of attention I did not immediately answer your letter. The truth is, I wished to consult some of the gentlemen to whom the management of Dr. Johnson's monument had been assigned, and had not opportunity of doing so till yesterday. The epitaph which you have written will, I have no doubt, be everything that they could wish ; but as they and the surviving executor (Sir Wm. Scott) cannot properly adopt any inscription without seeing and approving it, and as you might possibly not choose to submit it at all to their inspection unless upon a certain *assurance* of its being adopted, I thought it right to state the circumstance to you before you transmitted the epitaph. The persons I allude to are, Mr. Burke, Mr. Windham, Sir Joseph Banks, Mr. Metcalf and Mr. Boswell, who together with myself are nominated as curators of the monument, and who are all extremely indebted to you for your exertions on the present occasion."

Dr. Parr writes, at the same moment, that he will soon be in town.   Malone replies by inclosing a proposal from Sir William Scott, implying some difference of opinion as to the language employed, which produced cessation of correspondence for more than a month.   Malone then resumes his pen at greater length, fortified by the opinion of the club, that certain alterations should be made in order to suit the general views :—

"*May* 21, 1795.

" DEAR SIR,—Some very pressing business of my own has prevented me a long time from obeying Sir William Scott's desire, who being entirely occupied by the business of the term, requested me to convey to you our joint sentiments on the subject of the two letters with which you favoured us.   I may add, that I felt myself very unequal to the task, as indeed I have nothing more to say respecting the epitaph than what I have said already.

" However, as in a question of this sort authority may be of some weight in a matter where the appeal must finally be to the public, I may mention to you that, as Dr. Johnson had founded what is called the Literary Club, I thought they had a kind of peculiar interest in any inscription to his memory; and therefore took an opportunity, when there happened to be some of our most eminent members present, to repeat your epitaph; and Mr. Fox, Mr. Windham, Mr. Steevens, Sir Wm. Scott, as well as all the other members present, were decidedly of opinion that *probabilis* was an utterly inadequate epithet as descriptive of Dr. Johnson's character as a poet; and they were equally clear that some eulogium on him as a poet was absolutely necessary to the *integrity* of his character. I do, therefore, most earnestly request that you will give us some other epitaph; for the total omission is what none of his friends are willing to agree to. Permit me to add one other consideration, which perhaps when you turn it in your mind, as I am sure your candour will lead you to do, may have some little weight.

" The world in general consider Johnson as a great writer in prose and verse. Now, under the words '*preceptori recte vivendi gravissimo,*' his admirable powers as a writer of prose are not *necessarily* included, though I know they are large enough to comprehend them; but that his great excellence in this respect is not necessarily included in these words appears from hence—that Bishop Butler and Bishop Coneybeare may be both described very truly as '*preceptores recte vivendi gravissimi,*' and yet neither of them were eminent for purity, elegance, or strength of language. If therefore no character at all is given of Johnson as a poet (which I think seems rather to be your wish), and the other words do not necessarily imply an eulogium on him as a prose writer, will not his admirers, which are all the judicious part of mankind, have some reason to consider the inscription, however masterly in many other respects, as an imperfect delineation of him?

"I may add also, that the universality of his knowledge, the promptness of his mind in producing it on all occasions in conversation, and the vivid eloquence with which he clothed his thoughts however suddenly called upon, formed in my apprehension, as I formerly took the liberty of mentioning to you, a very distinguished part of the character of his genius, and placed him on higher ground than, perhaps, any other quality that can be named. This has been wholly omitted, on grounds which I by no means wish to controvert; but at the same time, it surely may be properly urged as a circumstance that entitles us, his ardent admirers, to hope that his character as a *poet* may not *also* be omitted; and I therefore only mention it as an auxiliary argument to induce you to be a little more *liberal* to us in that part of the inscription concerning which we differ.

"Thus, dear Sir, I have, as shortly as I could, though I fear very imperfectly, stated our sentiments on this subject. An amicable discussion of this kind does not stand in need of any apology, and therefore, I shall not take up your time in making any.

"Poor Mr. Boswell died on Tuesday morning, after an illness of five weeks. Just before he fell ill he had prepared a very civil answer to your letter in the last *Gentleman's Magazine*."

This clever and indeed unanswerable appeal, unlike the round-robin to Johnson himself on a similar occasion, overcame the self-will of the author. He gave way with a tolerably good grace; and Malone in July following thus expresses the satisfaction arising from the alteration :—

" I did not trouble you with a letter merely to say that Sir William Scott and I am much pleased with your alteration of the epitaph, and neither of us thought the new words at all too *honied*. The Greek line is most happily changed, and may set all cavil at defiance."

This accomplished for the dead, another difficulty remained as to the living, of which Malone writing to Dr. Parr, may still be the historian.

" The inscription has been in Mr. Bacon's hands for some weeks past, and I did not think you would have had any more trouble with it; but in that part which relates particularly to himself, he wishes not to be shorn of his Academical honours, and that posterity should know he was entitled to annex R.A. to his name. You will be so good therefore, as to Latinize this for him, and to say how it shall stand. The words are at present, Faciebat Johannes Bacon Sculptor Ann. Christ. M.DCC.LXXXXV."

The poor sculptor pleaded for retention of the Academic honours of art in vain. The magnate of Greek and Latin declined compliance; and Malone curtly communicates the reception of the denial. " I have called on Mr. Bacon, and he very reluctantly has

agreed to omit any notice of his being a Royal Acade-
mician."

In the summer (1795), desirous of subduing unpleasant recollections, he visited Oxford. The aim
was to do for John Aubrey, the antiquary, what he
also intended for Dryden and Pope—that is to tell all
that could be gleaned new of their lives and works.

To the superstitions of that laborious writer—the
apparitions, voices, omens, dreams, and other supernatural fancies, he paid no more attention than sensible men of the present day do to table-turning and
spirit-rapping. But he had great respect, as other
eminent men had, for his facts—for those obvious
and unmistakeable things which impress the eyes and
ears and memory—not such as spring from heated
imaginations.

In the *History of the Stage* (p. 166, Ed. 1790) he
speaks of his works, printed and manuscript, with
great respect. Many of the latter being biographical,
told of men who, when he wrote, had then but just
quitted the world, and of whom the information being
recent, was probably authentic. These he considered
might be edited with advantage, illustrated by his
own researches. To Lord Charlemont he writes:—

" Of the whole of Aubrey's biographical collections
deposited in the Ashmolean Museum, I made a transcript last summer, which will be hereafter laid before the public." To this project allusion is again
made in the *Life of Dryden*.* By letters which I

---

* " Mr. Aubrey, who was acquainted with Dryden, informs us in his
Life of Milton (which, together with his other curious accounts of English
writers, I hope speedily to give the public), that our author (Dryden),

have seen, some jealousy arose among certain literati, as if other transcribers of the same papers were to be excluded; but this idea had no sufficient foundation. The design as we know never took effect. In one of Thorpe's catalogues a MS. volume on this subject, said to be his, was priced at twelve guineas. In the catalogue of the younger Boswell's books, two lots are transcripts from Aubrey, which doubtless came from the same pen.

At this moment a subject fitted beyond all others to exercise the discriminative powers in which he excelled, came before the public in the alleged discovery of Shakspeare Papers by the Irelands, father and son. The fraud was sufficiently daring; the skill employed quite enough to impose upon ordinary persons; and it was carried on with unusual effrontery. But with a judge in the way so scrutinizing as Malone, the moment could scarcely be considered favourable for success in such a deception. No colourable guarantee could or would be given of authenticity. Of the internal evidence he was perhaps the most complete master then living, having spent much of a life in the study of all the essential points bearing upon the question of ancient English composition. Examined by these lights, added to the suspicious and strict secrecy preserved as to the supposed original possession, he soon pronounced the papers to be forgeries.

To Lord Charlemont, his usual depositary of lite-

before he wrote this drama *State of Innocence*, waited on the blind bard, and asked his permission to put his great poem into rhyme. 'Ay,' said Milton, ' you may *tag* my verses if you will.' "

rary intelligence, the fact was early communicated. His lordship thus adverts to it, July 1795 :—

> I have seen in the papers, which, by the way, my eyes will scarcely permit me to read, some account of the wonderful Shakspearian discoveries. And even before your argument convinced me of the forgery, I gave very little credit to it. It promised too much to keep its word ; and I am only sorry that Mr. Steevens is not proprietor of the manuscripts. The lines you transcribe as part of one of the sonnets would alone be sufficient to prove the absurdity of the forger.

Literary imposture occasionally finds a ready ear in our country. Whenever a good excuse offers, we are willing to add to the fame of a popular idol, and in the first moments of enthusiasm at a new discovery are prone to indulge rather our partiality than judgment. So it proved with many in respect to these documents. Every one was interested in them because Shakspeare was every one's author. But the gradual increase of successive " discoveries " led from surprise to suspicion ; and although antiquaries of name avowed their belief, while others continued in doubt, the great body of professed commentators,— Malone, Reed, Farmer, Ritson, Lord Orford, Bishop of Dromore, Bishop of Salisbury (detector of Lander's forgery),—and many more of the most distinguished men of the day, deemed them spurious.

Malone, as best fitted for the work, was persuaded to take the lead in disabusing the credulous. A few inquiries moderate in tone in the magazines, brought forth angry replies, sneers, and abuse. At length, early in 1796, the publication of a two-guinea folio of the Papers, the advanced guard of two more at the same price, threatened such an attack on the good sense and purses of the people, that he deemed it due to them and himself to take the field in form, and destroy the fabrication for ever.

The mode chosen was that of a letter to Lord Charlemont—*An Inquiry into the Authenticity of Certain Papers attributed to Shakspeare.* But the letter grew to a book of more than four hundred pages. From the almost inexhaustible stores of the writer he proves from "orthography, phraseology, dates given, or deducible by inference, and dissimilitude of handwriting, that not a single paper or deed in this extraordinary volume was written or executed by the person to whom it was ascribed."

Nothing can be more complete than the exposure. Not a point is neglected, not one remains doubtful; while many are suggested and solved which were new to those unaccustomed to such studies, and which may be brought into play should a similar cheat be ever attempted again. Not the least conclusive testimony was that of Steevens, whose candour overpowered former feelings of alienation or rivalry: "Mr. Steevens presents his best compliments to Mr. Malone, and most sincerely thanks him for his very elegant present, which exhibits one of the most decisive pieces of criticism that was ever produced."

In the meantime *Vortigern*, one of the spurious family, was accepted at Drury Lane, with a prologue from Sir James B. Burgess. Pye, the Poet Laureate, also a believer for a time, had written one, but was just in time to withdraw it. Merry wrote the epi-

logue, and Mrs. Jordan spoke it. Three hundred
pounds were given by the managers for the right of
representation. But Malone's book came out at the
moment, and being likely to mar its success, Ireland
issued a hand-bill attacking his opponent, and be-
speaking the candour of a British audience.* Assailed
at length by general discredit from the researches of
the Critic as well as public taste, persistence in the
fraud ceased. Its perpetrator, young Ireland, gave
the story of forgery in detail, confessing all the
fabrications to be his own, and begun at the age of
nineteen.

It is often amusing to see how little grateful are
dupes to those who undeceive them. So it was with
these papers. When critical proof and open confession of the forger no longer left a peg to hang a doubt
upon, pamphlets came forth little complimentary to
the detector of the fraud. Chalmers favoured the
public with an *Apology for the Believers in the Shakspeare Papers.* And Caldecott, under the name of
Samuel Ireland, father of the perpetrator of the
offence, with *An Investigation of Mr. Malone's
claims to the character of a Scholar or Critic; being
an Examination of his Inquiry into the Authenticity
of the Shakspeare MSS.* Two or three others had

* " *Vortigern.* A malevolent and impotent attack on the Shakspeare
MSS. having appeared on the eve of the representation of the play of
Vortigern, evidently intended to injure the interest of the proprietor of
the MSS., Mr. Ireland feels it impossible within the short space of time
that intervenes between the publishing and the representation to produce an answer to the most unfounded and illiberal assertions in Mr.
Malone's *Inquiry*. He is therefore induced to request that the play
of *Vortigern* may be heard with that candour that has ever distinguished
a British audience."

Q

preceded or followed them; and then this great "discovery" passed silently to deserved oblivion.

An impression prevailed that these forgeries had been long contemplated. In 1785, a rumour circulated among literary men that in an attorney's office in Warwickshire, wills had been found of the Shakspeare family, throwing new lights upon its history. Such a report drew many inquirers. Malone wrote privately (April 7?) to Mr. Nichols of the *Gentleman's Magazine* for information, who however could furnish little more than that some details had transpired through Mr. Samuel Ireland, in *Illustrations of the Avon*. The story then died silently away.

Now that it suffered violent death, he amused himself as chief executioner, by collecting all pamphlets and papers written on either side into volumes, which passed under the auctioneer's hammer at his sale in 1818.

On the first appearance of his book, a copy was sent to Burke, who thus replies :—

My dear Sir,—Your letter is dated the first of the month, but I did not receive it with the welcome and most acceptable present that came along with it, till late in the evening of yesterday. However, I could not postpone the satisfaction offered to me by your partiality and goodness. I got to the seventy-third page before I went to sleep, to which what I read did not greatly contribute.

I do not know that for several years I longed so much for any literary object as for the appearance of this work. Far from having my expectations disappointed, I may say with great sincerity that they have been infinitely exceeded. The spirit of that sort of criticism by which false pretence and imposture are detected, was grown very rare in this century.

You have revived it with great advantage. Besides doing everything which the vindication of the first genius, perhaps in the world, required from the hand of him who studied him the most, and illustrated him the best; you have in the most natural, happy, and pleasing manner, and as if you were drawn into it by your subject, given us a very interesting history of our language during that important period in which, after being refined by Chaucer, it fell into the rudeness of civil confusion, and then continued in a pretty even progress to the state of correctness, strength, and elegance, in which we see it in your writings.

Your note, in which for the first time you leave the character of the antiquary, to be, I am afraid, but too right in that of a prophet, has not escaped me. Johnson used to say he loved a good hater. Your admiration of Shakspeare would be ill sorted, indeed, if your taste (to talk of nothing else) did not lead you to a perfect abhorrence of the French revolution and all its works. Once more thank you most heartily for the great entertainment you have given me as a critick, as an antiquary, a philologist, and as a politician. I shall finish the book I think to-day.

This will be delivered to you by a young kinsman of mine, of Exeter College, in Oxford. I think him a promising young man, very well qualified to be an admirer of yours, and I hope, to merit your notice, of which he is very ambitious. I have the honour to be, my dear sir, with true respect and affection, your most faithful and very much obliged and humble servant,

EDMUND BURKE.

Beaconsfield, April 8, 1796.

Lord Charlemont writes a long letter in August; regrets having ordered " Ireland's magnificent and ostentatious deceit ; " thanks him for literary purchases; asks whether a Liverpool trader be a sufficiently safe conveyance for his treasures to Dublin; and refers to his correspondent's literary employments and those of some of their mutual friends.

I rejoice to hear you have so many things on the anvil; every one of them is a resource against *ennui*—of all human maladies the worst, since all other diseases affect the mind through the body, while this pest of our nature seems to originate in the soul. Your *Life of Shakspeare* will, I am confident, be curious, and, as that more immediately belongs to you, I think you are in the right to give it the preference of (to) *Aubrey.* I know nothing of particulars, but am really impatient for *Dryden's Prose,* as I regard his style as one of the first in our language, and wish that it were more read and imitated than it has been.

As to my dear Sir Joshua's works, I more than long for them, not only on account of their intrinsic merit, but because I was and am, in spite of fate, his friend.

Poor Burke! I never, indeed, expected that he would get the better of his loss,[*] and am happy to find that, at times, he can forget it. *There* was a man whose spirit seemed to be almost independent of body, though even he is weighed down by bodily infirmities. Yet his mind, too, must suffer greatly from the present torrent of French success; and I hear that his *Regicide Peace* is suppressed, since no publication could assuredly be worse timed.[†]

The death of Lord Orford, which, from your account, I cannot but fear, will greatly grieve me. As an old and kind friend, I shall most sincerely lament him. As a literary character, I must deplore a loss to the world which will be scarcely retrievable, since such a union of the scholar and the gentleman will with difficulty be found.

Why must Lord Macartney, spite of ill health and increasing years, be for ever, like Cain, sentenced to be a wanderer, after all his peregrinations of Europe, Asia, and America? Why must he be condemned to leave his bones perhaps in Africa, among Hottentots?[‡] Indeed, his English

[*] That of his son, and only remaining child.

[†] This proved to be unfounded. Few who knew Burke would believe its suppression; but his lordship's politics were strong the other way.

[‡] His lordship, who mingled much in literary and fashionable coteries, and to whom I find several references by Malone, had been recently appointed Governor of the Cape of Good Hope.

peerage is, in my opinion, purchased dearly.   I was in hopes that his Chinese work would have been published long since.

Towards the close of the year, his good offices in the introduction of a new tragedy, *The Conspiracy*, to Drury Lane, were again sought by his friend Jephson.   It was taken from *Metastasio*, and ran only three nights.   Of other details Malone must be the historian.

" On this story, from *Clemenza di Tito*, Mr. Jephson produced a tragedy.   It was performed twice (an error, thrice) at the theatre in Drury Lane, in 1796, and then laid aside.   The proprietors of the theatre having determined that authors should no longer have their third nights, but the ninth part of 300*l*. for each night of performance, Mr. Jephson was entitled to 66*l*. 13*s*., for which Mr. Sheridan, after repeated delays, gave his draft on his banker, which was never paid ; being the ' New way of paying old debts ' adopted in that theatre since he became possessed of it."

Occasionally, Lord Orford and Malone continued their former meetings ; for who could resist so attractive a story-teller, or doubt so retentive a memory ?   At seventy-nine, with much bodily infirmity, two months before death, we find it as vivid as ever.

" *January 3rd*, 1797.—Lord Orford told me that he had seen the letter of Anne Clifford, Countess of Dorset, &c., which he had inserted in the *World*, without mentioning his authority.   It was shown to him by Mr. West, who got it (not very honestly) from the second Lord Orford's papers.

" The old Lady Dacres whom he has mentioned as having conversed with, one who had seen the old Countess of Desmond, was the wife of Richard, Lord Dacres, who died in ——. She was his second wife, and married in 1624; therefore, probably born about 1600. Her daughter was married to a Mr. Chaloner, by whom she had a son, who became Speaker in Richard Cromwell's Parliament. From a descendant of this Mr. Chute (*sic*) Lord Orford derived his information.

" It was at his instance that Lord Corke published the *Memoirs of Cary, Earl of Monmouth*. Lord Orford read them once in MS., and remembers a passage which Lord Corke suppressed. Cary told that, being of the bed-chamber to King Charles, it was his duty to light him upstairs; and that the king having returned unexpectedly one night, when either Henry Jermyn or Henry Percy was with the queen (for both were her favourites), Cary, to save her majesty from being caught, dropped the candle out of his hand when ascending the stairs, so as to give the gallant an opportunity of getting off.

" Lord Hervey wrote very curious memoirs of his own time, which are yet extant in the hands of General Hervey, he believes. Lord Lansdown possessed them for two years; and, therefore, probably had the MS. transcribed.*

" Of the Marquis of Halifax's curious memoirs

---

* Published in 1848; and afford curious revelations of the intrigues and manners of the time.

there were two copies. One was destroyed by Lord Nottingham, the other remained long in the hands of Lady Burlington; but Pope, finding that in several places the Papists of the time of Charles II. and James, were represented in an unfavourable light, prevailed upon her to burn them."

The conclusion of the Ireland forgery left him free to pursue the more grateful employment of collecting and editing the works of his dear friend Reynolds. This had been early designed, sanctioned by the approval of Burke, as the most appropriate tribute to the memory of the departed. He had been two years employed also upon an enlarged and revised history of the stage—but this was put aside for a time. Reynolds commanded more immediate attention; and his eyes found relief in ceasing to decipher old papers. To Lord Charlemont the intention as usual had been communicated, who thus replies, November 1794:—"I am glad to find that our ever-to-be-lamented Sir Joshua's works are in such forwardness. I have read his *Journey to Flanders* which he lent me in MS., and like it extremely. It is the best *voyage pittoresque* now extant."

The work appeared in the spring of 1797. No methodical or extended biography was attempted. A plain, unpretending outline gives us the main facts of his career, followed by the *Discourses, Idlers, a Journey to Flanders and Holland, Notes upon Du Fresnoy's Art of Painting.* These were his own. But with them are printed, as Mason did in 1783 at York in order to complete the basis for Reynolds's notes—Mason's translation of *Du Fresnoy*, Dryden's preface to it, Pope's *Epistle to Jervas* on the same, Du Fresnoy's *Account of Certain Painters; Chronological and Alphabetical List of Painters.*

In a pretty long letter from Bath written in May under severe illness, Burke gives Malone all credit for his labours and discriminative remarks. But, alas! the writer himself, while exciting the sympathy of his fellow-mourner for one whom they so much loved, was soon called by death to mingle with those for whom that fellow-mourner was left also to lament. An affecting incident, characteristic · of the warm affections of this great man, is mentioned on this occasion by Malone. In writing to the latter about Reynolds, although so many years had elapsed since his death, *Burke had blotted the paper with his tears.* He had just returned from Bath to Beaconsfield to die.

Lady Inchiquin wrote to Malone soon afterwards of their mutual friend : " Alas! my dear sir, I can give you but a heart-breaking account of our poor friend Mr. Burke. We are anxiously awaiting the return of a messenger, who we have every reason to fear will bring tidings of his death."

Two days afterwards he received the following :—

SIR,—It is with the deepest affliction I am to communicate to you the death of Mr. Burke, who expired last night at half-past twelve o'clock.

The long and unshaken friendship which had subsisted between you and him renders this a painful communication; but it is a duty I owe to such friendship.

He died as he lived, great and good. His mind remained collected and calm to the last. Mrs. Burke exceeds even her wonted fortitude; and in this trying moment displays all the pious resignation of the Christian.

I am, Sir, your very faithful servant,

EDM. NAGLE.

Beaconsfield, Sunday, 9th July, 1797.

Lord Charlemont, in a long letter, in August, thus notices him among other friends in a mortuary list sent by Malone. The allusion to his early circumstances must of course be taken, as no doubt is meant, with many grains of allowance; and his lordship's politics speak for themselves. He occasionally flings a jocular sarcasm at the Tory propensities of his correspondent; and at the conclusion of this letter good-humouredly takes him to task on the subject at length. He complains also of the state of Ireland, of his poverty, of the poverty of those around him who have not the means to keep up their usual mode of living. Hence he begs that Málone will suspend his literary purchases for him for the present—"To which abstinence from the favourite food of my mind, you may be assured my poverty and not my will consents."

Your list of deaths is indeed a sad one—Poor Burke! one of my oldest and best acquaintances and friends! I knew him intimately long before he was a politician, and when without a crown in his pocket he was a happy man. I knew him intimately at his first introduction to the political world, when also he was as happy as the adoration of his friends and a perfect rectitude of conduct could make him. I have also known him intimately when he was not quite so happy. His heart was excellent. His abilities were supernatural; and a deficiency in prudence and political wisdom (!) could alone have kept him within the rank of mortals.

Lord Orford, to whose kindness and friendship I have been early and long obliged, was undoubtedly the most

pleasing companion I ever knew.   He has also, I fear, made
a chasm in society which it will be difficult to fill.

Mason, I thank fate, I only knew by his writings, which
are alone sufficient to ensure the regret of any man who
pretends to the smallest degree of note.   As for Dr. Warren, death owed him a grudge for the numerous victims
rescued from his dart; and at last revenged himself by that
fatal blow on the stomach.

Toward the end of the year Malone, as already
hinted, found an assailant in a pamphlet concerning
the papers of Aubrey in the Ashmolean Museum at
Oxford.   It was said he had acquired permission
from the authorities to copy them to the exclusion of
a Mr. Caulfield, although their transcription had
been accomplished by him before, and their exterior
expressly marked—" These fragments collected and
arranged by E. M. 1792."   But the charge came
from a portion of the Ireland party.

Letters from various correspondents at this time
indicate something of his various pursuits.   Jeremy
Bentham writes to know whether the charter of
Queen Elizabeth for the foundation of Westminster
School can be seen anywhere, in print or manuscript,
without formal application to the Dean and Chapter.
The no less celebrated John Wilkes assures him that
every assistance shall be rendered to his " curious
researches " that can be given by the city authorities,
superiors, and subordinates.   Lord Charlemont says
he has picked up an old play in Dublin, which, not
being in any of the collections sent him from London,
he presumes to be scarce:—*A Chaste Mayd in
Cheapside*, by Thomas Midelton, Gent., 1630.   A
criticism follows upon *Love in Ruins*, which is

founded upon the same story as Lord Orford's excellent tragedy, who however declares that it was taken
from the confession of one of Tillotson's penitents;
but to go farther back, the same tale appears in one
of the Queen of Navarre's novels. He will not,
however, receive anything against Lord Orford's
originality. To that nobleman the Irish peer, as
we have seen, was strongly attached; again notices
his death as a loss to writers of literary memorials
of his time; desires his special and affectionate
remembrance to him in many letters to Malone; and
amid others equally strong, thus says in November
1787:—"You do me perfect justice in supposing that
I should be sorry indeed to receive Mr. Walpole's
book at the price you mention. My most truly affectionate compliments and sincere respects to that most
amiable of men."

His lordship also shortly before Burke's death
had written to Malone in alarm at the chance of
being embroiled in politics with his old friend,
though by no fault of his own. An injudicious
Irish politician had addressed him a pamphlet, in
reply to one of the letters on a *Regicide Peace*,
intermingled with abuse of their celebrated writer.
But though the peer found fault with the politics
of the commoner, no attack upon him could receive
the slightest countenance. Should the piece become
known, Malone was to deny, in his lordship's name,
the slightest knowledge of its production. If it
escaped notice, let it remain so; and accordingly it
passed at once unobserved to that populous yet noise-
less region into which Fame declines to enter.

CHAPTER XI.

Correspondence—A Rapt Poet—Excursion to Brighton—Portrait by
Ozias Humphrey—State of Ireland—Earl of Clare—The Union—
Prose of Dryden—Letter of Lord Hailes—George Canning and the
Literary Club—A Visitor from Stratford.

AMONG his correspondents at this time on various,
though unimportant topics, were Bindley, Cumber-
land, Sir George Beaumont, Lord Harrington, Duke
of Portland, and a few others.   Some obscure writers
" pressed by difficulties " seek subscriptions for their
distress, or opinions upon forthcoming works.   Some
have " high opinions of your learning, your worth,
and your benevolent nature, which have been entertained by the ' mighty dead,' and by many of the
most wise and virtuous of the living."   One is from
an unfortunate Navy chaplain, who has sold off every
book and rag he possessed for the means of sub-
sistence :—" I have no resource, sir, for bread but
in Providence and my pen.   I possess no official or
other stated income.   I am old.   Neither my age,
my indigence, nor inclination allow of a return to a
sea life.   My few relations of fortune are far as India
from me.   My only alternative is to beg or to starve."

I extract this specimen of prosaic misery in contrast to another from a rapt poet—flighty as the
wildest who has trodden Parnassus—who seeks " an
inheritance on the Elysian heights "—" an asylum in

the arms of genius "—" while others are mad for a few weeds of fame and money !" We hear occasionally of the erratic and unworldly sons of song, but the specimen given below is worth preserving as a curiosity.*

* " Be so good as to excuse the freedom of a pen that springs forward in the present airy epoch,* from the pinion which never cut the fantastic winds of fortune or of fame ; a pen guided by the fingers of one who has been so happy as to enjoy himself serenely to the present moment in the pleasing circles of science and the Muses, careless of fame and the volant revolutionary system of interest—unknown to the world individually.

"I could not have ventured, I presume, to have taken upon me the liberty of writing to you under any other idea than that you delighted in the beauteous regions and temples of the Muses, wherein, also, I love to ramble. And, notwithstanding it was with much reluctance (fearful of offending) that I at length mustered courage enough to spring forward in laying this fragment before you. Since I have had the pleasure of knowing your name (which I esteem reciprocally), while being kept back by the potent arm of timidity, I thought, time after time, of sending you pieces, some written in rhyme, others in blank verse, which have since (as customary with most of my writings) been obliterated in the flames. The fire is the general repository of my Muse.

" And now, sir, since I have so far ventured upon your leisure, permit me to leave the piece, of which you have only a part, with these few encomiums, to battle through, and bring me clear from, the storms and shouts of impropriety in so doing.

" Sir, this (namely, the *Thunderstorm*, containing between eight and nine hundred lines) I have lately written for the purpose of entertaining myself through a secluded hour. But, after pondering over my papers, reflecting on the want of a friendly remark, and entertaining an opinion of the regard which perhaps you may have for a picture of this character, I extracted for you the first canto, wishing to have your opinion thereon. Meantime, I believe I have written, and may venture to recollect with little attention, better pieces, both in rhyme and blank verse ; thinking, sir, that my pen is capable of altering what may be found deficient,—not, surely, that I ever care anything for the press, but to entertain a friend so well myself, sometimes with a view reflected from gloom, from the dawn, or from the angry plains of wars; for my delight is in the epic system.

"I cannot wander into a commenting region of redundance, or to darken the paper with a cloud of words does not become *me*. But, sir, permit

---

* To you singularly ; and if not acceptable, will never be heard of more.

From these and similar taxations he was glad to seek refuge at the sea-side in a visit to his co-executor Metcalfe. *   Here a new scene opened in rank,

me to observe (after, young as I am, being in many parts of the world, abroad and at home, in most kinds of weather, and knowing well the plains of Salisbury) that there is nothing represented but what may be within the boundaries of nature.   That I think it necessary for you to trans-port your soul into the very body of a scene, since the piece is entirely in action, in order to see and enjoy every object in its true colour (for if it cannot withstand such, it will be unworthy of me) ; that, after being brought to the depth of the scene by this first canto, I have a second to introduce you therefrom, and I think with more pleasing and change of variety.

" In the second canto are seen the clouds, the lightning, the rain, and the wind to pass away by degrees, the village getting lighter, &c., &c. ; clouds, in patches, floating in the heavens; with several other representa-tions.   The whole ending with a view of *Emma*, dead, by the side of her weeping lover, and the plains, &c., &c. ; the sun shining, and the clouds level, reclined on the horizon ; which canto, containing about five hun-dred lines, remains among my papers, and to your service.

" Such lines, sir, have dropped almost spontaneously from my pen, and you have them nearly as they fell.   But, notwithstanding, be so good, if such be entertaining to you, as not to excuse but point me my errors and imperfections; for I can freely submit to your advice, and calmly guide my pen amidst either censure or praise.   Criticism is an ornament worthy of a bosom.

" The following section, sir, I will extract for you immediately on re-ceiving a few lines from you by post or otherwise ; tending to entertain you in the vacant time—a piece entirely novel, written in rhyme, which likely you will be more partial to.   Otherwise, if not agreeable, I will call and receive, begging pardon for the liberty taken.

" And now, after stretching out my hand to present you this extract, I once more return to the fields and society of the Muses, while others are mad with a few weeds of fame and money.   An inheritance on the Elysian heights, the fields of Nature, with an asylum in the arms of Genius, is the only desire and wish of,

Sir,

Your most humble and obedient servant

" *At Mr. Kendrick's,*   (while to you and all a stranger),
   Little Bath Street,   JOHN PHELPS TUCKER."
      Cold Bath Square,
         No. 5, ——n, 1797.

* Little of this gentleman appears to have been recorded, excepting that he valued and sought the best literary society, and kept—one of its pleasant accompaniments—a good table.   He was in the House of Commons several years ; his name appears in the round robin attached

gaiety, and female society. But there was nothing to win "a prepossessed mind." The letter is to his favourite sister Catherine, October, 1797 :—

"My excursion to Brighton was quite an impromptu. I stayed there three weeks, and had seventeen dips in a good sea bath, which is a hundred times better than the open sea on that coast. The mornings went off quick enough—the evenings rather tedious, as for want of my (illegible) candles I could not venture to read. Metcalfe generally went to Lady Jersey's to whist—Mrs. Stratford and Lady Heron her only companions—and sometimes to the play, whither I accompanied him two or three times for want of something to do.

"We dined one day at Sir Godfrey Webster's, who is not a bit depressed by the loss of his wife.*
. . . . We had some fine folks there—the Duke of Beaufort and his son, the Marquis of Worcester, who is married to a very pleasing woman, daughter of Lord Gower, and sister to her you met at Cheltenham. There were also Lord Lucan and his daughter, Lady Anne. . . . . Her sister, Lady Spencer, is an agreeable woman; very different in manners.

"I dined one day with the Prince of Wales (not at his own house) and had a great deal of talk with him. But this is an old story, as you have probably

---

to the epitaph on Goldsmith. He gave Dr. Johnson the occasional use of his carriage, and on one occasion took him in it on an excursion through the county of Sussex. His being, with Burke and Malone, an executor of Reynolds, speaks sufficiently for the respect entertained for his character.

* Afterwards Lady Holland.

heard it all from D. (Lord Sunderlin.)   His simple
object is the payment of his debts; and as Pitt will
not do that he has thrown himself upon Fox.   .   .   .
Yet the latter and his party are not very willing to
have anything to do with him.   He retailed all the
common cant about the grievances of the Irish
Catholics with sufficient dexterity and address.   But
I did not let them pass, and fairly told him that they
were merely imaginary, and that their people were
worked up into discontent and clamour about grievances by wicked and artful men for factious purposes.
I shall be, therefore, certainly no favourite at Carlton House.

" I was two or three times at the rooms, but I can
scarcely see anything in large lighted apartments.   It
is surprising how little beauty or attraction there is in
the world, at least to a prepossessed mind.   I dined
with three or four private families, friends of Metcalfe,
where there were ladies—at Lord Lucan's, &c. &c.
(Several parties of female acquaintance are here mentioned.)   And yet among all these various groups I
did not see a single woman, gentle or simple, but
Lady Worcester, that appeared to me to have the
smallest attraction.   How therefore should I ever
get a wife?   Or what ground have I to expect after
all that has happened that any but a mere dowdy will
accept my hand?   Yet I still keep on hoping that
something may happen—and unless it does, the new
peerage will be quite thrown away." *

---

* His brother, who had no children, had received in 1797 a new
patent as Baron Sunderlin of Baronston, "with remainder to his brother,
Edmond Malone, Esq., of Shinglas."

To a sisterly caution on avoiding increase of debts, he enters into a full detail of pecuniary circumstances and resources, by which it appears he was by no means incautious. "When this mortgage is got rid of I shall be one hundred and fifty pounds a year richer, and then my first operation shall be to diminish the sad arrear I owe you. Afterwards, in case of peace, I think I can so manage the Cavan estate as to pay all my debts, and have a *clear* income of from nine hundred to one thousand pounds a year."

How he became introduced to the Prince does not appear—perhaps through Admiral Payne, whose brother, a general officer, was an occasional visitor at Lord Sunderlin's seat in Ireland. The admiral figured a good deal in Brighton and Pall Mall; and few accustomed to stroll for amusement past Dighton's shop at Charing Cross, more than half a century ago, but will remember one of his sketches: "Jack P——, the little Admiral; taken on the Steyne, at Brighton." A reply of his to a visitor at Carlton House is still remembered. "I believe, sir," said the inquirer, "you were bred to the sea?" "No, sir; the sea was *bread* to me, and d—d hard bread it has been!"

Mr. Metcalfe, then his host, writes from Brighton to him in Ireland, two or three years later: "Jack Payne, for so the admiral is always called, is here with the Prince, and he was pleased with the good account you give of his brother, who I have always heard is an excellent cavalry officer." . . . .

"The Prince and Mrs. F. have been here all the season. He is making great alterations. . . The place is full, but not of the best company, for various

R

reasons; and the balls and rooms badly attended, though *they* go to grace them. Your old friend Mr. (or Mrs.) Spencer* is here; so is Baron Graham and his lady; but he has lost all taste for society:"

Another long letter from Lord Charlemont (October, 1797) greets him at Brighton, in which the present of a portrait from a grateful painter to his lordship, forms a more interesting portion of it than a lengthy dissertation on politics. These are no doubt honest, though strong and sadly one-sided. He writes, he says, as a *Constitutional Royalist*—" I hate the French. I detest their principles ;"—but has an utter antipathy to the war, the Ministry, all their policy and proceedings at home and abroad. We shall quote him, however, on more appropriate subjects :—

So little selfish am I, my dear Malone, and so much do I prefer your advantage to my own pleasure, that though your abode at Brighthelmstone suspended for a long time that correspondence which in my present situation is one of my principal comforts, still I rejoice in your country residence, and even in your idleness, both of which I consider as relaxations absolutely necessary to your health and spirits—to your mind and body. And if I can persuade myself to be content with your having postponed a jaunt of amusement upon my account, it is only because my opinion of your friendship induces me to believe that *chatting* with me is pleasant, and consequently salutary to you.

Indeed, my dear friend, you lead too sedentary a life, and do not sufficiently diversify your occupations. For though I be thoroughly of opinion that constant employment is the most universal of all specifics to you in its full effects, it should be often varied. You think also too much and too

---

* Probably the lady or her daughter, to whom he appears to have given refuge at a future day in mental derangement, besides leaving her an annuity.

deeply on politics; a subject of investigation which in the present state of affairs cannot fail of being extremely unwholesome to a man who, like you, loves his country, and loves mankind. In this, however, it must be confessed that, like other physicians, I do not follow my own prescriptions, being, Heaven help me! as much addicted as man can be to this detrimental exercise of the mind. And in truth, I am much the worse for it.

But to quit this *Recipe stile*, I will now proceed with pleasure to inform you that within these few days I have met with a gratification as great as it was unexpected. The case of books arrived from Liverpool; and with it another case containing a real treasure—no less than a portrait of you by Humphrey, as like as possible, and as well painted as I would wish him to paint. A letter from him immediately preceded it, requesting my acceptance of this, to me, inestimable acquisition, under the pressure of certain services which his grateful heart conceives I had done for him, but which in reality was nothing more than in not defrauding him in my general conversation of the applause so justly due to his merit. No person most assuredly was ever handed (?) with more gratifying circumstances. It is the exact resemblance of an absent friend whom I would wish never to lose sight of. It is an excellent picture, and as such must be highly pleasing to a lover of the arts. And it is a proof of gratitude which cannot fail to delight every man who wishes well to human nature: I have written to him, and beg you will tell him so, lest the miscarriage of my letter should make me appear negligent. . . . .

I long much to see your edition of Dryden's prose works, as I know of no compositions in our language which better deserve such an editor. Of Aubrey I know nothing. And as for Chalmers, his petulance not having travelled to Ireland has never offended me. But I take it for granted he is scarcely worth an answer, which may probably counteract your purpose, by raising him into notice.

From Lord Charlemont's impressions, and those of others less influenced by the politics of the moment,

our Critic felt serious misgivings about the state of
Ireland; and in case of disturbance, the probable fate
of those he loved. No condition could be more alarm-
ing—seething with the principles of rebellion,—ready
at any moment to burst forth into that open insurrection which speedily ensued; while invasion was likewise
hourly expected. Those of the gentry who had influence, or means, raised and led corps of yeomanry;
others sought the towns to avoid nocturnal violence
or murder. Catherine tells him they had adopted
the latter course ; but even in Dublin Theatre so
decided and fearless were the predilections of the
mob, that calls and clapping of hands were made for
" Buonaparte," "Arthur O'Conner," and others not
less offensive to loyalty and order. Previous to this
removal the tone of his sister's letters had been so
gloomy that he attributed it to the too diligent
perusal of religious books, of which he had transmitted some, especially *Wilberforce on Christianity.*
This idea Catherine controverts at great length. No
present, she says, could have been more gratifying
than that volume—none more soothing, refreshing,
and cheering—" The best thoughts expressed in the
most elegant language. It is written more to the heart
than any book I ever read in my life." They found
improvement by the perusal, even amid the alarms
which everywhere prevailed, and the distractions
experienced in every family circle of their acquaintance.

But the danger went far beyond even feminine apprehension. Statesmen saw the impending reality not
far distant; and prepared as they best could to meet

those terrible emergencies where passions of the most violent and painful nature are evolved, and where in war among brethren success is little less painful than defeat.

Nothing within the range of public duty can so much try the capacity of rulers as the judicious suppression of domestic rebellion. Foreign enemies may be met, foiled, and disposed of. But with our countrymen, our townsmen, even our acquaintance, in arms against authority, we scarcely know how to deal. Our wisdom and humanity are equally at stake; our decision, judgment, discretion, put upon the stretch to draw the line between what is just and what is vindictive, between mercy and resentment; to subdue, but not wholly destroy; to punish the leader rather than the follower; to save the loyal from the traitor, property from the plunderer, life from the murderer, age and infancy from the ruffian—all these, exercised with the forbearance of a good man, yet the firmness of a wise one, form one of the severest tests of human capacity. And who is he who may pass through such an ordeal, and wholly escape censure? Who, if he errs a little on one side or on the other, is not entitled to be considerately judged?

One of the Irish rulers devoted to obloquy on this occasion, and a youthful friend of Malone, was John Fitzgibbon, Earl of Clare. Chetwood, we have seen, alludes to him as conspicuous for dress; and I find one of his letters to Malone written early in life. Descended from a Romanist family which had conformed to Protestantism, and bred to the law, he early entered Parliament as the main stepping-stone to professional honours. Without perhaps commanding talents, he was busy, quick, bold, a prompt speaker, careless of the higher order of oratory, who being deemed useful in the House became Attorney-General under Lord Northington. A duel with Curran showed that, like so many other Irish members, he *fought* as well as *talked* his way into eminence. The regency question made him Lord Chancellor and a peer, but rent asunder all former political ties. An earldom followed when revolutionary principles took root in that country, and when a strong, daring, perhaps even unscrupulous hand became necessary to restrain their progress. These qualities he possessed, and nowhere was their exercise more required.

He appears to have had little sympathy with popular opinions. When unimportant things were started, he took no trouble to identify himself with the general voice. When doubtful, they encountered effectual opposition. He saw peace, order, security of person and property risked by men of little weight or wisdom in the country for love of the fanciful theory of republicanism, and as he hated the principle as well as the race that approved it, stood on no ceremony in putting down both with a strong hand. The scene was cut out for the man, and the man for the scene. As head of the law he was said to have attempted to stretch law beyond its limits under the plea of preserving the constitution from conspirators and traitors. Devoted to what he considered duty, he was willing in its exercise to brave any amount of odium. Influence, and the vigour by which it was exercised, gave the impression of his being less the organ of Government than the Government itself. Through life he was attached, like most other sound judging men, to the tie with England; for through that channel alone could the advancement of Ireland in commerce, knowledge, and the higher order of civilization be accomplished. Whether this attachment was disinterested has been doubted. In Ireland it is yet scarcely forgiven. It made him unpopular while living among her ephemeral and disloyal writers; and no pen of historical value has since appeared to balance merits against defects, and award fairly that approbation which there is little doubt is due to his energy at least, if not to his judgment.*

His early association with Malone probably ceased from dissimilarity of pursuits and change of abode. How it revived does not appear; but three communications were received from him during this year on the critical state of the country. Two were written in March. The first refers to a speech in the Lords in reply to Lord Moira, which "he is ashamed to say consumed three hours and a half in the delivery." This he has been induced by Lord

---

* Rumour, indeed, says that no materials exist for the purpose; that his papers, in short, have been destroyed from delicacy to many reputations, which would be most seriously damaged by the exposure of written documents to the public eye. This story, if true, tells not against the Chancellor, but rather against his countrymen who could thus descend to solicit favours from one whom they probably afterwards maligned, because he would not or could not accomplish their wishes. But it is another proof of the correctness of his judgment, which, in accomplishing the Union, carried the influence of the *Sectional*—as we may call it—to the *Imperial* Parliament, and thus extinguished those sources of corruption almost inseparable from all local legislatures, particularly that of Ireland—if we may believe all her politicians.

Camden (the Viceroy) to retrace and publish,—
" which has proved the most difficult and laborious
task I have ever undertaken,"—which, as he was
usually considered an extemporaneous speaker, or
nearly so, is probably true.

The second letter, which continues the subject,
was sent a week afterward. "Nothing should have
induced me to undertake the task (of re-collection
and publication) but the conviction that it is essential
to open the eyes of the English people to the state of
this country, which I am sorry to say gets worse
every day. Within the last week two magistrates
have been shot at noon-day. One of them, Sir
Henry Maurice, you may have known. The assassination took place (1798) on the high road within
half a mile of his house. . . . I think a crisis is
at hand. The rebels have assumed an unusual air
of confidence, and they have I am sorry to say succeeded completely in stirring up the savages in every
part of the country, and reviving the spirit of 1641.
. . . . Sir Lawrence Parsons chose to play
second fiddle to Lord Moira, on Monday last, in the
House of Commons, where he found eighteen fools to
join him."

The third letter is dated 20th June. As his
opinions here are more full, and expressed with that
characteristic bluntness and decision which never for
a moment hesitated to call what he considered questionable actions by the strongest names, it may be
given at length. Few of his remains are extant; and
notices of the outrages in daily perpetration show that
at such a moment such a man was in his proper place.

Dublin, June 20th, 1798.

MY DEAR MALONE,—I am not surprised at any act of profligacy in Mr. Sheridan, or of knavery and folly in the Duke of Leinster; but I own I was not prepared for the co-operation of the Dukes of Leeds and Devonshire with the Irish rebels. The latter of these worthies has more than twenty thousand pounds a year in Ireland; and neither he nor any of his mentors has thought it necessary to contribute by personal exertion, or by pecuniary aid in any manner, to the relief or defence of this kingdom. Nor is the one or the other acquainted with the internal situation or economy of it, so well as he may be with that of the most remote corner of the world.

The truth is that this rebellion has grown out of the corrupt interposition of individuals in Great Britain with Irish politics, and the strange and preposterous experiments which have been made upon Ireland by the British Cabinet for the last six years, against the strong and repeated remonstrances of every kind friend of British government in this country. And it is plain that the desperate gang of opposition in England have determined to play the game out. We expect every hour to hear of some decisive action with the rebels in the county of Wexford, where a force of more than ten thousand men has marched against them. They have heretofore fought with incredible fury and enthusiasm, to which they have been brought by their priests, who attend all their camps in great numbers. One of them was killed at Arklow fighting at the head of a rebel column.

Poor Lord Mountjoy was a sacrifice to the cowardice of his sergeant-major, who prevented the privates of his regiment from advancing to his support. Lord O'Neil, I fear, cannot recover. He was murdered in his chaise by his own tenants in the town of Antrim. I have often said, for the last three years, that the spirit of 1641 had revived again in Ireland, and the scene now too fatally verifies my assertion. There are very strong dispositions in the Houses of Lords and Commons to *animadvert* (?) on the proceedings of the Duke of Leinster and Mr. Sheridan. Whenever his grace shall ven-

ture to make his appearance amongst us, he will be treated
very roughly.

Yours always very truly, my dear Malone,

CLARE.

A letter has just been received by Lord Camden from
Lake (General), stating that all the columns of his army had
advanced, and that the rebels are completely surrounded.
Poor O'Neil is dead.

Irish politicians of other opinions, at this moment
seemed desirous of enlisting Malone in their views—
probably from his known friendship with Mr. Windham.   The topic indeed was a great and exciting
one—the union with England; for while it mortified
the national pride of the patriotic and really honest
class, on the other hand it threatened the happy
extinction of that corruption and jobbing, of which
public men whether truly or not loudly accused
each other.   Letters to him against it came from
Mr. Foster, Speaker of the House of Commons; four
from Mr. James Fitzgerald; and three or four from
others who evidently held high office, whose names
are not traceable in their communications.   Two of
the number during this correspondence, were dismissed from employment—one of them with this
explicit intimation to the critic—" Your opinion
decided me.   Ready to do anything to bind the
countries, but to reserve the right of a separate
legislature."   From this stirring theme, if he really
recommended a negative to his friends, he soon returned to more congenial studies.

So early as the completion of the edition of Shakspeare, he had formed the design of republishing,

with such additions as could be gleaned, the lives
and portions of the works of some of our poets. He
had Dryden more especially, and Pope in view. Inquiries were therefore commenced among literary
friends without explicitly disclosing his aims excepting to Lord Claremont, who thus replies so early
as June, 1794 :—

> If a new edition be wanted of Dryden's critical prose works,
> I know of nothing better worth republishing. The matter is
> for the most part excellent; the manner incomparable through-
> out. There cannot be a better antidote against our modern
> innovations in style than his compositions—perspicuous,
> graceful, elegant, humorous, and easy. His life will also be
> very acceptable, as nothing of the kind worth reading has
> hitherto been written.*

A still greater authority in eloquence, that of Burke,
held his pieces in high estimation, not only for the criticism, but for the richness and freedom of his style and
language. He was also considerate enough to offer
an apology for the manner of the poet's address to
his patrons.

In a conversation, says Malone, which I had a few
years ago with the late Mr. Burke, talking of Dryden's
dedications, he observed that the extravagant panegyrics which they contain were the vice of the time,
not of the man ; that the dedications of almost every
other writer of that period were loaded with flattery,
and that no disgrace was annexed to such an exercise of
men's talents, the contest being who should go farthest
in the most graceful way, and with the best turns of

* His lordship here, of course, means the *facts* of his life. Dr. Johnson acknowledged to Malone that he had failed in procuring such as he
wished. Neither was he young or perhaps zealous enough for such
pursuits when he wrote the *Lives of the Poets*.

expression. He added that Butler had well illustrated the principle on which they went, where he compares their endeavours to those of the archer who *draws his arrow to the head* whether his object be a swan or a goose. The plays, poems, and other productions that issued from the press from the time of the Restoration to the reign of Queen Anne, fully confirm this remark.

A previous application on this subject had been made to Lord Hailes of the Court of Session in Scotland—eminent for historical and biographical research—for such materials as he possessed. But no facts on the subject could be supplied. He had once formed similar projects, but found—alas! what man of letters does not find?—that life and health are too limited for their completion. His reply however is worth transcribing. It is dated October 1791; is introduced by Malone into his memoranda evidently for future use of some description; but being copied by another hand is in a few places illegible.

It would give me great pleasure, sir, to be able to aid you in any of your literary plans. But I am afraid that my assistance can go but a little way. I have hardly looked into Pope these twenty years past, having been immersed in business and in prose.

Pope was not a conscientious satirist. When an incident did not suit his purpose, he mended it. Of this there is a remarkable example in a publication called *Opinions of the Duchess Dowager of Marlborough,* where the poet converts an elegant bequest into a capricious lavishing of money. I am apt to believe that " If where I am going I could serve you, sir," is a true story perverted with still more malevolence. The late Lord Elibank told me, but I do not vouch the authority, that the dying man who would not leave a favourite

manor with the rest of his estates was "the rich Duncombe."
But the jest has been supposed to allude to Sir Godfrey
Kneller. He is also the justice of peace who committed
the man who exposed his watch in view of the thief. Yet to
the same Sir Godfrey, Pope inscribed "eternal nonsense
graved in Parian stone." "Stars other far than [illegible]
bear," i.e., Kent and Essex; the first the constant butt of the
Tories, as I remember, in the *Examiner*. I recollect to have
seen him, a very mean-looking man. But, party set aside, I
know not why he became the subject of satire.

I formerly imagined that Bufo meant G. Bubb Dodington;
but I have been since assured that it meant Charles Montagu,
Earl of Halifax. "Rosamond's bowl" I think respects Lady
Lechmere, of the Carlisle family, of whom you will see
enough on a marble tablet in the Westminster Abbey. "Each
widow asks it for the best of men" was Mrs. Rowe, the
sorrowful relict of the poet, who married a Colonel Dean.
It may well be supposed that the sin of Winnington was
his apostasy from the Tories.

As to the "unfortunate lady," it can serve no good purpose were one able to *deterre* her. Your MS. memorandum
seems the most consistent story that I have heard concerning
her, and there it may rest. Sir John Hawkins' story seems
to be Fanny Bradock's end grafted on some other anecdote.
You know it may be presumed that "poor Narcissa" is Mrs.
Oldfield, though here the poet has, according to custom,
added "a little red." Betty is Mrs. Charlotte Sanderson, an
inferior player. There is a curious letter from her in Curle's
Life of Mrs. Oldfield. Pope calls Dr. Middleton a schoolmaster, who, if I mistake not, quitted his party as Winnington
did—but *never* was a schoolmaster.

Bland, Master, and then Provost of Eton, and Dean of
Durham, was the schoolfellow of Sir Robert Walpole, wrote
for him in some of the party newspapers, and was well beneficed. His name occurs more than once in Pope's *Satires*.
Good is *Burnbain* Good, under-master of Eton, also a
schoolfellow of Sir Robert, and one of his writers. His
memory was fresh at Eton in my time as an oddity, but
beloved by the boys. Some of the older Etonians, as Mr.

Bryant or Mr. Cambridge, will be able to tell you more about him. Alsop was of Westminster; so out of my way, though I have heard little stories of him. He was a companion of my Lord of Yorke. He being a Whig does not fare so well as Alsop, though he could have "joked like Horace" as well as Alsop. "Steeped in port," when applied to Dr. Bentley, alludes to his drinking too much port in his later days. This is all that I can remember at present. Perhaps, if you put queries to me, I could remember more.

Let me be allowed to say this for my old friend Bishop Warburton, that he avows he *left undone* what he thought it unfit for him *to have done*. As to his finding out meanings which his author never meant, I suppose you allude to the *Essay on Man*, which Dr. Warburton wished Pope to make less exceptionable than it seemed to be—but he was under the guidance of Bolingbroke. I forgot to mention the famous couplet concerning Sir Thomas Burnet, which Pope was at last prevailed upon to omit, while he ridiculously preserved the line, "This shines a comet, &c." By that time Sir Thomas Burnett was one of the twelve judges of England, and high in the public favour. I never could learn whether Pope had a personal or political quarrel with Judge Burnett. The tract by Sir Thos. [illegible] Doggrel has nothing to do with Pope's *Homer*; so far as, after a long space from reading it, I can recollect. It is a ridicule on the Tory members of the House of Commons.

In former days, when I read without selection, I studied the State poems, &c. It is very possible that upon recollection I might be able to fill up many of the initial letters. But in such party collections, little is to be learnt beside the personal appearance of the parties satirized. I remember that I had formed to myself an idea of Dryden being a man of good height, such as in England is colloquially called a personable man. This notion was formed on his head, by Kneller, which I saw in Mr. West's dining-room, and which has been well engraved by Edylynck, Vertue, and Houbraken. But from the State poems I learnt not to put my faith in painters; for there it is uniformly Poet-Squab, a short, thick man.

Five-and-forty years ago I read a very dull dramatic piece called the *Temple of Dullness,* or some such thing. It is valuable by reason of a letter to the author from Mr. Southerne, giving an account of the poets of the day, and particularly of Dryden. I recollect that he censured Bishop Burnett for saying that Dryden was a " monster of impurity "—which respects his plays, not his morals; and in that sense the bishop is not far from his mark; for Limberham is more indecent than Etheredge's *She would if she could,* was hooted from the stage in the reign of Charles II., and is now, as we know it in the (present) edition, freed from all obscenity. Such as it is in its purified state, I suppose that no British audience, even in the Haymarket during the summer, would hear it to an end.

Southerne says, " Dryden was a very modest man. Often have I ate cheese-cakes with him and Mrs. Ann Reeves." Such, from my recollection, is what Southerne says. Your plan of memoirs is a good one. But I, as a much older man than you, say, " Quid brevi fortes . . . . I have felt the truth of this *opera interrupta* . . . [illegible] *ingentes* hang over me on every side. I have projected more than enough for a century, and no part of it will be performed. Should you choose the plan of memoirs [illegible] I can help you. My old correspondent, Guthrie, was very innocent. By talking on a subject he thought he understood it. I do not believe the anecdote of the [illegible] and I am sure that no vestige of it will be found in the Advocates' Library.

A few more replies to applications appear in this year among his letters. Two of length from Lady Dryden; from Rev. Mr. Blakeway; John Kemble, who had been looking over Powell's plays for an attack upon Dryden and tells him not to forget half-past five—the dinner-hour; from Bishop Percy, as to Dryden's letters to Walsh; from Mr. Caldwell, and several others. None however were able to communicate the information literary or personal of which he was in pursuit.

In the club, occasional difficulties occurred in the election of new members, often not unusual in such associations. The friends of some, with or without cause, find opponents in others; and to some gentle mediating spirit is given the task of soothing asperities and explaining away misunderstandings. This office often fell to the lot of Malone. Mr. Windham, Sir Joseph Banks, Boswell, and a bishop or two, on former occasions, sought his kind offices when their friends were in danger of rejection by adverse votes, and succeeded. Sometimes his popularity ensured a call to fulfil more social duty, as appears by the following note of Mr. Canning :—

Spring Gardens, Monday Night, March 12, 1799.

DEAR SIR,—You must not infer that I am likely to become an inattentive member (however I may be an unworthy one) of the club, from the circumstance of being unable to attend to-morrow and to take the chair, which, I find, I am called upon to fill. But I am not my own master on a post night; and a post night, after the arrival of fifteen mails at once, will confine me too strictly to the Foreign Office to allow me to partake of the convivialities of the Thatched House.

Will you permit me to request, if a substitute is necessary, that you will have the goodness to take the chair for me; and if any apology can be required for my most unwilling abdication of so high an office, that you will have the goodness to make that apology in my behalf, by stating the occasion which prevents my attendance?

I beg your pardon for giving you this trouble, but I know not to whom I could apply with so confident a reliance upon their good nature and good offices.

I am, dear Sir,

Your very sincere and faithful humble servant,

GEO. CANNING.

A humble and once useful visitor from the country found a ready reception from his hospitality. This was "good Mr. Jordan" of Stratford, who in many notes and messages of kindness sent thither, was not forgotten. In 1797 Malone directs one of his inmates, being too busy himself on the works of Reynolds, to send Jordan a print of himself and of Lord Southampton. Another honour appears likewise to have been in store for him—for it is added, "Mr. Harding has not yet engraved your portrait. When he has, I will endeavour to fulfil your request."

Two years afterward (July 1799) Jordan found his way to London. Thence he describes to Mr. Peyton, one of the assistants in the hunt after Shaksperian affairs, his reception by the critic, whose kindness gratified, while his skill in working out ancient materials for his purpose appears to have puzzled him.

According to promise before I left Stratford, I write this to inform you that I breakfasted, dined, drank tea, and supped at Mr. Malone's last Thursday; and am happy to inform you that I was treated in the most respectable and genteel manner by that truly great, good, and honourable gentleman, who very politely acknowledged the receipt of my letter from Stratford; and made a very satisfactory apology for not returning me an answer while I was at Stratford, by both assuring and *showing* me that his time is wholly employed in the publication of the works of Dryden.

He has postponed the life and works of our immortal poet till the others are published, but he has not declined or given it up, as he convinced me by showing me the manuscript copy of the *Genealogy of the Shakspeare Family*, in which he has already proved to a demonstration that they resided at Rowington at a very early period. By what means he pro-

s

cured his materials it is out of my power to inform you.   But
you will probably. hear from him before he begins to print the
work, and the corporation may be assured that all their papers
will be faithfully restored, and that the work, when it is published, will certainly confer an additional lustre on the town
of Stratford.*

* I have been informed by Mr. Halliwell that Jordan was accused, in
Stratford, of some *inventions*, rather than facts, in statements to Malone.
This certainly could not be in matters of moment, as we find nothing
suspicious in the first edition; neither in the second.   Malone was too
keen in such inquiries to take anything of the smallest importance upon
trust from almost any quarter; and, from the concluding passage in the
above letter, it would seem that Malone surprised Jordan—not Jordan,
Malone—by the nature of his materials.

CHAPTER XII.

1799—1805.

Dr. Burney—Publication of Life and Prose Works of Dryden—R. Bell's
late Edition of his Poems—Pope—Visit to Ireland in 1801—Andrew
Caldwell—Mr. Wraxall and Lord Whitworth—Disappointed in a
public appointment—William Gifford—Sale of part of his Books—
Letters to his Sister—Notices by Rev. J. Jephson—Letter from
Gifford.

WHILE writing notes to a new edition of Boswell, the
subject of this memoir wished to describe the interior
of Thrale's house, so immortalized by its many fre-
quenters, and applied to Dr. Burney for his recollections. This information the reader will find below
from a note written in December 1798. It is worth
its space. Few suburban mansions have acquired so
much celebrity. Its site perhaps is too low, but
Tooting Common opens pleasantly in front; and
often while resident for several years in the vicinity,
have I lingered around it for hours as venerated
ground.*

* "I would not," says Burney, "take my *corporal* of it; but, as far as
I can remember, Johnson's account of the prints in *the* Thrales' drawing-
room was accurate. The family lived in the library which used to be
the parlour. There they breakfasted, &c. Over the bookcases were
hung Sir Joshua's portraits of Mr. Thrale's friends, of whom Boswell, I
believe, has given a lift. From these portraits the room has by painters
been called the Thrale Gallery.

"The *drawing-room*, if memory does not deceive me, was hung with
plain bright sky-blue paper, ornamented with a very gay border, somewhat tawdry; and the room in which dinner was served when large
parties were invited which, I believe, Johnson means, was I believe,
hung with prints. Family dinners without company were served in a
more small and plain room. I forget now what I said, and of course

Close application to a new work, added to the illness of Lord Charlemont, probably interfered with
the correspondence of this old friend. He died in
August, 1799, in the heat of the contest about the
Union. His biographer (Hardy) applied to Malone
in May, 1804, for such notices or materials as might
be interesting to blend with the narrative. These
however for some reason now unknown, appear not
to have been supplied. Had he any intention of
undertaking the work himself? With his large stores
of information, such a design may have been formed,
though interrupted soon afterward by illness. Hardy
alludes to him as a correspondent of his lordship, but
says nothing of refusal of assistance.

In the spring of 1800 came out in four volumes,
*The Critical and Miscellaneous Prose Works of
John Dryden; with an Account of the Life and
Writings of the Author.*

The praise of research always unwearied, as much
as possible exact, and industrious almost to a fault,
were given him without hesitation. His aim, he
tells us, was to delineate the *man*, not the *poet.*
The latter had been inimitably accomplished by the
greatest critic of the age, or perhaps of any age.
Nothing, in the estimate of his powers, could be
added to the pages of Dr. Johnson; but there was
much to fill up and rearrange in those incidents of
life and character common to us all, about which the

thought, concerning the French Horn. But that and anything else
which I scribbled down during my last perusal of Boswell's life of our
friend, were given more as queries than positive assertions . . . .
It (a cold) prevents me from calling on you to talk over Johnsonian
matters."

mass of readers are often as anxious as upon ordinary points of criticism. There were also the order and dates of his works; his letters; his friends; his literary adversaries; and their contests, to ascertain in a long and distinguished, though unhappily for his comfort, a contentious career.

The notes to the *Prose Works*, in addition to those of the *Life*, tells us all of him of any importance that we are likely to know. No source of information was left untried. When unsuccessful himself on particular points, he has given some clue for others to follow. But when we consider how much on all subjects remains buried in family archives; how difficult it is to get them examined or suffered to be examined, by their owners; and how often it is that what are discoveries in literary eyes are not deemed so by the uninitiated, we must not be surprised at the slow pace at which they emerge into light from old boxes and closets. We must be thankful for what has been done. All literary men agree that none but Malone could have accomplished so much. To his pages all must turn who want accurate information upon the life and works of Dryden.

Merits such as these might be supposed to pass with general applause; but there is a large class of persons who feel disposed to decry what they have not virtue to imitate; and on this occasion the ridicule which had been so largely directed against the poet himself during life, took aim in another way at his biographer. He was, in fact, deemed to be too particular. Yet on such a subject we want facts whenever they can be fathomed—not romance or conjecture. Truth is always worth some trouble in the pursuit. So thought Dr. Johnson. He praises the judge I have just quoted (Lord Hailes) "as a man of worth, a scholar, and wit, whose exactness excites my wonder . . . whose book (*Annals of Scotland*) has such a *stability of dates, such a certainty of facts, and such a punctuality of citation,*" &c. These are precisely the merits of Malone. They will be the merits of every one who has courage to quit the hard-trodden path of commonplace book makers and will plunge for knowledge into an exploratory track of his own.

Qualities which had drawn the commendation of Johnson, were not permitted by one of the supposed "wits" of the age, Mr. George Hardinge, to pass muster in the *Life of Dryden*. Wits are seldom noted for being exact or particular in anything. Precision with them is akin to offence. So on the present occasion the censor·made minute detail the subject of ridicule in a bulky pamphlet, *The Essence of Malone*. This was followed by another; and again by a similar piece levelled at *Shakspeare*.

A jest at an antiquary may occasionally run happily enough; but expanded to two or three hundred pages becomes the butt of the ridicule it is meant to convey. Jests of such length are found to be no jests at all; on the contrary, they are serious taxes on patience. He that reads them will suspect spleen, cavilling, envy, captiousness to be the basis of the performance—especially when, as in this instance, the page is studded with such a crop of notes of admiration and interrogation, as if much of the wit or wisdom lay in these silent symbols of immature genius !

In such imitations there is no novelty, and very little wit. Many of our most distinguished writers —Dr. Johnson among others—have furnished occasional amusement to such as felt disposed to exercise their ingenuity as literary caricaturists. Even the straightforward style of Boswell has found an imitator in Mr. Alexander Chalmers. But such things must be taken for what they are really worth ; and no one whose productions are not in themselves ridiculous, need fear their effect. The smile they occasionally excite forms but a polite and speedy dismissal to oblivion.

No reply came from Malone. He had at first intended it, as I find by a letter from the Rev. Mr. Blakeway, who supposed him (January, 1801) occupied with—"Your proposed and well-deserved castigation of Mr. George Hardinge, which I have been expecting with some impatience to see announced in the papers." ' The Bishop of Dromore also writes— " I read with pleasure the article signed ' W.' which I conclude was intended to have had the signature of *Sciolus*. Can you guess who was your maligner ? He took great pains to gratify his ill-humour, for which I neither envy him his success nor his motives."

A genius of superior order has however estimated his labours as they deserve. Sir Walter Scott found it vain to delve in a mine where Malone had been a workman with the hope of finding anything new. He accepts his facts ; and interweaves his own narrative with such notices and criticisms of the poets and

dramatists of that and the previous age as their contentions and rivalries drew forth.

" In the biographical memoir," he says, " it would
have been hard to exact that the editor should rival
the criticism of Johnson, or produce facts which
had escaped the accuracy of Malone . . . whose
industry has removed the clouds which so long hung
over the events of Dryden's life." Such is and has
been the general opinion. The laugh, if any arose,
soon ceased. The book remains a standard of authority of the times and matters of which it treats. And
there are few who profess attachment to letters or
to knowledge of many of the writers or writings of
that day, but confess their obligations to the *Life
of Dryden.*

To a second edition of this work, improved by new
materials, he looked forward with interest. One of
these acquisitions* was a letter of Dryden sent by
correspondents named Smith, which he traced as
having been addressed to the second Earl of Der-
wentwater, on a question of poetical translation. In
return, wishing to be grateful, he transmits an autograph of Pope; laments he has not a line of Shakspeare to bestow; but sends a fac-simile of his name
to his will and to a law-deed, March 1612-13; and
adds in allusion to piracies :—

" The printed copy (of the letter) is very inaccurate, de-
viating in several minute particulars from its archetype. I
hope some time or other to publish a second and improved
edition of my *Life of Dryden,* and of his letters and prose
works. To the collection of letters which I had infinite

* Now in the possession of R. Monckton Milnes, Esq.

trouble in making, and which has since been made so free
with, I have several others to add that have never appeared;
and I will take care that they shall not be used in the same
manner the former were."

His own copy of the work, largely annotated, is now
in the Bodleian. One of the additions is a notice of
Dryden's sister, second wife of Dr. Lawton, who died
in December 1710. She had previously buried her
only son. Dryden gave him an epitaph in Catworth
Church characteristic of her extreme grief; and
which not being included in his works, may find
place here—

> " Stay, stranger, stay, and drop one tear,
> She always weeps who laid him here;
> And will do till her race is run :
> His father's fifth, her only son." *

Pope formed the next name on his list for a similar
tribute of respect. Both, as we have said, were
commenced about the same time, but the vein of
information chanced to run deeper in one than the
other. Probably also Dr. Joseph Warton informed
him early of being engaged on that edition of the
younger poet which came out in 1797, in nine

---

* Some additions to the facts of the life have been made by the diligence
of Mr. Robert Bell, in his annotated edition of the *British Poets*, which
supplies one of the wants of the age. These are chiefly from the family
of the poet—letters from Honor and Ann Dryden; copy of his marriage
licence at St. Swithin's Church ; letter of William Walsh on his poems ;
and besides others, an Exchequer warrant by which 100*l.* per annum
was added to his salary as poet laureate in May 1684. This grant
coming from Charles II., relieves him from the charge of changing his
religion for a pension under his successor—the latter being, in fact,
simply a confirmation of the previous gift. It is pleasant thus to be
enabled to exonerate genius from imputed unworthy motives. Lord
Macaulay, not always accurate, will therefore, no doubt, from this discovery of Mr. Bell, withdraw the charge against him of corrupt motives,
however lightly he may otherwise think of the " renegade." While this
is passing through the press, his lordship's death is announced.

volumes. To this, I have no doubt he contributed aid.

It is certain that the fragment of an unpublished poem of Pope, copied by Malone among his anecdotes some years before, appears in that work. I have consequently omitted it in this volume. A few other memoranda of the poet, in verse, not quoted by Warton, are retained as specimens of his first thoughts. Both came from an early friend of Malone, Dr. Wilson,* of Trinity College, Dublin, who thus writes:—" This poem I transcribed from a rough draft in Pope's own hand. He left many blanks for fear of the Argus eyes of those who if they may not find, can fabricate, treason. . . . It was lent me by a grandson of Lord Chetwynd, an intimate friend of the famous Lord Bolingbroke, who gratified his curiosity by a boxful of the rubbish and sweepings of Pope's study."

Popiana, the name given to his own collection of fragments, were embodied in two memorandum books. To these were added various loose papers, anecdotes, and straggling notes jotted down as communicated, some of which may still emerge into life from the stores of the curious. He had likewise collected three volumes of tracts, twenty-one in number, connected with the same poet, said to have contained much curious matter, and which passed into the possession of a new owner at his sale in 1818. Fresh from his own hand, cohering and shaped into form, with life breathed into them by his own kindly spirit, we should have perused the details with more satisfaction.

* This gentleman I have mentioned in a previous page; also in the *Life of Goldsmith*, vol. i. p. 63 : Murray, 1837.

Delayed for a time by the attack of Hardinge, many literary and private friends were gratified by his visit to Ireland the following year. He looked fondly to her improvement—to her advances, notwithstanding recent misbehaviour, to a higher grade of civilization in industry and commerce. Discontent and rebellion had been actively at work since he had last crossed the Channel, and left their usual fruits behind—the country and social organization at a standstill—latent and not always veiled hatreds between classes of society—a subdued but not quiet populace—and the probability, soon proved by the event, of these starting once more into active hostility.

Poor Ireland had not yet recovered her sanity. The maddest of all projects—that of casting of alliance with England to become if successful inevitably the slave of France and more especially of Rome—still lingered among her bolder but unwise spirits. The meteor of a republic gleamed in the horizon; the emblems of power danced before the deluded eye of men of ambition, who fancied themselves patriots without the elements of common capacity for such affairs; nor could they be convinced of inherent weakness and unfitness for self-government till rebellion proved it impossible. In one class, the mistake might be accounted for by the unquestionable supremacy which success must have given to the Roman Catholic body. But that Protestant gentlemen should be so blinded to the results—their own certain persecution and degradation—made them the laughing-stock of Europe—the greatest of simpletons, or the maddest of maniacs.

Among his Dublin friends was Mr. Andrew Caldwell, a lawyer, although not actively taxing the law
for a maintenance.   His father, in that usually well-
paid profession, had performed the duty before him:
and although likewise called to the bar himself, he
thought it more satisfactory to sit down to the enjoyment of the paternal inheritance rather than aim to
increase the store.   His tastes, like those of Malone,
were literary.   He acquired a good library; frequented booksellers' shops; read much; and selected
companions of similar pursuits, who in his retreat
in Cavendish Row, often found a social dinner set off
with considerable learning, friendly disposition, and
gentlemanlike manners.   Where seed is thus plenti-
fully sown, we expect in time to see a crop.   But it
was not so with Caldwell.   He produced only one
or two trifles; one of which, an account of Athenian
Stuart's escape from some intended Turkish mur-
derers, was corrected by Malone.

He annually visited London, sought out that friend
as his guide in literary purchases, and enjoyed such
social dinners as he himself bestowed.

"I dined," he says to Bishop Percy on one occasion, "with Malone on Sunday, *tête-à-tête* . . . .
I had just begun his *Life of Dryden;* but got only
through a few pages when obliged to come away.
No writer, I think, ever took more pains to establish
facts and detect errors.   When he offers himself to
the public it seems to be his aim to employ the
utmost diligence of research to be useful and to
merit favour.   He tells me he does not escape; and
has already been attacked for the very circumstance

that does him honour." In a few months he again says to the Bishop, "I have been much gratified with Malone's curious *Life of Dryden*. It is a most remarkable instance of diligence and accuracy. The numerous anecdotes, and the accounts of noted persons and families interspersed, are highly interesting."

When the scene changed, and Malone sought Dublin, Caldwell faithfully attended his book-shop explorations.

In 1801, he tells Bishop Percy of one of these— " Mr. Malone was in town for two days on his way to London. I accompanied him one entire morning in researches in which we were not very successful." In June, another well-known topic is mentioned in their correspondence—" I have had a long agreeable letter from Mr. Malone. He mentions a curious sale of the farrago of the famous Samuel Ireland, the *Shakspeare Papers*, in three immense volumes bound in Russia, green boxes without end, old leases, deeds, seals, and playhouse accounts, to take in the hunters of curiosities."

On another occasion, they had an elaborate though vain examination together of the royal library for a scarce author. But a previous mischance in such researches acting upon impaired habit of body from over-study, created among the friends of our subject, for a time, serious fears of the consequences. Archdeacon Nares writes to Bishop Percy—" Malone has been nearly destroyed by an accident apparently insignificant, that of breaking his shin in getting out of a coach at the Museum. It has been very un-

willing to heal, and sometimes has shown a threatening tendency."

In Ireland he saw little to allure those of studious
habits to a long stay. No retreat for a quiet man
was there. All were politicians. Some of small
talent and without an atom of experience could even
believe themselves statesmen ; happy only when indulged with a fling at that Union which was to extinguish for ever their small importance. To his
friend Mr. Philip Metcalfe hints were dropped toward
the end of the year that things were not as he wished,
who replies—

" Your picture of that country removes my apprehensions of your leaving us for any length of time ;
for its reform of manners must be too slow for our
time of life to hope to see accomplished."

In 1802, paragraphs in the newspapers intimated
that two letters of Shakspeare, written in 1606 and
1607, had been found in the *Dorset* papers, addressed
to the Lord Treasurer Buckhurst, Earl of Dorset.
Mr. (afterwards Sir Nathaniel) Wraxall had been
it appeared in possession of these papers ; and to
him Malone applied, but found the newspaper statement erroneous. He mentioned however that in the
Middlesex papers which formed part of the Dorset
collection, he found a petition from *Sarah* Shakspeare to the Lord Treasurer Cranfield, Earl of
Middlesex, but whether she were a relative of the
poet did not appear. The duke, he said, entrusted
him with the papers in 1797 for the selection and
publication of such as were of public interest. His
grace died in 1800, and in December following the

whole of them had been withdrawn from him by
the duchess.   Previous to that event he had, in
company with her grace and Mrs. Wraxall, opened
a large chest or coffer at the top of the house
(Knowle) filled with old letters and papers, of which
he drew out a few, but whether anything of Shakspeare mingled with them he had never since been
permitted to ascertain.

A second letter from Malone produced another
from the same gentleman with slight additions to
his previous report.   The petition alluded to consisted
of about twenty lines requesting succour for her necessities ; no note is made, as on several others, whether
relief was rendered ; no intimation supplied whether
spinster or widow ; but highly probable that she was
widow or wife of Gilbert Shakspeare ; date of the
petition he thinks 1623.

A zealous antiquary is not easily baulked on a
favourite topic.   Animated by hopes from the " coffer" in question, Malone induced Mr. Windham to
write to Lord Whitworth, then in Paris, for information whether anything of Shakspeare had been
found among its contents.   The reply (March 1803)
was a negative.   They had withdrawn the papers he
said " from the plagiaristick hands of Mr. Wraxall,"
and believed they contained nothing of public interest.
" For my own part I will confess to you that, from
what I have seen of it, this may be comprised in a
very small compass."   Wraxall, with whom some
quarrel had evidently taken place, and who tells
Malone that if annoyed by newspaper paragraphs
from that family, he will publish the whole of the cir-

cumstances, thinks differently.   He tells Malone that
there is much curious and interesting matter in the
collection. But the critic, to his great regret, received
no invitation, then or afterward, from the owner of
Knowle, to examine either letters or papers.*

A whim seized him about this time (1802) to
change his diet.   Severe dyspepsia, which so often
haunts the steps and dashes the triumphs of genius
and study, induced him to forsake solids for soups,
broths, gruel, and similar fare.   The success of the
scheme, as may be supposed, was not great; but the
economy, had that been an object, considerable.   " I
have been living," he writes to his sister, Jan. 1803,
" upon nothing for a good while past.   My butcher's
bill for this whole year comes to but thirty-three
pounds, and of that only seven guineas have been
spent since July."

Soon afterward he unexpectedly failed in securing
a public appointment, without disturbance of his usual
constitutional equanimity.   The office had become
vacant by death; his succession to it was promised
and said to be certain; till just on the point of being
inducted, it was discovered to be not in the gift of
the nobleman who claimed the patronage, but in that
of Lord Hawkesbury.   " Lord Pelham," he writes to
his sister, " would unquestionably have had the disposal of it had not his predecessor, the Duke of Portland, granted the reversion of the first clerkship of the
Signet that should fall, which took place on Fraser's

---

* A hint in the letter to Mr. Windham from Paris plainly shows
that his lordship was not easy in his communications with Napoleon—
" and the sooner I am relieved from this place the better."

death, and this passed for the turn of the Secretary (of State), and of course of Lord Pelham, who stood in his shoes. . . . . I state all this because you and dear Hetty wish to know the particulars, and not because it makes any impression on my mind. I am sure that W. [Windham] whenever he comes into power, will make me compensation for the disappointment. Besides, I shall have a rise of between one and two hundred a year on the Cavan estate; so I consider that *a place*, and shall think no more of the other."

Criticism on certain passages in Shakspeare came opportunely to divert attention from this disappointment. The writer was an old and eminent friend, Dr. Michael Kearney, of Trinity College, Dublin, who had retired from his duties to those of a country pastor, where his leisure was employed in *reading* books—neglecting, as is too frequently the case with members of Trinity, to *write* them, as they are well fitted to do, for the instruction of others. Distinguished for classical learning and talent, he was not less conversant with our great dramatic poet. On this occasion he notices an anachronism in *King John*. Louis VIII. of France, who succeeded to the crown in 1223, is called Dauphin; whereas Dauphiny, whence the name is derived, was not resigned to France till 1349. This, he observes, may suit the commentators; but signifies little to that great genius whose powers rose above all time and place. He controverts Dr. Johnson's criticism on Dover Cliff in an ingenious and philosophical passage; and concludes with queries on some expressions in the first part of *Henry IV*.

T

An acquaintance soon afterwards commenced with Mr. William Gifford, the sharpest critic of his day, who from satire and censure in the *Anti-Jacobin*, had tamed down his hand to the calmer employment of editing *Massinger*. He was well fitted for the work, as his edition sufficiently evinces. But he saw in Malone a superior in research, added to the possession of materials conducive to his own success. They were previously unacquainted; but both being strongly tinctured by similar political sentiments, a letter of inquiry answered the purpose of more formal introduction. The immediate subject was an imperfect drama of Massinger in manuscript, to which the possessor replied in February, 1803 :—

"Mr. Malone presents his compliments to Mr. Gifford. He has sent the *Parliament of Love* by his servant for Mr. Gifford's inspection and transcription, if he should think it worth that trouble. This piece is however in such a mutilated state, wanting the whole of the first act and part of the second—to say nothing of other defects from damp and time—that it is feared it can be of little use."

Gifford put his ingenuity to work, and in six weeks returned a fair copy to the owner with the following :—

March 18, 1803—*James Street.*

Sir,—It is so long since I received your very obliging letter that I am almost ashamed to recur to it; but in truth, I was desirous of returning the MS., which I cannot sufficiently thank you for; at the same time, the transcription of it took up so much more time than I was aware of, and drew me on so from day to day, that I fear you have thought me either very negligent or very ungrateful.

I now, sir, return the *Parliament of Love.* It has never been out of my hands, and I have copied it all myself. You will be pleased to know that less of it is lost than you imagine, as there are still four pages of the first act remaining. I hope I have made it out pretty well. Indeed, with the exception of the six last broken lines of the first page—which better eyes than mine may still read perhaps—and a contraction in the twenty-fourth line of the last page but one, which my little acquaintance with old MSS. disable me from reading, I flatter myself that all has been copied. I was desirous of sending you a fair copy, but I have been disappointed by the person to whom I intrusted my manuscript. The instant it is brought me, I will take the liberty of enclosing it to Queen Ann Street.

I am infinitely obliged to you, sir, for the two volumes which accompanied your letter. The notices they contain are very precious to me, as well as those you have kindly set down in your last favour. The two volumes, with your permission, I will yet withhold, as they contain three plays of the first editions which I was not before possessed of. I will take all imaginable care of them.

Many years ago, when I first read your *History of the English Stage,* I was so convinced of the truth of what you urged respecting what we now call scenery, that I wondered how Mr. Steevens, a man of infinite sagacity, could attempt to controvert it. Since I have looked into the early editions of Massinger I have been frequently reminded of it. The marginal hints, scattered up and down for the use of the property man, furnish the most ridiculous proofs of the poverty of the ancient stage.

With every good wish, and every feeling of respect, I remain, sir, your truly obliged and obedient servant,

WM. GIFFORD.

The English critic has recorded some further acknowledgments to his industrious brother of Ireland. " And Mr. Malone, with a liberality that I shall ever remember with gratitude and delight, furnished me unsolicited with his valuable collection, among which I found all the first editions." In another place we find—"From Mr. Malone, from whose historical account of the English stage—one of the most instructive essays that ever appeared on the subject—many of these notices are taken."

In this year (1803) he appears to have found constant accumulations from book-marts to be either inconvenient to his shelves, or unnecessary for such purposes as he had in view. From a purchaser, therefore, he became a seller. In one of Thorpe's trading announcements (1841), there is the following insertion:—"Catalogue of a collection of English poetry, &c., part of the library of Edmond Malone; sold by Mr. King; h. b. neat, scarce, 5s. 1803." Many of the articles were, no doubt, duplicates; or portions of the refuse with which literary, like other diamonds, are often intermixed.

Particulars of the insurrection in Ireland in July created momentary apprehensions for the safety of his family. But these were soon dispelled by correspondents in Dublin. Never did discontent take the field with less of wisdom than in this wrong-headed and wicked affair. The intellect of Ireland most assuredly lies not among her rebellious sons; for not one of the number has shown himself of the slightest capacity as a leader; and happily for her that it is so, and that it may never be otherwise.

In 1804 his sister Catherine, after a visit to Queen Anne Street, proceeded on an excursion to Scotland in search of an imprudent lady-friend who had failed to manage her own affairs in the most prudent way.

Kind advice and active assistance appear in the proceedings of brother and sister. Money is transmitted by both; and as a small mark of delicate
attention to the wants of a lady, he sallied forth himself in search of the most expensive tea and coffee to
be found in London to forward to the same quarter.

During her absence (July) he made a journey to
Cambridge, in pursuit of old books and papers—dined
out four days in the week—was busied in daily researches from nine till four o'clock—is on the whole
pretty well satisfied though certain papers evaded his
vigilance—and means to visit Mr. Bindley to talk
over his discoveries. Has had a dinner-party or two
—dines with the Windhams; with Lord Cowper,
though unwell; with Sir W. Scott; and from the
former, "went in the evening with Mrs. Crewe to
Holland House—a fine piece of antiquity in its way,
but much in want of the expenditure of five or six
thousand pounds to make it a really handsome
antique."

In August he writes again, but with an eye to
business. Thanks "Kate" for a promised letter of
Congreve, and desires her to ask Lady Clark for
copies of others in possession of the Duchess of Buc-
cleugh. "They will add to my literary stores, and I
may extract some good out of them."

"Yesterday," he adds—and even in the anecdote
we see Shakspeare and the drama prominent in
thought, while that of Mr. Windham is no less
strongly characteristic—"I dined with the Windhams at Mr. Woodford's, at Vauxhall. There was
a rowing-match on the Thames for a prize left by

Dogget, the player. Windham, being bred at Eton, is a great swimmer and rower, and necessarily much interested in the contest. We sat for an hour in a boat under one of the arches of Westminster Bridge awaiting the contending parties, who no sooner appeared than he dashed in among a hundred boats, shouting, splashing, and pulling about to keep pace for a moment with the rivals. Afterwards, while crossing to Vauxhall, we found one of the defeated men, overcome by the event, sitting with his head upon his knees in an agony of tears. He was from Bankside, where Shakspeare's plays used to be acted, and his name was *Still*, the same as that of the author of the first English comedy ever written—so was doubly interesting to me. We gave him half-crowns —all the comfort we could. It was delightful to see what interest W(indham) took in the sport, to prevent obstruction or interference with the boats engaged, totally regardless of the safety of his own."

Toward the end of the year he again became affected with intense burning pain in the nerves of the arm, shoulder, and side. His eyes were giving way to labours upon old and minute penmanship; and sleep had nearly deserted him. These ills he believed were caught in work; that is, in profuse perspirations caused by long walks to Stationers' Hall to copy their books in rooms not often aired or tenanted. But he made light of all personal ills, as usual, to his sister. Convalescence came in about two or three months; and then he tells of his visitors, Lord Cowper, Luttrell, Metcalf, Windham, Dr. Burney and his son Charles, Bindley, Caldwell, and others, either dining with them or they with him. Their talk even alleviated twinges which Drs. Heberden, Blane, and Sir James Earle assailed in vain.

His sisters, however, had become uneasy. His health continued indifferent, his spirits depressed, and the constant presence of a friend, in whom they could all place implicit confidence, seemed the only mode of allaying their apprehensions. With this view, a protégé of the family, the Rev. J. Jephson, was summoned from Westmeath to London, who sketches for his wife a few notices of the scene.

I intended you (May 3) a long letter to-day, but Lord Sunderlin and Luttrell both called, and occupied me some hours; and then Mr. M. (Malone) and I sat down to books, papers, and criticism, which we have barely left within half an hour of the post going out.

He then mentions, as indicative of their studies, having solved a passage in *Valerius Maximus* which had defeated Malone, Windham, Luttrell,* and others.

* Of this gentleman, once well known in the higher circles of London life, little has been made public. But an eminent literary friend favours me with the following notice :—

"Luttrell I knew well. He was the natural son of a nobleman, Lord C.; sat in the Irish Parliament when a young man ; and subsequently was sent to the West Indies by his father, to manage estates there. He soon found himself fit for a larger sphere. On returning to England, he found an introduction to the celebrated Duchess of Devonshire—was constantly at her parties, and at all other fashionable assemblies of those days, was admired as a lively and intelligent, if not brilliant talker. Nor was he less a favourite with those of the next generation. Indeed, he continued to visit in, and be admired by, the very highest society in London till illness compelled him to stay at home. He died, if I mistake not, about a year before Rogers. He was twice married ; by the first wife he had a son ; the second wife, more advanced in life, proved an excellent nurse in his last illness. Though he published two poems of considerable merit—*Letters to Julia* and *Crockford House*,—he was, and I believe wished to be thought, a man of fashion, of attractive conversa-

The Malones urge my stay—but listen to my reasons for
not protracting it as much as they wish.   I dine to-day with
Lord Sunderlin.   The ladies put me down at night on their
way to Lady Clonmell's.

It was my intention (May 6) to write daily to you, but
was prevented by a visitor, who occupied the only time I had
left.   I dined yesterday at Lord Sunderlin's; Luttrell and
Courtenay were of the party—but the irreconcileable differences between their notions on politics, morals, taste, &c.,
and those of Mr. M., rather dullified the day, though not altogether.

In the midst of much discomfort, he gained patience
to endure it by contrasting with his own the afflictions of his friend Mr. R. M. Jephson, settled at
Gibraltar, from whom accounts were at this time
received.   His situation was indeed deplorable.   Pes-
tilence in the form of fever had visited that fortress
and made hideous ravages in every class of the popu-
lation.   His wife, child, brother, and many intimate
associates perished in what he calls " this charnell
house."   Even a dear friend (chief medical officer of

tional powers, rather than a literary man.   Moore consulted him about
destroying Byron's autobiography. . . . . I may mention that he had
a bad temper: so had Rogers; and they were ever and anon falling out.
On one occasion I was the innocent cause of a dreadful quarrel, during
which they used such language to each other as none could have expected from the lips of two men who had associated not only with the
highest nobility, but with kings and queens."

In Rogers' *Table Talk*, Mr. Dyce quotes the old poet on the literary
qualifications of this gentleman. . "What a pity it is," said he, "that
Luttrell gives up nearly his whole time to persons of mere fashion!
Everything that he has written is very clever.   Are you acquainted with
his epigram on Miss Tree (Mrs. Bradshaw)?   It is quite a little fairy
tale :—

" ' On this *Tree* when a Nightingale settles and sings,
          The *Tree* will return her as good as she brings.'

Luttrell is indeed a most pleasant companion.   None of the talkers
whom I meet in London society can slide in a brilliant thing with such
readiness as he does."—p. 280, third edition.

the navy), in whose house he and his family took refuge when driven by despair and death from their own, shared the general fate.   No scene could be more terrible.   So indeed the medical records of that time amply testify. 'He even asks for death at the hand of Providence ; he has no other refuge ; is alone in the world ; cares not for society ; children—boys, young men—unfit to soothe grief. " Women alone fit for comforters and companions on such occasions."   Four letters of this description within a month, filled with wailings, disease, and death, give a melancholy picture of deep suffering, little short of the extremity of despair.

Letters and literature, as usual, deadened the sense of his own personal afflictions.   Two of the former came from Gifford, in his blandest mood, apologizing for the author—infirmity of retaining borrowed volumes too long ; and for the delays of those incurable clogs upon their labours, unpunctual printers.   The first of these (May 1805) may be given :—

I am extremely sorry I was not at home when you did me the honour to call—more especially as I was anxious to make my best apologies to you for the unconscionable time I have detained your valuable volumes.   One plea I may now offer, which is, that I was desirous of bringing you a set of Massinger, at the same time that I waited upon you with my best thanks.   This I hoped to have done long since ; but you who have had somewhat more experience than I have, need not be told that no set of men can vie with printers in deranging the most confident calculations—and I have been led on from month to month, and from week to week.

To-day, however, puts a termination to the business ; and as soon as a set can be made up, I shall have the pleasure of waiting on you with it and of returning your little collections,

which I may truly say have been to me invaluable.—I remain, dear sir, with the sincerest esteem, your ever obliged
and obedient friend and servant."

A month afterward, the same critic thanks his brother
labourer for friendly emendations:—" You could not
have given me a more sincere or a more pleasing
proof of your kindness than the corrections and additions which you transmitted in your last favour; and
of all which I shall be most anxious to avail myself. . . . ." Is there anything peculiar implied
in the last part of the following passage? " It (Mal-
kin's *Almahide and Hamet*) is in my possession, and
very much at your service; indeed, I would send it to
you, but I am without a servant—

> ' A malady
> Most incident to —— what shall I say?'—"

The Bishop of Dromore, Dr. French Laurence,
Mr. Sayers, author of the *Life of Mortimer* (who
writes through Mr. Amyot), Mr. Caldwell, and Dr.
Mansell, Master of Trinity College, Cambridge, and
afterwards Bishop of Bristol, plied him variously
with literary inquiries, or answers, as the case might
be. To the latter he had complained of some accuser
as to an alleged slip of the pen, and receives from
that classical church dignitary a handsome testimony
to the general merits of his style.*

---

* " Whether you wrote cingulus or cingulum, I really do not recollect.
But this I *do* know, that if to be master at will of every classical image
and sentiment—if to write simply, purely, and with the very properest
words in their places—stamps the best acquaintance with all that is best
and worthy in what is called *classical*, then I think *you* have very little
occasion to trouble yourself about fifty or five hundred *lapsus calami*, of
which no man is more guilty than myself, and unhappily without such
sets-off. . . . . I congratulate you much upon the acquisition of
the first edition of the *Venus and Adonis*, and agree with you that
no one of this land could ever think of giving such a turn to their story."

CHAPTER XIII.

1805—1810.

Venus and Adonis (ed. 1593)—*Life of Shakspeare*—Bishop Percy—
Notices of Malone, by Rev. J. Jephson—Letter to his Sister—Pam-
phlet on the origin of *The Tempest*—Parliamentary Logic and Right
Hon. W. G. Hamilton—Thomas Moore and Kilkenny Theatricals—
Right Hon. W. Windham.

THE allusion in the last chapter by the Bishop to
Venus and Adonis, applied to a new Shakspearian
acquisition made by his editor. In the little volume
itself, now in the Bodleian (325), we find the following memorandum :—

"Bought of Mr. William Ford, bookseller, in
Manchester, in August, 1805, at the enormous price
of twenty-five pounds.

"Many years ago, I said that I had no doubt an
edition of Shakspeare's *Venus and Adonis* was published in 1593 ;* but no copy of that edition was
discovered in the long period that has elapsed since
my first notice of it, nor is any other copy of 1593
but the present known to exist.

"E. MALONE."

In December, he writes to the Rev. Mr. Davenport, of Stratford, of the new edition, "in twenty-
three volumes, royal octavo," flitting before his san-

* In the edition of Shakspeare (1790) he fancied the first edition was
1594, though entered at Stationers' Hall 1593.

guine hopes, and of which Shakspeare's *Life* is to form an important part; but the stubborn volumes required even more than the stubborn labour he gave them to start into active existence.

"I have still been in hopes of bringing my work to a conclusion, but have been delayed by a thousand unforeseen consequences. . . . . If I can but live to finish it, I shall think nothing of the labour. I hope to put it to press about the middle of summer."

Just eleven years before (1794), he told the same friend he had been almost equally sanguine on the *Life of Shakspeare*, and a hint is dropped as if some essential discovery in his history had been made. "One half of it was written and fairly transcribed; but when I had brought him to the door of the London theatre, a fancy struck me to give a history of the prevailing manners of the English world when he first came on the town. . . . . My plan will have the advantage of novelty, for I think I shall be able to overturn every received tradition respecting this very extraordinary man."

Another friend, Bishop Percy, reduced to blindness and the necessity of employing a friendly pen, is not less active and inquisitive than before. Two long letters in the spring, treat of Dean Vincent and the *Periplus of the Erythrean;* Bruce, the traveller; a *Hermit's Meditations*, copied by him when a boy though the author continued unknown; *Norton Fulgate*, written probably in ridicule of Bentley; Malone's obvious advantage over Steevens as to Shakspeare's conversation; the Society of Antiquaries; Sir Joshua Reynolds's monument; the condition of the Club with his usual *Esto perpetua;* and reply to a proposal from Malone to have his (the Bishop's) portrait engraved. Acquiescing in the request, it was forwarded to town by his daughter in Northamptonshire. The Bishop adds an Anglo-Iricism considering his complaint, "I hope you will allow me to *see* there are no mistakes in the narrative"—stating that several had crept into some notes of Dr. Anderson printed in Edinburgh. This engraving and memoir, under Malone's inspection, were meant for an edition of the *Reliques.*

In the following year (1806) the print was completed, and gave satisfaction to the Bishop's Irish friends. To Malone he wrote as usual, in that tone of apology always employed in adverting to a work the introduction of which, to literary life, required no apology, and which, in fact, forms the basis of his literary reputation. " The Bishop cannot see the print, but his friends think it is neatly engraved. Not having the picture to compare it with, they cannot judge of its fidelity. He cannot by any means think that such a solemn figure is fit to be prefixed to the sportive subjects of the *Reliques*— the gay amusements of early youth, of which he is now frequently reproached by his brethren and other serious persons."

In the beginning of winter, renewed apprehensions of their brother's condition prevailed in the Baronston family. His health became unsatisfactory, exercise was discontinued, and his spirits depressed. A

cheerful companion and counsellor was again sought
in their reverend friend (Jephson) from Westmeath,
whose spirits were as cheerful as his personal attachments were sincere. He was therefore again summoned to London, and gives his wife as before,
some lively notices of the incidents of his stay :—

I sit down (November 4th, 1805) to write my dearest girl
an account of myself in Mr. M.'s study, after having sent off
Miss Spencer* without much difficulty to Hockston (*sic*),
where she is to be received in an excellent establishment for
persons in her situation. I think I am of use to Mr. M., and
if so, my whole object has been attained. I have hitherto
never stirred from him, and to-morrow night am to be in the
house. . . . . London looks, for that is all I shall see
of it, as cheerful, gay, and riant as possible.

Whether Luttrell be yet in town or not, I know not. I
dine to-day with Mr. M., Mr. Plumptree, a Cantab, and I
believe young Boswell. Now for my journey. It was ridiculous enough during my Italian mania that I found myself
placed in the coach at Holyhead, next to a native of Tuscany,
of most agreeable manners, so that in walking up and down
the Welsh hills, I had plenty of pronunciation, idiom, and the
analogy and philosophy of languages, which you know is so
much to my taste. . . . .

November 19*th.* — I had this morning packed up the
greater part of my things, and with an impatient heart was
getting ready for the Shrewsbury coach, which sets off at
three o'clock this day, when I received a letter from Miss C.
Malone, so earnestly recommending my further stay, that I
was staggered in my resolution, and upon showing my letter
to Mr. M., and pressing him to know how he felt upon the
subject, the result is that I must submit to a little further
absence from my dearest of dear girls.

Though Miss Malone, naturally enough, is more appre-

* Daughter, it is supposed, of a former acquaintance, alluded to by
Mr. Metcalfe in a letter from Brighton, and now believed to have been
thrown on the humanity of Malone.

hensive for her brother's spirits than happily she need be, I now find that my presence for a little while longer is more material than Mr. M.'s extreme delicacy suffered me to imagine before, and I shall therefore mitigate my impatience to be with you again by reflecting that I am acting at once more rightly and beneficially to the best of friends. And now, my love, that I am disappointed of telling you myself all that I have seen and done so soon as I expected, I will write in continuation what I hoped to have related with the interruption of a thousand kisses. You know to whom my whole heart belongs, and you shall have the rummaging of your own property, and look, as you have a right to do, into every corner of it.

To begin with my reception by Mr. M., I found him in his study at about eight o'clock; his manner was kind, but not remarkably warm. After a little conversation he told me that he began to smell a rat—and that I had been sent over by the Baronston lord and ladies. I assured him that was not the case, but did not tell him exactly that I had come to help him, not liking to place him under an obligation, and quite satisfied with conversing and drawing off his thoughts from melancholy objects. A few days after he received a letter from Miss C. (Catherine Malone). I came into the room, when he seized my hand, and rated me for not telling him how much he was my debtor. This you see was at once the best and most agreeable way of our coming to a right understanding; and the greatest possible degree of cordiality and confidence immediately commenced, which has increased with uniformly accelerated motion ever since.

Our first company was a very lively Mr. Boswell, and Mr. Plumptree, a Cambridge author. The first business I set about was collecting materials for my uncle's life,* and the opportunity, which will not recur, proved such a stimulus that, aided by Mr. M.'s zeal, I have succeeded in point of dates and events completely to my wish. I soon saw Mr. Courtenay, and, added to a good deal of amusement from his conversation,

* Captain (or Mr.) Robert Jephson, the dramatist, who has been already introduced to the reader, and died in 1803

sucked out of him something for my Life, together with the promise of a very interesting letter, relative to Mr. Burke and my uncle, which will greatly enrich my volume. The Trafalgar victory, and the death of Lord Nelson, occupied every one, and I had the pleasure of talking it over with Mr. Trevor, late ambassador at Turin, who knows all continental business, and the probable effects of our naval success upon them, as well as any man in England.

In a day or two after Luttrell arrived from Lord Egremont's with Lord Cowper. He ran to me in an absolute ecstasy; next morning introduced me to Lord C., whom I like better, I think, than any one I ever met upon a short acquaintance. Luttrell dined next day with Mr. Malone; and the day but one after, gave a dinner to Lord C., Mr. M. and myself. It was absolutely delightful; and we sat till near twelve in a perpetual talk, and of the best kind. You cannot often, my dearest Anne, see such men as Lord C., but I am a little out of luck about him. He has lately married Lord Melbourne's daughter, and is fitting up his house, residing till it is finished with Lord Melbourne. He lamented over and over again this circumstance, which prevented him giving me certain dinners, which he assures me are at my service whenever I come again to London. Lord Melbourne's house was inaccessible, on account of the Prince of Wales, who lived there all the time Lord C. staid in town, and must not have new personages to dine with him. I should otherwise, I believe, have had an *entrée* here. Lord C., Luttrell, and I, however, had a long and very pleasant walk to Kensington, and consequently a lot of talking.

I have been twice to the play; once because Mr. M. passed the evening abroad. It was at Drury Lane, a new play, dreadfully bad—*The Prior Claim;* but Bannister very diverting in Molière's *Médecin Malgre Lui.* The next was to hear Braham. I was delighted with him and Storace. He is in appearance so like Harvey Daniel, that I was thinking myself every moment at New Forest. I have not been at the Opera, but will give you a variety of reasons for not doing what you desire, beginning with the last, namely, that

there will be no more till January. Luttrell and I chose you
a few musical things.

The day before yesterday Mr. M. and I went to Hoxton
and sat with poor Miss S. for half an hour. She is much
better, but still evidently deranged; she kissed us both on
our going away. Yesterday Mr. Windham came to town.
He dined with us and sat all the evening. We had a great
deal of conversation together of the most satisfactory kind,—
to me extremely flattering on his part. I was to have dined
to-day with Mr. Ward, Lord Dudley's son, and to have met
Mr. Spencer, the author, but my proposed departure prevented
it. He is the liveliest man I ever met, and we harmonized
amazingly one evening at Luttrell's. I must tell it in my
dearest dear's ear, that my reception here with these sort of
people has been uniformly so flattering, and so favourable,
as to astonish even my vanity. Lord C. called upon me
while I was out, and spoke of me most ludicrously well to
Mr. M.

I have dined twice with Dr. Hume and Anacreon Moore.
Once I brought Mr. Malone at his desire. I like his wife
much, and Moore without bounds. Once also with Woodward, where I met Lord Mountcashell hot from Germany.

After an impassioned passage of affection to his
wife, Mr. Jephson again writes:—

November 30*th*.—You are right in your opinion of Mr.
M.'s mind, and of the excellence of his heart. His kindness
to me is unbounded, and the unqualified confidence in which
we live together, with our many hours of talk which our
mode of life induces, have certainly strengthened those bonds
of amity that before subsisted between us.

To return to my journalier account of myself. We dined
a few days since with Mr. Metcalf. He is principally remarkable for *La cuisine douce*, of which we certainly had a
very good example. A Mr. Cromle, formerly Steward of the
Household to Lord Carlisle when Lord-Lieutenant of Ireland,
was the only stranger. He seemed to me a perfect model of

U

that species of man which is formed by exclusive habitudes with the very highest ranks of society, operating upon a mind very moderately qualified by nature. He is, as Shakspeare expresses it, " a man of most soft society," and might be well administered as a sedative to irritable nerves, without anything of those angular manners and ungraceful abruptnesses that give me the sensation of jolting at every step. Compared to his host, Mr. Metcalf, he was as a well-hung, double-springed coach to the wheel part of a jaunting car without springs. We were placed together at table, and had a great deal of intercourse. I think I have a sort of advantage from taking all manner of things in their own way, not wilfully excluding all pleasure but such as comes in such a particular shape.

The day before yesterday Mr. Courtenay and Mr. Windham dined here, or rather, the latter came in after dinner and drank wine. He brought an account of Bonaparte's arrival at Vienna, the probable death of the archduke, and seemed really depressed upon public affairs. He would hardly allow me to state Trafalgar as a good set off, according to the legal phrase.

Were not you diverted, dearest, to see me making a figure in the fashionable intelligence of a London newspaper? Who informed the public of so important an event as my visit to Mr. Malone, I cannot guess; but there I was, to my own great surprise and amusement. I feel extremely obliged to Miss C. Malone for her good-nature to me, and still more for her kindness to you. She rates much too highly my attempt to be of use to the best and most affectionate of friends; but that overrating is a further cause of gratitude on my part, which I most sincerely feel.

Mr. M. begins to talk rather peremptorily of sending me away during the next light nights. I shall not at this moment directly oppose him, but certainly shall not leave him till I am quite convinced that he really wishes it. S. S.* is a great deal better. A Miss Legard, a friend of hers, saw her the day before yesterday, and says that she thinks her quite

* The lady who had been placed at Hoxton.

well. I know that this appearance is fallacious, and have tried to instil that opinion into Mr. M. that he would do nothing without precise directions from Dr. Willis. We shall go to see her together on Monday next.

An advertisement of a *Life of Dr. Johnson* written by himself drew attention from the Dublin critics as a probable forgery. Malone, as an authority, was appealed to by two or three of the number; and he ascertained it to be that juvenile sketch which is now admitted to be authentic.

Dr. Kearney again enters upon Shakspearian criticism, deeming the Poet, the more he read him, to rise higher and higher in mind.

When I read him (Shakspeare), I think that I find many deep and philosophical maxims which, if they were prosaically expressed and incorporated in the writings of the severest masters of reason, even in Bacon, would appear to be the profoundest and best established observations. . . . I do not mean remarks on manners, &c., which might be expected in the writings of a man engaged in the world, but such as might offer themselves to a studious, contemplative mind, absorbed in meditation on the subjects of science.*

* Among numberless others, perhaps the following passages may support my notion (edition 1793) :—

"The sense of death," *Measure for Measure*, act iii. scene 1, p. 271.
"Nature is better made," *Winter's Tale*, act iv. scene 3, p. 125.
"Oh, vanity of sickness," &c., *King John*, act v. scene 7, p. 178.
"Before the curing," &c., *King John*, act iii. scene 4, p. 113.
"All things that are," *Merchant of Venice*, act ii. scene 6, p. 444.
"Each substance of a grief," *Richard II.*, act ii. scene 2, p. 247.
"For if our virtues," &c., *Measure for Measure*, act i. scene 1, p. 185.
"Too subtle," &c., *Troilus and Cressida*, act iii. scene 2, p. 321.
"The heavens themselves, *Troilus and Cressida*, act i. scene 3, p. 252.
"Who can hold," &c., *King Richard II.*, act ii. scene 3, p. 222.
"Reason not the need," &c., *Lear*, act ii. scene 12, p. 134.
"Impediments in Fancy's way," *All's Well*, act v. scene 3, p. 363.
Many more will present themselves to you.

Toward the end of 1806, a visit from his friend Jephson and family from Gibraltar, deranged the systematic quietude of an old bachelor. "My whole time," he writes, "has been taken up. *Shakspeare* is at a stand. On his account alone, I shall not be sorry when they are settled in their own house. However, I have the pleasure of reflecting that though inconvenient in housekeeping details, I have done a kind thing."

"I am still," he writes again to his elder sister, "as you see, in town, though I had thought of going to Taplow Court for a few days. Lady Thomond * is a good deal here, attending her aunt, who is very ill and not likely to live long. Lord Thomond is uneasy without her society, so she does as well as she can, going to and fro occasionally. This matter might be adjusted by removing Mrs. Reynolds to the country, were she not confined to bed, and near eighty years old. However, if I find Lord Thomond at home the latter end of next week, I believe I shall then go to them.

"The Windhams are still in town, but are positively to set off for his house in Norfolk next Monday. I dined with them twice this week. As usual, old Mrs. Cholmondeley, who is grown quite foolish, was there, and tiresome enough. I met there the two Miss Berrys, renewed our acquaintance, and dined with them and their father in North Audley Street last week. They have a pretty little place in the country, on the banks of the Thames, which Lord Orford gave them, called *little* Strawberry Hill;

* Niece to Sir Joshua Reynolds.

and they pressed me much to visit them there. So has their neighbour, Mrs. Damer, of *great* Strawberry Hill. But I am a wretched visitor."

Frequent remonstrances came from friends upon the undue labours given to his eyes. Lord Charlemont, who suffered from similar infirmity, often remonstrated with him. "Five hours a day employed in transcribing from obscure manuscripts! How in the name of wonder do your eyes hold out?" His sisters often ask the same question, intermingled with sisterly exhortations to amend; but the species of recreation given them seems pretty much akin to work. "I have not pressed them hard these three weeks, for I have been almost daily at a book auction, the library of Mr. Reed, the last Shaksperian except myself, where my purse has been drained as usual. But what I have purchased are chiefly books of my own trade. There is hardly a library of this kind now left, except my own and Mr. Bindley's, neither of us having the least desire to succeed the other in his peculiar species of literary wealth."

While in search of the publications of the age of Elizabeth, he discovered some tracts connected with the settlement of the colony of Virginia. These on further consideration led to the belief of their bearing upon a curious Shaksperian question—the origin of the play of *The Tempest*—in the shipwreck of Sir George Somers and Sir Thomas Gates on the Bermuda Islands in a violent storm. This impression became at length conviction. A paper was drawn up embodying the circumstances, with extracts from one of the pamphlets alluded to, which were shown at the

time to a literary friend whom he does not name, who
fully participated in the opinion.

This discovery he deemed to be exclusively his own.
It was therefore hoarded for the long-promised second
edition of the Poet ; but just at this moment the publication of Mr. Douce's *Illustrations* disclosed that he
also had arrived at a similar conclusion. No time was
to be lost in announcing through the press his claim
to originality.* The tract was therefore printed early
in January, 1808, and all honour paid in it to " the
learned and ingenious critic " who had thus acciden-
tally preceded him.   Copies, however, were still withheld from the public.   That to Lord Sunderlin, now
before me, and others also have this intimation on
the fly-leaf : " It is requested that this pamphlet may
not be inadvertently put into the hands of persons
who may be likely to publish any part of it." It did,
however, eventually transpire.   From some misapprehension of Archdeacon Nares, a review of it appeared
in the *British Critic* in the following year in conformity, as erroneously supposed, with the wishes of the
author, which produced two or three letters of amicable explanation between the parties, though Nares was
declared to be wrong in giving part of the merit of
the discovery to Capell.

This essay proved a momentary diversion from
another subject.   In 1796 he had lost his friend Mr.
William Gerard Hamilton, who had acquired during
life high private repute with apparently little labour.

---

* Malone assigned the date of the *Tempest* to 1611; recently Mr.
Joseph Hunter believes that an earlier date may be assigned to the
Tempest, perhaps 1596 or 1597; but other authorities say certainly not
till after 1603, and more probably not till 1611, the time stated by Malone.

Among many of his manuscript remains submitted to Malone, one only appeared fit for the press, *Parliamentary Logick*. To this were added a few poetical pieces printed after leaving college; and a short notice by Dr. Johnson of the corn-laws of that day (1767), which had been found in his own hand-writing among Hamilton's papers.*

Malone edited these, and was constitutionally fitted for an editor—for his friendships survived his friends. He was proud of their names and their remains being equally remembered. He and the deceased had travelled down the hill of life together without finding cause to part company by the way. They valued each other, were in habits of intercourse, visited in the same circles—that is, the best informed societies in London,—and he wished now to test whether public opinion would stamp as sterling that reputation which in private life had been freely awarded him.

Hamilton was one of those men whose history presents some anomalies in English public life, not always easy to reconcile. Elsewhere I have glanced at the earlier portion of his career. He has left us little of himself to contemplate; and if the portrait be unsatisfactory, the fault can scarcely be laid to the charge of the limner.

* Boswell, in one of his letters to Malone, written just before the publication of Johnson's life, thus writes of Hamilton:—"That nervous mortal, W. G. H., is not satisfied with some particulars *which I wrote down from his own mouth*, and is so much agitated that Courtenay has persuaded me to allow a new edition of them by H. himself, to be made at H.'s expense." On this Mr. Croker remarks—"Mr. Hamilton's *nervousness* increases our regret at not being able to penetrate the secret of his political transactions with Johnson. It was clearly something that he did not like to reveal." This, however, is probably an error. It was more likely temperament—a nature painfully fastidious about small matters.

He was clever; and no ordinary judge of clever-
ness in others. He sought out those who possessed
it, and aimed to draw around and secure such as might
be employed for his own special uses. Accession to
office in the Board of Trade about 1755, after a
popular speech or two, kept him for five years afterwards silent. An Irish sinecure kept him equally
tongue-tied after his return from office in that
country above thirty years more. Though mute,
he contrived to retain fame as an orator. Unknown
to the press, he obtained the character of a first-
rate writer even so far as to be considered "Junius"
—no one could tell precisely why,—yet comparison
with that writer he deemed injurious to his own
powers. He claimed to be a statesman, but did
nothing and attempted nothing common to the character. In private life, none more freely discussed
public affairs. In the Senate he said nothing. None
more narrowly watched there the conduct of public
men, their sentiments, speeches, and modes of speaking, yet never gave the country the benefit of his
opinions on the momentous proceedings of one American and two French wars—not even the small
contribution of a set speech once or twice in a
session. He saw a former friend of whom he had
hoped to make a tool, ascend equally by his tongue
and his pen, step by step, and day by day, to unrivalled celebrity throughout Europe, yet never
once attempted a struggle for former eminence as
a speaker, or attempted to do anything as a writer.
He appeared to live upon the past, yet is said to
have kept a lively eye upon the future. Office—after

his sinecure had been exchanged for a pension—he did not for a long time deem beyond his grasp; and had Richard, Earl Temple, constructed a ministry he would have probably become his Chancellor of the Exchequer.*

The chief incident of his life was in becoming the first official patron of Edmund Burke. From volunteer studies at the Board of Trade—for Burke had no appointment—he carried him to Dublin; profited by his large capacity; procured him a pension " after six years of laborious attendance " in both countries; exacted its resignation when he refused to become permanently subservient; and the quarrel ceased in what Burke, writing to Flood at the moment, said should be an " eternal separation." The demand made upon him was unprecedented—in fact, to sell himself for life—for three hundred a year. He, however, felt confident in his own powers to ensure distinction whenever an appropriate stage should open for their exhibition. The "patron" may have thought the same; but presuming on the adhesive power of the pension to keep its holder in his train, carried his demand farther than a man of spirit could brook. Hamilton thus lost the services and friendship of the most accomplished intellect in Europe. With such an ally and counsellor, added to his own

* Mr. Thomas Grenville in reply to Malone's inquiries writes (March, 1807):—" Long as I have known Stowe, and much as I have been accustomed to see Gerard Hamilton there from my earliest days, yet have I no recollection whatever of any picture or drawing of him at that place. I have, however, written to Lord Buckingham to inquire." The result was the engraving prefixed to the posthumous work by Malone.

influence and talents, he may have lost much fame and honour in public life. He could not indeed have had the remotest conception that the rise of that luminary should prefigure his own decadence, nay prove, from whatever cause, the extinction of his eloquence and consequent political importance in the country.

In the esteem of the Grenvilles, he took a high place. No guest was more frequent or favoured at Stowe. Many eminent men of the day spoke of his talents as first-rate. Select circles of good society made him an oracle. Dr. Johnson admired his conversation and encouraged his visits. He left behind several volumes of *Adversaria*, none of which but that mentioned here found its way into the press.

Of such a man, who spoke little in public while living, and has left nothing behind to earn reputation, what shall we say? Probably that he was overrated. Critical justice can scarcely award celebrity where there is nothing of moment to warrant it. He observed keenly and discriminated minutely; but if we are to take *Parliamentary Logick* as a specimen— though it contains useful precepts for young members of Parliament—he appears prone to note the forms rather than substance of things—the manner of a debater more than his matter—in fact, that he was a mere rhetorician. Otherwise, how can we conceive that a really powerful mind should be profoundly taciturn between 1756 and 1761, and again from 1763 to 1796 in the British House of Commons, when the most exciting topics ever discussed in Europe were daily before him? Or if too nervous to speak, which has never been alleged, that he should not have aimed to enlighten the country through the press?

Lord Charlemont, in writing to Malone (1792), is equally unable to suggest any probable motive for his inactivity—"For the precarious state of my old acquaintance Hamilton, I am most sincerely grieved.* There was a man whose talents were equal to every undertaking; and yet from indolence, or from too fastidious vanity, or from what other cause I know not, he has done nothing." Further conjecture is now vain; we are left but to one derogatory supposition— that having reaped the material fruits of statesman-ship in a sinecure place afterwards exchanged for an "equivalent," he was willing to remain undisturbed by its contests and labours.

In the preliminary notice to the volume it is re-markable that Malone is silent on the connection of the writer with Burke. Neither did he affix his name as editor. Mrs. Burke still survived. Hamilton had formed no family ties. But as the friend of both, he was probably unwilling to revive any un-pleasing recollections at Beaconsfield, or on the other hand tell a story of one who, in that instance at least, had exhibited none of the feelings of a high-spirited or liberal man. A few of his remarks appear in the subsequent anecdotes.

With the usual keen eyes of ladies on domestic matters, the Misses Malone discovered in their London

* An attack of paralysis; yet in 1794 he still wished to remain in the House of Commons! and became dissatisfied by the seat being given to another.

visits that their brother's house was becoming more
and more that of an old bachelor—an accumulation
of books; rooms not in spruce order; furniture
rather in the rear of the fashion of the age. One
rallies him on the unthriftiness of not paying off
debts instead of investing money in the funds. The
other, for not spending savings in refurnishing and
beautifying Foley Place. He makes the best defence
he can—the want of female superintendence. Catherine on her way to England, returns to the charge
in writing from Dublin—

Mr. Forth* told me he had sent you a pretty round sum
of one thousand pounds. My answer to him was that I
wished he had not sent you so much at a time; for that you
would only be more profuse in buying *old* books, and think
it would never be out. Is not this true enough? Well, if
money ever did you good, this will certainly. He has paid
us a hundred and twenty pounds on your account; so you
have got out of your estate this moment eleven hundred and
twenty pounds.

Again she writes, that having been on a visit to
the Bishop of Meath (O'Beirne), they heard so much
of Kilkenny theatricals from visitors in the house as
to produce general desire for an excursion thither.
A party for the occasion had been therefore formed
by Lord Sunderlin and some of the family, which,
with one of the Jephsons, she meant to accompany.
The Bishop stayed at home. But in a long letter to
Malone soon afterwards, his lordship concludes with
an allusion to the most celebrated member of the
Kilkenny amateur group.

* His land agent.

We have had a visit very lately from our friends at
Baronston, and the only drawback on the pleasure we always
enjoy in their society was the absence of the good and
worthy Miss Malone, who was not well enough to accompany them.   All Miss Catherine's cheerful spirits and good-
humour, Lady Sunderlin's sound sense and understanding,
your brother's warmth of heart, and Jephson's jokes, could
not make us forget her.

I dare say they will have made the theatricals of Kilkenny,
and the final close of that very classical scene, the subject of
some of their late letters to you.   My daughter has copied
for you Mr. Moore's verses on the effect of national music,
which he recited on the stage there, as I heard from every
one, in a most masterly manner.   I do not much admire
that little gentleman ; and I am apt to believe, with a most
excellent judge of character, that Tommy Moore will never
become Thomas.   But I think some of the verses of the
Melologue, as he foolishly calls it in the cant phrase of the
day, are extremely beautiful and true poetry.

The prediction happily was not fulfilled.   Tommy
grew to be Thomas ; the supposed pigmy became a
giant among admiring nations, equally valued for
fancy, and sweetness, and often for strength.   How is
it that Irishmen are thus prone to form such undue
estimates of each other ?   Why do not the gifted class
more frequently travel to England for reputation—
that England so often abused and vilified by the idle,
the uninformed, and the bigoted of their country?
There, when they deserve it, they will obtain it.   No
party or religious feelings which poison the sources
of liberality elsewhere, can in her keep down the
intellect of man to the narrow dimensions which interested bigotry and superstition prescribe at home.
In England, the mind may expand to the length,
and breadth, and depth which Providence may have

ordained for its widest and highest exercise, because
untrammelled by a despotic priesthood. Let not
Irishmen be misled by their provincial notions or
peddling politics to look no farther than Ireland for
the reward of their talents. England is the natural
sphere for capacious views and enlightened labours.
She opens widely her arms to every man who does
honour to his kind; and from her, when their conduct and character merit it, are sure to obtain their
reward.

Amused by these accounts of theatrical exhibitions
on one side of the Channel, he was not at all disposed to submit to censures of it on the other. One
of his friends, Archdeacon Plumptre, was accused of
this in sermons preached at Cambridge. Malone
lost no time in defence and remonstrance. In reply,
the Archdeacon denies the charge; alleges that he
assails only *abuses*, not *uses*, of the stage; that he
had quoted Archbishop Tillotson, and other eminent
authorities holding the same sentiments, in opposition
to Wilberforce, Witherspoon, Law, Mrs. More, who
took extreme views of the subject; and for his own
part, believed that many portions of an audience
would be worse employed than in witnessing a
well-written play. The critic was soothed, and
sent him an additional sheet to the tract on the
Tempest.

Amid correspondence on various topics—with the
learned though eccentric Dr. Barrett (of Dublin)
on certain historical incidents, Lysons on mistakes
in the *Monumenta Vetusta*, Rev. Mr. Blakeway,
Archdeacon Nares, Dr. Burney, Chetwood, and

others—the death of Mr. Windham gave a severe shock to his enjoyments. No adverse influences had shaken mutual esteem and intimacy during thirty years. From the turmoil of public business, the statesman often sought repose in the quiet study or the conversation of the man of letters. There, sincere affection and admiration at all times awaited him—such as were due to one of the most accomplished gentlemen and manly spirits of the age—from one of the most amiable and unassuming.

Mr. Windham formed the *beau ideal* of an English gentleman of the highest class. Well born, well educated, endowed with superior faculties, in addition to those goods of fortune which command consideration everywhere and often of themselves serve to open the portals to fame, he possessed judgment to turn these advantages to the best use. As a boy, he sought distinction, and as a boy obtained it, in being leader of all those sports which make the ambition of school-boy life. At college he became a student of no ordinary attainments. While resident for a season in Scotland he took to mathematics. At Oxford, and through life, he pursued with success the study of its higher branches. At twenty-three, he started with the future Lord Mulgrave on a voyage to the North Pole. He ascended, in 1785, in a balloon. At the siege of Valenciennes, he perilled himself freely in surveying the enemy's works ; and at an earlier period, ran personal risks in subduing mutiny in a militia regiment of which he was major. Even his death arose from the same fearless spirit exhibited through life. While assisting to rescue valuables from the house of a friend on fire, he sustained injury eventually requiring a surgical operation, under which he sank ; but with characteristic consideration for the feelings of his wife, the operation was performed during her absence from town. And in the same Christian spirit, he received the sacrament previously in a private room from the Rev. Dr. Fisher, of the Charter House.

Equally frank and generous ; graceful in address and high in principle ; chivalrous and resolute ; the patron and promoter of manly pastimes and character, he seems to have been cut out by nature for a favourite of the people. But he would not yield to their prejudices or errors. Hence he was occasionally unpopular ; but the courage displayed in opposing their wishes often made him nearly as much a favourite as those who gave way to them.

His career in the State, open and uncompromising, left no doubt as to his opinions. In Parliament, his abilities commanded the greatest respect. Often eloquent and logical, he was sometimes too refined —sometimes too sincere and unreserved for a working statesman. In quitting office he took nothing for himself or his friends. As Secretary at War he was too low in the scale of office, though a seat in the Cabinet partially remedied the defect. But it was not known even to Malone till a year or two afterward, that he declined the Seals as Secretary of State by deferring to the Duke of Portland; and twice the title of viscount in the peerage. He conscientiously filled public places—not by playing the patron to his friends—but with the fittest men he could find for the duties.

The regard and companionship of one so characterized conferred honour on any man.   To lose such a friend when ourselves advanced into the vale of years, leaves a miserable blank in the breast.   So Malone felt it.   And when the first emotions of grief were subdued, he set about doing honour to the departed by embodying a few of the leading points of character in a memoir.   A short statement was first printed in the *Gentleman's Magazine* to correct erroneous rumours regarding the manner of an event so little expected by the world.   This, with additions, was reprinted as a pamphlet, and sent to many mutual friends and various members of both Houses of Parliament, all of whom, however opposed in party attachments, paid the honour due to one who stood in the foremost rank in public esteem as in worth and independence.   He left a journal which rumour said was not to be published.

The correspondence of our author during this year appears to have been less active than usual.   Mr. J. Taylor, of the *Sun* newspaper (author of *Monsieur Tonson*), refers to a passage in *Cynthia's Revels* so closely resembling what Anthony says of Brutus that it seems plain the one poet borrowed from the other.*   Interested, as he says, in the researches of the critic, he would not fail to point out any things bearing upon Shakspeare.   Ritson is taken to task soundly for his abuse ; and the writer, who had given

---

* Crites, a creature of the most perfect and divine temper—one in whom the *elements* are peaceably met, &c. &c.

x

him previous information upon the supposed connection between Shakspeare and D'Avenant, thus breaks out in a stanza against Malone's unhappy assailant.

TO EDMOND MALONE, Esq.,

ON THE ATTACKS OF A VIRULENT SCRIBBLER.

Proceed, Malone, thy Shakspeare's page to clear,
  Nor heed what Ritson's cankered spleen can say;
So may the Sun of our poetic sphere
  Shoot through the mists of time its faintest ray.

CHAPTER XIV.

1810—1812.

Proposed Life of Mason—W. Gifford—Notes upon Books—Conversational Memoranda—Illness—Letter to Lady Ailesbury—Letter to a Lady in Ireland—Letter to Lady Sunderlin—His Death—Character—Person and Manners—Collections—Will—Gift of his Brother to the Bodleian Library—Letters and Papers.

ABOUT two years after the death of Mason the poet, one of his executors (Rev. John Dixon of Boughton) applied to Malone on the propriety of republishing the translation of Du Fresnoy's *Art of Painting*, which with the notes of Reynolds, had been previously published by the former in his works. This led to further correspondence. Hearing that he knew Lord Orford's executors, the same gentleman requested him to urge on them the return of Mason's letters to his lordship, which the will of that nobleman directed, but which they had applied for in vain. Malone complied, but also failed in his application—from what cause does not appear.

This eventually led (1811) to the project of a Life of Mason. But who was to write it? Few were deemed sufficiently disposed, or in other respects qualified for the office. At length Gifford, the sharp editor of the *Quarterly Review*, was proposed, apparently by Malone; but he declined. Could a fiery Tory do otherwise to a Whig no less fierce? But he had ample excuse. The *Review* was of recent date.

All his energies were required to secure contributions from the best writers; or to put in what is
technically called the *plumbs*—that is, point, satire,
or virulence—into such as required it, so as to aim
at destroying that monopoly in the martyrdom of
books hitherto enjoyed by the literary butchers of
Edinburgh.   The refusal however was couched in
terms satisfactory to the reverend friend of the poet :

> Though not successful in your application to Mr. Gifford,
> I think myself indebted for the trouble you have taken to
> make it so. I should have been well satisfied if so able a
> man had undertaken to write Mr. Mason's life; he is so
> competent, from genius, knowledge, and taste, to execute it
> well. . . . I will thank you to mention, when you see
> him, that I am obliged by his answer to your application;
> and gratified by the sentiments of a man of genius and taste,
> relative to Mr. Mason.

Hitherto we have seen Gifford only in his blander
moods—bent on being amiable in return for the
assistance cordially rendered to his studies by a
stranger.   But these were weaker moments—the
tiger assuming the bleat of the lamb.   The gall in
his system lay too near the surface not to ooze
through the thin layer of suavity upon the smallest
provocation.

Malone, it will be remembered, had confessed to
Mr. Whalley twenty years before, that he had no
taste for the productions of Ben Jonson; that he
had doubts whether his professions of friendship for
Shakspeare were sincere.   In this he was not singular, as several of the biographers and writers of
the time had arrived at a similar conclusion.   But

when Gifford became the editor of Jonson, all these, as well as more modern men, were to be overthrown —Headley, A. Chalmers, Davies, Capell, Hurd, and others. While, as one of the late and principal offenders, Malone, then in his grave, became the primary object of abuse. The late eulogist of the living man became his reviler when dead. The terms " false, mean, base, malicious," were liberally applied; and simple difference of opinion upon the literary merits of a writer who had lived two hundred years before, was thought sufficient to warrant language applicable only to the perpetrator of a serious moral offence. Such are some of the men who claim to be critics by profession. Habits of irresponsible abuse in anonymous criticism increase by indulgence. Native acerbity or vulgarity, thrust by accident or impudence into the chair of mere opinion, form examples not to imitate but to shun.

In reference to this gratuitous asperity, the younger Boswell justly writes :

Mr. Gifford knows not Mr. Malone's notions of friendship. I regret that, he did not know him better; for he was truly a man to be loved. I regret still more deeply that the grave has closed over a long catalogue of illustrious men, whose esteem and regard accompanied him through life, and that my feeble voice must offer that testimony to his notions of friendship which would have been borne with affectionate warmth by a Reynolds, a Burke, and a Wyndham. He was indeed a cordial and a steady friend, combining the utmost mildness with the simplest sincerity and the most manly independence. Tenacious, perhaps, of his own opinions, which he had seldom hastily formed, he was always ready to listen with candour and good-humour to those of others. That suppleness of character which would yield without conviction, and that roughness of temper which cannot tole-rate dissent, were equally foreign from his nature.

An amusement of his more lonely hours largely exercised about this time, was the annotation of books under perusal—general remarks, anecdotes, or details gleaned from sources not generally familiar. These, after the discontinuance of his regular memoranda, diversified the labours on Shakspeare. *Spence's Anecdotes* were thus taken in hand, and such notes added as came within range of his reading or conversational sources, and were published by an anonymous editor in 1820. Another was Mrs. Piozzi's *Anecdotes of Dr. Johnson.* His leanings here, as already noticed, are all against the lady whose accuracy, though there seems little to find fault with, has been on many occasions impeached. Mr. Caldwell, writing to Bishop Percy (Sept. 1806), says, on Langbaine's catalogue of old plays—" Malone told me he had copied all the notes from the original, and has besides added thrice as many as all his predecessors."

From statements of the junior Boswell, it appears that in conversation on the versification of Shakspeare, so many freedoms had been taken with it by the caprice of editors, that Malone was induced to undertake an express essay on his metre and phraseology. Some progress was made when death arrested this among other critical contributions. There is, however, a paper on the subject in the last edition of which we may deem Boswell to be the writer.

Another and more favourite occupation was in revising and noting reprints of Boswell's *Johnson.* In this work he was more at home than with Spence.

He had aided in its arrangement; added much of his own matter; revised large portions of the volumes as we have seen ere they issued from the press; and friendship for the author, added to unbounded admiration of the great man whom it commemorates, rendered success as dear to him as a production of his own. It became further dear by the request of the dying author that he would give such advice for the disposal of any of his works as his judgment should decide. This charge he faithfully fulfilled. Successive editions passed under his eye, particularly the third, fourth, fifth, and sixth, in 1799, 1804, 1807, and 1811.

His notes in a small recent edition which trench not on Mr. Croker's labours, amount to no less than two hundred and twenty-six, exhibiting his customary research and accuracy. The younger Boswell felt grateful for the labour; and by a species of poetical justice, repaid the debt of his father by editing, according to the wish of Malone, his great work, the second edition of *Shakspeare* in twenty-one volumes.

Early in their acquaintance, he carried through the press the second edition of Boswell's *Tour to the Hebrides*, when the author was absent in Scotland. To this likewise he gave a few notes. One is on the wit of Burke, written as if by Boswell, who, however, insisted that the credit should be surrendered to the actual writer.

In the early part of 1812 his health, which had been gradually declining, seriously gave way. Without being wholly confined, he could take little exercise; his appetite failed; the stomach imperfectly fulfilled its functions otherwise ; and wasting of the frame, without material pain, ensued. Still his studies were but slightly intermitted. What ·he had once done he aimed to improve, when and wherever the opportunity offered. The following note, written in the spring of the year respecting some letters of Dryden kindly procured for him by a member of the Royal family, displays the pains he took in not merely accomplishing an object, but in doing it so completely that there should be as little room as possible for future improvement.

" Mr. Malone presents his compliments to Lady Ailesbury, and requests that her ladyship will accept his sincere thanks for the copies of· Dryden's letters and Lord Chesterfield's answers, which she has had the goodness to transmit to him, and which he should have acknowledged some days, but that he has been since Friday last much out of order. He is extremely concerned to find that Lady Ailesbury has had so much trouble in obtaining these papers. Indeed, had he conceived that this could possibly have been the case, he hardly would have ventured to solicit her ladyship to undertake so difficult a negotiation.

" Were he master of those happy turns of expression for which his author was so justly celebrated, he might perhaps have endeavoured to express his sense of the goodness of her Royal Highness the Princess Elizabeth in taking so much concern in this matter. Without, however, any pretensions of that kind, he trusts he may be permitted to say that her Royal Highness's condescension in exerting her powerful influence for the purpose of procuring copies of these literary remains of the great Dryden, evinces not only the benignity of her disposition, but her good taste and love of letters, one of the surest sources of happiness to the possessor, and no inconsiderable ornament of the highest station.

" Whenever an opportunity shall offer itself, he requests that Lady Ailesbury will have the goodness to express to her Royal Highness the sentiments of gratitude and respect imprinted upon his mind by her Royal Highness's gracious interposition on the present occasion, which has obtained these memorials of one of our most celebrated English poets that otherwise, perhaps, might have been lost to posterity.

" *F. P. Monday, March 2nd,* 1812."

Soon afterwards he proceeded to the country; but the scene, or the season, failed to give relief. Excess in long-continued study had doubtless induced aggravated dyspepsia—what hard student has escaped it?—with more or less permanent disease of the stomach. Emaciation and exhaustion of the animal powers succeeded. Instead of throwing off study, seeking home-travelling, horse exercise, seaside residence, and frequent change, the routine of remedies already adopted in town was continued. Thus we find him a solitary, comfortless patient in the middle of April, in a letter to Mrs. Smith, an intimate friend of his sisters, and near relative of the Jephsons. The utter absence of self to save the sensibility of his sisters in this extremity, evinces the thoroughly amiable qualities of this very amiable man.

"*Foley Place, April 17th,* 1812.

"MY DEAR MADAM,—I cannot tell you how much I am obliged for your care and discretion in not mentioning my illness to my sisters, from whom I have taken great pains to conceal my present situation; for my poor Kate is in great distress about her sister, and it would quite break her heart to learn how ill I have been, and indeed am.

"Such has been my situation ever since the latter end of January, or beginning of February, under Sir Henry Halford's care. All of a sudden I lost all my colour, and much of my flesh and strength. Halford for some time tried the usual medicines, but with little effect, and then wished I should change the air. As I have an abhorrence of public places which some recommend, I borrowed from Lady Thormond (who is in town) her house at Taplow Court, near Maidenhead, on condition of being my own purveyor; and I remained there from the 17th of March to the 13th of April (last Monday), during which I had not one soft or genial day; and though strictly following my physician's prescriptions, do not think I derived any benefit from this movement.

"My course was half a pint of new milk in bed at half-past seven. About half-past eight I rose, dressed for the day, and walked about half an hour before breakfast. From eleven to half-past one I devoted to the newspaper and a letter or two, and a few pages of *Shakspeare*. Then appeared a bark draught; after that I walked two or three miles if the weather would at all permit; dinner at five; tea at eight; the bark again at ten; and so to bed. All this promised well, but had no effect, not for want of being well planned, but from that disposition, or rather indisposition, which had no tendency to be cured by medicine or air. I therefore came to town on Monday, and had a long conversation with Sir H. Halford on Wednesday, who was so good as to give me half an hour before he went to Windsor.

"He said that had happened to me which must happen to himself some time hence, and to all mankind—that there is a time with every human creature when the powers of digestion weaken, and the whole system becomes less energetic. That if I weathered this attack (and he saw no reason why I should not) he could not promise me ever to be again as in times past, but that I might live some years with tolerable health and strength. This appeared to me extremely sensible. He then ordered a new course of medicines.

"From my earliest years I have been accustomed to communicate to my dear Kate every sentiment of my heart. You may easily, therefore, conceive how distressing it has been not to let her know my real state; but it would be a terrible aggravation of her present distress; and, therefore, as soon as it is determined either that they can come to England, or not come, I will inform them of the truth. I have had two or three visitors since I began this, and it is late. My kindest love to my dear Shakspeare associate, and believe me ever,

"My dear Madam, &c. &c.,

"E. MALONE."

About a fortnight more elapsed ere the secret was
disclosed by himself to Lady Sunderlin. The heaviest
of pressures was upon him. The shadow of the destroyer flitted around, and obviously influenced the
tremulous hand that aimed to tell its story of suffering without inflicting painful recitals upon others.
With the ease of his dear sisters ever in view, he
attempts to prescribe for the one, and hint something
like consolation to the other. The allusion to Mrs.
Smith respecting his studies is almost affecting. It
is, indeed, love to the last—Devotion to Shakspeare
in the struggle with Death !

" London, Monday, May 4, 1812.

" My dear Lady Sunderlin, — I have this moment received a letter from Catherine, of 28th April,
in which she calls on me for all the comfort I can
give her. But, alas! I wanted comfort myself; and
the concealment of my own illness for near three
months was a sad and heavy weight on my own
mind. I wrote to K. (Kate) and to my brother on
the 29th April, and I think it probable they will set
off before this letter can reach Dublin, and that my
poor Harriet may be in bed, and that even the reading a letter may be troublesome to her, and I therefore direct this to you; and if my brother and sister
should not have set off, you will, of course, on reading
it communicate it to them, so that nothing will be
lost.

" K. in her letter mentions that poor dear Harriet
suffers excruciating pain in the coach from certain
movements in the hip. Now, might not this be
prevented by her going to the salt-water bath in a

sedan chair, the men being instructed not to swing her high. With respect to the hip pain, which is described as similar to one that I had there when I (rode?) some twenty years ago, I believe the camphorated volatile liniment would do it some good; so pray ask Dr. Percival about it, and if he approves, apply it. As to the salt-water hot-bath, I have myself no great faith in it; for to a very weakly person, as much is lost by the relaxation as may be gained on the other side for the malady. However, we must obey the physicians. But I have great faith in the rubbing, and have proof of it in myself, for one of my symptoms has been swelling in my insteps and ankles, which have been very much removed by rubbings morning and night.

"If my brother and sister should not have set off when this arrives, I beg you will exhort them not to agitate themselves about me on their journey; for though my illness has been long and is attended with great weakness, yet there are several favourable symptoms, such as a steady, good pulse, my being able to take a good deal of nutriment at different times in the course of the day, and my sleep in general being tolerably good, though not always. My kindest love to my dear Harriet; and believe me, my dear Lady Sunderlin, most faithfully and affectionately yours,

" E. MALONE."

His brother and sister Catherine soon reached Foley Place, and rendered such aid and sympathy as devoted affection could bestow. But the dart had

been thrown with too fatal precision.   An exhausted
frame could not long sustain itself against increasing
debility, former excesses in study, sedentary habits,
and the weight of seventy-one years.   He expired
on the 25th May, 1812.

No place of sepulture had been named in his will;
but Lord Sunderlin remembering a former conversation where something fell from him on the preference due to family burial-places, the body was
removed to Baronston for interment.

None who knew the man but regretted the event.
He had made no enemies but the worthless—such
as aimed by fraud to impose upon public credulity.
Those who possessed merit or character found in him
a sincere friend.   A kind disposition and gentlemanly manners enabled him to pass through life with
few of its almost inevitable bickerings.   Several
tributes to his worth found their way into print.
The following from an unknown correspondent, with
a few additions by its editor, appeared in the journal
(*Gentleman's Magazine*) to which he had been a
frequent contributor :—

Mr. Malone had the happiness to live with the most distinguished characters of his time.   He was united in the
closest intimacy with Dr. Johnson, Mr. Burke, Sir Joshua
Reynolds, Lord Charlemont, and the other members of a
society which, for various talent and virtue, can never be
surpassed. . . . . As an editor, this is the peculiar fame
of Edmond Malone, that he could subdue the temptations
to display his own wisdom or wit, and consider only the
integrity of his author's text. . . . . He adhered still
more pertinaciously than Mr. Steevens to the ancient copies.
To obtain them was the great effort of his life; and a large

part of his very moderate fortune was devoted to purchases, to him of the first necessity—to many collectors, of idle curiosity. His library was accessible to every scholar; and in any difficulty, his sagacity and experience were received and gratefully acknowledged by men themselves of profound erudition. . . . .

Since the year 1790, he had been zealously continuing those labours which in that year produced his edition of *Shakspeare's Plays and Poems*. Had he lived to carry a second edition through the press, the world would have received a large accession to its knowledge of Shakspeare. From the careful habit which he had of entering every new acquisition in its proper place, and the accurate references which he made to the sources of his information, it is apprehended there will be little difficulty in carrying this design into effect. With such a stock of materials as perhaps no other man than Mr. Malone could have collected, the executor of his critical will can have no other than a delightful task.

Few men ever possessed greater command of temper; it characterized his virtues; they were all of the gentle yet steady kind. To form new friendships could hardly be expected from one who had survived the most distinguished ornaments of the world; but they left their principles to him as a legacy. . . . . His reputation as a critic will vindicate itself—as a man he needs no vindication.

As ready to communicate as to acquire information, he has left us in no doubt as to personal appearance. " I weighed at Hall Barn" (Mr. Waller's), he says, " Oct. 4th, 1791, eleven stones two pounds. Height five feet six inches and a half." Again, in August, 1796, "weight as before."

His face, I learn from surviving friends, was bland, quiet, and rather handsome; his manner no less agreeable and winning. The portrait by Sir Joshua in the possession of the Reverend Thomas R. Rooper of Brighton, is a good resemblance, doing him no more than justice, and has been twice engraved. One is a correct copy of this picture and has been widely circulated. The other, smaller and less pleasing, has place in Bell's *British Poets;* said also to be from Sir Joshua's pencil and engraved by Bartolozzi.* The date given to this print is May, 1787. It will be seen by the preceding pages that another portrait was executed by Ozias Humphrey and transmitted to Lord Charlemont, of the fidelity of which his lordship speaks highly. I have not, however, seen it. In his collection of prints of the Literary Club, his own stands number thirty-one.

The lady already mentioned, now resident in Ireland, who with her father visited him during childhood in London, thus describes his exterior :—

His countenance had a most pleasing expression of sensibility and serenity. When I saw him, his dress was unlike that of most other gentlemen of the time. He wore a light blue coat, white silk stockings, and I *think* buckles in his shoes. His hair was white and tied behind. I remember him taking some pains to make me recite effectively before Mr. Windham, some lines which he had taught me from one of Bishop Heber's prize poems. . . . .

The death of Mr. Windham was deeply felt by Mr. Malone. Indeed, all his attachments were strong and durable, never neglecting their interests or gratification in smaller as in greater matters. His habits were methodical. He loved London, and seldom left it excepting for occasional excursions during the summer. James Boswell (the younger) was a frequent visitor at his house when we were there, and likewise Mr. Courtenay. . . . . That house was in Queen Anne Street East, and the only one I believe he ever inhabited in London, though one end of the street became

---

* Among his letters is a note from Bartolozzi, requesting payment for some of his labours, being then, as he said, hard pressed for money.

changed to Foley Place. I remember his saying in a letter
that he had gone to bed in one street, and rose in the morning
in another. The house seemed to my young ideas what that
of a literary man should be; handsomely, not showily furnished; a good library; and excellent pictures, chiefly I think,
portraits. Everything seemed in order. He gave dinners
frequently, and all said they were remarkably pleasant.

By others of riper years he was often adduced as
representative of the race of English gentlemen of
the old school, and became a favourite into whatever
society he was thrown. Boaden, who knew him well,
adverts to some of his characteristics in the *Life of
Kemble*.

I had the melancholy task of announcing to him the death
of our excellent friend, Mr. Malone. I am unable to name in
the large circle of Mr. Kemble's acquaintance, any gentleman
for whom he had a more perfect esteem. He frequently
alluded in conversation to the elegance of his manners; and
delighted to quote him as one of the best illustrations of the
old school. As a commentator on Shakspeare, Mr. Kemble
greatly preferred Mr. Malone, because he saw in him unwearied diligence and most scrupulous accuracy; with an
utter rejection of that self-display which had discredited, on
too many occasions, the wit, learning, and labour of some of
his rivals.

Some early defect of vision, increased by constant
occupation on books and manuscripts, tended to keep
him away from the theatre more than might be supposed. He saw no advantage in the increased size
of theatres. " Whenever, after the play, he walked
round to Mr. Kemble's dressing-room where I have
joined him, his usual complaint was, ' I dare say it
was a very perfect performance, but you have made
your houses so large that really I can neither hear nor

Y

see in them.' On these occasions when speaking even of Garrick, he would with the natural feeling of his country, honour Barry with a parenthesis of praise so as to extract a smile from Kemble. The chief theme seemed to be the wonderful beauty of his voice, and its effect in the thrilling ecstacies of love."

He had no airs of assumption or presumed superiority—never put on the learned garb to silence or alarm the less knowing. " He talked of literature without a tinge of pedantry, with a seeming imitation of the laughing manner of Sir Joshua Reynolds." Again, Boaden says, " I met at Kemble's hospitable board with such men as either, for instruction or amusement, will not be easily excelled, with Mr. Malone and Dr. Charles Burney."

Malone forms a striking example of a life devoted almost to one literary pursuit. The object indeed was not personal but national, having employed more pens and given birth to more readers and admirers in our island than any other literary topic whatever. For this he forsook law, wealth, and probably station for unprofitable literature ; and proved beyond most other men fitted for the occupation. He set out with the determination that whatever his employment, its duties should be faithfully fulfilled—that his business in life was *to work*. A memorandum which I found among his papers, signed with his name, contains this maxim :—" All the importunities and perplexities of business are softness and luxury compared to the incessant demands of vacancy and the unsatisfactory expedients of idleness."

If our ancient poetry and drama be really objects

of national interest as the most eminent scholars maintain, we owe him serious obligations. He brought many useful qualities to the investigation— laborious habits, keen spirit of research, love of antiquity, and determination to explore farther and dive deeper than any of his predecessors. He saw as he advanced many new points of inquiry opening before him. A placid persevering spirit carried him cheerfully onward to exhume from oblivion such information, in print or manuscript, as inquiry proved to exist. From the solid volume to the tract of a few leaves, nothing was unexamined that could be procured. He purchased, read, studied, and turned to its proper uses everything bearing upon his subject in the opinions, language, and manners of the olden time. The very quiet of the pursuit kept a mind occupied and at ease which painful private circumstances might have caused to prey upon itself. A competent provision left nothing to apprehend on the score of poverty; and learning, family, and connections gave him at once that standing among the educated and well-born which it might have cost others less fortunately situated some trouble to acquire.

Emendations of Shakspeare's text, though the principal, was not solely his object. The drama as but a representation of life, required life in all its phases to be gauged with all the accuracy which an attentive survey of its peculiarities, habits and general social condition could give. Hence much ampler reading than merely dramatic reading, was required. Poems and plays could supply only a part of the knowledge necessary to full acquaintance with the age. An apparently slight fragment, a passage, an epigram, a song, a jest, an allusion, threw light upon a speech in a play which had puzzled or misled previous commentators. Plots were to be traced to history or romance; characters to national feelings of the time; incidents to traditions then existing, or received in the era of the supposed events. This labour pursued as he pursued it, enormously increased the duties, though it as deservedly increased the fame of the critic. He disdained in fact to skim the surface of any subject as writers of credit are too often found to do even in matters of moment. He worked for facts as men in certain positions now labour for *nuggets;* and truth to him was scarcely less valuable than gold to the others.

Inseparably connected with the written drama was the Stage for its representation. Yet though beyond all others the most intellectual amusement of the people, and thence had found its way to the highest quarters in rank and station, few inquirers had given full attention to its earlier years.

Here was another enterprise for his persevering spirit—curious, unworked, and to the literary antiquary interesting in a high degree. Materials were scanty, but his exertions unwearied. Wherever documents or books of the time existed fitted to aid his pursuits, there was he to be found—whether in libraries, less frequented repositories, or unaired and unfurnished rooms. His business was to explore and note—to feast at home in the evening upon discoveries of the day, and fit them into form and consistence for the public eye. Unwearied assiduity produced its usual effects. He has left a history of the stage such as few thought could have been written, and none but whom have admired.

Burke, as we have seen, was one of the first. His large views and comprehensive information had foreseen the difficulty; and so great was his curiosity that on receiving the work, although in the midst of serious engagements, he went nearly through it at once, and immediately as we have seen, testified his gratification. Writers who have since touched this theme, amid endless differences upon all other points, have uniformly borne similar testimony.

Malone, therefore, had the merit of originating and completing a great work in the history of letters, as one of our greatest authorities has testified. " The stage," said Burke on this occasion, " may be considered as the republic of active literature, and its history as the history of that state." What was thus accomplished no pains were spared by our author to improve; for much of his subsequent career was spent in fishing out for a second edition all that could be supposed wanting in the first. As to Shakspeare he mainly devoted his life, so to his skirts he may lawfully cling for a touch of that immortality which his principal has so wonderfully earned.

Among other pursuits of taste and leisure was a collection of engraved portraits of persons in English history; chiefly poets and others of literary eminence. These, now in the possession of the Reverend Thomas R. Rooper of Brighton, I have looked over with much interest. One large volume contains four hundred and sixty-three of various merit. Twenty-three are of Shakspeare, eleven or twelve of Dryden, nine of Pope. The rarest are about forty in number; noted as of Gower, Howard, Shakspeare, Donne, Chapman, Fanshaw, Cowley, Overbury, Dryden, Prior, Addison, and others. Occasionally he purchased works of cost to cut out such portraits as were rare or good. Members of his own "Literary Club" were of course not forgotten—those at least which were procurable and of sufficient note in public life. They are preserved in a separate volume.

The researches involved by his pursuits necessarily led to the formation of a good library. He became a purchaser to some extent of Reed's, Farmer's, and other collections that promised anything rare. Upon these most of his savings were spent; and notwithstanding this acquisitive spirit says—"He should lament to acquire others, as implying the loss of his friend (Bindley), and he was quite sure he would feel equal regret at seeing his in the market."

His mission however as collector was less general than special. Anything of the age of Elizabeth, her predecessors or indeed successors even to his own time bearing upon poetry and the drama, formed the business of his life to obtain. No research was spared, no sale unattended, no novelty unexamined, no money grudged to glean information from every source. Whenever one collector died off who was rich in curious rarities, another was in the field to acquire them. The longest purse was usually successful; and as Malone without being rich was not often straitened for money, and competitors were then comparatively few, his acquisitions were of the rarest description.

The gift of the Misses Malone to the younger Boswell, accounts for the dispersion of much of their brother's correspondence and of other literary papers known to be in his possession. In the sale of the former gentleman, May 1825, we find two hundred and eighty-seven letters addressed to the critic by various correspondents—Burke, Windham, Farmer, Tyrwhitt, Steevens, the Wartons, Burney, Kemble, and many more.

So likewise were disposed several of his transcripts and notes upon books. These, which in intervals of leisure he took the trouble to make more or less complete, were no doubt destined to future use; some to illustrate other pieces; a few for new editions. Among them were *Kempe's Nine Days' Wonder, Sayings of Hobbes, Extracts from Spence,* with manuscript notes, afterwards printed; *Milton's Letters of State,* 1649–59, *annotated;* interleaved copy of *Johnson's Poets, with Notes.* Among others with which he amused himself were—A folio volume of autograph collections in illustration of Shakspeare, with papers by Steevens and Boswell; a quarto volume of extracts from old household books of Baptist May, Privy Purse to Charles II., with items of losses at play of his Majesty and Lady Castlemaine; Diary of Philip Henslowe in Dulwich College of theatrical companies, with notes and corrections; a memorandum book from Dodsley's papers, illustrative of literary history, and notes upon Shakspeare. And others doubtless exist of which no record is preserved.

One, however, must not be forgotten. It is a collection of " Tracts," above seven hundred in number, comprised in seventy-six volumes. These chiefly proceeded from, or are connected with, persons of his own or the preceding age. Many are freely annotated; and the whole passed into the world at his sale in 1818. They came again into the book-market in 1833, under the auspices of Thorpe, the well-known dealer in such literary wares. He gives an outline of their authors and contents, which will be found in the appendix; and making allowance for the usual eloquence of trade, forms a fair summary of both. Such a collection, embracing many things now scarce or unattainable, should find place in some public library.

His will was made in 1801. Lord Sunderlin is named sole executor, to whom he leaves the Shinglas and Cavan property; three thousand pounds to each of his sisters; an annuity to Mrs. Susanna Spencer; memorials to Mr. and Mrs. Windham, Mr. Forth; his servants; and earnestly recommends his sisters to the affectionate care of their brother.

His library he valued very moderately at two thousand pounds; and would wish it to remain an heirloom at Baronston, the family seat. But remembering there was no immediate descendant—no child of his brother, sisters, himself, or particularly valued relative, and that such want might be fatal to its integrity, he then mentions Trinity College, Dublin. But not desiring to make it an absolute trust, finally leaves the disposal to Lord Sunderlin.

The result was that his lordship, deeming so remarkable a collection more accessible to scholars in England than in Dublin, or in compliment to the

spot where he finished his education, offered it to
Oxford in 1815. The tender met respectful acceptance from the Vice-Chancellor and other assembled
officials; and in 1821, when the younger Boswell had
finished the edition of *Shakspeare* intrusted to him
by Malone, the remainder of the books still in his
possession were transferred to the Bodleian Library.
The collector himself terms it "The most curious,
valuable, and extensive collection ever assembled of
ancient English plays and poetry." This is quite
true. We have nothing like it or approaching to it
elsewhere; nor could a second such collection probably be formed. He told Caldwell, who repeats
the remarkable fact, that he had procured every
dramatic piece mentioned by Langbaine, excepting
four or five—the advantage, observes that gentleman,
of living in London.

The number of printed volumes and tracts in a
folio catalogue of forty-six pages printed by the
University, amounts to about two thousand seven
hundred.* The majority poetical and dramatic. He
did not however turn aside from other pieces of
ancient date bearing upon manners, opinions, or events
of the time; and the hunter after such literary curiosities may here make some gratifying discoveries.

The manuscript list, which embraces several copies
from his own pen, comprises chiefly miscellaneous
poetry—songs, epistles, addresses, ballads, love verses,
epigrams (very numerous), elegies, and epitaphs. The

---

* Estimated, however, in a note to me by the Rev. H. O. Coxe, of the
Bodleian, by whom my inquiries were assisted, at three thousand two
hundred. I am likewise indebted to the attentions of Dr. Bandinell.

volume numbered 13 has fifty-seven pieces of that description; number 21, ninety-six; * 14, thirty-two; † forming altogether, perhaps, about three hundred or more. Appended to some are explanatory notes, as, for instance, "This manuscript appears to have been written, or at least a part of it, about or after the year 1644. In p. 91 is an allusion to Sir Edward Littleton, then Lord Keeper, going from London to the King at Oxford, which was in 1642; and in p. 38, the pulling down of Cheapside Cross is mentioned. This was, I think, in 1644.— EDMOND MALONE."

In the Bodleian, they remain a distinct collection —creditable alike to the industry, taste, and patience by which they were brought together. Nor can we but feel respect for that preservative spirit and taste of our ancestors by which so many small pieces of a remote age should have been snatched from that hasty oblivion to which such things are commonly destined. The catalogue bears date 1836.

Such was the life of a scholar. Careless of the bustle of human existence, he was active only to read, hear, and note the progress of its letters. He loved them for their own sake; for the inquiries induced—the thought and knowledge evolved—the enlargement of mind acquired by the successful cultivator—the innocence as well as amusement of the occupation. His topics promised well for the quietude he loved. While others lost their temper or good manners toward each other in critical pursuits, nothing of that description escaped from him.

* Ninety-eight.—H. O. C.   † Thirty-three.—H. O. C.

A few, not acquainted with the peculiarities of his line of studies, deemed them little more than dalliance with letters—a kind of agreeable disporting over the green fields of literature. They knew not the labours it involved; the occasional difficulties of access to the places where deposited; the interminable research, the exhausted patience, eyes, and frames of which I have in him endeavoured to depict an outline. None of his predecessors had attempted what he accomplished. Few of his successors have, on most points, added materially to our knowledge. When assailed for excess of accuracy by the idle or superficial, he disdained reply.

He was studious, and selected an object of popular study; inquiring, and left nothing unexplored likely to afford information; reflective, and therefore usually accurate in drawing conclusions where positive testimony was at fault. His talents were steady and practical; his learning extensive; his critical judgments, as we have seen in the preceding pages, sound. He who could throw light upon the career of Shakspeare and Dryden—give us the first and best history of the Stage—and leave, for our study and guidance, volumes at Oxford which no other spot supplies, must be considered no small benefactor to letters.

MALONIANA.

INTRODUCTORY NOTICE.

UNDER the date of 1783, notice has been taken in a previous page of a new occupation by the subject of our memoir—that of taking notes of such incidents not generally known in life, literature, manners, and character as conversation or inquiry should offer. The design was not new; and with the majority of persons popular, having furnished much information and amusement not otherwise attainable ; and the " Club," as well as the general society in which he mingled, promised that it should not be with him unproductive.

Few familiar with London life but would gladly store in recollection portions of what they have heard in its varied society. To many it is at once the most agreeable and popular mode of communicating familiarly what may be otherwise sought in vain. Not that it is of historical, but rather of biographical value. We see and hear men of note talk, or are talked of ; yet how rarely are such things retained ? How fluent are the majority of speakers present at a metropolitan party ! How rare the industry neces-

sary to fix their stories on paper and transmit them
to future inquirers! New stories and new relators
drive their predecessors from recollection. The tale
of to-day is forgotten to-morrow. Yet how much wit
and wisdom, facts and opinions, incidents that illustrate life, manners and letters, are thus consigned to
oblivion almost from the moment of birth! At a
London dinner-table are heard things which may not
transpire elsewhere. Men and women who form a
puzzle to contemporaries as well as to posterity, commonly find some one there to explain what is curious,
obscure or anomalous, and thus throw a ray of truth
over what was previously error or conjecture. We
view them and their associates face to face, not
through the haze of rumour or antiquity, their persons—not an unimportant part of the portrait—as
well as characters.

I may illustrate this by a celebrated public man
of the last century. Lord Chesterfield is familiar to
every one. We know his wit, pleasantry, gallantry,
letters, intrigues, and libertinisms; and from these if
unexpectedly questioned might suppose he was a man
of personable or winning exterior. What is the fact
as described by his contemporary, Lord Hervey?

"With a person as disagreeable as it was possible
for a human figure to be without being deformed, he
affected following women of the first beauty, and the
most in fashion; and if you would have taken his
word for it, not without success. . . . . He
was very short, disproportioned, thick, and clumsily
made; had a broad, rough-featured, ugly face, with
black teeth, and a head big enough for a Polyphe-

mus." * Such a portrait, pictorial or literary, prefixed to his letters, would have gone far to extinguish
all taste for his principles !

And why should not such men and their peculiarities be noted? Yet I have lately heard the
practice censured in the very scene of enjoyment—a
London dinner-table—by one of our highest authorities in rank and letters. The occasion was a few
memoranda in the *Memoirs of Thomas Moore*. What
the poet put down, though now not of the slightest
moment, was condemned as breach of confidence and
the reserve due to private society. In vain I adduced
the example of Boswell—what the world would have
lost had he been as idle or indifferent to what was
said as his then more celebrated associates. In reply,
it was said he was an exception for a purpose—that
he was destined for a biographer, and but pursued his
calling in amassing materials.

In the Life of Jeffrey it is stated in one of his
letters that something similar in character took place
at Holland House. The noble owner had assented
to notices being made of the chat of the parties
in the manner of Boswell. Curiosity or comparison
formed the motive—but the emphatic remark is
made, "*It would not do.*" Why, we are not told.
Dulness or grossness in such society is not to be
supposed. If too much tinctured by party spirit, or
secret history, or scandal, or of questionable authenticity, or with disclosures likely to pain or injure the
living, those are circumstances wide of the purpose

* *Memoirs of George II.*, vol. i. p. 96. 1848. Edited by Rt. Hon.
J. W. Croker.

in view. We wish to hear what is curious or not commonly known—whatever may amuse or instruct —what men of a certain note in the world say and how they say it; in fact, how eminent actors in the scenes of life exhibit themselves on familiar occasions. Such anecdotes are not history, but they illustrate it. Where the reported party speaks truth and sense, or is simply amusing, he has nothing to fear from the curious reporter. But of such materials, true or false, there is certainly no danger of an abundance. Men are too idle for that. Not one in ten thousand will voluntarily sit down to recapitulate or express upon paper what he has heard verbally the day before, although calculated to strengthen memory, amuse his friends, and enlighten posterity.

Malone was not one of that class. Many judged him to be over-diligent—the gentleman who was rarely to be seen at home without a pen in his hand or a book at his elbow. He found himself associated with the most eminent men of the time; he felt that even their more familiar moments produced something for future information or inquiry; and he was not above the labour of recording such particulars as might throw light upon their own or the previous age. To evince the precision of the narrator even in anecdotes, his authority is usually given.

He commenced the business of noting about May, 1783, and continued it, with occasional intermissions, till the death of Sir Joshua Reynolds, in 1792. Sincere grief for that loss, added to active occupation as one of his executors, drew attention away so long that it was never resumed with the same spirit as before.   Occasionally he took up the pen, but only in short notices, to which other depressing influences no doubt contributed.

They are here transcribed in the order in which the principal collection was written, excepting such portions as appeared to belong more immediately to the order of time in the narrative.   Others, gleaned from various manuscript sources, are appended. But many additions may yet be made from detached papers and notes upon books once in his library.

[Notices of Dr. Johnson occur early in the *Maloniana*, which appear either in preceding pages, or which have been introduced into Boswell.   But as nothing relating to such a man should be lost, I replace them here by an original anecdote of interest which has escaped the research of three such indefatigable inquirers as Boswell, Malone, and Croker. The reader is indebted for it to the Honourable Sir George Rose.

[Johnson, it appears, was willing to exchange the air of Bolt Court for that of a suburban palace.   He therefore applied for a retreat where several parties of small means and of some public claims turn their eyes with similar expectations of finding a home. He failed—whether with the knowledge of his Majesty is doubtful.   The following is the letter of application, and reply :—]

[" My Lord,—Being wholly unknown to your lordship, I have only this apology to make for

z

presuming to trouble you with a request, that a stranger's petition, if it cannot be easily granted, can be easily refused.

["Some of the apartments are now vacant in which I am encouraged to hope that by application to your lordship I may obtain a residence. Such a grant would be considered by me as a great favour; and I hope that to a man who has had the honour of vindicating his Majesty's Government, a retreat in one of his houses may not be improperly or unworthily allowed.

["I therefore request that your lordship will be pleased to grant such rooms in Hampton Court as shall seem proper to

" My Lord,

" Your lordship's most obedient,

" And most faithful humble servant,

" SAM. JOHNSON.

"April 11, 1776."

[Indorsed, "Mr. Saml. Johnson to the Earl of Hertford, requesting apartments at Hampton Court. 11th May, 1776." And within, a memorandum of the answer.

["Lord C. presents his compliments to Mr. Johnson, and is sorry he cannot obey his commands, having already on his hands many engagements unsatisfied."

*   *   *   *   *

[How this curious incident escaped the prying biographer who would have made so much of it, is difficult to surmise. The presumption is that it was withheld from his knowledge by the pride of Johnson, who we find by referring to dates, was in constant communication with him personally at the time. Perhaps Boswell had some private reason for its suppression.

[By his own memoranda, it appears he arrived in London from Scotland, March 15th, 1776; saw Johnson the following day; set out with him on the 19th on an excursion to Oxford, Lichfield, Ashbourne, &c., and returned on the 29th in consequence of the death of Mr. Thrale's son, which prevented that family proceeding to Italy, whither Johnson was to accompany them. He and Boswell met on the 31st March, 3rd, 4th, 5th, 7th, 10th, 11th, and 12th April, probably oftener; so that they were little apart when the letter was written. About the middle of April, Johnson accompanied the Thrales to Bath. Boswell soon followed. While there they were almost constantly together. On the 4th May, they returned to London; and Boswell occasionally slept at Johnson's house. On the 7th, 8th, and 9th May, they dined together at the houses of mutual friends. A day or two (15th) afterward, he planned the amusing meeting of Johnson and Wilkes at dinner at Dilly's on the 15th May; and shortly afterward set out for Scotland. He was therefore in town at the time of Johnson's application—during all the period of its consideration—and when it was refused.]

EDMOND MALONE, 1783.

" Conviva est, commessatorque libellus."

MARTIAL. lv. epig. 16.

It is not generally known that Middleton, in his *Life of Cicero*, was much indebted to a book entitled *De Tribus Luminibus Romanorum*, written by a Scotchman named Bellenden, and printed at Paris, in folio, 1633. It is a history of Cicero's life and times, extracted from his letters and orations, and in his own language. It was, I believe, the writer's intention to have published two other works of the same kind, but not having seen the book,* I know not who the other two Luminæ were. A gentleman who was acquainted with Middleton (who has not mentioned this book, though so much indebted to it), in order to try him, once told him he wondered among all the authors he had examined when he was compiling his *Life of Cicero*, he had never looked into Bellenden. He seemed very much disconcerted, and, after recollecting himself a little, only said, "he did not know how it happened."

Dr. Warton, in his *Essay on Pope*, has mentioned that three of our celebrated poets died singular deaths. He might have added Shenstone to the number. He had a housekeeper who lived with him in the double capacity of maid and mistress; and being offended with her on some occasion, he went

* Since this was written I have purchased it, but it gives no information relative to its title.—*Mal.* M. de Quincey in one of his essays adverts to the subject of Middleton's obligations to Bellenden.

out of his house and sat all night in his post-chaise in much agitation, in consequence of which he caught a cold that eventually caused his death.

Mr. Hamilton (Chancellor of the Exchequer in Ireland) informs me that Johnson has written *his own life.** He once saw it on his table. He had thoughts of writing a second part to his admirable work, *Rasselas*, but I know not whether he ever executed it.† It is much to be lamented that he did not translate *Tacitus*, a work that I have heard he once had thoughts of undertaking. How well he would have done it, may be collected from his translation of part of Milton's *Panegyric on Cromwell*.

I should be glad to see some of his very earliest prose productions before he came to London, in order to ascertain whether from the first he adopted the style by which he has been so much distinguished. *Lobo* being a translation from the French, is not a fair specimen. In the preface to it his style is clearly discernible. I imagine there are three periods or epochs in his style. At first he was certainly simpler than afterwards. Between the years 1750 and 1758 his style was, I think, in its hardest and most laboured state. Of late, it is evidently improved.

His last work, the *Lives of the Poets*, has all the vigour and energy of the *Rambler*, without so much artificial niceness in the construction of the sentences, and without the hardness of phraseology that distinguishes that work. He formed his style, I imagine,

---

* This was doubtless the sketch of his childhood, recognized as genuine.

† I have since found that he never did.—*Mal.* Mr. Hamilton was William Gerard, noticed in the Life.

on Hooker, Sir Thomas Brown, and the author of the *Decay of Piety*—an admirable writer, who deserves to be much more studied than he is, on account of the energy of his style, and the very lively imagery in which he everywhere abounds, both in the work already mentioned and the *Government of the Tongue*. There is a little too much of cant in his works, and somewhat too *gloomy* and austere an enforcement of religious doctrines. Had he written on any other subject than religion, he would have been, I believe, a very popular author.

Mr. Hamilton, the gentleman above-mentioned, is master of an admirable style, and very happy in short characteristick expressions. Being asked what he thought of the two most distinguished orators of the present day, Mr. C. Fox and young Mr. Pitt, he said the oratory of the latter appeared to him only "languid elegance;" that of Mr. Fox, "spirited vulgarity."

It is a striking circumstance and presumptive proof that Mr. Fox * is little better than a popular declaimer, and ready and dexterous parliamentary disputant (which he is universally allowed to be), but with no pretensions to the character of a *real orator;* that no marked or singularly happy expression of his has ever been quoted after any debate in a period of ten years. This was not the case with Lord Chatham, Mr. Charles Townshend, Mr. Flood, and

* When I wrote this, I had not often heard Mr. Fox. I have since, and now think him, if not a consummate orator, a most able, vigorous, and impressive speaker. He is always logical, acute, various, rapid, copious, and energetick, and perfectly exhausts, though he seldom *adorns* his subject. He is also uncommonly dexterous and able in displaying the weak parts of his adversary's arguments.—*Mal.*

Mr. Hussey Burgh (the last two of Ireland), the most distinguished orators of the present age.

Mr. Hamilton, in conversation with the late Bishop Warburton, asked him, what his opinion was of *Eikon Basilike?* That he was almost afraid of delivering his own sentiments of that work, but that really it appeared to him, notwithstanding all the noise made about it and all the editions it had gone through, to have very little merit. " You are very right," said the bishop ; " it has mostly been supported by the cry of party." " Well," said Mr. Hamilton, " since I find I have the sanction of your lordship's concurrence so far, I will venture to go a little farther, and own that I cannot see any very extraordinary merit in another much talked of and much admired work—Lord Clarendon's *History of the Civil Wars.*" " Ah, now you have undone yourself with me," replied the bishop. " It is one of the finest compositions that was ever written. I have read it at least a dozen times, and filled every leaf with manuscript observations."

Mr. Hamilton, talking to me on this subject, said he still continued of the same opinion. Speaking of the endless parentheses and tedious length of his sentences, he observed, in his usual marked manner, that " there was not only all the formality of the old courtier and Lord Chancellor in the work, but his very wig, and gown, and band, and mace, too."

I agree with him entirely with respect to the style, and yet surely the book is worth reading for the sake of the characters alone. The simplicity and probity of the writer, too,* conspicuous throughout the work, are very captivating. Hume says very justly, that " he is not near so partial in fact as he appears to be," for he shows a perpetual *wish* to apologize for Charles, and yet, in truth, states fairly and correctly enough all those enormities, which afterwards cost him his crown and his life.

[The Clarendon's *History* above-mentioned, with Warburton's Notes, he bequeathed to his friend Dr. Hurd, in whose possession it now is.]

Dr. Warburton had scribbled a good deal in many other of his books. He bequeathed them, I think, to be sold for the benefit of the Bath Hospital; but his wife having notice of it, and the old man being for the two or three last years of his life in nearly a state of dotage, she disposed of them in his lifetime, if I mistake not, to Payne, the bookseller, and they are now dispersed.

He inherited all Mr. Pope's copies of the old quarto editions of *Shakspeare*, which he bound up in two volumes; but in 1766, on Mr. Steevens republishing them, he disposed of those valuable copies to Payne, who put them into the sale of Mr. Mallet's books, which at the time were selling by auction. They were not numbered in Mallet's catalogue, but sold at the end of his quarto plays for three guineas; but I never could learn to whom.

* " Yet still I love the language of his heart," is fully as applicable to him as to Cowley.

⌐ Pope's collection of the pieces written against him, on account of the *Dunciad*, are in Bishop Hurd's possession.

—————

Mr. Warburton, about the year 1750 or 1752, being in company with Quin, the player, at Mr. Allen's, near Bath, took several opportunities of being sharp upon him, on the subject of his love of eating and his voluptuous life. However, in the course of the evening, he said he should be obliged to Quin for "a touch of his quality," as he could never again see him on the stage. Quin said that plays were then quite out of his head; however, he believed he remembered a few lines of *Pierre;* on which he got up, and looking directly at Mr. Allen, repeated *ore rotunda—*

" Honest men
Are the soft easy cushions on which knaves
Repose and fatten."

Warburton gave him no further trouble for the rest of the evening.

—————

The late Lord Bath (formerly Mr. Pultney) used to say that Quin was incomparably the best performer of *Sir John Brute;* Cibber, the worst; and Garrick, next to Quin.

—————

I have never been able to meet with any person who had seen Betterton or Booth; but am persuaded that their manner was very pompous and false, and that they spoke in a high, unnatural tone. Yet if we are to believe the *Tatler's* description of Betterton's *Hamlet,* it was all nature. I am, however, incredulous; because Booth, undoubtedly, copied Betterton; and old Cibber copied both in tragedy as well as he could. *He* was, indeed, a very *bad tragedian;* but from his manner, though unhappy and extravagant (and there are some now living that remember him), one may form some guess what effect the same general manner, more chastened and correct (as it probably was in Betterton), would have. Ryan, who died about the year 1758, was the last actor of the old school.

Mr. Glover, author of *Leonidas,* told me he well remembered Garrick's first appearance at Goodman's Fields. He was then intimate with the old Lord Cobham. This nobleman had seen Betterton ; and told Glover that Garrick was infinitely a better actor; and that till he appeared, no performer had even attempted the quick, lively, and natural display of the passions for which he was so much distinguished.

Mr. Pope also saw Garrick in 1743, and was greatly struck by him. He said the young man would be in danger of being spoiled, for he would have no competitor.

Lord Mansfield told Mr. W. Gerard Hamilton this winter (1783), that what he most regretted to have lost by the burning of his house (at the time of the riots, set on foot about three years ago by that wicked canting hypocrite Lord George Gordon) was a speech that he had made on the question how far the privilege of Parliament extended; that it contained *all the eloquence* and *all the law* he was master of; that it was fairly written out; and that he had no other copy. Mr. Daines Barrington informed me that the book here alluded to contained *eight* speeches made in the House of Lords; all fairly written for the press, *and now* irreparably lost.

When Lord Mansfield (then Mr. Murray) was examined before the Privy Council about the year 1747, for drinking the Pretender's health on his knees (which he certainly did), it was urged against him, among other things, to show how strong a well-wisher he was to the cause of the exiled family, that, when he was employed as Solicitor-General against the *rebels* who were tried in 1746, he had never used that term, but always called them *unfortunate gentlemen.* When he came to his defence he said the fact was true; and he should only say that "he pitied that man's loyalty, who thought that *epithets* could add to the guilt of treason!" an admirable instance of a dexterous and subtle evasion.

Lord Mansfield's general method in his speeches in the House of Lords is to lay down some clear first principles, commonly those which the adverse party have most relied upon. He allows all the force of the precedents quoted, and the propriety of the *general* doctrines in favour of constitutional liberty for which the patriots of the last two centuries have struggled so hard; and then by some nice and subtle distinctions, to show that the particular case

under consideration is distinguished from all former
ones, and that no ill precedent can be established
by agreeing to the proposal made by the minister
of the day, whoever he happens to be. The late
Mr. Charles Townshend happened one day to be
in the House of Lords, when he was speaking on
some great constitutional question. After parading
for a good while in the manner I have mentioned,
on the high ground of general liberty, he all of a
sudden slided into the doctrine that it was necessary
to maintain, in order to prove what the Ministry
had done to be constitutional. "*What a damn'd
crane-necked fellow it is!*" said Mr. Townshend,
who stood within a few yards of him. Mr. Hutchinson (the late Prime Sergeant and present Provost
of the University of Dublin) generally pursues this
method in the House of Commons of Ireland.

———

Lord Mansfield told Mr. Hamilton that what
Dr. Johnson says of Pope, that "he was a dull companion," is not true. "He was very lively and entertaining when at his ease; and in a small company
very communicative." *

———

Pope talking once to Lord Mansfield about posthumous fame, said that the surest method of securing
it would be to leave a sum of money to be laid out
in an entertainment to be given once every year

* Lord Mansfield's account is different from every other, and I believe
not true. He is not to be trusted on this head; for he must then have
been greatly flattered by being in Pope's company. Besides, his own conversation was never very brilliant, and he was always very fond of bad
jokes and dull stories, so that his *taste* and judgment on this subject may
be suspected.—*Mal.*

to the first form of Westminster School for ever; and that the testator would by this means ensure eulogiums and Latin verses to the end of the world.

The late Lord Chatham (when Mr. Pitt) on some occasion made a very long and able speech in the Privy Council, relative to some naval matter. Every one present was struck by the force of his eloquence. Lord Anson, who was no orator, being then at the head of the Admiralty, and differing entirely in opinion from Mr. Pitt, got up, and only said these words, " My lords, Mr. Secretary is very eloquent, and has stated his own opinion very plausibly. I am no orator, and all I shall say is, that he knows nothing at all of what he has been talking about." This short reply, together with the confidence the Council had in Lord Anson's professional skill, had such an effect on every one present, that they immediately determined against Mr. Pitt's proposition.

A few weeks before Lord Chatham died, Lord Camden paid him a visit. Lord Chatham's son, the present celebrated W. Pitt, left the room on Lord Camden's coming in. " You see that young man" (said the old lord); " what I now say, be assured, is not the fond partiality of a parent, but grounded on a very accurate examination. Rely upon it, that young man will be more distinguished in this country than ever his father was." His prophecy is in part accomplished. At the age of twenty-four he was Chancellor of the Exchequer; and before he had attained his twenty-fifth year had been offered, and refused, the place of First Minister.*

When the late Mr. Harris of Salisbury made his first speech in the House of Commons, Charles Townshend asked, with an affected surprise, who he was? He had never seen him before. "Ah! you must, at least, have heard of him. That's the celebrated Mr. Harris of Salisbury, who has written a very ingenious book on *grammar*, and another on *virtue*."—"What the devil then brings him here? I am sure he will neither find the one nor the other in the House of Commons."

Mr. Townshend knew Mr. Harris well enough; but it was a common practice with him, as with other wits, to lay traps for saying good things.

Mr. Lees (of the post-office in Ireland), who was originally a clerk in the Townshend family, told me that it was Mr. Charles Townshend's usual practice to dictate speeches on every great question; that he had himself frequently written down for him three or four speeches on the same subject; that afterwards he used to ride out and converse with various people, both those who were likely to be on the same side with himself, and those of the opposite party. When he had sucked all their arguments out of them, he would then dictate another speech on a different side of the question from that which he had before taken. In the House, however, he never spoke any of these

* Afterwards, in 1784, he was appointed First Lord of the Treasury and Chancellor of the Exchequer, and continued in office till January 1802.—*Mal.*

speeches; but some of the language he had employed
in dictating them, would naturally recur to his mind,
and he always interlaced a great deal of new matter
in answer to what had fallen in the course of the
debate. This method seems unquestionably the best,
having all the sprightliness of extempore speaking,
with the grace and elegance of composition. This
kind of preparation was peculiarly proper for a man
who did not always know when he came into the
House, on which side of the question the convenience
or circumstances of the day might induce him to get
up to speak.

I have heard that the best speech he ever made was
after drinking two bottles of champagne in the Parliament coffee-house. There is nothing of his now
remaining, I believe, except a pamphlet, entitled a
Defence of the Minority, on the question of General
Warrants, published I think in 1766; the inscription
on his brother, Roger Townshend, in Westminster
Abbey; and two or three small poems in Dodsley's
collection.

———

Some little management and dexterity is necessary
even in telling truths. Secretary Craggs used to
relate of himself that, when he first came into office,
he made it a rule to tell every person who applied to
him for a favour the exact truth;* that he was either
engaged to give the place in question to some one
else, or if that were not the case, that he could not
possibly promise the office, as other persons with
superior pretensions might have a claim to it. But

* Statesman, yet friend to *truth*, &c.—POPE.

he found by experience that this method rendered him universally odious; and that the only way of being popular, is—whether you comply with men's solicitations or not—to soothe them with *hopes* and *fair speeches*.

Lord Chesterfield, when Lord-Lieutenant in Ireland, being asked one day whom he thought the greatest man of the time, said—"The last man who arrived from England, be he who he might." There is some truth in this. Dublin depends a great deal on London for topics of conversation, as every secondary metropolis must; and the last man who arrives from the great scene of action (if of any degree of consequence) is courted as being supposed to know many little particulars not communicated by letters or the public prints. Every person in a distant county-town in England experiences something of this on the arrival of a friend from the metropolis.

The late Lord Southwell (Thomas, third lord), who was a relation of Lord Chesterfield, told me that he had left *Memoirs of his own Times* behind him, which he (Lord S.) had seen in the possession of Sir W. Stanhope, Lord Chesterfield's brother. But they have never been published.

Lord Bath's *Memoirs* of the same period are, I believe, in the hands of Dr. Douglas, his chaplain;* and I know not why they are kept from the world. The only piece that I have seen of his writing is,

* Since made Bishop of Carlisle, and afterwards removed to Salisbury.

Seasonable Hints from an Honest Man, published about 1761. He wrote some of the papers of the *Craftsman,* but I know not which of them.

Quin, the player, might have been mentioned in addition to Cibber, as proof of the false taste and bad manner of the old actors. He came on the stage about the year 1720, and of consequence played some years with Booth, whose manner therefore in tragedy probably bore some *general* resemblance to his. Quin, like all the other actors of that time, used to make inordinate long pauses by way of adding weight and dignity to a passage. When Garrick first came on the stage, the admirers of the old manner could not reconcile themselves to the new mode of playing introduced by him, and were clamorous in all public places in praise of Quin. At last it was fixed that they should perform in the same piece, and the admirers of the old stage had no doubt they should be triumphant. The *Fair Penitent* was the play chosen, in which Garrick performed *Lothario,* and Quin, *Horatio.* The first act took up an hour in the performance, from the contention between the parties who should be loudest and longest in the applause of their favourite; and from Quin's slow and solemn recitation. At last a trivial circumstance gave Garrick the victory. In the last scene of the second act, *Lothario* challenges *Horatio:* "Two hours ere noon to-morrow, I expect thee." Quin, with his usual stateliness paused so long before he gave an answer, that some simple fellow in the gallery grew impatient, and cried out: "D— your blood! why don't you tell the little gentleman whether you'll meet him or no?" This entirely disconcerted Quin, and the contest was decided in favour of his rival.

Mr. Jephson,* who knew him, told me however that his manner of reciting in private, though pompous, had a certain natural weight and dignity which, after you were a little used to it, was not disagreeable. He was fond of quoting Milton—the only English poet that he much studied except Shakspeare; and so little was the latter author read at that time, and so false the taste of that age, that Quin, who very frequently used to repeat passages of *Macbeth* in company, always quoted the wretched alteration of that drama made by Sir Wm. Davenant and published in 1674. Probably he had never read the original play. So little relish had the nation in general for the real beauties of Shakspeare, and so little was he read, that this insult to his memory was suffered to keep possession of the stage for nearly seventy years. It is a singular circumstance that the late Mrs. Pritchard, who was celebrated in the part of *Lady Macbeth*, owned not long before she died that she had never read the play, nor knew any more of it than what was contained in her own part, written for her by the prompter.

Darius Tibertus, an Italian, abridged the Lives of Plutarch, in Latin; but I have never met with the book.

* The dramatist.

I have never been able to find out in what author a line that is often quoted is to be found—

Solamen miseris socios habuisse doloris.

Probably it is in some modern Latin poem.

[Here is recorded the introduction of Dr. Johnson to Lord Chesterfield. The slight of being kept waiting in his hall, &c., which from being generally known, is not necessary to reprint. It appears that Malone heard these and other particulars not through the medium of Boswell, but previous to their acquaintance.]

Lord C. is supposed to have had Johnson in his thoughts in his description of a very awkward literary man in one of his letters to his son.

Johnson was also offended that his lordship, though engaged in writing occasionally in the periodical paper called the *World*, did not recommend the *English Dictionary* to the public till it was on the verge of publication. A few weeks before it appeared he wrote two essays in its favour. "While I was floating on a tempestuous ocean" (said Johnson on that occasion) "he would not afford me the smallest succour; but when I had got within sight of land, and almost touched the shore, he sent out two little frigates to my assistance."

Soon afterwards he wrote a letter to Lord Chesterfield not inferior to any of his compositions; but he was prevailed upon not to print it. "In my first address to your lordship" (says he in some part of it) "having exhausted all the compliments that an uncourtly and sequestered scholar could devise, I

expected a different return than personal slight and
neglect, or the more mortifying condescension of a
lukewarm patronage.   At length indeed you have
thought proper to recommend me to the public; but
your recommendation comes too late.   The notice
which your lordship has been pleased to take of me
and my labours, had it been early, would have been
kind; but it has been protracted so long as to be
neither a service nor a favour; till I am indifferent
and cannot enjoy it; till I am solitary and cannot
impart it; till I am known and do not need it."*

These few passages of this celebrated letter were
repeated to me by a person to whom Dr. Johnson had
read it.

When Lord Chesterfield's *Letters to his Son* were
published, Dr. J. said they inculcated the morals of
a strumpet, and the manners of a dancing-master.

Some other wit has not unhappily called them the
Scoundrel's Primer.

After all, these Letters have been, I think, unrea-
sonably decried; for supposing a young man to be
properly guarded against the base principles of dis-
simulation, &c., which they enforce, he may derive
much advantage from the many minute directions
which they contain, that other instructors and even
parents don't think it worth while to mention.   In
this and almost everything else, the world generally

---

* This story has been long familiar in the pages of Boswell, but when
written by Malone, in his *Memoranda*, was little known.   It is retained
here in proof of his sources of information being good, and his notes
accurately made.

seizes on two or three obviously ridiculous circumstances, talks a great deal about them, and passes over all the valuable parts that may still be found in the work or in the character they are criticizing. I have heard persons laugh at the noble writer's laying weight upon such trifling matters as paring nails, or opening a dirty pocket handkerchief in company. Yet trifling as these instructions are, I have observed these very people greatly negligent in those very particulars.

Lord Chesterfield however by his perpetual attention to propriety, decorum, *bienséance*, &c., had so *veneered* his manners, that though he lived on good terms with all the world he had not a single *friend*. The fact was I believe that he had no warm affections. His excessive and unreasonable attention to decorum and studied manner attended him almost to his last hour. Nearly the last words he spoke were, "Fetch Derolles a chair." Derolles had been patronized by him, and came to see him and sit by his bedside in his last illness.

The heart, however, is a much better preceptor for politeness (which is nothing but attention to others, and preferring them often to yourself) than all his lordship's lessons. I have never met with a really *good-natured* man that was not perfectly polite and well-bred in the true sense of those words though he had never seen St. James's. Lord Charlemont is the politest man I have ever seen. In him politeness is no effort. It arises naturally and necessarily from his warm and affectionate heart.

Mr. Melmoth, in a very entertaining book, *Fitz-osborne's Letters*, has many criticisms on Pope's translation of Homer. However great its merit—and a most admirable work it undoubtedly is—he sometimes praises it injudiciously. It has been often said that Pope's version is beautiful, but not sufficiently *Homerick*. The following passage is a remarkable instance of the peculiar force and energy of the original being lost in the graces of the translation. "It is quoted" (says Melmoth) "by a celebrated author of antiquity as an instance of the true sublime. I will leave it to you" (he adds) "to determine whether the translation has not, at least, as just a claim to that character as the original."

Ως ὁὸτε χειμαρροι ποταμοι κατ'υρεσφι ρεοντες,
Ες μισγαλκειαν συμβαλλετον οβριμον υδωρ,
Κρουνων εκμεγαλων, κοιλης εντοσϑε χαραδρης,
Των δε τε τηλοσε δουπον εν ουρεσιν εκλυεποιμην,
Ως των μισγομενων γενετο ιαχη τε φοβος τε.

As torrents roll, increas'd by num'rous rills,
With rage impetuous down their echoing hills,
Rush to the vales, and pour'd along the plain,
Roar through a thousand channels to the main;
The distant shepherd trembling hears the sound;
So mix both hosts, and so their cries rebound.
POPE.

It is observable, as an ingenious friend remarked to me, that Pope has here omitted some of the circumstances that give peculiar force and propriety to this simile, and introduced others that *are inconsistent* with Homer's idea.

In the original, *two* torrents are particularly mentioned (as is marked by the dual number being used), corresponding with the two armies described. Pope has lost this propriety by using a general term, *torrents.* These torrents too, in Homer, are *winter* torrents, which the translator has overlooked. Afterwards, however, these torrents become swollen. By what?—By "num'rous RILLS," the *prettiest* word he could have chosen. What do they do?—They rush to *the vales*, and then are dispersed through a thousand different channels till they reach the ocean. In the original there is not a word of this. The two torrents rush from the mountains into a hollow *valley*, and being there *pent up*, the mountain shepherd is stunned by the noise of the *conflicting* waters. But a very close translation with which the same gentleman furnished me, will best prove how the beautiful simile has suffered in Pope's hands.

> " As when two winter torrents from the height
> Of neighbouring mountains, rush with rapid might,
> And mix their foaming waves with stunning sound
> Struggling within some valley's hollow bound ;
> The mountain shepherd hears the din from far ;
> Such the tremendous shoutings of the mingled war."

It is rather extraordinary that so good a critic as Mr. Melmoth overlooked these circumstances, and should have chosen these lines of Pope's in particular for so high an eulogium.

———

When Dr. Johnson was struck with the palsy a few days ago (June 1783), after the first shock was over and he had time to recollect himself, he attempted to speak in English. Unable as he found himself to pronounce the words, he tried what he could do with Latin, but here he found equal difficulty. He then attempted Greek, and could utter a few words, but slowly and with pain. In the evening he called for paper, and wrote a *Latin Hymn*, addressed to the Creator, the prayer of which was that so long as the Almighty should suffer him to live, he should be pleased to allow him the enjoyment of his understanding; that his intellectual powers and his body should expire together,—a striking instance of fortitude, piety, and resignation!

On one of Sir J. Reynolds's friends observing to Dr. Johnson (who had long lived in great intimacy with that excellent painter) that it was extraordinary the King should have taken so little notice of him, having on all occasions employed Ramsay, West, &c., in preference to Sir Joshua, he said he thought it a matter of little consequence,—" His Majesty's neglect could never do him any prejudice ; but it would reflect *eternal disgrace* on the King not to have employed Sir Joshua Reynolds."

The following sarcastic lines on William III. (which I believe have never appeared in print) are so much in the manner of Swift, and agree so exactly with his political Tory principles, that I strongly suspect him to have been the author of them:—

ON KING WILLIAM III.

Here lives a man, who, by relation,
Depends upon predestination;
For which the learned and the wise
His understanding much despise;
But I pronounce with loyal tongue
Him in the right, them in the wrong;
For how should such a wretch succeed,
But that alas! it was *decreed?*

Vita Ambrogii Commandolensis, par l'Abbe Mahus, printed at Florence, in folio, in 1772, contains, as

Dr. Stock informs me, a fuller account of the manner in which the original MSS. of the Greek and Roman classics were discovered and preserved than any other book extant.

———

Dean Tucker's *state* of the great leading principles on which the present dispute between the Crown and the House of Commons—which has a few days since (March 24, 1784) ended in a dissolution of the latter —is in Lord Mansfield's opinion perfect. It is preserved in the *Gentleman's Magazine*, vol. 54, p. 202.

———

Mr. Flood, himself one of the greatest orators of the present age, speaking to me on the subject of the distinguishing characteristics of the two eminent persons mentioned in a preceding page (Mr. Pitt and Mr. Fox), said that neither of them appeared to him to merit the title of *eloquent* speakers. Mr. Pitt's speeches, he called *didactick declamations;* those of Mr. Fox, *argumentative conversations.* Mr. Pitt's style of eloquence, he said, had something of an historical cast. It was a compound of the perspicuity and precision of Sir Wm. Blackstone, with the elegance of Robertson; and his periods particularly reminded him of that writer, whom he thought he resembled much more than he did Bolingbroke, Cicero, or Demosthenes. Mr. Fox's style of speaking he did not think the *best,* but that he was *perfect* in that style. Mr. Pitt's style of eloquence he considered much *superior,* but then he was *not* near so perfect in that style as he might be.

———

The celebrated Mr. Wilkes, about the time when

his *North Briton* began to be much noticed, probably when the first fifteen or twenty numbers had appeared, dined one day with Mr. Rigby, and after dinner honestly confessed that he was a ruined man, not worth a shilling; that his principal object in writing was to procure himself some place, and that he should be particularly pleased with one that should remove him from the clamour and importunity of his creditors. He mentioned the office of *Governor of Canada*, and requested Mr. Rigby's good offices with the Duke of Bedford, so as to prevail on that nobleman to apply to Lord Bute for that place. Mr. Rigby said, the duke had not much intercourse with Lord Bute; neither could it be supposed that his lordship would purchase Mr. Wilkes' silence by giving him a good employment. Besides, he could have no security that the same hostile attacks would not be still made against him by Mr. Wilkes' coadjutors, Lloyd and Churchill, after he had left England. Wilkes solemnly assured him there need not be the least apprehension of that; for that he would make Churchill his chaplain, and Lloyd his secretary, and take them both with him to Canada.

The duke, at Rigby's request, made the application. Lord Bute would not listen to it, and even treated the affair with contempt. When this was told to Mr. Wilkes, he observed to Mr. Rigby that Lord B. had acted very foolishly, and that he might live to lament that he and his colleagues had not quitted England, as much as King Charles did that Hampden and Cromwell had not gone to America, after the famous representation of the state of the

nation in 1641; for now he should never cease
his attacks till he had made him the most unpopular
man in England. He kept his word.

[From the information of Mr. J. Courtenay, who
had it from Mr. Rigby.]

The following epigram on Mr. Wilkes, in consequence of becoming a favourite at Court in April
1784, and having once more come into Parliament
for Middlesex in conjunction with the *Court candidate*, Mr. Mainwaring, is better than the generality
of newspaper productions :—

POLITICAL CONSISTENCY.

What! Liberty-Wilkes, of oppression the hater,
Call'd a turncoat, a Judas, a rogue, and a traitor!
What has made all our patriots so angry and sore?
Has Wilkes done that now which he ne'er did before?

Consistent was John all the days of his life;
For he loved his best friends as he loved his own wife;*
In his actions he always kept self in his view,
Though false to the world to John Wilkes he was true!

Selemnus, a river in Achaia, is said by Pausanias
to have possessed the quality of making those who
bathed in it forget the object of their affection. Were
there really such a water, how valuable would it be!

Lexiphanes, which was written in ridicule of Dr.
Johnson's style, is by many supposed to have been the
work of Mr. Kenrick; but it was really written by a
Mr. Campbell, son of a Scotch professor; and who
was likewise the author of a book entitled *The Sale of
Authors*. He some years since went to the West Indies
or North America, in one of which places he died.†

* Whom he married for money, and deserted.
† He is said to have been a purser (now called paymaster) in the Royal
Navy.—P.

The concealed author of *Lyrick Odes*, by Peter Pindar, Esquire, is one Woolcot, a clergyman, who abjured the gown, and now lives in Great Queen Street, Lincoln's Inn Fields, under the character of a physician. He is likewise author of a scurrilous epistle lately published, addressed to James Boswell, Esq., March 4th, 1786. He is noted for impudence, lewdness, and almost every species of profligacy.

Dr. Johnson was no admirer of the Duke of Buckingham's *Rehearsal*. On a high eulogium being once pronounced upon it in his presence, he said: "It had not wit enough to keep it sweet; it had not sufficient vitality to preserve it from putrefaction."

Mrs. Thrale has caught something of this story and marred it in the telling, as she has many other of her anecdotes of the Doctor just now published. On the whole, however, the publick is indebted to her for her lively, though very inaccurate and artful, account of Dr. Johnson.

After Pope's death, Lord Bolingbroke, in consequence of a clause in his will, had the command of his study. Among the sweepings was the following Satire, which was left unfinished by the poet. It fell after Bolingbroke's death into the hands of a kinsman or friend of his, and has since by some strange accident strayed into Ireland. I saw it there about the year 1774, in the possession of the Rev. Dr.

Wilson, Senior Fellow of Trinity College, Dublin, together with a pocket-book of Parnell's, Dryden's *Limberham*, corrected by himself, Pope's *Farewell to London*, and several other papers found in the same drawer.* The Satire I have copied by Dr. Wilson's permission. It is in Pope's handwriting, and I have followed closely all his interlineations, corrections, alterations, &c. &c. His MSS. in the Museum are often found in the same state. This in short is a *facsimile* in every respect except the handwriting which I have not attempted to imitate.

[Here follows a transcript of the Satire *One Thousand Seven Hundred and Forty*, which as it was printed in 1797 in Dr. Warton's edition of Pope, need not appear here. Malone gave him the clue to its depository with much other information for his volumes. Dr. Wilson in communicating it, writes thus to Warton :—

[" This poem I transcribed from a rough draft in Pope's own hand. He left many blanks for fear of the Argus eyes of those who, if they cannot find, can fabricate treason; yet spite of his precaution it fell into the hands of his enemies. To the hieroglyphics there are direct allusions, I think, in some of the notes on the *Dunciad*. It was lent me by a grandson of Lord Chetwynd, an intimate friend of the famous Lord Bolingbroke, who gratified his curiosity by a boxful of the rubbish and sweepings of Pope's study, whose executor he was, in conjunction with Lord Marchmont."

* They were lent to Dr. Wilson by Lord Chetwynd.

[To the transcript Malone appends this note:—
"Lord Marchmont in his conversation with Dr.
Johnson relative to Pope, mentioned this Satire.
He said he and Lord [indistinct] had often heard of
it from Pope, and much lamented that he could not
find it among Pope's papers."

[The following specimens give us some idea of the
poet's idler hours.]

From the same collection (Pope's manuscript).

"*An me ludit*," &c.

What pleasing frenzy steals away my soul?
Thro' thy blest shades, Latour, I seem to rove;
I see thy fountains fall, thy waters roll,
And breathe soft zephyrs that refresh thy grove.

I hear whatever can delight, inspire,
Vilette's soft voice, and St. John's silver lyre.

From a letter of Pope to Bolingbroke.

From the same collection (this in Pope's handwriting).

To
His most sacred Majesty!
Not God, but
George II.
By divine, hereditary right,
King of Great Britain,
And France (when he can get it),
And to
His more sacred Minister,
By divine, that is, royal permission,
King over him,
These
Gazetteers,
In defence of corruption and abuse of liberty
(Drawn for and from the said Minister),
Are here offered
Bound and sold
(Like their authors)
'By both their Majesties'
Sworn and devoted
Subjects and hirelings,

B. Courteville, W. Papple.

J. Morley, Th. Cook, W. Billers, Th. Cibber, &c. &c.

From the same collection (this in Pope's handwriting.)

Epitaph on a Man's Wife, the tomb being set up by himself.

Tom T——y has set up this thing for his wife:
The first thing he set up for her all his life.

Swift's Imitation of Hor. b. xiv. b. 1.

" Such was Jerne's claim as just," &c.

Stood thus :—

So when Hibernia made her claim like thine,
Her sons descended from the British line,
Her martial sons whose valour still remains
On French records for twenty long campaigns;
Led captive to a prison from a throne,
Gain'd Europe's liberty to lose her own.

From the same collection.

Earl of Dorset's mottos for the pictures of Tragedy and Comedy in the playhouse.

Quoth Dorset, what mottos your pictures become,
You would know if your brains were not addle:
Under your Tragedy write *humdrum*,
And under your Comedy *fidde-faddle*.

From the same.

POPE.

More tyrants they, who use a woman ill,
And those more fools who let have her will.

Joy's but a flutt'ring pleasure at the best,
That some few moments beats about the breast
Sad thought, or thoughtless folly all the rest.

Fragments : Education too early in the World.

Desirous all to see the world they seem,
And ne'er consider that the world sees them.
Compassion lessens not the truly great,
Gold easiest melts, but melting keeps its weight.
How to get in th' ambitious aim no doubt,
Let them consider how they shall get out.
Some men's wits run away with them like,
Compassion lessens not the truly great,
So melts the gold, but melting keeps its weight.

Verbal scholars in nudo verbarum cultu ludent.

GREAT PARTS.

To want for ever, turn which way you will,
An able judge or abler second still.

Amusement is the happiness of those that don't think Gaming is the amusement of fools and the art of knaves.

What shame can harbour where the great resort,
Otes walked Whitehall, and never blush'd at *Court.*
Who's next a knave? who with a knave will dine.
Who next a harlot? she that drinks her wine.
Know in their heart that he that she adore,
The wit of knaves, the courage of a whore:
And trust my word, that woman or that man
Will be the thing they worship if they can.

Bridgeman, unskill'd in wit's mysterious ways,
Knows not, good man, a satire from a praise;
Yet he can make a mount, or turn a maze.

Belinda, beauteous and admir'd by all,
Gay in the box, resistless in the ball, &c.

When the Quaker who purchased the property of Mr. Thrale's brewery, &c., asked Dr. Johnson, who was one of the executors, what it was that he was going to purchase—how many were the brewing tubs, drays, &c. &c. " Sir," says Johnson, " I cannot enumerate them; but it is of more consequence to you to know that you have the potentiality of growing rich beyond even the dreams of avarice."

Mr. Burke told me he was well acquainted with David Hume, and that he was a very easy, pleasant, unaffected man, till he went to Paris as secretary to Lord Hertford. There the attention paid him by the French *belles savants* had the effect of making him somewhat of a literary coxcomb.

Mr. Burke said that Hume in compiling his history did not give himself a great deal of trouble in examining records, &c.; and that the part he most laboured at was the reign of King Charles II., for whom he had an unaccountable partiality.

When some one observed to Foote that Garrick's features still had great effect notwithstanding his age, " Yes," said Foote, " wonderfully so, considering all the wear and tear they have gone through."

On Lord Kelly, a remarkable red-faced, drunken lord, coming into a room in a coat much embroidered but somewhat tarnished, Foote said he was an exact representation of Monmouth Street in flames.

" Who is this Pope that I hear so much about?" said George II.; "I cannot discover what is his merit. Why will not my subjects write in prose? I hear a great deal, too, of Shakspeare, but I cannot read him, he is such a *bombast* fellow."

Dr. Beattie, with whom I dined at Sir J. Reynolds' in July 1787, mentioned that Mr. Hume was a very tall, large man, near six feet high, and his countenance rather vacant. All that knew him concur in opinion of his having been a very unaffected, good-humoured man. He acknowledged to Mr. Boswell that he did not take much pains in examining the old historians while writing the early part of his history. He dipped only into them so as to make out a pleasing narrative. It is manifest to me on reading Bacon's *Life of Henry VII.*, that *that* was the model on which Hume founded his plan. Bacon particularly recommends to the historian a review at the end of every reign of the laws enacted; of the progress of manners, arts, &c., which Hume has so successfully followed.

It is surprising, on examining any particular point, how superficial Hume is, and how many particulars are omitted that would have made his book much more entertaining; but perhaps we have no right to expect this in a general history. For my own part, I am much more entertained with memoirs and letters written at the time, in which everything is alive, and passes in motion before the eye.

Mr. Burke, speaking of Dr. Warburton, told me he was so much struck by him the first time they dined together in company, that he conjectured it must be Warburton who was talking and sitting next him. After some little conversation, he could not help exclaiming, " Sir, I think it is impossible I can mistake. You must be the celebrated Dr. Warburton, *aut Erasmus aut Diabolus.*" Warburton, though so furious a controversialist in print, was very easy and good-humoured in company, and sometimes entertaining.

Mr. Burke, who avowed he knew little of art, though he admired it and knew many of its professors, was acquainted with Blakey the artist, who made the drawing for the frontispiece to Warburton's edition of Pope's works. He told him it was by Warburton's particular desire that he made him the principal figure, and Pope only secondary; and that the light, contrary to the rules of art, goes upward from Warburton to Pope. A gentleman who was present when Mr. B. mentioned this circumstance, remarked that it was observable the poet and his commentator were looking different ways.

Mr. Lock, of Norbury Park, well known for his collection of pictures, statues, &c., was a natural son. On his marriage with the daughter of Lady Schaub who had been very gallant, Horace Walpole said very happily, " Then everybody's daughter is married to nobody's son."

On Mr. Pulteney's complaining to old Lady Townshend that he had been much out of order with a pain in his side, she asked him which was *his side*, for that she never knew he had one. " Oh," said he, " you must at least acknowledge that I have a *nether* side." " I know nothing about it," replied Lady T. " All the world knows that your wife has one." The allusion was to the well-known anecdote of Pulteney's insisting upon having some papers read in the House of Commons, one of which turned out to be a letter dated by one of his wife's gallants, concluding with a distich too coarse for quotation here.

[Some other anecdotes of the previous age are noticed as examples of the licence of language not uncommon then even with ladies.]

Few classical quotations have ever been more neatly applied than the following: Mr. Burke had been speaking in the House of Commons for some time, and paused. He soon proceeded, and some time afterwards paused again so long (which with him is very uncommon) that Sir Wm. Bagot thought he had done, and got up to speak, " Sir" (said Mr. B.), "I have not finished." Sir W. B. made an apology, and said, "As the hon. gentleman had spoken a long time, and had paused unusually long also, he imagined that he had concluded, but he found he was mistaken. Some allowance, however, he hoped would be made for him as a *country* gentleman, for

> "' *Rusticus* expectat dum defluat amnis ; at ille
> Labitur et labetur in omne volubilis ævum.' "

Let it, however, be remembered that this was a mere happiness of *application*, for in truth the " labitur" and "labetur" of Mr. B., though inexhaustible, is never tiresome, but always teeming with the richest stores of knowledge of every species, ornamented with a profusion of the happiest imagery almost running to waste.

The following verses, written by the Hon. Thomas Erskine, have not I believe appeared in print. They were written on a Yorkshire lady, known by the name of *Peg Waldron* in that county, who is supposed to be worth two hundred thousand pounds and is remarkably dirty :—

Accept, dear Peg, my humble lays,
The thanks a grateful heart repays,
Thou useful lesson to defy
The charms of vain philosophy.

Oft has my soul, puffed up with pride,
The truths of sacred writ deny'd;
And to myself I still have said,
Sure mankind ne'er of dirt was made;
But you, dear Peg, reverse my creed,
And show me, we are *dirt* indeed.

For these last five years, that is from 1782 to 1787, scarce one of the monthly publications have been without some extravagant praise of two very moderate versifiers, Mr. Hayley and Miss Anna Seward; and generally they have written the most high-flown encomiums on each other.

Some of the old Italian writers would have condemned them in a future state to lash each other from morning till night with nettles, for their folly and vanity. A modern wit, a few days since, inflicted on them a milder punishment.

Dialogue between Miss Seward and Mr. Hayley.

" Tuneful poet ! Britain's glory,
  Mr. Hayley, that is you——"
" Ma'am, you carry all before you,
  Trust me, Lichfield Swan, you do——"
" Ode, didactick, epick, sonnet,
  Mr. Hayley, you're divine——"
" Ma'am, I'll take my oath upon it,
  You alone are all the Nine !"

                  Nov. 1787.

The celebrated writer Sterne, after being long the idol of this town, died in a mean lodging without a single friend who felt interest in his fate except Becket, his bookseller, who was the only person that attended his interment. He was buried in a grave-yard near Tyburn, belonging to the parish of Mary-lebone, and the corpse being marked by some of the *resurrection men* (as they are called), was taken up soon afterward and carried to an ana'omy professor of Cambridge. A gentleman who was present at the dissection told me, he recognized Sterne's face the moment he saw the body.

Mrs. Bracegirdle, being once in company with Mr. Garrick, happened to quote from *Hamlet*—

> Oh, woe is me!
> To have seen what I have seen, seeing what I see?

which she spoke in the manner of our own time, and so ill, that Garrick told Mr. Langton he was sure from that specimen she could not speak a single line as it ought to be spoken.

She lived, I believe, till the year 1760.

Dr. Young, the poet, who was born in 1681 and had often seen Betterton, told Mr. Langton that Garrick was *but a boy* to Betterton as an actor. Lord Cobham, however, who had seen both, gave a very different account of their respective powers.

Hume, the historian, had not the least relish for Shakspeare, nor any sense of his transcendent merit. His criticism on him in his history was originally much more severe and tasteless than now appears. It was much qualified and softened by Lord Kames, who feared the historian would have been disgraced by confessing total insensibility to what the English nation has so long and so justly admired.—(From Mr. Boswell, who had it from Lord Kames.)

Mr. Burke told me a few days ago that the first Lord Lyttleton informed him, that Lord Bolingbroke never wrote down any of his works, but *dictated* them to a secretary. This may account for their endless tautology. In company, according to Lord Lyttleton, he was very eloquent, speaking with great fluency and authority on every subject, and generally in the form of *harangue* rather than colloquial table talk. His company all looked up to him, and very few *dared* to interrupt or contradict him.—*Dec.* 1787.

Mr. Soame Jenyns, who died a few days ago, had (as Mr. Wm. Gerard Hamilton, who sat for six years at the Board of Trade with him, informed me) no notion of ratiocination, no rectitude of mind; nor could he be made without much labour to comprehend an argument. If however there was anything weak, or defective, or ridiculous in what another said, he always laid hold of it and played upon it with success. He looked at everything with a view to pleasantry alone. This being his grand object, and he being no reasoner, his best friends were at a loss to know whether his book upon Christianity was serious or ironical.

He twice endeavoured to speak in the House of Commons, and every one was prepared with a half-grin before he uttered a word; but he failed miserably. He had a most inharmonious voice, and a laugh scarcely human. He laughed all his life at patriotism and public spirit; and supposed all oppression of the people by those in power was merely imaginary. Among other whimsical collections he had forty-seven Petitions or Remonstrances of the City of London complaining of grievances, *all* of which he said had the same, that is, no foundation; for in each it was mentioned that if the measure complained of were pursued, the constitution would be annihilated. He was so great a coward that at an election at Cambridge, he was almost ready to faint at some huzza of the mob lest they should assault him, as his counsel, Mr. Graham, told me.

Mr. Garrick always took care to leave company with a good impression in his favour. After he had told some good story, or defeated an antagonist by wit or raillery, he often disappointed people who hoped that he would continue to entertain them and receive the praise and admiration they were ready enough to give. But he was so artificial that he could break away in the midst of the highest festivity, merely in order to secure the impression he had made. On this part of his character it was well said by Coleman, that he never came into company without laying a plot for an escape out of it.

The part of the *Clandestine Marriage* which he wrote was *Lord Ogilby* and *Mrs. Heidelberg*, as Cautherly, who was in his house at the time, told Mr.

Kemble. Cautherly was employed to transcribe the parts for the use of the theatre.

In the *Jealous Wife* he assisted by writing the character of *Major Oakley*. In that play as written originally, the whole of the farce of the *Musical Lady* was introduced; but Garrick persuaded Coleman to leave it out.

Having lately read over a great number of letters written by various friends to my father near fifty years ago, and among others several from Dr. Taylor, of Isleworth, with whom he was very intimate, I became desirous of seeing him once more and having some talk about old times. I have been acquainted with him several years, and occasionally had slept at his house, but never happened to converse on the events of former days. I was even doubtful whether he still lived; and therefore wrote a note that I would call upon him on Saturday, January 12th, 1788. He replied by a most cordial invitation, saying he should be very glad of the meeting, but must receive me in his bedchamber, being afflicted with the rheumatism and St. Anthony's fire.

I did not reach his house till past three (in consequence of paying a visit elsewhere first), and wished to have passed the evening with him; but he was in such pain, that I feared it would have been troublesome, nor indeed did he ask me. He however gave me a mutton chop (for he had himself dined), but I was sadly disappointed with respect to intelligence of former days. I well knew that he was a superficial, good-humoured, easy man, who had never thought or read much ; but there was a chance at least of having some few anecdotes from him.   He told me however but one worth recording.   He married my father to Miss Collier at Greenwich in 1736.   Old Mr. Collier was a very vain man who had made his fortune in the South Sea year, and having been originally a merchant, was very fond after he had retired to live upon his fortune, of a great deal of display and parade.   (Here is told the story of the wedding already given.)

His story is a curious trait of the manners of the times.   For I suppose the whim only of an individual was answerable for the *excess* in numbers ; and that it was *common* for the party at a wedding-dinner to visit the bride and bridegroom in bed.   Taylor, nearly the same age with my father who if he were living would be eighty-three, remembered my grandfather, Richard Malone, very well, but could give no discriminative account of him.   He had never heard him plead.   He resembled he said his third son, Richard, more than his other sons ; a tall, black, handsome man, with much dignity in his appearance.

Dr. Taylor remembered Swift very well ; the print done for him in Ireland (a mezzotinto) he thought very like.   The only anecdote he mentioned of the Dean was, that a very well-dressed man having come to St. Patrick's Cathedral on a Sunday, and being seated in one of the vacant stalls during the time of service bowed frequently to different persons in the church.   When Swift came out he called the verger, and desired him never to permit that person (pointing to him) to come into his church again, *for he was sure he was not a gentleman.*

About the year 1735, when Dr. Taylor was in Dublin, the people used to run after Swift's coach to get a sight of him, as they did in London after Lady Coventry when she appeared in public.

I asked him whether he (Taylor) could amuse himself by reading? No, he said, he could read nothing but the newspaper. "What, at his time of life, should he read for?"

I have in general observed that very few old people can bear to read—a very melancholy circumstance! for what a relief would this be to pass away tedious hours! Dr. Taylor several years ago lost his only child, and ten years since his wife. Almost every friend of his youth is now dead; but luckily for himself he has by no means a feeling mind. If a man has a turn for literary pursuits, and possesses a benevolent heart, he may in some measure defy old age. The mines of science are inexhaustible; and objects for the exercise of beneficence may for ever be found.

Those who have not been early tinctured with letters, and have been much immersed in politicks or other business, cannot, any more than the aged, derive much pleasure from books.

———

Sir Robert Walpole, after he ceased to be minister, endeavoured to amuse his mind with reading at Houghton. But one day when the present Mr. Welbore Ellis was in his library, he heard him say with tears in his eyes, after having taken up several books and at last thrown away a folio just taken down from a shelf, "Alas! it is all in vain; *I* CANNOT *read*."

Having heard much of there being an original picture of Shakspeare at Teddington, near Strawberry Hill, in the possession of Mr. Douglass, I called there before I went to Dr. Taylor's, by which means (it proving to be two miles farther than I reckoned) I was too late at Isleworth. However, as I might not soon again have an opportunity of seeing this picture, I was glad I had not omitted to go. It is a small picture about 18 inches by 14, on canvas. It is not I think an original, but I suspect the very picture which was formerly in the possession of Wright, the painter and printseller in Covent Garden, from which the handsome mezzotinto was made by Simon. That picture according to Wright was painted by Zoust or Zoast, but *he* lived in the time of Charles II. The earliest known picture of Zoust is painted in 1657. He died about 1681; Shakspeare in 1616. The only thing that looks original about this picture is the hard manner in which it is done, and the size, which is one of which the old painters were so fond —a size smaller than life yet not miniature. This picture has quite a different air from that belonging to the Duke of Chandos; no earrings; a very small collar or band, no strings to it; the hair on the crown of the head negligently thrown about without any appearance of baldness.

There was a picture of Shakspeare painted by Sir Godfrey Kneller, and presented by him to Dryden;

but I have never met with it. Perhaps it fell into Congreve's hands. Kneller probably copied the picture which Betterton then had, and which the Duke of Chandos now possesses. It might however have fallen into the hands of Charles Earl of Dorset, Dryden's patron; and it may be the very picture of Shakspeare now at Knowle.*

Swift used often to make extempore distichs. Having preached one Sunday at St. Ann's Church, in Dublin, where there is only the basement of a tower without any spire, the building never having been finished, the present Archdeacon Mahon who was then a boy, followed Swift from curiosity when he went out of the church, and heard him grumble out—

> A beggarly people!
> A church and no steeple!

(*Ex relatione* Mr. Downes, brother-in-law to Mr. Mahon.)

Mr. Drumgoold, who had resided long at St. Germains, told Mr. Burke that old Grammont, whose memoirs are so entertaining, was a very cross, unpleasant old fellow. Count Hamilton, who really wrote the book, *invented* several of the anecdotes told in it, and mixed them with such facts as he could pick up from the old man, who was pleased to hear these tales when put into a handsome dress.

When Sir J. Reynolds, Mr. Garrick, Mr. Burke, and others went to Lord Mansfield's house to bail

* The pictures of Mr. Douglass were sold by auction by Christic in January 1792, but this picture of Shakspeare was not sent with the rest.

Baretti, his lordship, without paying much attention to the business, immediately and abruptly began with some very flimsy and boyish observations on the contested passage in *Othello*, " Put out the light," &c. This was by way of showing off to Garrick, whose opinion of him however was not much raised by this impotent and untimely endeavour to shine on a subject with which he was little acquainted. Sir J. Reynolds, who had never seen him before (who told me the story), was grievously disappointed in finding this *great lawyer* so *little* at the same time.

Mr. Gibbon, the historian, is so exceedingly indolent that he never even pares his nails. His servant, while Gibbon is reading, takes up one of his hands, and when he has performed the operation lays it down, and then manages the other—the patient in the meanwhile scarcely knowing what is going on, and quietly pursuing his studies.

The picture of him painted by Sir J. Reynolds, and the prints made from it, are as like the original as it is possible to be. When he was introduced to a blind French lady, the servant happening to stretch out her mistress's hand to lay hold of the historian's cheek, she thought, upon feeling its rounded contour, that some trick was being played upon her with the *sitting* part of a child, and exclaimed, " Fidonc ! "

Mr. Gibbon is very replete with anecdotes, and tells them with great happiness and fluency.

It would be very satisfactory if contemporaries would hand down to posterity their opinion concerning the likenesses of portraits of celebrated men of their own time. It is for that I have introduced Mr. G.'s portrait above. Sir J. Reynolds is in general as happy in his likenesses as he is masterly in the execution of his pictures. His portraits of Dr. Johnson, of Mr. Boswell, Lord Thurlow, Lord Mansfield, Lord Loughborough, Lord Camden, Mr. Fox, Mr. Windham, Mr. Garrick, Mr. Burke, Charles Townshend, Dr. Burney, Baretti, Foote, Goldsmith, Mr. W. Mason, Mr. Andrew Stuart, and Mr. Pott are all extremely like. Concerning all these I speak according to the best of my judgment from personal knowledge. I do not think the portraits of Dr. and Thomas Warton are like.

Mr. Raftor, the brother of Mrs. Clive, the actress, was but a bad actor, but had some dry humour. Having described some wretched situation in which he had once been, Garrick said he had no patience with him for not having made some effort to relieve himself. "Why, what would you have me do?" replied Raftor; "I was cut down twice!"

Harward, the Irish lawyer, with the help of a great brogue, a strong and a peculiar cough, or long h-e-m, was sometimes happy in a retort. Harward had read a great deal of law, but it was all a confused mass; he had little judgment or discrimination. Having however made one of his best harangues and stated, as he usually did, a great deal of *doubtful* law, which yet he thought very sound, Lord Chief Justice Clayton,

who though one of the weakest and most ignorant
boors I have ever known, had got the common black-
letter of Westminster Hall pretty ready, as soon as
Harward had done, exclaimed, " You don't suppose,
Mr. Harward, that I take this to be law?" " Indeed,
my Lord," replied Harward, with his usual shrug and
cough, " I don't suppose you do !"

April 15, 1788.—Mr. Courtenay happening to dine
yesterday with Lord Lansdown, took occasion to mention the *Harley Papers* which his lordship was said to
have bought from the executors of Mr. West. The
fact was so; but the much-talked-of letter of the Duke
of Marlborough was not among them. Lord Lansdown said that Harley intended at first to have sent
the original letter to Lord Duplin, but on second
thoughts substituted an exact copy, lest the duke
should destroy the original. When this *copy* was
shown to the duke, he desired it might be given to
him, and is supposed to have destroyed it. (See
further particulars on this subject, p. 440.)

When the thermometer is as low as thirty-six, all
vegetation ceases.—*Sir J. Banks.*

In a late conversation with Mr. Flood, speaking
of my late uncle, Anthony Malone, he observed that
such was Mr. Malone's perspicuity and method, that,
during the many years they sat in Parliament together, Mr. Flood never remembered a single instance
where any one part of Mr. M.'s speech could be transferred with advantage. Every part seemed to follow

what preceded it so naturally that no change could be made for the better.

On my mentioning what I have said in the character I have given of this extraordinary man in the new *Irish Peerage*, that he seemed to argue with somewhat less of his usual vigour when engaged on the wrong side of the question, Mr. Flood happily observed that " he could not escape from the force of his own understanding."—*Feb.* 1789.

Pope had an original picture of Bishop Atterbury painted by Kneller. Of this picture he used to make Worsdale the painter make copies for three or four guineas; and whenever he wished to pay a particular compliment to one of his friends, he gave him an *original* picture of Atterbury. Of these *originals*, Worsdale had painted five or six.—(From Mr. Walpole.)

The origin of venison being sold by fishmongers was this. Many noblemen having more bucks than they had occasion for, wished to dispose of them, but were ashamed to take money. They therefore sent them to their fishmongers, and received fish in return. This practice commenced about forty years ago; and the fishmongers still continue to sell venison, though they do not obtain it in the same way. For the owners of parks now feel no reluctance in receiving cash for a certain number of bucks every season at a stipulated price.

Soon after Pope's acquaintance with Warburton commenced, and the latter had published some of his

c c

heavy commentaries on that poet, his friend Lord Marchmont told him that he was convinced he was one of the vainest men living. "How so?" says Pope. "Because, you little rogue," replied Lord Marchmont, "it is manifest from your close connection with your new commentator you want to show posterity what an exquisite poet you are, and what a quantity of dulness you can carry down on your back without sinking under the load."

When Sir Robert Walpole was attacked in the House of Commons in the latter end of 1741, Sir Spencer Compton though ill of a fever, got out of bed and went down to vote for him, as Mr. Horace Walpole told me. He thought much to Sir Spencer's honour, as they had been rival candidates for the place of Prime Minister on the accession of King George II.*

Sir Robert lived about three years after being dismissed from office and created Earl of Orford. He spent about half the year at Houghton and the remainder in London. Being afflicted with the gravel he could not take much exercise, but sometimes rode out.

[The following anecdote has been noticed in a previous page, but it is satisfactory to have this verification of it, with additional circumstances.]

Having heard from Mr. Courtenay, who had it

* He was then, and had been long before, Lord Wilmington. The struggle—if such it can be called—of the rivals for power is told at length by Lord Hervey.—*Memoirs of George II.*, vol. i. chap. i. to iv.

from Mr. W. Ellis, that Lord Orford had once taken up three or four books in his library, and at length threw down the last of them, with tears in his eyes, exclaiming, "It is all in vain—*I cannot read!*" I was curious to know the truth of this story, and therefore mentioned it to Mr. Walpole (March 15, 1789). He said he was about twenty-two years old when his father retired; and that he remembered very well his offering one day to read to Lord Orford, finding that time hung heavy on his hands. "What," said Lord Orford, "will you read, child?" Mr. Walpole, considering that his father had been long engaged in publick business, proposed to read some history. "No," said Lord Orford, "don't read history to me; that can't be true."

He read Sydenham's works, and admired him much; but this admiration was the cause of his death; for meeting with Dr. Jusin's pamphlet on Mrs. Steevens' medicine for the stone, and thinking that Jusin's hypothesis agreed with Sydenham's, he took the medicine which dissolved the stone, but lacerated his bladder in such a way as to be the cause of his death. He was near seventy years of age, and had been very handsome. I could not find from Mr. Walpole that his father read any other book but Sydenham in his retirement; so probably Mr. Ellis's anecdote is true.

Mr. Hamilton once observed to Bishop Warburton that he thought Pope was a cold man, notwithstanding all his talk about friendship and philosophy.

c c 2

" No," said the Bishop, " you are entirely mistaken ;
he had as tender a heart as any man that ever lived."

(Query—Is the Bishop a fair and impartial witness on this point?)

Warburton told Mr. Hamilton that Pope and
others had undoubted proofs that Walsh at one time
was reduced to such distress by prodigality as to become the hostler of an inn.

When Bishop Secker spoke in the House of Lords
in favour of the Gin Bill, among other of the evils
arising from its immoderate use he with great
gravity mentioned that it occasioned promiscuous intercourse of the sexes. The House could not stand
this, and burst into a fit of laughter.

Secker was very irritable in temper, and in order
to guard himself against passion he made it a rule
always to speak in a very slow and measured tone,
which had the effect he wished.

The two portraits which Sir Joshua Reynolds has
lately painted of Mr. William Windham, of Norfolk,
and Richard Brinsley Sheridan are so like the originals, that they seem almost alive and ready to speak
to you. Painting, in point of resemblance, can go
no farther.

Mr. George Selwyn, who is now seventy-three or
seventy-four years old, remembers Mrs. Oldfield,
and was once carried by her in a coach to the play,
which was *Mary Queen of Scots.* He says she had

very fine eyes, and that her son, the present Colonel
Churchill, is very like her. Him I have seen, and
he is certainly not handsome. Mr. Selwyn being
once in the green room with Quin, asked him
whether he had seen Betterton, and his opinion of
him. Quin replied that he was certainly a great
actor but added, "He would not, however, do *now*."
—(From Mr. Kemble, April 26, 1789.)

This conversation was probably after Garrick had
appeared in 1741 ; for in 1741 Selwyn was but about
twenty-five, at which time he probably did not go
among the wits of the green room, nor was he probably much interested about the merits of the old
actors. Quin himself had acted with Booth, who
had acted with Betterton ; and Quin's manner was
formed on Booth's, as Booth's was upon that of
Betterton. Quin therefore could not mean that
between the death of Betterton and the middle
period of his own acting, which was about 1735,
the publick taste was altered, and must have alluded
to the very different mode of acting introduced by
Mr. Garrick. The conversation, therefore, probably
passed about the year 1744 or 1745.

The first book that gave Sir Joshua Reynolds a
turn for painting was the *Jesuit's Perspective*, a
book which happened to be in the parlour window in
the house of his father, who was a clergyman. He
made himself at eight years old so completely master
of this book that he has never had occasion to study
any other work on the subject ; and the knowledge of

perspective then acquired has served him ever since.—
(From Sir J. R. himself.)

In one of his Italian tours, Baretti picked up at a
house where he stopped for refreshment a little book
which his host let him have for a trifle, and which
contained the *seeds* of Ariosto's great poem. He
afterwards gave the book to Mr. Croft, and it was
sold at the auction of his books to Mr. Steevens for
some exorbitant price. I forget the title of the book.

When Cuzzoni* was somewhat in the decline of
her reputation on her second visit here, Baretti went
with a friend to see her. She was leaning pensively
on her arm; on which Baretti's friend asked her
how she came to be in such low spirits. "How can I
be otherwise," said Cuzzoni, "when I have had no
dinner, and have not a shilling to buy one?" "Well,"
said the other, "I am not very rich; I have but two
guineas in my purse; here is one of them, and let us
hear no more of your low spirits. You can now dine
as soon as you will." Cuzzoni rang the bell, gave her
servant the guinea, and bade him go to a famous wine-

---

* Or (according to her married name) Sandoni, once a celebrated
opera singer, of whom and Handel an amusing story is told. Handel
had composed for her the song of *Falsa Imagine* in *Otho*, which occasioned so severe a dispute between them on account of her refusing to
sing it, that at last Handel threatened to throw the refractory signora
out of the window; telling her "that he always knew she was a *very
devil*, but that he should now let her know, in her turn, that he was
Beelzebub, the Prince of Devils." He then seized her by the waist and
lifted up the sash. Alarmed at this process, Cuzzoni now consented, and
by exquisite grace and pathos, added to the ornaments with which she
executed and diversified the few simple notes that compose the air, added
more to her reputation than by any other performance.

merchant, and get from him a pint of cape (*sic*) wine and a penny roll. The man after some time returned and said the merchant would not let him have a roll—that he was not a baker, but had sent the wine. " Get you gone," said Cuzzoni; " unless he sends me a roll I'll have no wine." " Well," said the wine-merchant, on the boy's return, " since she insists on it, there is a penny; go to the next baker's and buy her a roll." On getting her bread and wine she poured the cape (which cost a guinea) into a bowl, and crumbling the bread into it drank off the contents. Not many years afterwards Baretti saw her *selling greens* at a stall at Bologna.

May 8, 1789.—I little expected when I dined with the man mentioned in the preceding pages, that he would so soon be numbered with the dead. Baretti, on the day on which I met him at Mr. Courtenay's, seemed in remarkably good health. He told us then I think that he was in his seventy-third year. He was very entertaining; and a good deal of that roughness for which he was formerly dis-tinguished had gone off. He died last Tuesday, 6th instant, at his house in Edward Street, of gout in his stomach, of which he had complained but a few days. He was in indigent circumstances. He had a small pension of 80*l.* per annum which was his chief support. He had lately revised his dictionary and made it (as he told us at Mr. Courtenay's) a much better work; the original having been copied from the dictionaries that had gone before. By re-trenching several faulty expressions, &c., he reduced

tho size from two volumes to one which tho booksellers, who estimate works by their *bulk*, did not much
approve of. He was to have 100*l.* for his labour, and
having delivered in his MS. complete to Messrs.
Cadell and Robinson, and being distressed for money,
he pressed for the payment. Some words which
passed between him and the latter of these booksellers inflamed him so much as in some measure
to prey upon his mind and accelerate his death.
Cadell at length relented, and sent 50*l.*, half the
money agreed upon, but it did not reach Baretti's
house till after his death.

He was certainly a man of extraordinary talents,
and perhaps no one ever made himself so completely
master of a foreign language as he did of English.
He came to England, I imagine, about the year 1750,
and resided here principally ever since. He has, I
find, given particular directions to prevent his body
falling into the hands of the surgeons.

Not very long after the institution of the Club,
Sir J. Reynolds was speaking of it to Garrick. "I
like it much," says he, "I think I'll be of you."
When Sir J. R. mentioned this to Dr. Johnson, he
was much displeased at the actor's conceit. "He'll be
of us," says Johnson, "how does he know we will
permit him? The first duke in England has no
right to hold such language?" However, when
Garrick was regularly proposed some time afterwards,
Johnson warmly supported him, being in reality a

very tender affectionate man. He was merely offended at the actor's conceit.*

On the former part of this story it probably was that Sir John Hawkins grounded his account that Garrick never was of the Literary Club, and that Johnson said he never ought to be of it. And thus it is that this stupid biographer, and the more flippant and malicious Mrs. Piozzi, have miscoloured and misrepresented almost every anecdote that they have pretended to tell of Dr. Johnson.—(The fact from Sir J. Reynolds.)

Soon after Gainsborough settled in London, Sir J. Reynolds thought himself bound in civility to pay him a visit. Gainsborough took not the least notice of him for several years, but at length called and solicited him to sit for his picture. Sir Joshua sat *once;* but being soon afterwards affected by a slight paralytick stroke, he was obliged to go to Bath. On his return to town perfectly restored to health, he sent Gainsborough word that he was returned; to which Gainsborough only replied that he was glad to hear he was well; and never after desired him to sit, or called upon him, or had any other intercourse with him till he was dying, when he sent and thanked him for the very handsome manner in which he had always spoken of him; a circumstance which the President has thought worth recording in his fourteenth discourse. Gainsborough was so enamoured of his art that he had many of the pictures he was then work-

---

* I mentioned this anecdote to Mr. Boswell, and he has introduced it into his *Life of Johnson.*—M.

ing upon brought to his bedside to show them to Reynolds, and flattered himself that he should live to finish them.—(From the same.)

He was a very dissolute capricious man, inordinately fond of women, and not very delicate in his sentiments of honour. He was first put forward in the world, I think by a Mr. Fonnereaux, who lent him 300*l.* Gainsborough having a vote for an election in which his benefactor had some concern, voted against him. His conscience however remonstrating against such conduct, he kept himself in a state of intoxication from the time he set out to vote till his return to town, that he might not relent of his ingratitude.— (From Mr. Windham.)

On mentioning to Sir Joshua Reynolds the conversation that I had had with Baretti, on my return from Mr. Courtenay's about the Lord's Prayer, he said, " This turn which B. now gives to the matter was an after-thought; for he once said to me myself, ' there are various opinions about the writer of that prayer; some give it to St. Augustine, some to St. Chrysostom, &c. What is your opinion ?' "

On examining the indexes at the Signet Office yesterday (June 19, 1789) to ascertain when Sir George Buck was made Master of the Revels to King James the First, I happened to turn back to the reign of Elizabeth, and under the year 1590, was surprised to find in the letter S., " Edmund Spenser Penson." On examining the minute of the grant, I found it entered as follows : "Feb. 1590 (*i. e.* 1591) An Annuity of 50*l.* per ann. to Edmund Spenser during life."—(D. Aubrey.)

This particular has, I think, escaped all our biographers. Fifty pounds a year was then, all circumstances being considered, at least equal to 200*l.* a year now, so that he could not be in such extreme poverty at his death as is usually represented. I suppose that contemporary writers meant he was *comparatively poor ;* for he had possessed a large estate in Ireland which was lost in the troubles. He was in Ireland in 1598, as appears by a curious letter from Queen Elizabeth which I found in the Museum, recommending him to be Sheriff of the County of Cork in that year. . . . . (See it in my *Shakspeare.*)

Yesterday (June 19) I passed an hour very agreeably in Furnival's Inn with Mr. P. H. Neve, a young gentleman who has lately printed some miscellaneous observations on the English poets, and is much devoted to literary pursuits. His chambers look on the garden of Furnival's Inn, a very sequestered spot which I had never before happened to look at. Yet he complained that it was not private enough, and talked of moving elsewhere. He showed me many rare autographs, and a curious memorandum which he found lately in Milton's book in defence of the people of England; in which the former possessor of the book says in Latin, that Milton's brother (who was, I think, a judge of one of the courts at Westminster) told him that with all the *legal* arguments in that book, Milton was furnished by the celebrated Bradshaw, president of the court that put Charles I. to death.

Dr. Donne, the poet, in 1602 married the daughter of Sir George Moore privately against her father's consent, who was so enraged that he not only turned him and his wife out of his house, but got Lord Chancellor Egerton to turn him out of his office as Secretary to the Great Seal. Donne and his wife took refuge in a house at ——, in the neighbourhood of his father-in-law, who lived at Lothesby, in the county of Surrey, where the first thing he did was to write on a pane of glass—

> John Donne
> An Donne
> Undone.

These words were visible at that house in 1749. It should be remembered that Donne's name was formerly pronounced Dun.—(From a similar notice found by Mr. Neve in an old book.)

Mr. Welbore Ellis, who was well acquainted with the late Twisden, Bishop of Raphoe, assured me at the Marquis Townshend's about a month ago, that the strange story which has been long current in Ireland, of the bishop being shot in attempting to rob on the highway in England, was an absolute falsehood. Mr. Ellis said he saw the physician who attended him, who told him he died of a fever.

The stories which are told of this bishop's levity or vivacity are probably however true; for Mr. Ellis owned that Twisden once laid a wager that he would leap over a cow as she lay in the field. Just at the instant of the attempt, the cow got up, and the bishop dislocated his shoulder.*

"Pope's house at Twickenham," says Dr. Taylor (who is now living at Isleworth, and eighty-five years old) in a letter to my father in Ireland, written soon after the poet's death, "I believe will be bought by Sir William Stanhope. They say the whole purchase will come within 1,500*l.* Pope died worth 4,000*l.* The King of Sardinia's watch, which is mentioned in his will, is a common plain gold one, not worth twenty guineas."

"People here," he adds in the same letter, "do not talk of the Anglesey affair in the same strain they seem to do in Ireland. The verdict here is generally condemned. Bacon told me he heard Sir John Strange lately say at Tom's that he had read the printed trial, and that the Pl. appeared clearly from thence to him to be a bastard; and that he was astonished at the charge and at the verdict.— Concanen arrived in London last night."

Mr. Parsons, an ingenious picture cleaner and painter from whom I bought eight drawings yesterday done by the elder Richardson called upon me this morning, June 2nd, 1789. He says that the great sale of Richardson's drawings was in 1746-7.

* It was often said formerly that many of the bishops sent from England to fill Irish sees were such as would not have been tolerated in England.

At that sale the younger Richardson was a considerable purchaser, and he afterwards added greatly to his collection, which upon his own death about the year 1772, was sold by auction. There Mr. P. bought the drawings; two of Pope; two of Milton, one of them very highly finished; two of Shakspeare, one of them from the picture now in the Duke of Chandos' possession, and the other from the print prefixed to his poems in 1640; one of the elder Richardson; and one of the late Dr. Birch.

Mrs. Thrale has grossly misrepresented the story which she has told of Dr. Johnson's saying a harsh thing to her at table (*see* her *Anecdotes*). The fact was this. A Mr. Thrale, related to Mr. Thrale, Johnson's friend, for whom they both had a great regard, had gone some time before to the East or West Indies. Dr. Johnson had not yet heard of his fate; and Mrs. Thrale very abruptly while she was eating some larks most ravenously, laid down her knife and fork—"Oh dear, Dr. Johnson, do you know what has happened? The last letters from abroad have brought us an account that poor Tom Thrale's head was taken off by a cannon ball in the action of ——." Johnson, who was shocked both at the fact and at her gross manner of telling it, replied,—"Madam, it would give you very little concern if all your relations were spitted like those larks, and dressed for Presto's supper." Presto was the dog which lay under the table, and which Mrs. Thrale was feeding just as she mentioned the death of Mr. Thrale's cousin.

Mr. Boswell has mentioned in his *Journal of a Tour to the Hebrides*, that Johnson once met with an Italian in London who did not know who was the author of the Lord's Prayer. The Italian, whom Mr. Boswell out of tenderness forbore to name, was Baretti. As I walked home with him from Mr. Courtenay's, he mentioned that the story as told gave an unfair representation of him. The fact he said was this. In a conversation with Dr. Johnson concerning the Lord's Prayer, Baretti observed (profanely enough) that the petition, *lead us not into temptation*, ought rather to be addressed to the tempter of mankind than a benevolent Creator who delighted in the happiness of his creatures. " Pray, sir," said Johnson" (who could not bear that any part of our holy religion should be spoken lightly of), "do you know who was the author of the Lord's Prayer?" Baretti (who did not wish to get into any serious dispute, and who appears to be an Infidel), by way of putting an end to the conversation, only replied,—" Oh, sir, you know by *our* religion (Roman Catholic), we are not permitted to read the Scriptures. You can't therefore expect an answer."

The two drawings of Pope are marked at the back with Richardson's R—, but have no date. Milton is in profile, " 13th February, 1737 R." The other Milton, " 4th December, 1734 R." The Shakspeare from the old picture, " R., 21st April, 1733." The copy from the print thus : " From an old print before an early edition of his poems, R. — Shakspeare, 20th October, 1732." " Richardson, senior, 24th August,

1736." " Mr. Birch, R., 21st November, 1739." I have put these dates down here lest, being written in pencil with which the drawings were made, they should hereafter be defaced.

Mr. Parsons had a university education, and was originally intended for the Church, but his love of painting led him to his present profession. He set out as a painter, and copied in his youth a vast number of Sir Peter Lely's pictures which have deceived some connoisseurs, and were taken for originals. Being carried down by Lord Craven about thirty years ago to view his great collection of old pictures, he found them in a miserable condition, and cleaned them so well that he has ever since had so much employment in that way as to have had scarcely time to paint an original picture. He has however made a great many copies in that time ; amongst others, one of Fenton, the poet, for a Mr. Fenton in ——. Fenton, of whom I did not know there had been any picture, was he says a very handsome man. Addison's daughter, he informs me, is now living in Warwickshire, and is possessed of an original picture of Dryden, which belonged to her father, and which Parsons copied some time ago for a Mr. Sneyd of Staffordshire.

He has been lately much employed by Lord Warwick and Lord Scarsdale, and sold the latter about six months ago a very great curiosity, a portrait of Shakspeare by Vandyke. It is now at Lord Scarsdale's, in Derbyshire. It was brought to Parsons last winter by a dealer with two or three other old pictures; and having been much conversant with Vandyke's pictures he knew the hand at once.

He is equally clear that it is a portrait of Shakspeare. It has more resemblance he says to the picture said to be painted by Zoest, of which there is a mezzotinto by Simon, than to the Duke of Chandos' picture. Vandyke came to England, I think, about the year 1630;* so that he must have copied this picture from that from which the print prefixed to the first folio, 1623, was made, or from the old picture formerly in the possession of Davenant, and now belonging to the Duke of Chandos, or from some other original. There is, Parsons says, great spirit in the portrait; it contains a hand which, according to Vandyke's manner, is spread on the left side of the body. The drapery is black without any figure or flowers in it.

My two ruins of Rome, Parsons thinks were done by Viviani, after Panini; and he inclines to think that my Duke of Monmouth which in my grandfather Collier's catalogue is called Sir Peter Lely's, was painted either by Mrs. Bale or the elder Richardson. The landscape, in the large picture of the Creation painted by De Foss, was done he says by ——, who always was employed by De Foss in that part of his pictures.

I had thought my large landscape by Abraham Houdens, 1687, was a great rarity as well as a very

* Probably before that time; for in 1632 he was in high repute, was knighted, and received a pension.

D D

fine picture, because Mr. Walpole has said he painted very few pictures, or that there are very few of his hand in England; but this is not so; Mr. Parsons has had above a hundred of his go through his hands. He allows the picture however, though it has not the merit of rarity, to be admirably executed.

On looking a few days since over the *General Advertiser*, 1748, for Macklin's letter relative to Ford and Shakspeare which I have proved to be fiction, I found Mrs. Pritchard, the actress, was in that year weak enough to think of performing the part of *George Barnwell* for her husband's benefit. However, before the day came she thought better of it, and performed *Lady Macbeth* instead.

Mr. Fenton mentions in his notes on Waller's *Poems*, pp. 29, 46, that Spencer was matriculated at Cambridge, on the 20th May, 1569; and supposing him to have been in his sixteenth year, he concluded that this poet was born in 1553; but at that time it was much more common to go to the university at *twelve* years old than at sixteen. If he was but twelve in 1569, he was born in 1557. His birth took place in East Smithfield in the parish of St. Botolph. I examined the register of that parish in vain for his baptism. I did not commence I found till 1550.

There is I suppose some mistake with respect to the portrait shown as Sacharissa's at Mr. Waller's house; for on my mentioning to Lord Macartney at our club, how little she was entitled to Waller's praise, he told me that two fine pictures of her and her sister by Vandyke were at Petworth in Sussex (Lord Egremont's), and that Sacharissa appeared to have been very handsome.

———— —

Lady Falconberg, Cromwell's daughter, lived till the year 1712. Old Lord Ilchester told Lord Macartney that he remembered her when he was a boy visiting at his father's, and that all the younger part of the family used always to get near her on account of her having a great quantity of perfumes about her.

————

Sir J. Reynolds when he called on me yesterday (July 10), on looking over the elder Richardson's drawings, said he understood his art very well scientifically; but that his manner was cold and hard. He was Sir Joshua's pictorial grandfather, being Hudson's master. He was always drawing either himself or Pope, whom he scarcely ever visited without taking some sketch of his face. His son was intended for a painter, but being very near-sighted soon gave up all thoughts of that profession. He was a great news and anecdote monger; and in the latter part of his life spent much of his time in gathering and communicating intelligence concerning the King of Prussia and other topics of the day; as Dr. Burney, who knew him very well, informs me. His *Richardsoniana* are not uninteresting.

I this day (July 24, 1789) perused Wentworth Lord Roscommon's will at Doctors' Commons. He having been once the owner of my estate in West-meath, in Ireland, I feel an interest about him, and should be glad to meet with his picture by Carlo Maratti which is somewhere extant. His will is very short. He expresses the strongest hope of a resurrection and redemption by the merits of our Saviour, and commits his wretched body to the earth. He makes his (second) wife Isabella (daughter of Matthew Baynton, Yorkshire, Esq., whom he mar-ried in 1674) his executrix, and bequeathes her all his estate real and personal after payment of his debts. His will was made January 4, 1684–5, and proved the latter end of that month.

Knightly Chetwood, who has left MS. memoirs of him—now in the public library at Cambridge—was one of the witnesses to his will. I think he says in those memoirs that Lord Roscommon resembled his uncle Lord Strafford in the countenance. His widow married the father of the late Thomas Carter, Master of the Rolls in Ireland, and died in Dublin in 1722. I hoped to have found her picture in the possession of Mr. Carter's heir, but he has it not.

Sir Joshua Reynolds was born at Plympton in Devonshire, in 1723. One of the first portraits he ever painted is in the possession of a Mr. Hamilton, nephew to Lord Abercorn. As he himself told me, when about the age of nineteen or twenty, he became very careless about his profession, and lived for near three years at Plymouth in a great deal of dissipation with but indifferent company, at least such company as from whom no improvement could be gained. He now much laments the loss of these three years. However, he saw his error in time, and sat down seriously to his art about the year 1743 or 1744. Soon afterwards he painted the portrait above-mentioned, Captain Hamilton being a naval officer who married the present Lord Eliot's mother.

This Captain Hamilton was a very uncommon character; very obstinate, very whimsical, very pious, a rigid disciplinarian, yet very kind to his men. He lost his life as he was proceeding from his ship to land at Plymouth. The wind and sea were extremely high, and his officers remonstrated against the imprudence of venturing in a boat where the danger seemed imminent. But he was impatient to see his wife, and would not be persuaded. In a few minutes after he left the ship, the boat was upset and turned keel upward. The captain being a good swimmer, trusted to his skill, and would not accept of a place on the keel in order to make room for others, and then clung to the edge of the boat. Unluckily he had kept on his greatcoat. At length, seeming exhausted, those on the keel exhorted him to take a place beside them, and he attempted to throw off the coat, but finding his strength fail, told the men he must yield to his fate and soon afterwards sank while *singing a psalm.*—(From Lord Eliot.)

Hayman, the painter, though but an ordinary artist, had some humour. Among the set with

whom he lived much, there was one who was always
complaining of ill-health and low spirits without
being able to assign any particular malady as the
cause.   One evening at Hayman's club, it was mentioned that this *maladie imaginaire* had been married the day before. "Is he! and be d———d to him!"
said Hayman; "now he'll know what ails him!"—
(From Sir J. Reynolds.)

Mendez, the Jew poet, sat to him for his picture,
but requested he would not put it in his show-room,
as he wished to keep the matter a secret.   However,
as Hayman had but little business in portraits, he
could not afford to let his new work remain in obscurity, so out it went with the few others that he
had to display.   A new picture being a rarity in
Hayman's room, the first friend that came in took
notice of it and asked whose portrait it was?
" Mendez'." " Good heavens!" said the friend, "you
are wonderfully out of luck here.   It has not a trait
of his countenance."   "Why, to tell you the truth,"
said the painter, " he desired *it might not be known*."

The present Duke of Marlborough has been
always remarkably shy and reserved.   Among other
small talents that he possesses he plays *Quinze* uncommonly well.   He told Sir J. Reynolds one day,
when speaking of the defect in himself already mentioned, of which he is very sensible, that having once
made a master-stroke at that game by which he
should have made a hundred pounds, he put his
cards into the heap, and lost what he had set on
them, knowing that if he had shown them, which

it was necessary to do to win the money, all the company at the different tables would have come round him, and the fineness of the stroke have been their topic for half an hour. This he acknowledged he could not stand; adding, however, "*I am not so shy now.*" And yet to common observers he is still unaccountably so, considering his birth, education, and commerce with the world.—(From Sir Josh. R.)

Captain Hamilton, half-brother of the present Lord Eliot, gave a still more extraordinary proof of the force of *mauvaise honte.* He was appointed governor of some foreign settlement—Newfoundland, I think. During the voyage he often talked of the embarrassments of such a situation, and how painful it would be to him to have a concourse of people perpetually about him, and to be so marked an object as he must be whenever he stirred out. All this lay very heavy on his mind; however, he endeavoured to shake off his apprehensions during the voyage; but when he came near the shore, and saw the crowd of people ready to receive him, and heard their huzzas, it entirely overcame him, and he retired into his cabin and shot himself.—(From Sir Josh. R.)

Serjeant Davy was often employed at the Bar of the House of Commons. On one occasion he called a witness to prove some point, and put a question of no great importance which was immediately objected to by the opposite counsel. The counsel on both sides, according to the usual form, were

ordered to withdraw, and the House began to debate
on the propriety of the question. The discussion
lasted for *some hours;* but at length the determination being in favour of Davy, he was called in,
and the Speaker informed him he might put his
question. " I protest, Mr. Speaker," replied Davy,
" *I entirely forget what it was.*" This, as may easily
be believed, threw the House into a roar of laughter.

His brother-serjeant, Whitaker, was still more
celebrated for his wit, or rather dry humour. On
some contested election before the House of Commons, he argued that the testimony of a Mr. Smith
would be very material for his client. The adverse
party were very desirous that the witness should
not be produced, and urged that he was in so bad
a state of health it might be extremely prejudicial
to him to remain for some hours in so hot a place
as a full House of Commons. At length it was
determined that Mr. Smith should be examined;
and to give a colour to what had been alleged, he
was brought in muffled up, and supported by a friend.
All the members were very attentive when Whitaker
rose to examine him, expecting some question that
would get to the bottom of the business. The
serjeant got up with great gravity, and began his
examination with—" Pray, Mr. Smith, how do you
do? " The greater part of the House being in the
secret, or at least suspecting that his illness was
mere pretence, burst into a roar of laughter not
less violent than that produced by Davy's sally on

a former occasion.—(This and the former from Mr. Gerard Hamilton.)

Petrarch observes in one of his letters (*Epist. Fam.* l. ii. ep. 2) that the Romans before the time of Sylla were buried entire in the earth, and that the practice of cremation began with the dictator, who apprehending that some of the Marian faction would treat his own remains as ill as he had done those of Marius, ordered his dead body to be burned.

Dr. Arthur Charlette in the last age corresponded with almost all the celebrated persons of that time, and preserved all their letters. An immense collection of them, which he had made and bound in several folio volumes, fell into the hands of Mr. Ballard, author of the *Memoirs of Learned Ladies of Great Britain*, and are now in the Bodleian Library. They contain, as Mr. Warton informs me, many curious anecdotes.

August 6, 1791.—I dined at Sir William Scott's in the Commons, with Mr. Windham, Mr. Erskine, Sir William Wynne, Sir J. Reynolds, and a Mr. De Vyme. The latter, who was the son of a French refugee, and spoke English perfectly well, had lived in Portugal for forty years, and was at Lisbon at the time of the earthquake; of which he gave us a curious account.

It happened about ten in the morning on All Souls' Day, when many of the people were in the parish churches. He was sitting in his counting-house in his night-gown, and the first symptom he heard was a very loud whizzing noise; soon afterwards he found his house shake, and called immediately to his clerks to follow him. They all ran out behind his house, and proceeded as fast as possible to a high ground, where they remained in safety and saw the town falling on every side. After continuing there about forty-eight hours, he ventured to go down into the town, where generally there reigned total silence. Almost every step he took was over a dead body. Among other shocking scenes he saw a woman dead with a child at her breast without its head. He made his way however through the ruins to his own house, which being situated on a rock, he hoped might not have been wholly destroyed; and with the help of eight or ten persons who had escaped like himself and whom he paid highly, cleared away the rubbish sufficiently to get to his strong box in the counting-house, from which he carried away notes to the amount of eighteen thousand pounds. He, however, by the inability of others to fulfil their contracts, lost 40,000*l.* that day.

Very soon after the first shock, the air, by whirl-winds of smoke and dust from the city falling and taking fire (for the small pans of coals with which they warm themselves soon produced that effect), became entirely dark; and the first sensation of every one was that the end of the world had arrived. The total number of inhabitants of Portugal is about two and a half millions, so that it is less populous than Ireland, where about four millions are now reckoned. The people of Lisbon amount, as is supposed, to one hundred thousand, of whom about eleven hundred perished in the earthquake. The town is built upon seven hills, and was twice destroyed by earthquakes before.

After the last visitation it was proposed to the minister, Pombal, to rebuild the town on a new site, two miles inland, and more distant from the sea; but from some unknown motive he adhered to the old position; and there is no doubt that the same causes which operated before will at some time or other destroy the town again.

Mr. De Vyme having now quitted Lisbon, on account of his health, and settled in England, wishes to sell his country-house in Portugal, but such is the poverty of the people that he cannot get a purchaser. It is almost a palace, the purchase-money required being above 30,000*l.* The Queen herself wishes to be the owner, but it has been represented to her that if she should spare so much money from building churches (for she is a great devotee) she ought rather, for the good of her people, to lay it out in building one herself. Mr. De Vyme was the first who introduced pineapples into Portugal. He, the Queen, and one of her ministers, are the only persons who now grow them.

The Portuguese have a great quantity of specie among them, and yet are not very rich. Spain, he said, at present contains about eleven millions of people, and is capable of sustaining at least twenty-two millions. While he was in Portugal he spent two hundred and forty thousand pounds. He brought home with him one hundred thousand; and left in the house at Lisbon twelve hundred thousand.

August 9, at Mr. Windham's. — The company, Sir William Scott, Sir Joshua Reynolds, Dr. Laurence, Sir Henry Englefield, and myself. A very pleasant day.

Sir Joshua and Sir W. Scott, in talking concerning that despicable woman Mrs. Piozzi, mentioned the letter which she wrote to Johnson in answer to his objurgatory one relative to her proposed marriage with an Italian singer.* She has suppressed both letters in her book, and hers to Johnson happened by some accident not to be returned to her with the rest of her letters. She said in it among other things, as both Sir W. Scott and Sir Joshua agreed, that however she might have disgraced *Miss Salisbury* by marrying the brewer, she could not disgrace *Mrs. Thrale* by marrying Piozzi—that his profession was a liberal one which could not be said of the other; and she was told he excelled very much in his own way.

Of this kind of excellence however she all her life affected to be so little of a judge, as always to join with Dr. Johnson in inattention to musick; and soon after her present *caro sposo* came to England, she said once to Dr. Burney, as he told me, " We are all mightily pleasant and happy; but there is no bearing that fellow squaring his elbows at the harpsichord." This was at Dr. Burney's house; and the fellow was Piozzi.

* Piozzi—the story so well known in literary history.

When she first resolved to marry him, Miss Burney
(the authoress) lived with her, or was there on a
visit; and on being consulted, remonstrated strongly
on the impropriety of such a step. At length a promise was solemnly given that she would relinquish
all thoughts of it. In a day or two afterwards she
acted like a bedlamite, tore her hair, knocked her
head against the wall, &c., and told Miss Burney she
could not survive unless she had Piozzi. Soon afterwards she married him; and Miss Burney and she
are now entirely alienated. She is now wholly unconnected with all her former friends.

Mr. Lysons, though a great friend of hers, showed
Dr. Laurence who dined with us this day, a little
account of her pretty poem, *The Three Warnings*.
Of this piece, Lysons said, from some information
he had got, that " the first hint was given to her by
Johnson; that she brought it to him very incorrect;
and that he not only revised it throughout, but supplied several new lines." Under this account, which
was written by Lysons and shown to Mrs. Piozzi,
she had added with respect to the statement of its
being suggested by Johnson, " *That is not true*," ac-
knowledging by the exception that the rest was true.
But she was careless about truth, and therefore not
to be trusted.

Dr. Akenside, as Sir J. Reynolds told me, soon
after the publication of Goldsmith's *Traveller*, was
very liberal in its praise. A report then prevailed
that it was in fact written by Johnson; but Akenside maintained that it was impossible, and he par-

ticularly relied on two lines which he said Johnson would not have written—

> " Or onward, where the rude Carinthian boor,
> Against the houseless stranger shuts the door."

Perhaps Johnson would not have used the familiar but forcible expression in the second line ; and yet it is not Goldsmith's, but Shakspeare's—

> "Who should against his murderer shut the door,
> Not bear the knife myself."—*Macbeth*.

And " houseless" he had from *King Lear*.

Akenside however, while he pointed out these lines as unlike Johnson's manner, had not sagacity enough to observe some others which at once discovered his vigorous pen and cast of thought—

> " Still to ourselves in every place consigned,
> Our own felicity we make or find."

Johnson, in fact, wrote about sixteen lines of this beautiful poem, and no more, as he himself told Mr. Boswell.*   But Akenside never found this out.

Mr. Cator, the money-lender, once speaking about drunkenness, instead of enlarging on the common topics, the universality of it, its obscuring men's faculties, producing quarrels, &c., observed that it was a most injurious practice, and might be attended with very bad effects ; for no man who goes into company and indulges in wine, can know when he may be called out to make a bargain !

* In this, Malone or Boswell slightly errs.   The latter says : " In the year 1783, he (Johnson) at my request marked with a pencil the lines which he had furnished, which are only line 420th : ' To stop too fearful and too faint to go,' and the concluding ten lines except the last couplet but one."

Sir William Scott having occasionally mentioned that Sir William Blackstone composed his *Commentaries* with *a bottle of port-wine before him*, Mr. Boswell has inserted this anecdote in his new *Life of Dr. Johnson*. Sir William felt concerned at the disclosure, and wrote to his family to apologize. He was sorry that Mr. Boswell had inserted it without apprising him, as from the words employed it might be inferred that Sir William Blackstone was a drunkard, which was by no means the case.

The fact, as Sir W. Scott observed, was, that Blackstone was of a languid, phlegmatick constitution, in consequence of which he required a cheerful glass of wine to rouse and animate him; and after he returned from college in the evening to his chamber, had some wine frequently left in the room while writing, in order to correct or prevent the depression sometimes attendant on close study. That he did not use it to excess the *Commentaries* themselves, one of the most methodical, perspicuous, and elegant books in our language, clearly show. The late Dr. Lowth, Bishop of London, in this respect resembled Blackstone, being very indolent, taking little exercise, and eating heartily; in consequence of which he generally drank what is called a cheerful glass of wine.

Thomson, the poet, was so extremely indolent, that half his mornings were spent in bed. Dr. Burney having called on him one day at two o'clock, expressed surprise at finding him still there, and asked how he came to lie so long?—" Ecod, mon, because I had no *mot-tive* * to rise," was his sole answer. (From Dr. Burney.)

The late Lord Chesterfield's *bons mots* were all studied. Dr. Warren, who attended him for some months before his death, told me that he had always *one* ready for him each visit, but never gave him a second on the same day.

The late Duchess of N—— was very large and fat, had good sense, but was not very refined or delicate in her expressions, nor much addicted to reading. At one of the great assemblies in N—— House, Lady Talbot, a very slight, delicate woman who affected literature, happening to stand near a door where there was a great throng, exclaimed, "Good Lord, this is as difficult a pass as the Straits of Thermopylæ!" "I don't know what *street* you mean," replied the duchess, "but I am afraid I shall never get my —— through it." The consternation of the learned lady may be easily conceived.—(From Mr. Burke.)

It happens sometimes to celebrated wits by too great an effort to render a day from which much was expected quite abortive. Not long before Garrick's death, he invited Charles Fox, Mr. Burke, Mr. Gibbon, Mr. Sheridan, Sir Joshua Reynolds, Mr. Beauclerc, and some others to dine at Hampton. Soon after dinner he began to read a copy of verses, written by himself on some of the most celebrated

---

* So our Scottish brethren pronounce the word *motive*.

men of the time, including two or three of those who were present. They were not very well satisfied with their characters, and still less when describing Lord Thurlow, who was not present, he introduced the words "*superior parts.*" Mr. Burke, speaking of his own character, said afterwards to Sir Joshua Reynolds, that he was almost ready to have spat in his face.

Garrick, finding the company uncommonly grave, in consequence of his unlucky verses, before they had drunk half a dozen glasses of wine proposed to adjourn to his lawn, where they would find some amusement. When there, the whole amusement consisted in an old man and a young one running backwards and forwards between two baskets filled with stones, and whoever emptied his basket first was to be the victor. Garrick expected that his guests would have been interested and have betted on the runners; but between ill-humour with his verses and being dragged from table the instant dinner had been finished, no interest whatever was expressed in what, from the anticipations of their host, so much had been expected. All was cold and spiritless—one of the most vapid days they had ever spent. If Garrick had not laid these plots for merriment, but let conversation taken its common course, all would have gone well. Such men as I have mentioned could not have passed a dull day.—(From Sir Joshua Reynolds.)

Sir Joshua Reynolds remembers Quin in *Falstaff*, and also remembers being exceedingly disappointed by him in that character. Some of the graver part of the character he did well, but had none of the natural festivity of Falstaff, and in all the gayer part was very inefficient.

From a slight specimen which Garrick gave of Falstaff when the *Jubilee* was represented at Drury Lane, Sir Joshua thinks he would have played it inimitably well, could he have sustained the continued effort during the whole part necessary for assuming the voice of a very fat man, &c. He had often thoughts of playing that character.

It has long been a question who was the author of the letters which appeared under the signature of *Junius* in 1769 and 1770. Many have ascribed them to Mr. Wm. Gerard Hamilton, who is certainly capable of having written them, but his style is very different. He would have had still more point than they exhibit, and certainly more Johnsonian energy.[*]

Besides, he has all his life been distinguished for political timidity and indecision. Neither would he, even under a mask, have entered into such decided warfare with many persons whom it might be necessary afterwards to have as colleagues. What is still more decisive, he could not have divested himself of the apprehension of a discovery, having long accustomed his mind to too refined a policy, and being very apt to suppose that many things are brought about by scheme and machination which are merely the offspring of chance. He would have suspected that even the penny post could not be safe; and that

---

[*] See the answer which he wrote (with some aid from Mr. Burke) for Lord Halifax, when as Lord-Lieutenant of Ireland, he refused an addition of 4,000*l.* a year to his salary. *Gent. Mag.* 1762, p. 133—also p. 224.—*M.*

Sir W. Draper or any other antagonist would have managed so as to command every one of those offices within the bills of mortality.

Many have supposed *Junius* to have been written by Mr. Hamilton's old friend, the well-known and deservedly celebrated Edmund Burke. Dr. Johnson being once asked whether he thought Burke capable of writing *Junius,* said he thought him fully equal to it; but that he did not believe him the author because he himself had told him so; and he did not believe he would deliberately assert a falsehood.

Mr. Burke however, it is extremely probable, had a considerable share in the production of those papers in furnishing materials, suggesting hints, constructing and amending sentences, &c. &c. He has acknowledged to Sir Joshua Reynolds that *he knew the author.* Sir Joshua with very great probability thinks that the late *Mr. Samuel Dyer* was the author, assisted by Mr. Burke, and by Mr. William Burke, his cousin, now in India. Of Mr. Dyer, a long character may be found in Sir John Hawkins' *Life of Dr. Johnson* (pp. 222–231, 1st ed.), greatly overcharged and discoloured by the malignant prejudices of that shallow writer, who having quarrelled with Mr. Burke (who in p. 231 is darkly alluded to, together with his cousin, under the words, "Some persons of desperate fortunes"), carried his enmity even to Mr. Burke's friends.

Mr. Dyer was a man of uncommon understanding and attainments, but so modest and reserved, that he frequently sat silent in company for an hour, and seldom spoke unless appealed to; in which case he generally showed himself most intimately acquainted with whatever happened to be the subject. Goldsmith the poet, who used to rattle away upon *all* subjects, had been talking somewhat loosely relative to musick. Some one of the Literary Club (for this happened before I was a member) wished for Mr. Dyer's opinion, which he gave with his usual strength and accuracy. "Why," says Goldsmith (turning round to Dyer, whom he had scarcely noticed before), "you seem to know a good deal of this matter." "If I had not," replied Dyer, "I should not, in this company, have said a word upon the subject."

Mr. Dyer was one of the original members of our club about the year 1762, when it only met once a week on Friday evening, and then it was, I believe, that Mr. Burke's acquaintance with him commenced —an acquaintance which afterwards grew up into the strictest intimacy.

Mr. Dyer, by the favour of M. Chamier of the Treasury, got the place of commissary, or other office connected with the army; and it is observable that Junius in his second letter displays an intimate acquaintance with the then state of that department. It is also observable that there are one or two Gallicisms in *Junius*, that the author was apparently much used to French reading, for when he has occasion to divide his paragraphs numerically, he adopts the French mode 1°. 2°., &c., of which I have never met with an instance in any other English writer. Dyer was two years abroad; was a complete master of French and Italian; and one of his first literary attempts was the translation of *Les Mœurs*, of which however he performed but a part from dislike to its drudgery. It has long been supposed that the author of *Junius* died soon after the papers were discontinued. The first letter of *Junius* is dated "21st Jan. 1769," and the last "21st Jan. 1771." Dyer died Sept. 15th, 1772. Immediately after his death, Mr. William Burke went to his lodgings, and cut many of his papers into very minute fragments, there being no fire then to destroy them. Sir J. Reynolds saw these broken papers strewed all over the room.

The hypothesis now stated explains many circumstances which have puzzled all the conjecturers on this subject. It accounts for the accurate and quick intelligence which is exhibited in these letters shortly after the event, or negotiation, or whatever else is the subject of discussion. From this some have argued that the author must either have been closely connected with those in immediate opposition to Government, or have been himself one of the opposers; for Dyer lived in such intimacy with Burke, that from him he could learn everything that was going on, or even meditated. It accounts also for the *novelty of the style*. It is not likely that Mr. Burke, though he could easily imitate any known style, should have originally struck out a new one for these letters, so totally differing from his own. He might however in corrections and intercalations have adopted the style of his friend; and now and then there certainly may be found passages extremely *Burkish*.

It accounts also for the minute knowledge which Junius shows of *Irish* matters and phraseology, and particularly for the passage in his fourth letter (the seventh of the collection), "a job to accommodate two persons by particular interest and management *at the castle.*" This local phraseology, though the familiar language of Hibernians, and of men much conversant with Ireland, would not have occurred to an Englishman.

The *castle* is the residence of the Lord-Lieutenant of Ireland, and answers to *St. James's.* It accounts likewise for many images which any one well acquainted with Mr. Burke would almost swear to be the offspring of his mind. I particularly allude to that passage where the Duke of Grafton is said to have gone through each of the *signs* of the zodiac, and at last settled in *Virgo;* and another where the sacramental cup is mentioned. It may have given origin also to the *kind of law* which Junius so often displays; frequently strong and well applied, but not always perfectly sound. It is not the law of a practiser, but of one who had laid in considerable stores of legal and constitutional knowledge, but never followed the profession. This was precisely Mr. Burke's case; and certainly whatever legal knowledge Mr. Dyer possessed must have been of this kind.

Mr. Dyer translated two of *Plutarch's Lives* for the edition printed by Tonson in 1758, *Pericles* and *Demetrius,* and revised the whole work. The former which I have lately read with a view of comparison, is admirably executed; but in a translation, an author's own manner is less discernible. He also, as has been said, translated part of *Les Mœurs.* I know not whether he ever published anything original but *Junius,* if that be his, as from all these concurring circumstances is in the highest degree probable. I think there appears in *Junius* something of a personal enmity to the Duke of Grafton, quite distinct from any consideration of his political character. I remember when I first read these letters that it occurred to me as probable that the author was connected with some woman who had been ill-treated by the duke. Mr. Dyer, if Sir John Hawkins is to be trusted, was sufficiently likely to have been connected with such a woman; and at some future time perhaps this circumstance may be discovered, and furnish an additional proof to the many here collected on this subject.

Sir J. Reynolds painted the portrait of Mr. Dyer, which is now in Mr. Burke's possession. There is a mezzotinto from it, which has been copied for the *Lives of the Poets* by mistake, as if it were the portrait of John Dyer, author of a *poem* called the *Fleece.**

---

* In the numberless discussions about *Junius*, many of the surmises here thrown out by Malone will be familiar to the reader, though their source is now first made public. They had stolen forth unappropriated; but the majority were made known to me for the second edition of the *Life of Burke*, vol. i. pp. 186-198. A strong impression then prevailed in the family of Burke that he was more or less concerned in the authorship, and I thought it proper to state in detail all that they knew bearing upon the subject. More recent circumstances have dispelled this impression—none more perhaps than by the recently printed letters addressed by Junius to Mr. Grenville, noticed in my fifth edition of Burke's *Life*. These clearly evince that the writer could not be Burke. Neither would he probably countenance anything bearing so severely upon the Duke of Grafton, who while a minister exhibited kindly feeling, and recommended him strongly to office under Lord Chatham, "as the readiest man upon all points in the House."

In the alleged avowal of knowledge of the author by Burke to Sir Joshua, there is probably some misapprehension. All the parties save Dyer were alive (1791) when Malone wrote his notes; and he does not expressly say that Reynolds made *him* any such communication. Who it was made to, if ever made, does not appear. Malone enjoyed his

It is not commonly known that the translation of
Bacon's *Essays* into Latin, which was published in
1619, was done by the famous John Selden; but this is
proved decisively by a letter from N. N. (John Selden N.) to Camden (*See Camden Epistol.*, 4to, 1691,
p. 278). In the *General Dict.* and several other
books, this translation is ascribed to Bishop Hacket
and Ben Jonson. One Willymot, a schoolmaster,
was foolish enough to re-translate these essays into
English in the beginning of this century. The first
edition of these admirable essays was in 1597, the
next in 1598, another in 1606, another in 1612,
another in 1618; in the dedication to which he speaks
of *several* editions having been then printed.

The last and most perfect is in 4to in 1625, the
year preceding the author's death. There are a great
many changes and additions in all the editions subsequent to the first.

September 19*th*, 1791.—I met Dr. Percy, Bishop
of Dromore, at Sir Joshua Reynolds', and had a good

highest confidence and esteem, in proof of which he made him an executor; and therefore, if he ever expressly mentioned the avowal to any
one it would have been to him. The whole is probably conjecture or
hearsay—and Sir Philip Francis may still stand first on the list of candidates for the authorship of *Junius*.

The following is Burke's notice of the death of Dyer: " On Tuesday
morning (14th September, 1772) died at his lodgings in Castle Street,
Leicester Fields, Samuel Dyer, Esq., Fellow of the Royal Society. He
was a man of profound and general erudition; and his sagacity and
judgment were fully equal to the extent of his learning. His mind was
candid, sincere, and benevolent, his friendship disinterested and unalterable. The modesty, simplicity, and sweetness of his manners rendered
his conversation as amiable as it was instructive; and endeared him to
those few who had the happiness of knowing intimately that valuable
and unostentatious man, and his death is to them a loss irreparable."

deal of conversation with him relative to Mr. Dyer.
He said that they all at the Club had such a high
opinion of his knowledge and respect for his judgment as to appeal to him constantly, and that his
sentence was final. At the same time he was so
modest and unassuming that everybody loved as well
as respected him. His manner was uncommonly
happy. With respect to Sir John Hawkins' character of him, that it was on the whole a gross misre-
presentation.

The bishop concurred with every other person I
have heard speak of Hawkins, in saying that he was a
most detestable fellow. He was the son of a carpenter, and set out in life in the very lowest line of the
law. Dyer knew him well at one time, and the
bishop heard him give a character of Hawkins once
that painted him in the blackest colours; though
Dyer was by no means apt to deal in such portraits.
Dyer said he was a man of the most mischievous, un-
charitable, and malignant disposition, and that he
knew instances of his setting a husband against a
wife, and a brother against a brother; fomenting
their animosity by anonymous letters. With respect
to what Sir J. Hawkins has thrown in that he loved
Dyer as a brother, this the bishop said was inserted
from malignancy and art, to make the world suppose
that nothing but the gross vices of Dyer could have
extorted such a character from him; while in truth
Dyer was so amiable that he never could possibly have
lived in any great degree of intimacy with the other
at any period of his life. After Dyer's death, Mr.
Burke wrote a character of him, which was inserted

in one of the publick papers, I believe the *London Chronicle*.

A few days afterwards I had some conversation with Sir J. Reynolds relative to both Hawkins and Dyer. He said Dyer had so ill an opinion of Hawkins, that latterly at the Club he would not speak to him. Sir Joshua observed that Hawkins, though he assumed great outward sanctity, was not only mean and grovelling in disposition but absolutely dishonest. After the death of Dr. Johnson, he as one of his executors laid hold of his watch and several trinkets, coins, &c., which he said he should take to himself for his trouble—a pretty *liberal* construction of the rule of law, that an executor may satisfy his own demands in the first instance. Sir Joshua and Sir Wm. Scott, the other executors, remonstrated against this, and with great difficulty *compelled* him to give up the watch, which Dr. Johnson's servant, Francis Barber, now has; but the coins and old pieces of money they could never get.

He likewise seized on a gold-headed cane which some one had by accident left in Dr. Johnson's house previous to his death. They in vain urged that Francis had a right to this till an owner appeared, and should hold it *in usum jus habentes*. He would not restore it; and his house being soon afterwards consumed by fire, he *said* it was there burnt. The executors had several meetings relative to the business of their trust. Sir John Hawkins was paltry enough to bring them in a bill, charging his coach hire for every time they met. With all this meanness, if not dishonesty, he was a regular churchman, assuming

the character of a most rigid and sanctimonious cen-
surer of the lightest foibles of others. He never lived
in any real intimacy with Dr. Johnson, who never
opened his heart to him, or had in fact any accurate
knowledge of his character.

If the person who erects his own monument has
any vulnerable point of character, the experiment is a
dangerous one. The following epitaph, affixed about
thirty years ago on a tomb which Dr. Cox, Archbishop of Cashell, in Ireland (second son of Lord
Chancellor Cox, the historian), had erected in his
lifetime to his wife, leaving a vacant space for an
inscription on himself, may serve as a caution against
challenging in this manner the pen of the satirist :—

> Vainest of mortals, hadst thou sense or grace,
> Thou ne'er hadst left this ostentatious space,
> Nor given thine enemies such ample room,
> * To tell posterity upon thy tomb,
> A truth by friends and foes alike confess'd,
> That by this *blank* thy life is best express'd.

Mr. Gilbert Cooper was the last of the *benevolists*,
or sentimentalists, who were much in vogue between
1750 and 1760, and dealt *in general* admiration
of virtue. They were all tenderness in *words ;* their
finer feelings evaporated in the moment of expression,
for they had no connection with their practice. He
was the person whom, when lamenting most pite-
ously that his son then absent might be ill or even
dead, Mr. Fitzherbert so grievously disconcerted by
saying, in a growling tone, " Can't you take a post
chaise, and go and see him ? " Mr. Boswell has

recorded this anecdote, but did not know the name
of the complainer.   He was much in the world then,
and used to depreciate Johnson as much as he could,
by terming him "Nothing more than a *literary
Caliban*."   "Well then," said Johnson, when this
was told him, "you must allow that he is the
Punchinello of literature."

Cooper was round and fat.   He was, as Mr.
Burke, who knew him well, told me, a master of
French and Italian, well acquainted with the English
poets, and a good classical scholar ; but an insuf-
ferable coxcomb.   Dr. Warton one day, when dining
with Johnson and Burke, urged these circumstances
in his favour: " He was at least very well-informed,
and a good scholar."   "Yes," said Johnson, "it cannot be denied that he has good materials for playing
the fool ; and he makes abundant use of them."

The history of the Duke of Portland's house at
Bulstrode, near which I now write, is singular.   It
was built by *Praise God Barebones*, for a gentleman
of the name of Bulstrode.   It was then purchased
by the infamous Chancellor Jeffries, who used to
hold his seal in the great hall, and made the equity
lawyers at the end of the term come down twenty
miles to attend him there.   From his son, Lord
Jeffries, it was purchased by King William's favourite,
the Earl of Portland.

Sir Joshua Reynolds once saw Pope.   It was
about the year 1740, at an auction of books or
pictures.   He remembers that there was a lane

formed to let him pass freely through the assemblage, and he proceeded along bowing to those who were on each side. He was, according to Sir Joshua's account, about four feet six high; very humpbacked and deformed; he wore a black coat; and according to the fashion of that time, had on a little sword. Sir Joshua adds that he had a large and very fine eye, and a long handsome nose; his mouth had those peculiar marks which always are found in the mouths of crooked persons; and the muscles which run across the cheek were so strongly marked as to appear like small cords. Roubilliac, the statuary, who made a bust of him from life, observed that his countenance was that of a person who had been much afflicted with headache, and he should have known the fact from the contracted appearance of the skin between his eyebrows, though he had not been otherwise apprised of it. This bust of Roubilliac is now (1791) in possession of Mr. Bindley, Commissioner of Stamps.

Speaking of Sir Godfrey Kneller, on whom the conversation turned last night when we had done with Pope, Sir Joshua observed that he painted so very carelessly during the latter part of his life that his pictures done at that time were wretched in the extreme. On the contrary, several of his early pictures were equal to the best of Vandyck.—*Nov.* 1, 1791.

It is remarkable that of twelve passages objected to in Spencer's *Essay on the English Odyssey*, two

only are found in those books which were translated
by Pope.—(This comes from Mr. Langton, who had
his information from Mr. Spence.)

The books of the *Odyssey* which Pope translated
were the third, fifth, seventh, ninth, tenth, thirteenth,
fourteenth, fifteenth, seventeenth, twenty-first, twenty-
second, and twenty-fourth.   Fenton translated the
first, fourth, nineteenth, and twentieth books. Broome
the second, sixth, eighth, eleventh, twelfth, eigh-
teenth, and twenty-third.

When Spence carried his preface to *Gorboduck*,
which I think was published in 1736, to Pope,
he asked the poet his opinion of it.   Pope said, "It
would do very well ; there was nothing *pert* or *low*
in it."*   Spence was satisfied with this praise, which
however was an implied censure on his other writings,
and not without foundation ; for in his *Essay on the
Odyssey* (the only piece of his that I at present
recollect to have read) he appears very fond of the
familiar vulgarisms of common talk.   In this respect
he is the reverse of Johnson.   The book however
is not without merit.   Mr. Cambridge, who is now
above seventy and was acquainted with Spence, says
he was a *poor creature* though a very worthy man.

The late Dr. —— informed Dr. Warton that
when Warburton resided at Newark, he and several
others held a club, where Warburton used to produce
and read weekly essays in refutation of Pope's *Essay
on Man*.   This poem he afterwards found it conve-

* From Mr. Langton.

nient to defend in the *Works of the Learned.* Such palinode, it is well known, gained him Pope's friendship, and finally by his introduction to Allen, made his fortune and station in life.

Sir William Blackstone, as Sir Wm. Scott of the Commons observed to me a few days ago, was extremely irritable. He was the only man, my informant said, he had ever known who acknowledged and lamented his bad temper. He was an accomplished man in very various departments of science, with a store of general knowledge. He was particularly fond of architecture, and had written upon that subject. The notes which he gave me on Shakspeare show him to have been a man of excellent taste and accuracy, and a good critick. The total sum which he made by his *Commentaries,* including the profits of his lectures, the sale of the books while he kept the copyright in his own hands, and the final sale of the proprietorship to Mr. Cadell, amounted to fourteen thousand pounds. Probably the bookseller in twenty years from the time of that sale will clear ten thousand pounds by his bargain, and the book prove to be an estate to his heirs.

Blackstone made 600*l.* a year by his professorship and lectures, which however he thought it wise to relinquish for the chance of succeeding in Westminster Hall. Not having acquired a facility of expression, nor promptness of applying his law by early practice, he was always an embarrassed advocate. There were more new trials granted in causes which came before him on circuit, than were granted on the decisions of any other judge who sat at Westminster in his time. The reason was that being extremely diffident of his opinion, he never supported it with much warmth or pertinacity in the court above, if a new trial was moved for. With the little failings already mentioned, he was one of the finest writers and most profound lawyers that England has produced, considering law merely as a science. He was also a strictly conscientious honest man. In his *Commentaries* he was much indebted to Hall and Wood (particularly the latter) for the method and arrangement he has observed; but the perspicuity, the vigour, the luminous statement, the elegant illustration, and the classical grace by which his *Commentaries* are so eminently distinguished, were all his own.—*Dec.* 20, 1791.

———

[The notice of the death of Reynolds occurs here—but he goes on with remarks on the symptoms and treatment.]

A depression of spirits is, I am told, the usual accompaniment of any disorder of the liver, as is also loss of appetite, fulness, and indigestion. With all these indications, that the physicians should not have been led to explore that part, and to apply such remedies as the *Materia Medica* furnishes, is unaccountable any way but one. In the East Indies, by anointing the body with mercury, extraordinary cures have been performed in this disease; and had a consultation been held in December to investigate his malady and the remedy been tried, the world would

probably not have been deprived of this most amiable
and accomplished man for some years.

At length, about a fortnight before his death,
this consultation was called, and *then* the two physicians who had uniformly declared that he had no
particular or specific ailment, concurred with Dr.
Heberden and Dr. Carmichael Smith in saying that
his liver was affected. Soon afterward when almost
in the languor of death, mercury was applied in vain.

Though during his whole illness from December
to 23rd February, he *felt* and therefore thought that
his malady was mortal, he submitted to the Divine
will with perfect resignation, at the same time following the prescriptions of his physicians, though with
little or no hope of their being useful. He died with
very little pain.

From the time of our being first acquainted, he
always showed me great kindness and partiality.
Beside our usual and very frequent intercourse during
the winter, we were drawn for several years past still
more near to each other in the summer, the greater
part of which we both passed in London, my late
edition of Shakspeare, on which I was employed from
1784 to 1791 (I mean in the business of the printing
house), not permitting me to be long absent from
town. He was as fond of London as Dr. Johnson;
always maintaining that it was the only place in
England where a pleasant society might be found;
and no one I believe ever drew together a more
pleasant and distinguished society than he did.

I remember one day to have sat down with fifteen
persons at his table, the greater part of whom had

made a conspicuous figure in the world. Mr. Burke, Mr. Gibbon, two Wartons, Sir William Scott, Mr. Erskine, &c. &c. He was the original founder of our Literary Club about the year 1762, the first thought of which he started to Dr. Johnson at his own fireside. His having made me an executor to his will in conjunction with Mr. Burke and Mr. Metcalf (with the former of whom he had lived in great intimacy for thirty-four years, and with the latter for thirty-eight years), I consider as a very great honour, and hope my children if I should have any, will carefully preserve that memorial of his friendship which he has bequeathed me.*

He took very particular pains in drawing my picture.† I think I did not in the whole sit for it less than twelve or fourteen times. He painted it first in the year 1778, when I sat seven or eight times. Again, about ten years afterwards, he repainted it, making several alterations in the hair, drapery, &c. The last three pictures which he painted of persons much known, were those of our common friend Mr. Windham, of Felbrig, in Norfolk; Mr. Cholmondeley, Commissioner of Excise; and Mr. R. B. Sheridan, all of them master-pieces of art.‡

* The choice of one of his pictures.

† Now in the possession of the Rev. Thomas R. Rooper—said to be a good likeness, and bearing evidence of the pains bestowed upon it. An engraving of it is prefixed to this volume.

‡ On a question of art, I find the following note among Malone's letters:—

"DEAR SIR,—I always thought Sir Joshua Reynolds had Paul Veronese in view when he painted those pictures for the Dilletanti, particularly that next the door; and upon applying to him one day there at dinner, he told me I was right.

On the Tuesday after his death our club happened to meet; and I was much pleased that the members present unanimously concurred in a motion which I made, that a marble bust or portrait of our much-lamented founder should be procured at the expense of the body and placed in our club-room.

His will was made on the 5th November, 1791, and begins with this melancholy paragraph:—" As it is probable that I shall soon be totally deprived of sight, and may not have an opportunity of making a formal will, I desire that the following memorandums may be considered as my last will and testament."— *Feb.* 28, 1792.

MALONIANA.
Part II.

[The following is his introduction to the second part of these Memoranda, for the shortness of which he thus accounts. But, added to its brevity, he never resumed the work with the same spirit as at first.]

The former part concluded with an account of the death of my poor friend Sir Joshua Reynolds, which was for a long time left imperfect. The loss of that most valuable and amiable man I have felt almost every day since; and being unwilling again to recur to the subject, I for three years wholly discontinued

" P. Veronese delighted much in representing his figures as they appear in the open air or under the slight shade of an open portico without any forced effect of light and shade, such as (for example) Rembrandt sometimes used. I write this in great haste, almost too late for dinner.
" Ever yours,
" Sunday. " St. Beaumont."

my former practice of recording such anecdotes as I could collect from those friends with whom I conversed. Of some few, however, I made short notes on loose scraps of paper, and shall begin this volume with a transcript of whatever I collected during that period, *i.e.* from February 1792, to August 1795.

Dr. Douglas, Bishop of Salisbury, told me that about forty years ago he was acquainted with a gentleman then very old, who in travelling in the Apennines had met with a retired Jesuit, who acknowledged that about the time of Monmouth's rebellion he had been sent into Scotland, where he assumed the disguise of a *Covenanter*, and often preached to the people in fields, &c., to excite them to disturb the Government.

This agrees with the account given by Du Moulin of the conduct of the Jesuits previous to the murder of Charles the First.—(See *Kennet's Register.*)

Dryden has himself told us that he was of a grave cast and did not much excel in sallies of humour. One of his *bon-mots*, however, has been preserved. He does not seem to have lived on very amicable terms with his wife, Lady Elizabeth, whom, if we may believe the lampoons of the time, he was compelled by one of her brothers to marry. Thinking herself neglected by the bard, and that he spent too much time in his study, she one day exclaimed, "Lord, Mr. Dryden, how can you be always poring over those musty books? I wish I were a book, and then I should have more of your company." "Pray,

my dear," replied old John, "if you do become a
book let it be an almanack, for then I shall change
you every year."—(Mr. Horace Walpole.)

———

After Pope had written some bitter verses on Lady
M. W. Montague, he told a friend of his that he
should soon have ample revenge upon her, for that he
had set her down in black and white, and should soon
publish what he had written. "Be so good as to tell
the little gentleman," was the reply, "that I am not
at all afraid of him; for if he sets me down in black
and white, as he calls it, most assuredly I will have
him set down in *black and blue*."—(The same.)

———

The line in the *Bathos*,

———— and bob for whales,

was taken by Pope from his own *Alexander*.—(The
same, from Lord Harvey.)

———

The imagery in the *Messiah* was derived from an
old fabulous story relative to the celebrated cliff at
——, the seat of Mr. Wortley Montague, in Yorkshire.—(The same.)

———

Patty Blount was red-faced, fat, and by no means
pretty. Mr. Walpole remembered her walking to
Mr. Bethell's, in Arlington Street, after Pope's
death, with her petticoats tucked up like a semp-
stress. She was the decided mistress of Pope, yet
visited by respectable people.—(The same.)

———

Lord Radnor, who lived at Twickenham, and is
one of the subscribing witnesses to Pope's will, was

kept in subjection by the Poet, who he feared would ridicule his false taste. Pope availed himself of this, and used to borrow his chariot for three months at a time.—(The same.)

Conyers Middleton wrote a Treatise against Prayer, which he showed to Lord Bolingbroke, who dissuaded him from publishing it as it would set all the clergy against him. On this ground he counselled him to destroy the manuscript, but secretly kept a copy which is probably still in being.—(The same, from Mrs. Middleton.)

Congreve's *Double Dealer*, says Dryden in a manuscript letter to Walsh, is much censured by the greater part of the town, and is defended only by the best judges, who you know are commonly the fewest. Yet it gains ground daily, and has been already acted eight times. The women think he has exposed their bitchery, and the gentlemen are offended with him for the discovery of their follies, and the way of their intrigue under the notion of friendship to their ladies' husbands.

I am afraid you discover not your own opinion concerning my irregular way of tragi-comedy in my *dappia favola*. I will never defend that practice, for I know it distracts the hearers; but I know withal that it has hitherto pleased them for the sake of variety, and for the particular taste which they have to low comedy.—(MS. Letters from Dryden to Walsh, in the possession of Mr. Bromley, of Abberley Park, near Worcester.)

Richardson, the author of *Clarissa*, had been a common printer, and possessed no literature whatever. He was very silent in company, and so vain that he never enjoyed any subject but that of himself or his works. He once asked Douglas, Bishop of Salisbury, how he liked *Clarissa*. The bishop said he could never get beyond the Bailiff scene. The author, thinking this a condemnation of his book, looked grave; but all was right when the bishop added, it affected him so much that he was drowned in tears, and could not trust himself with the book any longer.

Richardson had a kind of club of women about him—Mrs. Carter, Mrs. Talbot, &c.—who looked up to him as to a superior being; to whom he dictated and gave laws; and with whom he lived almost entirely. To acquire a facility of epistolary writing he would on every trivial occasion write notes to his daughters even when they were in the same house with him.—(Bishop Douglas and Dr. Johnson.)

The paper published by Dalrymple in his appendix, p. 11, p. 78, and ascribed to Lord Nottingham, is not of unquestionable authority, being not in his handwriting. Dr. Percy got his copy from —— [not filled up].

When King William found himself much pressed and harassed by the Whigs who had put him on the throne, he one day exclaimed to Lord Wharton, that after all the Tories were the only true supporters of an English king. "True," replied Wharton, "but please your Majesty, you should recollect that you are not *their* king."—(Lord Ossory.)

January 29, 1793.—Dr. Douglas, Bishop of Salisbury, told me at the Club that two days before the death of Queen Anne, the Duke of Marlborough returned to England with a view to take measures for securing the succession to the Pretender-king. But a frigate being sent to communicate the event that was likely to take place every hour, all the Tories were dismayed; he prudently changed his plan, and when he landed, affected to be a firm Whig.

During the trial of Lord Oxford he discovered the letter from the Duke of Marlborough, mentioned in p. 384, and sent word to the duchess by Lord Duplin, afterwards Earl of Kinnoul, that if the trial went on this letter should certainly be produced. A consultation was then held among the Whigs, when it was agreed that by some means a disagreement between the Lords and Commons should be raised so as to give a pretence for putting an end to the trial. This was done accordingly. Lord Bath, who was then Mr. Pulteney, told the Bishop of Salisbury that not above three or four of the Whigs knew the secret; while the others were at a loss to discover the true sources of much that was done at that time.

Swift made several observations on the margin of Burnett's *History of his Own Time.* His copy is now in the hands of the Marquis of Lansdown. Lord Onslow has another copy filled with the remarks of his father the Speaker. Lord Lansdown has had these transcribed into his own copy, he lending in return his MS. to Lord Onslow for the same purpose. The Bishop of Salisbury has a transcript of the observations of Swift. They are short, he says, but very pointed and characteristick.

Hawkesworth, the writer, was introduced by Garrick to Lord Sandwich, who thinking to put a few hundred pounds into his pocket, appointed him to revise and publish Cook's *Voyages*. He scarcely did anything to the MSS., yet sold it to Cadell and Strahan, the printer and bookseller, for 6,000*l*. Soon after this he purchased some portion of India stock; and having made a speech or two at the India House, was much feasted by the directors, &c.

About this time he was severely attacked in the newspapers, particularly in letters signed "A Christian," for certain passages in the *Voyages*, from which it was inferred he did not believe in a Providence. These attacks affected him so much that, from low spirits he was seized with a nervous fever, which on account of the high living he had indulged in had the more power on him; and he is supposed to have put an end to his life by intentionally taking an immoderate dose of opium.—(From the Bishop of Salisbury. The opinion from Dr. Fordyce.)

He was originally a watchmaker, or some other mechanick trade. By reading Dr. Johnson's writings he acquired his style, and a certain moral and sentimental air, though nothing mortified him so much as to suppose that he was an imitator of Johnson. He lived much with him, and Johnson was fond of him, but latterly owned that Hawkesworth—who had set out a modest, humble man—was one of the many whom success in the world had spoiled. He was latterly, as Sir Joshua Reynolds told me, an affected insincere man, and a great coxcomb in his dress. He had no literature whatever ; and was so ignorant even of English history that, when he was employed in publishing three volumes of Swift's letters, the Bishop of Salisbury (as he told me) could not make him comprehend the difference between Lord Oxford and Lord Orford.

The Marquis of Halifax left behind him very curious memoirs of his own time. He kept a register every day of all the conversations he had with Charles II. and other 'persons. The loss, therefore, of this work by one who appears to have been an accurate observer of character is to be much lamented. He left two copies of it ; one of them remained in the hands of [blank], by whom it was destroyed ; the other came into the hands of Lady Burlington, who was persuaded by Pope to destroy it. —(From Lord Orford, March 26th, 1793.)

Sir John Germain was a mere soldier of fortune, who came to England from the Low Countries, and made his fortune by wives. He first married the Duchess of Norfolk, and after her death (1705) he married the celebrated Lady Betty Berkeley, sister of Earl Berkeley. He was so extremely ignorant that he thought St. Matthew's Gospel was written by Sir Matthew Decker. Lord Orford once asked Lady Viscountess Fitzwilliam, who was Sir Matthew's daughter, whether this strange story was true. She was a very cautious, prudent woman, spoke very slow, and not without a good deal of deliberation. She assured him it was, and mentioned as a confirmation of it, that Sir John at his death left Sir Matthew 200*l.* to be disposed of among his poor countrymen in London, having the greatest confidence in his honest execution of the trust, as he had already given the world such a proof of his piety in having written St. Matthew's Gospel. Sir John's gross ignorance in this respect, though almost incredible, is confirmed by what happened at his death. Lady Betty, being a very pious woman, proposed to him to receive the Sacrament. He asked would it do him any good? She said she had no doubt it would. Accordingly it was administered to him. Shortly afterwards he called his wife to his bedside, and said, with a sigh, " That thing you gave me has done me no good." He, poor man, took it for a medicine.—(From Lord Orford; who had the last particular from General Fitzwilliam.)

When Mr. Dowdeswell was made Chancellor of the Exchequer about 1765, in the room of Lord Lyttleton, who had possessed the office for a short time, Bishop Warburton observed to Mr. Hawkins Browne, that there was a curious contrast between these Ministers. " The one just turned out, Lord Lyttleton, never in his life could learn that two and two made four; while the other knew nothing else." This *bon-mot* has been given to others; but Bishop Douglas assured us he knew it was said by Warburton. Lord Lyttleton, though the accounts were all written down in *words* instead of figures, made such a miserable figure when he attempted, on the usual day, to represent the state of the nation and to demand a supply, that all his friends were greatly distressed for him.

It was said of the late Lord Anson that he never had any levees because he knew not how to talk, nor ever answered a letter because he scarcely knew how to write. This gives us a good idea of this famous navigator.

When the late Mr. Pitt, or Alderman Beckford, made a strong attack on the late Sir William Baker, Alderman of London, charging him with having made an immense sum by a fraudulent contract, he got up very quietly and gained the House to his side by this short reply: " The honourable gentleman is a great orator, and has made a long and serious charge against me. I am no orator, and therefore shall only answer him in two words—Prove it." Having thus spoken he sat down; but there was something in the manner and tone that satisfied the House the charge was a calumny.

One of the Townshend family, brother I believe to the present marquis, wrote home so absurd and inconsistent an account of an action in which he had been engaged, that on his own letter he was ordered to be brought to a court-martial for ill conduct. He was however most honourably acquitted, his officers bearing ample testimony to his cool and good conduct, and proving that his pen alone, not his sword, was in fault!

Bishop Warburton being asked by a friend to what profession he meant to breed his son, who died young—and many supposed him to be Mr. Potter's son—said it should be as he turned out. If he found him a lad of very good parts, he should make him a lawyer; if but mediocre, he should bring him up a physician; but if he proved a very dull fellow he should put him into the church.—(From old Lord Hilsborough, who knew Warburton, and once was intimate with Bishop Hurd.)

When Bishop Hurd once paid a visit to Bishop Warburton, Mrs. W., before the bishop came down, said to Hurd, " I am glad you are come, my lord, to pour a little of your oil into the bishop's vinegar."—(From the same, October, 1808.)

*　　*　　*　　*　　*

[Here the collection expressly termed "MALONIANA" ends. But several memoranda chiefly on similar subjects, and written upon loose sheets or half-sheets of paper, were found among his remains. Others are scattered in various volumes among collectors, or found in the Bodleian. None of these were paged, or regularly strung together. Many more no doubt have been lost from being in a disconnected state; or destroyed as useless from not having passed under regular literary examination when first dislodged from his repositories.

From this cause a few of the remarks, or anec-dotes, may have escaped into print; but the know-

ledge now of the source whence they spring will
add to their value.]

Swift, like some other poets—Congreve, Thomson,
Goldsmith, and many more, read his own pieces
badly. His deficiency in this respect is ascertained
from the testimony of George Faulkner, his Dublin
publisher, who in a note to the Irish edition of his
works, speaks of it as an acknowledged fact.

Edmund Spenser appears to have been born in
1557, for he was matriculated at Cambridge, where
be became a member of Pembroke Hall in May
1569. At that time they usually went to the University at twelve years old. William Webbe, in his
Discourse of English Poetrie, 4to., 1586, mentions
the following pieces of Spenser as being then in
MS.—"His *Dreams,* his *Legends,* his *Court of
Cupid,* and his *English Poet.*"

Mr. Narcissus Luttrell had formed a very curious
collection of ancient English poetry in twenty-four
quarto volumes, distinguished by the letters of the
alphabet. These were purchased some years ago by
the late Dr. Farmer, for twenty-four guineas. Being
cut up and sold piecemeal, they produced at the sale
of his books nearly, I believe, 200*l.* They contained
about three hundred articles. Five folio volumes of
lampoons, ballads, and occasional pieces, chiefly expressive of the opinions of the day, and published
between the Restoration and the end of the century,
were secured by Mr. Bindley.

It is remarkable that some of the worst plays in the English language have been ornamented with engravings. A few years after the appearance of Settle's tragedy (*Empress of Morocco*, the first play that was ever sold for two shillings, or printed with cuts), *Noah's Ark*, an opera, was embellished with similar decorations; and in the following century, *Scanderbeg*, a tragedy, was recommended to the public by the same ornamental appendages.

It is a singular circumstance that in writing the elegy on the Countess of Abingdon, called *Eleonora*, Dryden did not know that she died very suddenly at a ball in her own house in the midst of a gay assemblage of both sexes; a fact of which, had he been apprised, he would not have neglected to avail himself. He had never seen the lady; and wrote the poem at the solicitation of a nobleman with whom he was not personally acquainted.

A long note is given to Spenser in Winstanley's notice of him (1687) relative to his death, interment, and tomb, or rather supposed tombs. Camden, Fenton, Charles Fitz Geoffry, Sir Aston Cockaine, Sheppard (in his *Epigrams*, 1651), Warner, and Sir James Ware, are quoted, all varying in their testimonies as to facts. It seems there was no tomb erected for above twenty years after his death, and then by the Countess of Dorset. Discrepancies also existed as to his death, some making it 1598, some 1599. In 1802 Malone discovered the truth in the title-page of a copy of the second part of the *Faery Queen*, 1596, which the ancient owner appeared to have purchased in 1598, and in a Latin passage marks his death Jan. 16th, 1598.

The unmanly revenge of Lord Rochester in hiring three ruffians to beat Dryden is well known. " In a newspaper of the day," says Malone, is the following account of the transaction with which I have been furnished by Dr. Charles Burney, junior :—

" *Dec. 19th*, 1679.—Last night, Mr. Dryden, the famous poet, coming from a coffee-house in Covent Garden, was set upon by three persons unknown to him ; and so rudely by them handled, that it is said his life is in no small danger.   It is thought to have been the effect of private grudge rather than upon the too common design of unlawful gain ; an unkind trespass by which not only he himself, but the commonwealth of learning may receive injury." His own advertisement, with the reward of 50*l.* for the apprehension of the parties, did not appear till ten days afterward.   .   .   .   .

Pope, who in his earlier years made imitations of Chaucer, Spenser, Waller, Cowley, Rochester, Dorset, and Swift, did not attempt an imitation of Dryden.   His own poetry indeed was only Dryden's versification rendered by incessant care more smooth and musical, but less flowing and less varied.

The elder Cibber was, I believe, the most celebrated performer of Bayes in the *Rehearsal*.   To him succeeded Garrick, who though he doubtless departed in some measure from the original idea, made the representation incomparably pleasant. Lacy formed the original Bayes; after him Joseph Haines, celebrated for dancing and mimicry. . . .

The Duchess of Portsmouth (Louise de Querouaille), who was alleged to be an abettor of Rochester in the outrage on Dryden, returned to France on the death of her royal paramour. In 1699 she paid a visit to England, when according to Burnett, she told Mr. Anthony Henley, of the Grange in Hampshire, that Charles the Second had been poisoned. She died at Paris in 1728, much advanced in life.

Had not the whole of Lord Shaftesbury's political life made him so justly odious, Dryden's connections would naturally have led him to represent that nobleman in a favourable 'light. For Shaftesbury had married Margaret, daughter of William, second Lord Spencer; and Henry Howard, one of the brothers of Dryden's wife, married Elizabeth, another of Lord Spencer's daughters.

The discomfiture and flight of Shaftesbury to Holland in 1682, gave great satisfaction to the adherents of the Duke of York. It amounted in their view almost to a second Restoration. He had been represented on the stage in various evil imaginary forms; on one occasion with fiends' wings and snakes twisted round the body, while rebellious heads sucked poison out of his side which ran out by a *tap*. It appeared that previous to the Restoration he made a journey to Breda; was overturned; an abscess eventually formed in the side, which was obliged to be punctured, or *tapped*. With allusion to this circumstance and the hopes he was said to have once formed of being elected King of Poland, he figured often in the lampoons of the time by the name of *Tapsky*.

It is curious that so little of this remarkable man, who occupied so prominent a position in that day, should now be accurately known. Yet he used due diligence to be remembered by writing his memoirs. Like those of the Marquis of Halifax however the fire, not the press, became their destination; and this under the influence of two celebrated literary names. Pope, as guardian of the character of the Catholics, persuaded Lady Burlington to destroy the memoirs of the Marquis. Locke, afraid of having question-able papers found in his house such as Shaftesbury's were deemed to be, followed the example. Were those precedents generally followed, how little should we know of the secret springs which colour and influence history!

There is a tradition that when poor Otway died, he had about him the copy of a tragedy which it seems he had sold to Bentley, the bookseller; for there was an advertisement published soon after his death, at the end of one of L'Estrange's political papers, offering a reward to any one who should bring it to Bentley's shop.

A Lord Chancellor has occasionally dabbled in the drama. *Hecuba*, a tragedy, printed in 1726, was written beyond doubt by Mr. West, some time Lord Chancellor of Ireland. From the author's preface, it appears that the piece is a translation from Euripides, and that it was damned the first night.

Congreve is said to have been only nineteen when he wrote the *Old Bachelor*. It is announced as ready for the stage in the *Gentleman's Journal* (by Motteaux) for January, 1692-3; so it must have been written in 1692. But Congreve, instead of being nineteen as has been stated in all the books of biography, was twenty-three; for he was born some time in 1669, as appears from the register of the college where he was entered a student—Trinity College, Dublin—April 5, 1685, being then in his sixteenth year—" Annos natus sexdecim."

It has been scarcely noticed that Aaron Hill, besides his prose and poetical compositions printed in four volumes octavo, was the author of a periodical paper called the *Prompter*, the first number of which was published Nov. 12, 1734, and the last, I believe, June 29, 1736. These papers were printed in folio, and have never been collected into volumes.

Dryden was sometimes aided by the profits of the dramatic productions of his friends. Mr. George Granville wrote *The Jew of Venice* with that view; but Dryden dying before its representation, the profits were given to his eldest son. In like manner it is probable he gave him the profits of his two plays, *The She Gallants*, and *Heroick Love*, the former acted in 1696, the latter in Jan. 1697-8.   Before *Heroick Love* were some encomiastic verses by Dryden.   In the preface to the *She Gallants* Granville says that he gave the benefit of it to a friend ; and that if his friend had a *third* day to his satisfaction he had obtained his end.

(Of the correctness of this story he afterwards found some reason to doubt; but the main facts are probably true.)

Dryden, it appears, was not displaced from his offices by the strong hand of authority as generally supposed; but as he himself has told us, conscientiously relinquished them on the 1st August, 1689, by refusing to take the oaths of supremacy and abjuration which were appointed by the first parliament of King William to be taken by every person holding office under the Crown.

Addison, in his *Ode for St. Cecilia's Day*, has admitted the following lines, which were supplied by Hughes, as ascertained by a manuscript note in my possession.

> Such were the tuneful notes that hung
> On bright Cecilia's charming tongue;
> Notes that sacred hearts inspired,
> And with religious ardour fired
> The love-sick youth, that long suppressed
> The smothered passion in his breast.

Wycherley married twelve days before his death Elizabeth Jackson, one of the daughters and co-heiresses of Mr. Jos. Jackson, of Hertingfordbury, whose fortune was 1,000*l.*, not 1,500*l.*, as has been stated in books of biography. He settled on her a jointure of 1,000*l.* per annum. By his last will, which was made Saturday, Dec. 31, 1715, the day of his death and executed about two hours before that event, he leaves her, by the name of his dear and well-beloved wife Elizabeth Wycherley, after the payment of his debts and funeral charges, all the rest and residue of his estate, ready money, plate, goods and chattels whatsoever; and appoints his kinsman, Thomas Shrimpton, Esq., his executor. About three months after his death, she married that gentleman who was a half-pay captain. Mr. Wycherley's nephew (his brother's son) soon afterward filed a bill against Mr. and Mrs. Shrimpton, alleging that she was married to Mr. Shrimpton before she married Mr. Wycherley; that thus the old man had been imposed upon, and induced to settle a jointure on her without consideration, her fortune not having been paid to him. The defendants swore in their answer that he had received 190*l.* of it; and Lord Macclesfield finally decreed in their favour, so the allegation of her previous marriage must have been unfounded. The decree I believe was made in 1718.

Wycherley about six weeks before his death was arrested by an old servant, for a pretended debt of 30*l.*, which having lost the servant's receipt he was obliged to pay a second time. Not having the money, he solicited all his friends in vain to assist him, and at length was released by Captain Shrimpton. See a curious letter written by that gentleman, giving an account of these transactions, in Egerton's (*i. e.* Curlls's) *Life of Mrs. Oldfield*, p. 122. See also Major Pack's *Memoirs of Wycherley*, and Pope's letter soon after his death.—[Other writers vary this story considerably, and some with inaccurate details.]

* * * *

Mrs. Martha Fowke, *alias* Sansom, in her extraordinary memoirs of her own life, in which she gives a history of various lovers, says, p. 67:—"Here, at Bath (about 1714), I became acquainted with Mr. Wycherley, who had wit without politeness; and a levity improper for his age—seventy-four, it appears. He was very little to my taste. I was much more to his; and would love have consented, I might have been wife to that poet; but my heart was averse."—*Clio, or the Secret History of the Life and Amours of the late celebrated Mrs. S—n—m, written by Herself*, 8vo, 1752. It is singular that she also was a native of Hertingfordbury. Wycherley's paternal estate was situated at Cleve in Shropshire, about five miles from Shrewsbury, and was worth 600*l.* per annum.

———

Mr. Flood wrote and printed an *Ode to Fame* in 1775, which (ninety-four lines) has considerable merit. Also a translation of *The first Pythian Ode of Pindar*, about 150 lines. These, and some of his speeches, were presented (to Malone) by himself.

The speeches, says the latter, "On the Declaratory Act of Geo. II., 11th June, 1782;" and on Mr. Grattan's "Simple Repeal," are in my collection of *Tracts*, vol. 57. Those on the "Commercial

Treaty, 1787;" and on "Reform of the Representation," in vol. 60. They were never published. He
died December 2nd, 1791, at Farmley, in Kilkenny.
The edition, in the British Museum, is a thin quarto.

I have long endeavoured in vain to ascertain the
time when Lady M. W. Montague and Pope quarrelled. Circumstances seem to fix it at some period
between 1717, when Pope sent his verses on Addison
to him in MS., and 1719, when that writer died.
The advice she received from the latter was to avoid
Pope; otherwise he would certainly play her some
devilish trick. It appears certain that Pope was the
first to break off the acquaintance in form.

Song in ye Praise of Melancholy.—F. 80 Bod.
" Hence all your vain delights."
The author of this beautiful piece (Dr. Strode)
part of which has been ascribed unjustly to Fletcher,
because it is sung in his *Nice Valour*, was born about
the year 1600, and died Canon of Christ Church
in 1644. *Milton evidently took the hint of his
" L'Allegro" and " Penseroso" from it.*
No. 21 in Catalogue; 8vo, 96 leaves; Miscellaneous Poetry.

Pope's nephew has been mentioned by some. This
was, I suppose, the son of Mrs. Racket, Pope's half-
sister, or half-sister-in-law. None of the biographers
have told us whether Mrs. Racket was the daughter
of Pope's father by a former wife, or the daughter
of his mother by a former husband, or the wife of

one who was the son of either his father or mother. I believe she was the wife of Pope's half-brother; for I saw her once about the year 1760, and she seemed not to be above sixty years old. Since writing the above, I see Pope in his will calls her sister-in-law.

Aubrey, in his MS. *Anecdotes of the English Poets*, says, that Sir John Suckling, who fled from London to Paris in the troubles in 1641, in dread of being apprehended for conspiracy against the popular interests, was poisoned and died in that capital.

Creech did not translate *Manilius*. The version of that poet was done by Sir Edward Sherburne, I am informed.

Lady W. Montague corresponded with Dr. Young, the poet, who a little before his death destroyed a great number of her letters, assigning as a reason that they were too *indelicate* for public inspection.

Swift, in a letter to the Rev. Henry Jenny of Armagh, written in 1732, gives an extremely depreciatory view of the wretchedness of Ireland and her low order of civilization—all due, he will have it, to the tyranny of England; with a passing glance at the more immediate cause in remote districts—oppressive squires. When shown to Malone, he wrote a long comment upon it in 1808, explaining the causes of the misery of the people then and long afterwards, but there is nothing of particular interest to the reader to extract.

Mr. Nichols (of the *Gentleman's Magazine*), writing of Swift's *Life* about the same time, says : " I was much indebted to the friendship of Mr. Malone, who, besides many useful hints, obtained for me a very valuable *Essay on the earlier Part of the Life of Swift* by the Rev. Dr. John Barrett, Vice Provost of Trinity College, Dublin, with numerous articles written by the Dean in early life, and then first printed. From Mr. Malone also, I received a drawing of the very excellent likeness of the Dean, taken after his death; and an original letter to Dr. Jenny on the state of Ireland (1736), copied from one in the possession of Lord Cremorne.

In 1796 the Rev. James Plumptre of Clare Hall, Cambridge, " with high respect for his critical opinions," sends his *Observations on the Tragedy of Hamlet.* And John Kemble, not to be behind in complimentary offering, replies to an assailant of Shakspeare by an anonymous essay, *Macbeth Reconsidered*, inscribed to his master in the critical art, Malone.

[Desirous of doing all honour to the person and character of Lord Southampton, Shakspeare's patron, no opportunity was lost (see p. 179) of introducing both to our familiar acquaintance. With this view, one of his explorations for a picture of that nobleman was to Woburn, of which the following account is given to Ozias Humphrey. I am indebted for it to the kindness of Mr. Halliwell, but it came to hand too late for arrangement in chronological order.]

" DEAR SIR,—A celebrated Spanish philosopher,
Sancho Panza by name, I think says, ' He is a
wise father who knows his own child.' And some
other equally celebrated personage observes that
' books are often more learned than their authors.'
These remarks were brought to my mind by the
line you favoured me with from Strawberrry Hill;
for most assuredly there *is* an original picture of
Henry, Earl of Southampton, at Woburn Abbey;
and from *Mr. Walpole's book* it was that I first
learned such a picture, painted by *Wireveldt*, existed
there. He mentions it, I think, in the beginning
of his second volume.

"I knew of the picture at Bulstrode; and three
years ago went there on purpose to see it, with a
view to have it engraved in honour of Shakspeare;
but it is so disagreeable a picture that I gave up
all thoughts of it; and then got a copy made from
a bad impression (the only one I could get) of a
print by Simon Pass, in the year 1617. At the
time this print was engraving for me, I sent down
a proof to the Duke of Bedford's steward to compare
it with the picture; and from his account of the
correspondence between them, had no doubt that
the picture at Woburn was a genuine one. On
examining it this evening—for I am just now arrived
at my inn after walking through the apartments—
I am convinced that I was right; and lament much
that I had not the pleasure of your company to this
place to make a drawing. However, I will not yet
give up the point; but hope to do something in
it when I return from Ireland. There is here like-

wise an original picture of the celebrated Lord Essex, and some others worth your attention.

" You have made me very happy by the drawing of Shakspeare, for which I am extremely obliged. It struck me there was some little defect in one of the eyes, by too much of the white being shown, which gives the appearance of squinting, and which I do not recollect in the original. But I am no artist; and it is a hundred to one that I am mistaken. If I am right it can be easily rectified.

" I suppose you will not for some time look at old Shakspeare's face; but if any one can prevail upon you to copy what you have done, remember that I am to have the *original*. When Mr. Hall has done with it, and when next we have the pleasure of meeting, I will settle with you on the subject. In the meantime believe me, dear sir, &c. &c.

" *Woburn, Sunday night,*
 " *August 17th,* 1783.

" My address in Ireland is Baronston, Mullingar."

" Dr. Farmer, who had been enlisted in the same pursuit, sends some further information of his lordship with an apology for omitting his notes on the three parts of *Henry VI.*

" *Emanuel (College), August* 9, 1787.

" MY DEAR SIR,—I hoped to have seen you in my way through town, but I spent only one day there, and that at the other end of it.

" You should have heard from me a post or two sooner, but our Registrar was out of the University, and I could not earlier get into the office. I find

that Henry, Earl of Southampton, was admitted to
the degree of B.A. in 1589, and proceeded no farther;
and luckily examining the *Book of Matriculations*, I
at last fell upon 'Hen. Comes Southampton, impubes,
12 anᵒ. of St. John's College, Dec. 11, 1585.' Here
we have his age as well as college. Essex was of
Trin. June 1, 1579.   *   *   *

"Whatever you may have fancied, I solemnly declare to you that I always meant to send you my notes
on the *Henrys*, if I could find them, and I flattered
myself they might be among some papers at Canter-
bury. I cannot yet find them, and you want no
assistance. As I remember, you have some of my
arguments but not *all*. I have supposed the plays
originally *Marlowe's*, and altered after his death by
Shakspeare; this I argued from *style* and *manner;*
with many quotations from passages contradictory to
others in Shakspeare's genuine plays, and others
clashing in the *Henrys* themselves, which show
different hands," &c. &c.

Malone's aim at minute correctness we have seen
excited an occasional smile among the more fly-along
order of readers and writers. Occasionally he was
compelled to be exact, in consequence of being
watched. Steevens sometimes sought to find him
tripping. Hence the origin of the following note to
Isaac Reed, with which I am obliged from the stores
of Mr. J. H. Anderdon.

"Queen Anne Street, Feb. 16.

"MY DEAR SIR,—In a note on Dodsley's *Preface to
the Old Plays*, p. 11, speaking of the Curtain

Theatre, you refer to Sir John Hawkins' *History of Music*, iv. 67, but I can find nothing there upon the subject. I suppose there is an error of the press in the page referred to, and request you will let me know the true reference if you can light on it, as I have occasion to speak of the Curtain Theatre.

"I never could learn on what authority Mr. Steevens says the sign was a *striped* curtain. Perhaps you may know. The sign without doubt was a curtain, and it is of little consequence whether variegated; yet as we are henceforth to speak *by the Card*, one would wish to be *correct*. I sent my servant last night with the paper, that he might find you at home to inquire about the dreadful fire at Emanuel College. If you have had a line from Dr. Farmer, pray be so good as to let me know what the extent of the mischief may be. . . . I wrote a long letter to Dr. Farmer on Monday, but it must have reached his hands in the midst of the calamity," &c. &c.

Among the papers of Edmond, I have met with only one letter of his celebrated uncle Anthony Malone (see p. 3), of whom I am informed there are few remains, and which thence may find place here. It is a melancholy effusion to the elder sister of Edmond, written soon after the death of a wife to whom he was fondly attached; and in which we trace the sinking spirit in advanced life instinctively preparing to follow whither a beloved partner had preceded him.

From RT. HON. ANTHONY MALONE *to his Niece.*

MY DEAREST HARRIETT,—I had the favour of a letter from you yesterday, and was glad to hear you had got so well to the end of your journey, and in so good time, notwithstanding the disappointments you met with on the road, and that you found your father so well.

If the country, which you say looks very beautiful, be to you a melancholy place, consider in what light it must appear to me who have so lately lost my all—the faithful and affectionate partner of my heart—who alone could make either town or country pleasing to me. I have lost all relish for both; all plans are become quite indifferent to me; and I think it of very little moment to consider in what place I should indulge the melancholy reflections which attend my solitary hours, and which necessarily must accompany me wherever I go, especially when I add to them the disappointments I have lately met with where I least expected it. The only plan which my imagination could suggest as most likely to produce honour or advantage to my family, and a little comfort and satisfaction to myself, is by continuing that correspondence with friends which I have endeavoured, for the greatest part of my life, to cultivate and maintain, and which alone can alleviate my affliction, and make the short remainder of my life pass quietly.

But I will say no more. Perhaps I have already said too much; but you must excuse it, as being occasioned by the overflowing of a disturbed mind and disconsolate heart. In all events, however, you may be assured I am and shall continue your affectionate and sincere friend, and am, with love to your father and sister, my dearest Harriett, your very affectionate though disconsolate uncle,

ANT. MALONE.

Dublin, 5th Aug. 1773.

Ode

ON THE NUPTIALS OF IIIS MAJESTY GEORGE III.

SEPT., 1761.

BY EDMOND MALONE.

Vide p. 6.

DEEP in a lonely vale, beneath a bower
By nature formed for sweet recess and ease ;
Where every beauty that the eye can please
Conspired to gratify the royal power ;
What time the grey-eyed twilight o'er the glade
Spreads all around a glimmering gloomy shade,
 In contemplation George was laid ;
Long did suspense and doubt his mind possess
Wavering and unresolved, what blooming maid,
What soft associate, with his hand to bless.
When, lo ! far off two female forms he spies,
In flowing folds of silver light arrayed ;
Beauteous they seemed, of more than human size :
Such have the ancient poets oft pourtrayed.
The one advanced with solemn steps and slow,
With thought and meditation on her brow ;
Her air majestic, modest was her mien,
  Becoming Wisdom's queen ;
A decent veil concealed from human sight
Those virgin charms that ne'er beheld the light.
In such attire, before the son of Jove
Virtue appeared, at once commanding awe and love.

II.

Lightly the other moved, nor seemed to touch the ground ;
Her every look breathed beauty all around ;
Graceful her mien, and winning was her air ;
Softer her skin, more delicately fair.
A polished mirror in her hand she bore ;
A thin transparent robe of gauze she wore,
 Which made her charms more lovely show ;
Her eyes shone brighter than the morning dews ;
Vermilion dyes her blushing cheeks suffuse ;
O'er all her frame an air of health did glow,
Which simple nature only can bestow,
Which more commands and charms the heart
  Than all the tints of art.
In such a dress, in such a gay attire,
She used of old to meet the Trojan hero's sire.

III.

"Can doubt," said she, " divide thy wavering mind ?
In me immortal treasures shalt thou find.
Need I recount my merits or my fame?
Let it suffice that Beauty is my name.
Thy stream of life, if thou but follow me,
Shall peaceful flow from all rude tempest free,
   And all shall sunshine be.
What mighty bliss can sober Wisdom give ?
  What joys, alas! can she impart ?
With all her rigid precepts how to live,
  With all her vain and boasted art,
She cannot please the eye or glad the heart.
Attend my counsel, hearken to my voice,
And rule by me alone thy future choice ;
On thee eternal pleasures I'll bestow,
Pleasures which Wisdom ne'er can know,
   Pure and unalloyed with woe.
Such blessings will I shower upon thy head,
  Which none but I can give,
  If thou wilt with me live, -
And take a beauteous consort to thy bed."

IV.

"Cease, cease" (cries Wisdom), " thy delusive tongue ;
Heed not, my son, this charming syren's song ;
Let not the magic glass that she employs
  To throw a mist before thine eyes—
Let not insipid pleasures, empty joys,
Delude thy reason 'gainst my better voice.
  Let her not teach thee to despise
  What thou alone shouldst prize—
  The beauties of a nobler kind,
  The graces of the mind ;
These, these alone should be thy choice.
What will avail, alas! the skin of snow,
When the scarce-throbbing feeble pulse beats low
  Soon will the spring of life be past,
  And wintry age will come at last,
Of bloom and beauty that most bitter foe.
  But if from me, thy surest guide,
  Thou wilt receive thy future bride,
  One who will soften every care,
  And all thy sorrows kindly share,
  At once thy truest joy and pride ;
Then bliss refined, and happiness sincere
(The sure rewards of prudence and of truth),
Shall still attend thy youth ;
  And even at thy latest stage,
  Shall gild the evening of thy age."

V.

At this, slow raising up his thoughtful head,
    The youth, pathetic, said :
" What now, alas! avails my royal state ?
Hard is my lot, and, oh! severe my fate.
Contending passions now distract my breast :
Is this the boasted fruit of being great,
    The loss of peace and rest ?
    My raptured mind now Fancy sways,
    And all my soul her voice obeys.
Now Reason cries, ' Attend my sober strain.'
Cruel conditions! whichsoe'er I choose,
    The want of that which I refuse
Will quite corrode what I retain,
And late, perhaps, I shall repent in vain."

VI.

" Not so, my best beloved, my favoured youth "
    (Here interrupted Wisdom's queen),
" For such thy goodness and thy worth has been,
    Thy virtue, innocence, and truth,
    That thou deserv'st a nobler fate;
Nor e'er shalt thou, my son, too late
    Thy conduct past repent;
    If beauty of the brightest dye,
    If every graceful art
    That can attract the heart,
    Or charm the lover's nicer eye,
    Can give thy soul content.
For lo! to thee I now assign
Charlotte, the favourite of the Nine,
    Nor less beloved by me;
    Her do I now bestow on thee.
Nor can the Queen of Love refuse
    To join thy royal hand,
    In the connubial band,
    With this sweet daughter of the Muse;
    Since even from her earliest year,
    She still has been her darling care."
This said, they instant vanished from his sight,
And soon were lost in shades of endless night.

VII.

Smooth glide my verse, my numbers gently flow,
Nor harshly quick, nor querulously slow.
For see! where hoary Thames' translucent stream,
    His rushy-fringèd bank in silence laves,
    And all his crystal waves

Refulgent glitter with a silver gleam,
    The royal galley wafts her o'er;
The Naiads quit their coral beds,
And raise aloft their azure heads
      On the rejoicing shore,
To see the partner of the British crown,
    In all the gay and gallant pride
That erst conveyed th' Egyptian bride
      The silver Cydnus down;
    The wondering waves subside,
The green-haired sea nymphs round the vessel crowd,
    The winds adown the silken streamers glide,
      And sing their joy aloud.

VIII.

    The softly sighing gale
With gentle breezes fills the swelling sail;
    Now smooth it cuts the watery way,
Now wafts the Princess to th' expecting land.
      On either hand
The purple Loves and white-robed Graces play.
The rose-lipp'd cherub Health, with bosom bare
    And glowing cheek, was there.
And jocund Youth, fair Beauty's friend,
And meek-eyed Innocence, her steps attend.
    And lo! behind the blooming maid,
      With ever-verdant olives crowned,
    In all her tranquil charms arrayed,
      The matron Peace bestrews the ground.
Hark! now admiring thousands sing
    (While all the shores responsive ring),
" Long may Britannia's laughing plain
Proclaim that George and Charlotte reign."
Even Nature's self her homage gladly pays,
And joins the voice of universal praise.

SPEECH TO THE ELECTORS OF TRINITY COLLEGE, DUBLIN.
1774 or 1775.

Vide p. 42.

GENTLEMEN,—The honour that has been done me by being put in nomination for one of your representatives by the very respectable person who spoke last, at the same time that it demands my warmest acknowledgments, renders it necessary for me to say a few words. I am well aware to how judicious and distinguishing an audience I now address myself; I am fully sensible how much the arduousness of my situation is increased by the necessity I am under of speaking on the most difficult and ungrateful of all subjects—oneself. But there are some situations where silence would be criminal.

It was thrown out, gentlemen, early last summer, when I first took the liberty of proposing myself to your consideration, that I was nephew to Mr. A. M. (Anthony Malone), and therefore an improper person to represent this learned body. Perhaps it might be a sufficient answer to this electioneering artifice to say, that the character of that man should not seem very obnoxious to reproach, to whom the principal objection is that he is connected with as wise and able, and certainly as disinterested a man as any in this kingdom. But, gentlemen, though this short and decisive answer might be sufficient, I will not rest this matter here. I beg leave, with your permission, to consider this objection in all its parts.

Whatever failings this great man may have, no one can say that he has not acted on principle. No man perhaps ever supported administration so disinterestedly, or got so few favours from Government either for himself or his connexions. This indeed is so notorious, and the corruption and venality of the times are such, that men although they evidently see it is the fact are unwilling to believe it, and resort to the most improbable and chimerical suppositions in order to account for it. The persons too, who arraign the conduct of this great statesman, forget that it is necessary that the administration of affairs should be carried on by some persons or other; and that the gravity and moderation of this

H H 2

gentleman has often been of use to restrain the impetuous corruption of other men.

The enemies of this gentleman forget that the seat of a lord-lieutenant of the kingdom is besieged by men whose ready venality often outruns the wishes of Government; who, in addition to great present emolument, grasp at future and numerous reversions; who, not content with the highest offices in their own line, invade the offices of other men, thrust themselves into every department, civil, military, and ecclesiastical, and into stations for which the whole tenor of their lives and studies has rendered them wholly unqualified; who accumulate place upon place, and sinecure upon sinecure; who are so eager to obtain the wages of the day before the day is well passed over their heads, that they have emphatically and not improperly been styled ready-money voters; men that nothing is too arbitrary or illegal for them to varnish by their eloquence or support by their vote; men who are resolved at any rate to aggrandize themselves, and care not how soon they subvert the constitution of their country if they can but erect the fabric of their own fortunes on its ruins.

While our governors are surrounded by such men, surely, gentlemen, a wise and moderate and disinterested counsellor must be of some use to restrain their vicious ardour, and to prevent their headlong prostitution from subverting our liberties at a stroke. But however this may be, and though I have said thus much in justification of this distinguished character, I beg not to be misunderstood. I by no means insinuate that his conduct in supporting administration in general is such as I would myself follow. So far from it, gentlemen, that had I even been brought into Parliament by his interest, I should nevertheless have considered myself the trustee of the people, and perhaps there is no man that would have taken a more decided part than I should have done against that side which he generally espouses.

Gentlemen, I might call upon my worthy friend who has been put into nomination before me—whose truth and integrity are only surpassed by his abilities; I might call upon another gentleman, the greatest orator in this or perhaps any other kingdom—men whose testimony and approbation would set a seal upon any character; I could call upon these and many others with whom I have lived in intimacy to bear witness, that there are few persons who were not in Parliament that took a more active part than I have done against most of the measures of government for these some years past, particularly during the late unconstitutional administration of Lord Townshend. A man's zeal, gentlemen, must not always be measured by his situation; and persons moving even in an humble and private sphere of life like myself, have it sometimes in their power to molest an arbitrary administration.

But, gentlemen, I will go to the bottom of this objection, and will take it for granted that those who have thrown it out mean to insinuate that I was a *dependant* on another, and therefore not a proper object of your choice. And if this were the case, I would readily allow the force of the objection, and yield up all pretensions to your favour. But, gentlemen, this is as false as the rest; for a few months ago I obtained, at too high a price indeed, an honourable independence; nor shall any motive upon earth induce me to forfeit that independence.

If, gentlemen, I shall be thought worthy to represent this learned University on the foundation of which I had once the honour to be placed, I shall consider myself as the friend neither to this man nor to that—attached neither to this party nor the other. I shall consider no tie, no *relation*, but that relation which subsists between the electors and the elected. I shall consider myself as a friend to nothing but the liberty and the constitution of my country, to the support of which I shall devote my life and abilities, while in every part of my conduct I shall endeavour to approve myself no unprofitable and, I will be bold to say, no unfaithful representative.

I have a thousand apologies to make, gentlemen, for having taken up so much of your time. I hope that the necessity of explaining a matter which might have been misconstrued and misunderstood, will plead my excuse.

Collection of Tracts in 76 *Volumes made by* EDMOND MALONE.

" This truly valuable collection was formed by the above eminent literary character (Malone) during a life of the most ardent research, and contains many articles of the greatest interest and scarcity in every branch of literature. It is perhaps unrivalled in tracts relating to Ireland, parliamentary proceedings, politics, and the drama. It is also particularly rich in the classes relating to church affairs and divinity, prerogative of the crown, America, British colonies, affairs of Spain, trade, banks, coinage, history, army and navy, elections, peerage, antiquities, biography, poetry relating to Milton, legal treatises, languages, critical, universities of Oxford and Cambridge, origin of printing, prices of provisions, poor laws, rebellion riots, trials, regency, towns, naturalization, satirical jests, and other facetious productions, and various other classes, in which will be found the most complete collection of tracts by Burke.

" Also an extensive series by Dr. S. Johnson, Gibbon, and Ralph the historians ; Bishops Berkeley, Warburton, Lowth, Gibson, Sherlock, Burnet, Hurd, Burgess ; Deans Swift and Tucker. Also by Drs. Jortin, Lister, Lardner, Corry, Delaney, Campbell, Franklin, Z. Gray, G. Baker, Waterland, Woodward, Lucas, Clarke, Wells, Comber, J. Brown, E. Young, R. Bentley, J. Hill, Priestley. Also by Lords Grenville, Mount Norris, Duke of Portland, Thurlow, Chatham, Suffolk, Mansfield, Bath, Camden, Hardwick, Orford, Harvey, Molesworth, Earl of Kildare, Bolingbroke, Ormond, Essex, Ashburnham ; Honourables R. Boyle, C. J. Fox, T. Harvey, George Canning, H. Grattan, H. Flood, Tickel, Sir T. Hanmer, General Burgoyne, Governor Hutchinson, Duncan Forbes, John Wilkes, Sir J. Lowther, Sir T. W. Meredith, J. Holt, Wm. Temple, C. Bingham, R. Steele, R. Cox, W. Petty, Isaac Newton, A. Welding, L. O'Brien, R. B. Sheridan, Corbyn Morris, Macauley, J. Ponsonby, and Pery, Speaker of the Irish House of Commons ; also of Soame Jenyns, James Boswell, T. Warton, W. Pulteney, Quin, Derrick, Mason, Pope, Congreve, Cibber, Garrick, T. Sheridan, Prior, Sewel, J. Woodward, A. Malone, Oldmixon,

Foote, T. Davies, Upton Egerton, Macklin, Aikin, Theobald, and numerous other writers of note, the names of which alone would form a catalogue.

" Many of them are enriched with numerous highly interesting and valuable notes in the autograph of Mr. Malone. The life of Congreve is nearly re-written by him, and many others are much increased in value thereby. The collection was purchased in Mr. Malone's sale for 33*l.* 10*s.*"—*Thorpe*, 1838.

Notes written to Malone on Windham's Memoir, 1810.

Mr. Wilberforce (21st August, 1810) terms him " one of the most extraordinary men this country ever produced." Lord Wellesley, writing from Dorking, thanks him for an " interesting memoir, which he has read with great attention and satisfaction, and with all the respect due to its author and to its subject." Mr. Trevor (the last Lord Hampden) says, " I cannot offer you my sincere thanks for this obliging attention without expressing in common with all the friends of that great and amiable man my admiration of the just and honourable tribute which you have paid to his memory, and thence have equally gratified their feelings and your own." Lord Rosse writes from Parsonstown—" He (Mr. Windham) was undoubtedly the first gentleman in England, and fully merited everything you have said of him in your elegant panegyric. I regret it is so short, ... but hope it is only a foretaste of what we may hereafter hope to feast upon. . . . . The newspapers say that he has left many manuscripts. There is scarcely a subject he could touch which the magic of his imagination would not turn into something beautiful and valuable." Lord Whitworth says, " Although I had not the good fortune to live in habits of intimacy with Mr. Wyndham, yet I beg leave to assure you that you could not have bestowed your work on an individual more sensible of his virtues both public and private, or who laments his loss more sincerely."

The Bishop of Meath says, " I am grateful to receive from your own hands the tribute of praise you have paid to a man, whom to say I once had the happiness of knowing intimately, is to say I esteemed, admired, and loved. . . . . He was the last of the splendid constellations that shone in that part of the political hemisphere that most arrested my observation when I first knew London. . . . . What a void must he have left in your society!"

Mr. Canning writes from Hinckley, " I return you my best acknowledgments for the Memoir of Mr. Windham which I have read with great though melancholy pleasure. It contains some facts that were new to me. The sentiments are such as I have long and uniformly felt in common with you and with all who knew him well enough to value him as he deserved."

The Bishop of Dromore thanks him for " the tribute paid to his departed friend, Mr. Windham, whose merit as a man, a statesman, and a scholar, was above all praise."

Mr. Thomas Grenville expresses strong regrets for his " invaluable friend," whom, in another passage, he terms " the perfect model of an English gentleman," and adds, " The general regret which broke forth at the moment of his death, showed that his country was not insensible to the greatness of the loss which they had to deplore in him—a loss in some respects quite irreparable, as the extraordinary combination of his talents and character enabled him to do and say much for the public interests which no man now living can do or say with half the same effect or advantage."

Lady Crewe, the Misses Berry, and Mrs. Burke lament him as a most serious loss, the last pathetically as " a person I so sincerely admired and loved as I did Mr. Windham. I feel his loss most sorely ; for he was from his great attention to me almost my *last* support. But God's will be done!"

Lord Holland " feels it to be a flattering distinction to be reckoned among the sincere friends and admirers of Mr. Windham. It is said he has left a diary from the time of leaving college to the day on which the fatal operation was performed."

THE END.

INDEX.

I I

www.ingramcontent.com/pod-product-compliance
Lightning Source LLC
Chambersburg PA
CBHW032018110726
47901CB00004B/1132